THE MODERN MYTHOS ANOMALY

JUNIPER LAKE FITZGERALD

The Modern Mythos Anomaly
© Juniper Lake Fitzgerald

This novel is entirely a work of fiction. The names, characters, places, and events are the work of the author's imagination. Any resemblance to actual persons living or dead, events, or locations is entirely coincidental.

Copyright © Juniper Lake Fitzgerald 2023
Cover Illustration © Juniper Lake Fitzgerald
Illustrations, Maps, Symbols © Juniper Lake Fitzgerald

Cover Typography by Beauregard Saenz at Strange Suns Press
Edited by Rachel Fletcher & Josef Brühler at Strange Suns Press

Juniper Lake Fitzgerald reserves the right to be identified as the author and creator of this work.
All rights reserved. No part of this text may be reproduced or used in any manner without the permission of the publisher, except for the use of brief quotations in book review.

Using this publication for purposes of training artificial intelligence (AI) and machine learning (ML) technologies to generate text, including without limitation technologies that are capable of generating works in the same style or genre as the publication is expressly prohibited. The author & publisher reserve all rights to license or prohibit uses of this work for generative artificial intelligence training and development of machine learning language models.
First Edition: April 2023

Print ISBN: 979-8-218-15218-5

MEMORY'S HAUNT CONJURES THE MOST ARRANT OF GHOSTS

CONTENT WARNING

For those sensitive to certain topics, be aware of the following events contained within.
For those who do not wish to see spoilers, skip this page.

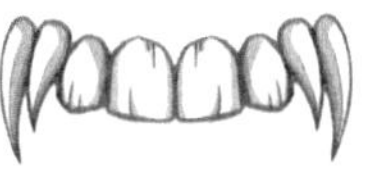

Content Warnings:

Alcohol consumption & smoking
Blood consumption, gore, violence, body horror
Cannibalism
Fire related trauma
Nightmares, repressed & relived trauma
Child labor
Public execution
Depiction of child physical & emotional abuse,
including corporal punishment

DEPRESSION, DISSOCIATION, PARANOID DELUSIONS & ANXIETY
BRIEF SUICIDAL IDEATION/APATHY
BRIEF USE OF ABLEIST LANGUAGE, BIPHOBIC DIALOGUE, &
MENTION OF SOCIETAL HOMOPHOBIA
BRIEF MENTION OF A SEXUALLY COERCIVE RELATIONSHIP

DEPRESSION, DISSOCIATION, PARANOID DELUSIONS & ANXIETY
BRIEF SUICIDAL IDEATION/APATHY
BRIEF USE OF ABLEIST LANGUAGE, BIPHOBIC DIALOGUE, &
MENTION OF SOCIETAL HOMOPHOBIA
BRIEF MENTION OF A SEXUALLY COERCIVE RELATIONSHIP

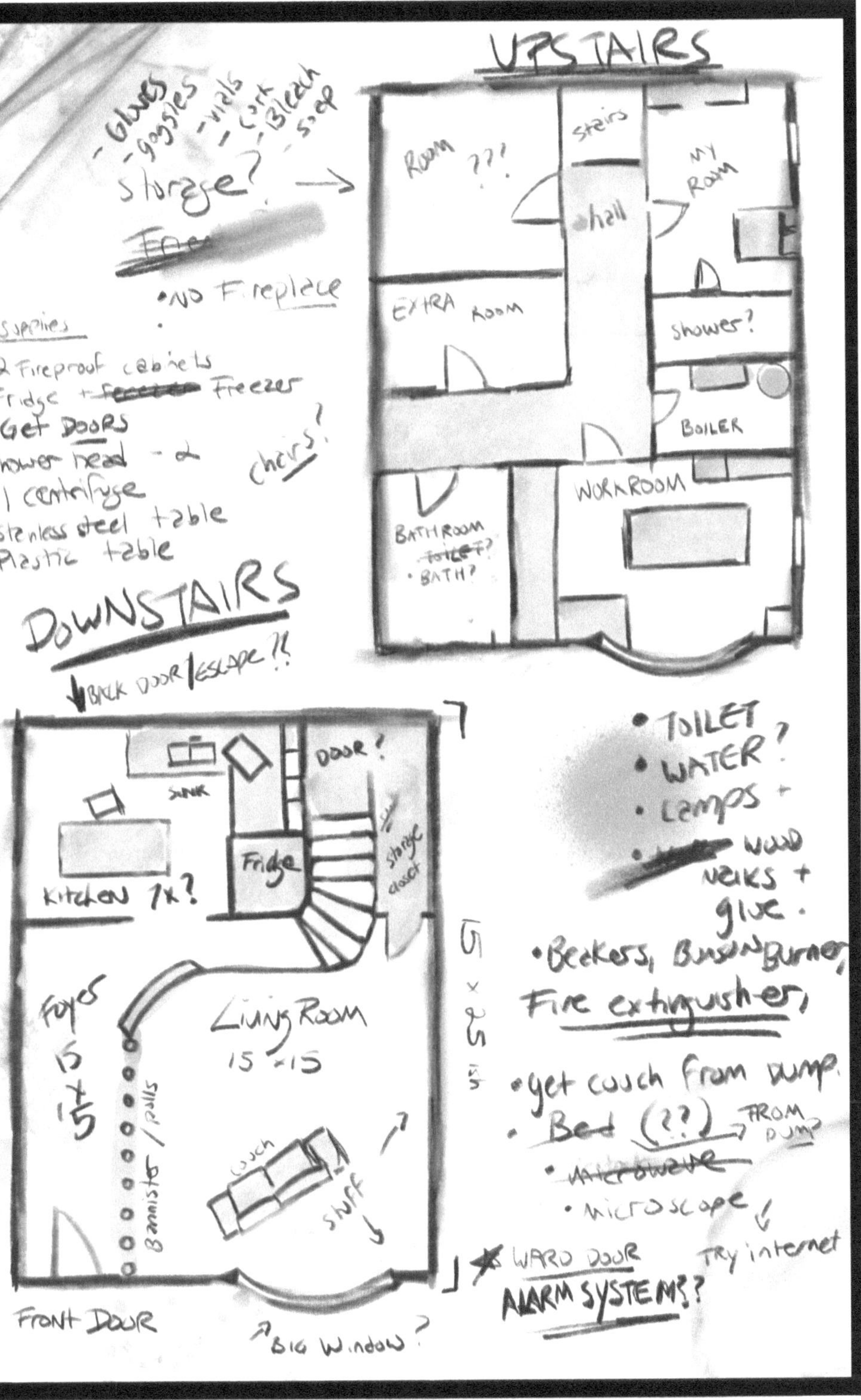

- Glues
- goggles
- vials
- Cork
- Bleach
- soap
Storage?
No Fireplace
supplies
2 Fireproof cabinets
Fridge + Freezer
Get DOORS
shower head - 2
chairs?
1 centrifuge
stainless steel table
Plastic table

DOWNSTAIRS
BACK DOOR/ESCAPE?!

UPSTAIRS
Room ??!
stairs
MY ROOM
hall
EXTRA ROOM
shower?
BOILER
WORKROOM
BATHROOM
TOILET?
BATH?

DOOR?
SINK
storage closet
Fridge
Kitchen 7x?
Foyer
15
x
15
Bannister / Rails
Living Room
15 x 15
Couch
SNIFF
Front DOOR
BIG Window?

15 x 25 = 15

TOILET?
WATER?
Lamps +
WOOD
NAILS +
glue.
Beakers, Bunsen Burner
Fire extinguisher
get couch from dump.
Bed (??) FROM DUMP
Microwave
Microscope
try internet
WARD DOOR
ALARM SYSTEM??

PART ONE
RELUCTANCE

CHAPTER

ONE

"Shit, shit, shit, shit! Shit!"

A cadence of curses perfectly matched the pace of footsteps flying rapidly across the blacktop and off the road into the woods.

He could usually outrun these kinds of fuckers by miles and stay ten moves ahead of any drunken mishap in the shape of a man that came his way. But it must've been something he'd eaten because he was tripping over his feet and had gotten turned around in a shit hole that he knew like the back of his hand.

That wasn't saying much—anyone who hung around here for more than a day could figure out a place that wasn't much more than three stoplights, a run-down gas station, a bar, and a grocery store. So, how the hell did he get so damned lost?

I really need to be more careful about what I drink, he thought briefly, tucking that nugget of wisdom away for later in a place he'd definitely forget to look. You'd think he'd get better at this, honestly. And to give him a little credit, he did there for a moment. He'd spent more time undiscovered and mostly unbothered in this truck-stop of a town than most others. A week is a record, right? It was hard to remember anymore, so many places blended together they ceased to have meaning or distinction. As long as he could keep track enough not to run back to a place he'd been chased from before, then he was happy not knowing where he was going or where he'd been.

This time though, he'd fucked up his chances here for good.

Nothing like getting caught with your teeth in the town's pageant queen claim-to-fame's neck behind a once-green muck-covered dumpster by a group of ego-bloated men with a couple of savior complexes and open carries between them. Even if he hadn't been drinking her blood, the sight of his lips on her neck was bad enough to ignite their rage at someone who dared taint the purity of a woman they presumed to put on a pedestal she didn't desire, even as her hand slid down the front of his pants to clench him in a vice grip similar to his own on her throat. He let her do it. She would quickly lose the strength to hold on for long anyway.

Sure, she was pretty, and even up close she could live up to the airbrushed posterized versions of herself plastered in the few local magazine pages taped up across dark sticky walls inside the bar that she leaned against as she pawed at his clothes.

If he were in any other mood maybe he'd indulge in more than just a meal. But she had taken something. Something synthetic and chemical that went straight to her bloodstream. Something that humans used in abundance, especially in dead-ends like this, to replicate a sense of euphoria and temporary meaning in life.

It tasted vile, of burnt plastic and antiseptic, stinging his throat and the sensitive roots of his teeth. It made his head swim and not in the way a pint of fresh blood simulated the rush of endorphins through his once-living flesh. He felt sick and jerked back from her upper-laced veins the moment the bumper sticker-covered back door kicked open to the sound of drunken guffaws and gurgling boasts. A sound that quickly turned to shouts of outrage as he became the target for a collective of alcohol-induced bravado, the men's makeshift team corralling against whatever would keep them from turning on each other instead.

His boots staggered unsteadily against the ground as he jerked his arm out of a slippery iron grip. He didn't need to try all that hard—he was stronger than them even on a bad day. But still, his vision was swimming and the trickle of blood down his chin was enough tinder to ignite an indignant tirade against him that was quickly growing violent. So, as one reached for a discarded bat and another played gentleman to the disheveled woman to the sound of a beer bottle breaking against the dumpster, Python righted himself, wiped his lips on the back of his sleeve, and ran.

He didn't make it far beyond the outskirts of town when the rancid blood began pounding in his ears, blocking out shouts of, "PERVERT!" "MOTHERFUCKER!" "GET HIM!" and replacing the sounds with a ringing whine that nearly knocked him off his feet.

He stumbled off the side of the crumbling asphalt and into a shallow ditch, clambering up the other side with razor-sharp claws extending in hopes of finding some kind of purchase. The tree line up ahead offered sufficient cover, but he wasn't quick enough, as the drunken-horde-turned-small-crowd spotted him making his escape.

Python didn't have a heading except *get away* and *throw up* as he stumbled blindly through the brush. The chorus of shouts and snapping twigs behind him pushed him forward even as his body was screaming for him to stop.

Then up ahead in the distance, tucked between trees and shrubbery and the shadows of moonlight, was a house. It stood as if on a tilt, threatening to fall over with the next thunderstorm wind, and the windows were lifeless and black. Abandoned and clearly slightly haunted, barely visible from its lopsided position in the overgrowth, it was the perfect hideout. Without hesitation Python ran to it, tried the door—that popped open with a soft angry groan—and slipped inside.

He didn't take the time to look around beyond the front hall before plopping down hard against the door and sliding to the floor. His chest was heaving in a pantomime of breath he didn't need. But the action did seem to help the way his stomach had landed upside down inside of him. He turned his head to peek through the slats in the old wooden door. Outside he could see the glow of flashlights and hear the grumbling of a frustrated posse of pricks.

He sat very still, watching carefully and hoping they wouldn't notice the run-down shack covered in vines that stood nearly ten feet in front of their whiskey-blinded sight.

Then something unexpected happened. The house began to shake. But not a shake from any wind or weather, rather it was as if the house itself had come alive. The door behind him began to rattle, trembling on its hinges and jolting violently against his back. In the darkness he heard glass break, falling from shelves or tables and skittering across the floor with a symphony of screaming scrapes. The whole thing creaked a loud moan of wood and nails and shuddered as if breathing against a persistent cough. Python planted his hands and feet against the wooden floor, and with his back as close to the rattling door as he could manage, squeezed his eyes shut.

It would be just his luck to die in some pathetic cliche manner like from a falling plank of wood through the heart, instead of something much more, I don't know, glamorous.

Then as soon as it began, it stopped.

The house squealed as it stilled, slowly settling down with a series of trembles and groans. As the silence slowly set in, still Python waited. The unexpected vibration drudged up bloody bile in his throat and the harsh scent burned his nostrils.

Oh, I'm gonna fuckin' hurl.

He willed himself to stand, continuing to lean heavily against the back of the door. He rubbed his eyes, forcing them to focus. Whatever that girl had taken really messed him up, as his usually impeccable night vision was sparking blue and white fractals behind his eyelids. But before he could find his bearings, his keen hearing caught a sound coming from upstairs, where it had been naught but quiet before. Footsteps. He froze with one hand on the doorknob and the other at his throat.

Someone else was in the house.

"Oh, what is it now…"

The haggard voice came from a rickety three-legged stool where a figure sat hunched over a workbench. Just what he was working on there well, it was hard to say.

The table was strewn with instruments of varying levels of antique and questionable states of cleanliness. Tipped over half-empty flasks were as common as the unbroken semi-useable ones. Some lie cracked and abandoned, contents dried in crusty rings around the edges—no doubt remnants of failed experiments or half-baked ideas that came the man in the middle of the night.

But now it was verging on early morning, and though deep in concentration between the beaker and notebook in front of him the man was rudely interrupted by a thunk coming from downstairs. In the house where no one else but he lived. In the middle of the woods. Where he specifically chose to be to avoid any kind of interruptions by creature or mankind alike.

Calysto sighed and slowly stood. His bent-over frame stretched into a long and wiry one and he could have been even taller still if he didn't slouch. He shuffled across the creaking wooden floors—on worn-out slippers that dragged with the tooth-aching grate of sand-paper—and made his way to the window.

The old hand-blown glass panels weren't ones for much visibility even when he wiped away a layer of dust with his sweater sleeve. It still didn't serve to do much, and only smeared grease from his sweater in thick streaks through the dirt.

With another heavy sigh and two substance-covered hands he lifted the window from the bottom, cracking it enough to peer into the open air. Cautiously, he looked back and forth between undulating vines of green and brown glistening blue in the moonlight. They served to hide his home from peering passersby and the random hunting party of belligerent assholes in tacky orange vests looking for a place to turn into their frat house for the night.

Men like that annoyed him to no end. Well, to be fair, most men did. Most people. There was more than one reason he chose such a remote place to call his home.

That's when he saw them. Flashlights, many of them, swinging with the fury of a chase and not the careful beam of a search.

A flashback remnant of torches in similar formation flashed in his mind, and he slammed the window shut.

"Fuck," he muttered.

Well, this was time enough in one place, anyway. This was always going to come. In all his years he'd never been able to settle down in one place for too long before his reclusive nature was criticized until he was vilified. Or he was found out. Or more accurately, his paranoia *convinced him* he was about to be found out.

Because Calysto wasn't your ordinary shut-in scientist. Calysto was a warlock. Yes, this rickety man who appeared as malnourished as a lone deer in winter, was what you might call a magical being. One that only exists in folktale and lore. Something unreal and truly unimaginable, with a real mystical power running in the veins beneath his skin. He could summon storms, conjure demons, make fire appear in his hands, and move things with his mind.

Well. That's what they say about warlocks anyway. You know, in the stories.

But this isn't a story nor a myth but a man, and as of yet there is no way of telling just what he can do. Though what he did next was not very what-you'd-imagine-to-be-warlock-like at all. Calysto slammed the window shut, yanked the worn cotton curtain closed, took a step back, and promptly fell on his ass.

What the fuck... !

An apparently invisible inch-thick test tube skittered out across the floor in an erratic spiral. It hit the wall with a loud thunk then proceeded to get stuck in a slat in the floorboards and jitter back and forth faster and faster until finally it fell still. Calysto just silently watched its journey with brows pinched in irritation.

"Are you quite done," he grumbled from a splayed-out position on his back.

He leaned up on his elbows and looked out across the room. Dimly illuminated only by the small magnifying glass lamp on his desk, everything glowed with an eerie bluish fluorescence that cast long bleeding shadows into the corners. Slowly, with movements that made him seem much older than his visible age, he climbed up off of the floor. A deep sigh escaped his lips and he rubbed his eye underneath his glasses.

Another thump closer beneath him reminded him of his more current and pressing predicament.

Fine, fine. Time to go then.

Calysto grabbed a small tube-like cylinder from off of his workbench and murmured a soft word. The end of it began to glow, pulsing with a reddish-orange light almost like a flare. It sputtered and jumped, flickering up and down as if trying to get his attention.

"Yes, Yes," he placated it. "I know, sorry it's been so long, alright? Now calm down, will you."

The light, seeming satisfied with his apology, steadied itself into an even glow, surrounding them in a warm haze.

Clasping the torch in one hand, Calysto shuffled across the workshop and out of the door. Down the hallway and to the right was small room— what was inside I cannot say—but Calysto scooted inside and closed the door. After a moments tinkering and another hum, a violet glow slipped out from underneath the crack in the door and the rickety house in which he lived and had spent countless of his days, began to creak. The tall wooden-planked walls groaned akin to how Calysto sounded when he fell on the floor. But then it did something no house would typically do. It shook, trembling, contracting, expanding, as if suddenly filled with a life of its own. The light from beneath the door grew brighter and brighter until a blinding flash erupted, consuming every inch of night.

There was nothing left to see after that. Not for a split second where everything was white. Then with a deafening bang the house ceased its strange breathing and stilled. The door opened and Calysto emerged, shuffling his way back down the hall and into his workshop, as if whatever had just happened was so routine he owed no explanation, and it offered no interruption. Simply part of his day. Or night. Or morning.

What was he even doing up? If the rings of blue under his amber eyes were any indication, whatever room his bed was in did not see much use.

Calysto plopped heavy back onto his stool, shoved his glasses back into place, and murmured to the torch to put it out. For a moment it was silent but the occasional clink of glass or scuffle of tools across the rough tabletop. Then, Calysto paused. He heard a noise coming from downstairs.

No, it was a voice.

He held his breath, strained his ears to focus, and heard it again. It was *definitely* a voice.

Someone else was in the house.

CHAPTER
TWO

"Who the fuck are you?" Python shouted towards the sound of dragging footsteps that approached from overhead. His whole body was on edge, tense, clenched around the angry contents of his stomach. He was fighting back an irritatingly persistent bout of nausea and the concoction of poisonous blood pounded through the veins behind his eyes.

"Who am I?!" A man's voice snapped. "You're in *my* house!"

"Well, *excuseee me.* This place looks abandoned to the pits of hell. Didn't think anyone lived here," Python snapped right back. He was *not* in the mood for this.

"Clearly you were wrong."

The voice came closer and despite his drugged-sick blood Python could see the figure clearly in the dim dawning light that crept in behind him from beneath the front door.

A man descended the stairs holding a jar of fluorescent liquid in his hand that illuminated his ghostly features in stark contrast. He looked no older than thirty years and was tall and wiry as a rail. Dressed in dirty too-big-for-him sweatpants, a hole-ridden black shirt covered in what looked like years of stains, a near-threadbare grey sweater, and a pair of sandals that flopped with each step like they should have been retired a decade ago.

His narrow face was pinched in annoyance and he glared at Python through a pair of cracked circular glasses. Golden-blonde hair was pulled haphazardly up in some chaotic semblance of a ponytail, or a bun. Whatever it was, it was a mess. *He* was a mess.

Python might've been a drifter and a mooch and an all-around bum, but at least he took pride in not looking like one, *thank you very much.*

This guy on the other hand... frankly he looked as awful and ragged as the house around them.

"You really live here?" Python asked.

The man stopped a step before the bottom and squinted over to where Python was still leaning dependently on the door.

"What business is that of yours." The man scowled, then quickly demanded, "Who are you?"

"Nobody of import." Python flashed him his best cheeky grin—at least he might have. He couldn't put much effort into it and his lips felt stuck to his teeth.

"If you're here for me I'm afraid I'll have to kill you."

This made Python laugh but it came out harsh and dry like a croak. Oh, he did *not* feel good. But still, where did this little fucking mold-ridden dweeb get off threatening him?

"I'd like to see you try."

The man still didn't move, but his frown sank further. "Your confidence is wasted, whatever you've been told."

"I don't know what you mean... what I've been told," Python bit the words out between the vice in his throat. "Look, once that mob outside passes I'll be gone and out of your fucking rats-nest hair, alright?"

The man ignored his insult and simply responded, "They are gone."

"Yeah?" Python shook his head, righting a piece of smoke-grey hair that dangled in his eyes. "How come you're so sure? They're a persistent bunch."

"I know," the man answered. He offered no other explanation.

The silence hung heavy and awkward between them. Python got the feeling this man was simply waiting for him to leave. The way an old man closes the door on the parcel delivery person then peers through the peephole until the car is out of sight. Just waiting. Suspicious, wary, and maybe slightly curious. Like someone who sees so little excitement they eat up anything that passes their way yet still sits by with reluctance, unwilling to engage beyond becoming a sponge to absorb the unfolding of events.

"Alright." Python decided to give up on this weirdo. A bit unsteady on his feet, he turned towards the door. His hand was on the knob when he paused. "How far's the closest town north?"

"I don't know," the strange and scraggly man replied.

Python sighed. "What do you mean you don't know, you live around here don't you?"

"No."

"Okay. Dick." Python twisted the knob and went to pull the door. "I'll get out of your fucking hair then..."

The door swung open and *FUCK what was I thinking!*

Dim morning sunlight washed over him with a warm comforting glow. No, sorry. Not comforting. Not for him.

Python tried to grab the door and shut it out but instead fell straight to his knees, projectile vomiting rancid black blood all across the floor. Even in the hazy overcast his skin was instantly burning, itching like a hundred thousand tiny bugs nipping and gnawing through the layers of his long-dead flesh. Finally, he was a meal for the worms that he'd eluded for so long. A thought he'd find somewhat funny if he had the wherewithal to process it.

Then the light was gone and the door closed with a click. His throat tasted of hot septic tank cleaner—not sure why he knew what *that* tasted like—and the bloody bile tingled where it leaked down his chin. A hand grabbed his bicep, hauling him back to sit against the foyer wall. Python's vision was blurrier than before but between hazy blinks he could make out the shape of the quiet man on the stairs reaching out to him with a rag. Python slapped his hand away.

"I don't... I don't need your h..." He coughed and spat. "Help."

"Sure," the man responded, sounding completely unruffled by his attitude. "I can see that. If that's the case then why don't you just get up and leave, like you planned."

Python took a deep breath he didn't need — it just felt good to do it. A little in-out reset. It was like sleep that way, unneeded but not necessarily bad.

He liked to compare it to one of those newer inventions. Smartphones. Turn it off, turn it back on again. It might not fix the deep-seated and ingrained fucked-upness of it. The screen still might be cracked despite the peeling protector plastered on top, and the contacts list was still as short as his mortal life should have been. The apps too few, the notes too full—stacked high with memories that he'd like to forget but still chose to transfer to each new number and each new sim card like he'd one day look back and it would be different. No, turning it on and back off again might not help that kind of shit. But it surely did make the whole thing run a little faster for a bit longer.

And right now Python really wanted to hit his own power button.

Just a quick little nap... just a little break and he'd get out of here and away from this... this asshole. He just... he just needed a quick...

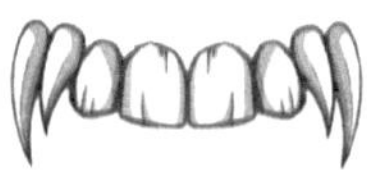

THE MAN who had so obnoxiously slammed open the door to his home, trampled inside, hitched a ride, insulted him, then threw up all over his floor, was now passed out at Calysto's feet.

Calysto set the glowing jar in his hand against the ledge in the foyer, using it as a makeshift flashlight. He crouched down with the rag still in hand to wipe up the liquid bile that was quickly seeping into the old dried out floorboards of his home. He took a couple of swipes, absorbing what he could, then paused.

Wait, what is this? Is this blood?

Calysto brought the rag closer to his face and sniffed. Oh, it was definitely blood. Then he realized something else. This man had just... wait, he had thrown this up?

What the fuck? What did he do, drink bleach?

He was definitely a dying, or very soon to be dead, man with this much blood loss. Calysto dropped the cloth and remained kneeling, observing the blood-soaked man in silence. He had shoulder length grey hair that was swept straight back from his face like a mobster from the past or a television cartoon vampire. His skin was a deathly pale and near translucent in the eerie lighting, and thin bluish-purple veins were clearly visible beneath the surface. Despite his hair he looked young, almost the same age that Calysto himself appeared to be.

He was dressed from head to toe in black and reminded Calysto of a kid from the 'goth scene' he knew very little about. But he knew enough to know this man's style was about forty years behind the current style. Calysto might be a recluse but he did find the time to pop on a movie or TV show of something relevant every once in a while.

Time passed so quickly anymore that there were no distinct days. Just times of being awake until there were times he couldn't stay awake any longer. Still, through the decades Calysto had made a half-hearted attempt to keep up with current affairs. Even if he didn't go outside and get involved in it, he did at least do his best to learn what the hell an e-mail and a tablet were. Tablets had definitely been something to come in handy. Though in the end the one he owned lay abandoned somewhere, not on its charger, in a house that definitely didn't get its power from being connected to an electrical grid.

A buzz came from the unconscious man and the deep black of his jeans glowed a soft blue.

Oh, a phone.

Maybe this guy had friends who could come pick him up. Calysto hesitated and glanced at the man's face before reaching for his pocket. He didn't look close to coming back to consciousness soon, so Calysto quickly dug his hand inside.

Ultimately it took him a few tries to get the phone out, as the pockets seemed built to fit either fingers or an object but certainly not both. Not to mention the pants were just too damned tight. The man groaned softly, head lolling limp to the side and Calysto froze. What would he look like if this guy woke up right now? A stranger crouched over him in the dark, his hand half in his jeans. Whether he was stealing from him or about to take advantage, it could be seen as either. Calysto quickly yanked the phone and sat back on the floor. He tapped the screen a few times and it came to life. Locked. There was a message on the screen, but not from any number this guy had saved though.

Where r u hon?

Two hours ago. Before the leap.

Shit, the leap.

Calysto checked the top corner of the screen. As expected there were no bars and it looked like the battery was on the way out, too. A crisscrossed crack ran horizontally across the glass like lightning and Calysto briefly wondered if that had happened just now when the man fell. There was no wallpaper background besides the standard stock photo of an obnoxiously oversaturated swirl of colors masquerading as artistic, and nothing else he could determine without the passcode.

Then, crouched beside him in the dark, Calysto realized something else. This guy wasn't breathing. He reached out his hand again, placing it carefully on his forehead. Cold as ice. Calysto sucked in a breath and moved his hand to the man's slender neck. No pulse either.

Fuck me.

This man had really just up and died in his fucking doorway.

Who was he? Would people be looking for him? If it was any indication from his phone message, then yes.

Shit, shit.

Calysto's heart raced in his throat. This was not something he needed right now. Or ever. He prided himself on keeping a low profile and going unnoticed. He didn't get wrapped up in other people's affairs, or other people at all. And he most definitely didn't need to be responsible for the corpse of a man who reeked of trouble on his heels, dead or alive.

Calysto didn't like attention and he certainly didn't like trouble.

Okay, he *might* have ruined that one hippie's bullshit 'medicine' shop. Just that one time. To be fair, that guy was really in there claiming that the clearly bathroom-grown ditch-weed bundle of sticks he was selling would cure all ails. From anxiety to cancer to fucking head lice. Like some kind of phony witch doctor, he floated around the shop shoving different shit under Calysto's nose and carrying on about it in a language he clearly didn't expect Calysto to be able to understand.

But he did. And when Calysto had insisted the man was overcharging for mediocre product, the drug-rug-clad half-baked idiot had the gall to tell Calysto he just couldn't *get* the 'science' behind the 'magic' of weed. So yeah, Calysto *may* have set up a *real* magical spark under that poor excuse for natural medicine on his way out.

It was a long time until he attempted to go out in public again after that.

The point is, it's not like Calysto had a clean record or could manage to entirely stay out of trouble. But I mean, really. That weed guy? He had it coming. This guy in front of him on the other hand—Calysto didn't have, or want, anything to do with.

But still, he was fucking dead.

Goddamnit.

Calysto sat back and spoke a few quiet words and the little wand he'd shoved in his pocket suddenly jumped up, splitting into multiple tiny lights that floated calmly in the air in front of his eyes.

"Please and thank you," Calysto spoke, and they dispersed across the room. They landed on various candlesticks and lamps placed in previously not-before-seen corners of the house. The whole room lit up and came to life, illuminating the lower floor in a crimson-orange hue.

"Alright..." Calysto placed the man's phone on the banister behind them and mumbling to himself, climbed to his feet. "Let's at least get you cleaned up, huh."

Calysto kicked off his sandals, sending them flying off into two opposite directions—landing in places that would surely elude his search for them later—rolled up his sleeves, crouched down and grabbed the man under the armpits and tugged.

Fuck, he's fucking heavy.

Well, that's what you get with dead weight. Calysto sucked in a breath and jerked the man's limp frame inch by inch across the floor and finally over to lean him up against the front of a worn-out old couch. Using his entire back to leverage the weight, Calysto climbed under the man's body and shoved him up onto the dusty and frayed cushions. It creaked loudly in protest at the sudden use.

"Yes, I know," Calysto panted. "He'll likely be the last."

Hard to say if the couch could understand him, or if he just talked to himself and everything in the house in the same manner whether it was magical or not, but the squeaking stopped as the limp body stilled. Calysto collapsed against the side, catching his breath for a moment. He had to figure out what to do. And preferably before anyone else found his fucking house. Again.

CHAPTER

THREE

Python shot up with a gasp and immediately choked on saliva and hot blood. Without thinking he turned and spat a heavy wad onto the floor. Oh, the floor. He squinted up in the dim orange light and blinked to clear his eyes. He was lying on a couch that looked like an antique from a hundred years ago, complete with wear and rat holes and dust and an arm that seemed to be held on by approximately three to five stitches. His head pounded as he turned to look around and to his right he was met with the sight of the rest of the room. It was mostly empty, only a small table at the foot of the couch, and a few lanterns glowing softly from their place on the floor.

What caught his attention was past that though. From the living room where he lay, he could see into a kitchen. And standing there in the entryway was that same raggedy looking man from before.

Oh, I must've passed out.

But the man was looking at him with a muted surprise that communicated he might have done more than that.

"What happened?" Python croaked. Damn his throat hurt. It would soon heal, but it fucking burned like road rash in the meantime.

Did I throw up?

The man didn't answer right away, and moved a few steps toward him without taking his eyes off of the couch.

"Well frankly, I thought you died," he finally said.

"Ha," Python barked. "It'd take more than that to kill me."

"More than what?" the man questioned. "Vomiting all your organs into my hallway?"

"Oh uh, yeah that, nah don't…" Python pushed his hair back and scratched his scalp. "Don't worry about it. Just ate something funny."

"What, raw meat?" The man squinted down at him as if observing him under a microscope. *Annoying.* "You weren't breathing, and you had no pulse. You were most certainly dead."

"Well, clearly I wasn't," Python snapped.

He didn't like the way this man was picking him apart with his creepy particular stare. Python's chest was sticky with bloody vomit and his mouth tasted like he'd just snacked on a pack of batteries and to make matters worse, he was fucking hungry again. Guess that's what happens when you upchuck your poisoned lunch.

Then, Python had a thought. This guy could do. He could just drain him dry and then haul his ass out of here, hopping over to the next town before that mob or anyone else was the wiser. He strained his hearing and found nothing but the sound of trees in the wind. They seemed to have gone. And he was out for long enough that the sun was again beginning to set.

"Alright" is all the man said in response and began to walk back toward the kitchen entrance. Python slung his legs over onto the floor and peered intently at the man's back, preparing to launch himself into his next meal.

"Your phone is by the door. There's a message," the man said as he shuffled away.

Python paused.

Message? From who?

His boots made a heavy sound on the hollow floor as he ran over and snatched it up.

"What the fuck," he croaked, and attempted to clear his throat. "You don't have service out here or what?"

The man didn't answer, having disappeared into the adjoining room.

"Hey!" Python called out. "Did you hear me?"

"Yes," came the short reply, and the man came back through the doorway glaring at him through the cracks in his glasses. "There is none, or can you not see that for yourself."

"You don't have a phone?"

"No."

"Ooookay," Python scoffed. "Old man."

The man ignored him. "Can you leave?"

"Yeah, yeah, I'm going," Python mumbled back while thumbing through his phone. "Don't give yourself a fucking headache."

Then he shut off the screen, shoved it into his pocket, and took three long strides towards the exit. As he left his voice carried out across the empty house, punctuated by the slam of the door.

"Thanks for nothing, asshole!"

Python stepped out into the cool early evening and inhaled sharply through his teeth, tasting the air and grinning wide. He enjoyed this—his freedom. The endless possibility the open night could bring. Being inside that house even for the short time he was there felt like a stuffy eternity of a special kind. The whole thing smelled of dust and chemicals, stale and stagnant and dead. And he was only one of those things. The other two he despised with a passion. He wasn't one for staying still and reveled in traveling, chasing, never settling down. Staying in any one place for too long just wasn't for him and he liked the fact that he didn't need to explain that fact about himself to anyone either.

Hungry and eager, Python didn't waste another moment before he took off through the surrounding forest on inhumanly swift feet. With any luck he could slip back into the trash heap town he'd been chased from for a quick bite and hitch a ride down the highway to the next one before the sun rose. Wind whipped through his silvery hair as he ran, leaving the creepy cabin and its weird little inhabitant far away in the dust, soon to be added to a long list of those forgotten. As unimportant to Python as he was to them and just the way he liked it. Untethered, unbothered. Free.

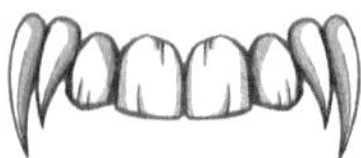

Finally. He was alone again. A familiar type of peace settled down around him in the house as Calysto climbed the stairs back up to his workshop. It's hard to say how long he sat there. Same posture, same position, same deathly silence. He didn't seem to mind, in fact, he seemed to prefer it this way. Eventually the need to pee got the better of him. Something he had clearly been ignoring for a while and forced himself to finally acknowledge, because when he stood it was so abrupt the stool flipped over behind him and he paid it no mind as he rushed down the hallway in an exasperated huff. Then, while relieving himself for what could be close to fifteen minutes straight there came another slam from downstairs.

Fucking hell. He cursed under his breath and pulled up the band of his sweatpants. *What is it now?*

"HEY!"

Oh for fuck's sake. Did he seriously come back here?

"What!" Calysto called out, emerging from his washroom. "What the fuck do you want!"

"What do I want?!" The grey-haired nuisance called back. "How about you tell me this first!" Calysto stopped in the hallway, watching with his hands in his sweater pockets as the man stormed angrily up the stairs to confront him. "How about you tell me where the fuck we are, huh?"

"I don't know," Calysto answered.

"What do you mean you don't know!" The man snapped his teeth like a dog then growled in the back of his throat. *Strange.*

"What... when I came in here we were like five miles outside of town, and that shit isn't there anymore. Plus these woods are different!"

"Different how?" Calysto pulled his sweater closed, hands still in his pockets. "How can you tell?"

"Wh— what kind of question is that? Don't try to distract me. You did something! What did you do? How are we in a totally different place?"

"I don't know what you mean."

"Y— Motherfucker I..." A little bit of color rose in the man's pale cheeks and as he stepped closer Calysto thought he could almost see an iridescent glimmer in his eyes. "You've got to be fucking kidding me."

"Watch yourself," Calysto said sharply as the man got within a foot's distance of him. "You did break into my house after all."

"*SO?! YOU FUCKING KIDNAPPED ME!*" The flush in his cheeks grew.

"How," Calysto leaned his shoulder against the wooden wall of the hallway. "Do you presume I managed to do that?"

"I don't know!" the man spat. His speech seemed to have gained a slight lisp. "Maybe... maybe the house! Yeah, I remember the house was shaking. What was that?"

This was turning from curious to irritating and the idea that Calysto had before he went pee was all but fleeing from his brain never to be seen again with every word that came out of this asshole's mouth.

"I don't need to tell you anything," Calysto narrowed his eyes. "And I don't want you in my house."

The man growled again and in a flash closed the space between them, slamming Calysto into the wall and knocking his glasses askew on his face. Their noses nearly touched as the man pinned his arms on either side of him. He smelled strange, of flesh and blood, but not the way a human smells of these things. Oh, what did Calysto know of the way a human smells? This was the first time he'd even been touched in... well. Who knows how long.

"Let me go," Calysto strained against his hold. *Damn, this guy is strong.*

"Not until you tell me what you did."

Calysto met his glare, and only then did he *really* see his eyes.

His pupils were bottomless and dead, an endless black ringed in irises of a deep crimson red. The cornea overlaying them glistened and flickered in the light like that of a cat, turning gold and silver and back to red again. It was unlike anything Calysto had ever seen.

Even this close Calysto felt no breath from the man's lips, just a strange cold absence of air.

But as he looked down, his struggling stopped and he froze.

Where before the man's lips had been as pale as his skin, they were now blushed. But what lie beyond them was even more startling. Teeth. No, fangs. Not just a regular set of human canines. But elongated, with an extra smaller set beside them. And in front of Calysto's eyes, they appeared to be growing longer and longer, as the mouth stretched into a hideous smile. Calysto felt his curiosity be quickly replaced with a paralyzing fear.

"Or I could just eat you whole," the man hissed.

Those teeth came even closer and much to his embarrassment, Calysto yelped.

"Alright!"

The man stopped and leaned back away from his slow trajectory in the direction of Calysto's neck. He smiled again, this time with a clear level of self-satisfaction.

"Well?" he said, the soft lisp was gone as those bizarre teeth disappeared inside his mouth.

"Let me go first."

"No."

Calysto inhaled, attempting to calm his nerves. "I moved the house."

"How?"

"It's hard to explain."

The man scowled. "How about you try."

"I don't need to tell you," Calysto snapped back. Danger though he may be in, he wasn't one to give up a hard-earned secret—or invention—for nothing. And besides, his wrists were aching from where the man held so tight. He was getting irritated. Again.

"Where are we, then?"

"I don't know," Cal answered, and the man gripped down tighter. "I don't fucking know, okay! I didn't... I don't plan it like that."

"What so you just, somehow move this whole house somewhere else and you don't even think about where?"

"Something like that."

"Just who the fuck are you?"

"Who are you!" Calysto snapped back, struggling a bit. "What're you, some kind of demon... no, vampire?"

The man instantly released him and stepped away, suddenly wary.

"How do you know that name," he demanded.

"Oh," Calysto righted himself, rubbing his wrists. "It was a guess. Something I've only ever read about. I didn't know you were real."

"I didn't say I was one."

"But you are." Calysto pushed up his glasses and cleared his throat, hopeful he was successful in hiding the excitement that just overcame him, and took another look at the man. "Pale skin, no pulse, no breath, fangs—double, that's interesting—the cat-like eyes. That wasn't your own blood you threw up before, was it?"

"You don't know anything about me," the man defended, weakly.

"Oh, but it seems I do." Calysto barely stopped himself from smiling. "Come, I'm not a threat to your no doubt secret identity. I'm simply curious. I thought your kind was a myth."

"Stop it."

"Stop what?"

"Analyzing me!" the man snapped.

"At least tell me your name."

The man seemed to be weighing his options. Calysto still wasn't too sure if he was still thinking about eating him. He wondered what that'd do, how the man would change. Did he change? Transform? Certainly cartoons and movies weren't all correct. He couldn't believe he'd guessed correctly on his first try. A vampire? Really? Calysto suddenly didn't give a single shit if he died in this moment. He had to know more. He had to.

"Tell me yours, first."

"Calysto."

"What kind of weird-ass wizard name is that? Your parents big fantasy nerds or something?"

Calysto didn't entertain him with an answer.

"Okay fine," the man sighed, shoving his hair back from his face. It was becoming clear this was some kind of nervous tell. Calysto was now drinking in every detail with rapt interest, watching as clawed fingernails fell to the man's side and noting the way the hands were long and veiny.

"My name's Python, happy?"

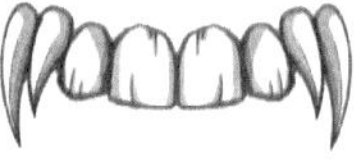

"A FITTING NAME FOR A VAMPIRE," the unkempt man named Calysto responded.

He was clearly trying to hide his excitement. Excitement over what? Most—no, all—people who found out what he was ran screaming in the other direction until he was forced to tear their throats out to silence them. Not that he let would anyone live after seeing him for what he truly was anyway. Not if he could help it.

This man looked like he had just won the lottery but hadn't told anyone yet, and his heartbeat had picked up speed, but not with the familiar sour smell of adrenaline-induced fear.

"Let me see." Calysto crossed the distance in the narrow hallway, and without meaning to Python shrank back, away from the outstretched hand reaching for his mouth. His pride would later demand a soothing for that little act of cowardice.

"Don't touch me." Python glared in hopes of scaring him off, but there was nowhere to go and Calysto didn't seem disturbed in the slightest.

Calysto lifted his lip and peered close. Python could smell his weird scent even more now. It was like musty leather shoes, old sweat, chemicals, and something... something he couldn't place. His thumb tasted like metal, warm against his cold gums.

"Can you do it again?"

"Wha—" Python spoke around his involuntarily curled lip. "I can'd do it unlesth I wanna bide' you."

"And you don't want to?" Calysto was a bit shorter in height and had to look up to meet him with a disbelieving glare. Python didn't respond but he let his fangs slowly appear. He would entertain this little man, for now.

"Ah!" Calysto brightened. This might be the first time Python saw him smile. Just ever so slightly. "Fascinating, really."

Python jerked his mouth away as the pulse in Calysto's hand became a little too apparent.

"Okay, you had your fun. Now answer something for me."

Calysto stepped back. "That's only fair."

"How'd you move this house?"

"Do you swear you won't touch anything," Calysto demanded defensively.

Python nodded once, eager to agree to whatever would let him on this secret.

"Follow me."

Calysto turned away from him and shuffled down into a dark corner of the hall. Python could still see him clearly, his frame bent with an age he didn't show on his face. He found himself wondering how long this guy had lived here alone. Then he decided he didn't care. He just wanted to see whatever the hell had the ability to move an entire house. Was it something like an airplane jet engine attached to the back? Secret wheels or some mysterious springboard mechanism?

Whatever idiotic guess he'd had still wasn't even close to what he saw.

Calysto stepped aside leaning against an open door and waved his hand towards the small space. He didn't bother to turn on a light, no doubt curious to see if Python could see so well in the dark. And, well yeah, he could. It seemed Calysto could tell—and did he seem delighted by it. In his controlled manner.

Python took a look around at what amounted to... basically nothing. There was a strange cylinder in the corner, almost like a copper hot water heater with various pipes and tubes coming from all sides. On a small coffee table was a piece of translucent purple crystal as big as a bowling ball, and next to it sat a small rack lined with corked vials full of differently colored liquids.

"This is it?"

"Do you even know what *it* is?" Calysto frowned.

"Well... no. But I fail to see how this has anything to do with, I don't know, moving an entire house. Don't you like, drive it or something?" Python looked around again, maybe he'd missed and important element. Like a gigantic windshield and accelerator and driver's seat? Anything?

"Technically, it's a cabin. Much less work." Calysto crossed his arms. "And no I don't drive it, that's absurd. It would take two days to drive fifteen hundred miles."

"Fif...." Python balked. "Are you telling me we moved *fifteen hundred miles*? In like ten seconds?"

"Yes." Calysto just watched him.

"HOW?!"

"You wouldn't understand even if I explained it."

Python felt dizzy again. Since he had run out of the house after their last parting, he was unable to find a town and was only blessed by some nonexistent god who probably hated him to find a random jogger out on a forest trail at night. No, he didn't kill the guy. Just knocked him out and took a bit of his precious life source, then continued on his way. But even after following the path all the way through the woods he saw no end in sight, and was running low on energy to explore in the other direction.

Damn I should have just drained that jogger dry.

He was still depleted from his possession-like projectile vomiting and was too weak to go on for the night. He could have risked it and tried to find a town. But fuck, if his best option wasn't running back to that fucking weirdo's house. Besides, he had to figure out just what the hell happened. So with a frustrated groan, Python turned on his heel and returned to the cabin in the woods.

Now, considering this house-traveling news, it was turning into one of the weirdest nights of his life. And for someone of his age and night-time occupation, that was saying something.

"Tell me this," Calysto's voice broke through his thoughts. "Can you run fast?"

"What?" Python leaned on the copper boiler.

"Don't touch anything!" Calysto snapped, suddenly alert.

"Shit," Python retracted his hand. "Okay, fuck. Touchy."

Calysto instantly calmed. "So can you?"

"Yeah," Python puffed up a bit, grinning down at the frumpy man. "Yeah, I can. Faster than a car on the highway."

"Huh."

Calysto didn't even seem impressed and nodded as if filing the information away in the database of his brain for later. This itched on Python's nerves. The guy *just* found out vampires exist, the least he could do was act like it was a *little* bit cool.

"Not good enough?" Python demanded.

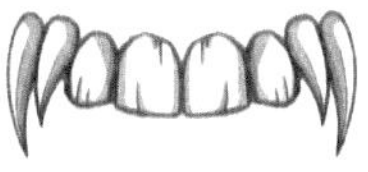

"Why, do you need my approval?" Calysto asked, motioning for Python to leave the room. The vampire glared back at him for a long tense breath before finally complying. He made his way down the stairs and Calysto could hear him grumble something under his breath as he passed.

"Listen!" Python stopped on the stairs and called out. "Just take me the fuck back!"

Calysto carefully closed the door and followed behind him. He rounded the corner and stopped to lean on the banister. "I can't do that."

"And why the fuck not!"

"I don't know where we were to begin with," Calysto admitted without shame. It wasn't ever really important to him where he ended up, just that he got away and was left alone for a while. He only got part of that this time.

"WH— " Python looked torn between complete disbelief and righteous anger. "What the fuck is your problem?" is all he managed to say in the end.

Calysto shrugged. As long as this vampire wasn't trying to eat him, his bravado was actually kind of amusing. For now, anyway. He seemed as volatile as a cornered snake.

Fitting name then.

Calysto huffed at the thought with a nearly imperceptible upturn of his lips.

"Is this funny to you?!" Python snapped.

"No." Calysto shook his head, turning his attention to Python fully. "Look, had I known you were in the house, I wouldn't have moved it yet. But I can't take you back."

Python deflated a bit. "Fuck... well, you did get me away from those assholes."

"Assholes...? They were after you?"

"Yeah, who else?" Python shrugged and gestured to himself. "Vampire, remember."

"Oh, of course." If Calysto were hiding something, he hid it well. "Well, in that case. You could say I helped you."

"You still owe me though," Python growled. "For the whole... displacing me thing."

Calysto didn't answer right away. He wanted to ask more questions of this strange creature but he also didn't want to get bit, and he got the impression that Python was constantly one wrong rub away from impulsively ripping his head off. If the ache in his wrists was any indication, Python definitely could do it too.

"Say I do owe you," Calysto said slowly. "What exactly would that be?"

Python didn't seem prepared for him to agree. "Oh uh... couch. I'm crashing on your couch."

"What? No. You can't live here."

"Not live here, idiot." Python rolled his eyes. "As if I'd want to. Just until I can find the nearest town."

"Oh..." Calysto relaxed slightly. Only for a few nights, then. He could probably handle that. "Fine."

FOUR

Aeris slowly sipped her drink, letting the heat of it burn the roof of her mouth and swirl around her tongue. It slid down her throat like rug burn to the esophagus but she didn't flinch. She simply swallowed and placed the crystal-cut glass carefully back onto the table that was sticky with ringed cup stains and smeared remnants of drunkenly consumed meals. She peeled her leather-gloved hand off of the surface with a soft *shlick*. From her position in the corner of the dive bar in which she sat, her dark eyes stayed sharp and observant.

She dipped a flimsy paper napkin into her glass, absorbing a bit of the melted ice from the bottom, and used it to wipe the heel of her glove. It was near autumn outside, and despite it being the season to acceptably dress like a character from a haunted Victorian mansion without garnering too many looks, she never changed this manner of dress. After all these years it had become not only a staple of comfort but of spite.

She wanted him to see her coming.

At this point, he knew who she was. And he knew she was after him. It had been so long now, after all. And she had gotten close a few times even. But somehow that damned vampire always slipped out of her grasp. Now, despite whatever drove her, and the fact that her very dated period dress made her stand entirely out of place, she continued to wear it.

Her long and heavy steel-grey canvas coat was lined with implements of her trade. Secret pockets and hooks, sewn in weapons and wards lined the inner jacket. Her vest covered the pistol straps that crisscrossed her chest, and she completed the look like a proper gentleman with tight-fitting black trousers and near-knee-high leather boots. Her flouncy once-white shirt was yellowed but the ruffled collar that rippled around her neck covered the evidence of something much worse than sweat stains underneath.

From her secluded corner, she watched the night unfold through the thick translucent rim of her glass, only moving otherwise to tap her cane on the floor in thought. Or impatience. It was unclear what she was waiting or looking for. But the bartender who went out of his way to oblige her request to bring drinks straight to her self-made outpost seemed to know better than to ask. His behind-the-bar bravado slipped away into timid obedience once in her presence, as he quietly replaced her glass with another and apologized without knowing what for or why. She didn't spare him more than one half-curious glance, observing him just enough to make sure to rule him out.

A crass and outdated country song rattled out of the worn-down never-that-good-to-begin-with house speakers. The singer twanged on about some long-lost love who never actually loved him in the first place. Aeris scoffed into her glass. Leave it up to some man to build an elaborate fantasy in his head before even talking to a girl, then hating her when she didn't play along. Typical shit. The few times someone had tried that on her, had been their last. Whether she would outright kill them or give them a scolding to leave their eardrums ringing for days was hard to say. Depended on her mood. And now, her mood was turning sour.

She stared at the black chipped paint flaking off from around the grimy push-bar of the front door and scowled.

Come on, come on.

She had followed his trail here not two days ago, punctuated and confirmed by the local spinning of tales that often happened in a vampire's wake. Apparently he'd gone after some cheerleader. Or homecoming queen. She didn't particularly bother with what, or who. Only that he'd definitely gotten himself in trouble by necking the most desirable neck in a low-life town. But that never meant that idiot learned his lesson. He'd be back. She was sure of it. Or at least she hoped she was sure. It had been two nights with no trace of the vampire whose thirst for alcohol nearly rivaled that of blood—not even in a place simply begging for someone like him to haunt.

Where the fuck is that asshole.

She cursed to herself, and this time set her glass down with a slam. The pathetic excuse for a table rocked back and forth on uneven legs under the force. It was nearing three in the morning, so basically lunchtime for her favorite hunt. But there was no sign of him, and no recent word spread through the cigarette-stained lips of the patrons who frequented such a joint. He wasn't here.

Had he actually learned his lesson for once? Moved on when he fucked up or things got too risky? No, that couldn't be right. Something must've happened to him. But what? What, or who—besides her—could take down the infamous Python? She bit her lip, wondering if that was it. Could some misfortune finally have befallen him?

Not that she cared.

It was only that... had someone else gotten to him first it was going to royally piss her off. No one—not a soul besides her—was allowed to get their hands on him. She was going to be the one to drive a stake through his heart, chop off his head, and stuff garlic down his bleeding neck. Even if that last part was only truly effective in stupid legends. She was going to do it. Her, and no one else, would get to slay that son of a devil himself.

Python is mine.

She stood abruptly, sending her chair jutting out from under her with a surprised squeak. No one looked her way as the warbling tenor of that delusional lovesick cowboy drowned out all other sounds. Though *literally any other noise* would be damned preferable.

She tapped her long black cane twice and then tossed it up, catching it in her leather-gloved hand. The silver snakehead pommel glimmered in the shitty pink and yellow neon lights behind her. The sign's lazy rhythm blinked on and off with a siren's call of *"BEER"* in big curly letters, and illuminated her black-clad frame in a shiny bubblegum-colored outline. She moved across the uneven bar floor of peeled linoleum and once-tan carpet strips with an even and authoritative gait. Not even the most obnoxious of late-week-night dive bar-goers got in her way. It was best for them that they didn't.

Outside, the moon shone down bright from behind a distant line of trees, but something else in the distance caught her attention. A smell in the air. Sharp and crisp, a pungent odor that tickled her memory with a familiarity she couldn't quite place. It traveled weak and fading over the gentle breeze, but with no other lead to follow she let the scent carry her.

Her irritation was only compounded by her solitude and the churning of her thoughts. She'd followed Python's trail to end after end, through age after age, and still, he eluded her. He was her final catch, her biggest prize, and the purpose that had driven her for countless periods of time. Yet even as the concoction of frustration and adrenaline traveled hot through her alcohol-laced veins, she felt the familiar and growing sense of exhaustion. She would capture him and kill him, of course. Then, she would finally rest.

Though her rage towards him fueled her relentless determination, she had to admit that after so long the promise of something beyond the quest for vengeance had its own kind of appeal. As far as what that appeal was exactly, or what a future without the chase would actually look like? Well...

Well, it's much easier to be fucking angry instead.

Aeris shoved her hat down harder on top of her curls and picked up her pace. She turned down a vacant street accompanied by nothing other than the sound of her footsteps on the pavement and the heading on her mind.

See you soon, sweetheart.

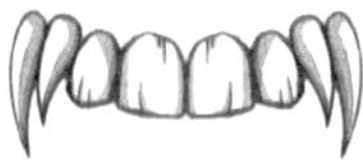

"CAL! CAAAALLLL!"

Calysto sighed so heavily he nearly dropped his head onto his desk. This vampire was going to be the death of him and of all his peace and good ideas. He had been crashing on Calysto's old couch for a few days now, leaving with a drag in his step for most hours in the night and returning with a vigor suspiciously revitalized before dawn.

"Hey! Cal!"

Python's head poked in through Calysto's workshop door, quickly followed by the rest of him. He sauntered over and leaned heavily onto Calysto's work desk, rattling the items on it dangerously. Calysto ignored him. Or, he tried to. He quietly scooted a screwdriver away from Python's intruding ass that leaned on the table edge and threatened to knock it off.

"Don't ignore me," Python whined.

Calysto didn't respond, didn't look up.

"What're you working on?"

Python leaned in closer and Calysto glanced over to see his eyes. They were practically glowing. His lips were blushed pink and his cheeky smile slipped a bit lopsided to the left. His fangs were still out —just barely.

"Are you going to bite me if I don't answer?"

This made Python laugh and he tilted his head back, giving Calysto a good look at the details of his long, pale neck. On the side usually hidden by his collar and hair, was an old scar. Bite marks.

Python's laughter ceased as he met Calysto's gaze and realized what he was staring at.

"I won't make you into one of me if that's what you're asking," he sneered. "Fucking nosey."

"Nosey?" Calysto frowned. "You were just demanding I tell you what I'm working on."

"I did no such thing," Python huffed. "I'm just curious. Can't a guy be curious?"

Calysto groaned under his breath. Python was simply unbearable. He hadn't made this much conversation in a countless amount of time and now he basically had a housemate. And a persistent, loud, and irritating one at that.

"It's a directional drive."

"A what?"

"To control the house." Calysto sat back, revealing the small hunk of stone and copper screws he had been hunched over. "To take you back."

"Oh, that tired of me already?"

"Yes," Calysto said simply and stood, tossing his tool onto the table.

He was barefoot now and though it was early autumn he wasn't all that keen on wearing shoes that weren't his slippers, and he couldn't find one of them from where he'd kicked them off downstairs. Still, he wore his trusty frayed grey sweater around him like a security blanket, shivering slightly against the damp chill that permeated the rickety house.

He could feel Python's glistening eyes on his back as he left the room and headed to the bottom floor.

In the small living space that Python had acquisitioned all for himself there were clothes strewn everywhere. The couch was now covered in a large blanket made of synthetic fur and stacked high with pillows of various shapes and sizes. Calysto had asked at some point where Python managed to get all this stuff, and the answer was a wickedly toothy grin punctuated by Python wiggling his fingers.

Calysto still didn't know how far they were from the nearest town, nor had the desire to find out. But at the speed and quantity in which Python had collected—stole—all these goods made him think they weren't too far. Though Python also did say he could run fast. Maybe there wasn't much to worry about then.

Calysto picked up a discarded velvet turtleneck with his toes and slung it in the direction of the couch.

"Hey! What the fuck don't! Touch that! With your nasty feet!" Python called out from behind him.

So, he followed him down here as well.

"Then don't leave it on the floor," Calysto said back in monotone. He heard Python huff.

"I'm hungry…" Python whined again, his voice suddenly appearing right behind Calysto's head, making him jump.

"Don't do that," Calysto barked. "Didn't you just eat? That's what your red lips mean, isn't it?"

Python scowled and tucked his lips into his teeth. "Stop observing me. It's invasive, weirdo."

"You give a lot away," Calysto shrugged, crossing the threshold into the kitchen. "I don't really have to try."

The kitchen was well… as barren as the rest of Calysto's house.

Lit with an artificial fluorescence it bled blueish-white down the walls, coating everything with the same restaurant walk-in sterile light. The counters were covered with half-made half-abandoned projects of mysterious purpose and origin. The space where a stove should've been was simply barren. The floor was a raw stone foundation, grey and grimy with stains and pot-hole-sized nicks deep enough to break an ankle in. Years of dirt and colonies of mold spread out in spindly trails across the walls like a nature-made wallpaper pattern.

Countertop space that wasn't taken up by some strange experiment was strewn with trash. Discarded bottles, cans, wrappers, and bags were stacked high, stuffed in and around every corner. The only furniture in the strange half-lab half-hoarders-nightmare was a flimsy white fold-out plastic table. The kind of table you'd find in a kid's craft room, or more likely, missing a leg and sticking out of someone's trash. It had clearly been that way when Calysto found it, as its surface was dinged up with scrapes, blotches of paint, and something brown that had soaked into the surface. It was hard to say if that particular marring was from Calysto or not. Either way, it didn't seem to faze him. He wasn't one for caring much about the decor.

In front of the table was a wooden chair likely dug from the same trash pile, and its legs were repaired in a similarly haphazard manner. Python slung himself down into it with the confidence of a man who didn't know how broken it had been. The only space in the kitchen clean of some kind of debris was the little area on the table that Python had cleared right in front of the chair.

"I did just eat," Python finally answered one question, choosing to ignore the others. "But, that doesn't mean I don't want food."

This made Calysto pause. He leaned a shoulder against the yellowed exterior of the once-white refrigerator which may or may not have been turned off for over a decade or longer and peered curiously at the vampire across from him.

"You eat regular food?" he asked. "Like human food? I thought that was impossible."

"Yeah well, just a few days ago you thought me, as a concept, was impossible," Python responded with a lazy wave of his hand. "So, this shouldn't be too hard to wrap your brain around."

"But," Calysto rubbed the skin of his nose beneath were his glasses rested. "You still have to drink blood, right?"

"Well yeah, food is just for fun." Python grinned then spread his arms out wide and in a mock-polite voice said, "Um yes, let me get a cheeseburger with fries, extra ketchup, and a large side of O-Negative please?"

Calysto rolled his eyes.

"So?" Python kicked his feet up onto the table, sending something on a loud journey to the floor. "What have you got?"

"See for yourself." Calysto motioned to the cabinets.

Python leapt up and began slinging open the cabinets that still had doors attached. It was already evident that the open ones had nothing inside. But as he searched the others his face began to fall. He slung one empty cookie container out onto the floor then slammed the last door shut and held up a ripped and wrinkled probably-stale bag of plain potato chips in his hand.

"Calysto. What the fuck is this?"

Calysto had already busied himself with something else taking up residence in the once-sink.

"Huh?"

"This is it?"

Calysto could hear the crinkle from Python shaking a bag from behind his head. He slowly turned, resting his hands on the counter edge. It was just his luck to get stuck with not only a high-maintenance diva of a vampire stowaway, but one who was also a picky eater.

"You don't like chips I take it."

"That's not what I mean!" Python snapped his teeth. "What are you a vampire, too? Or do you have some secret stash, 'cause this isn't anything for a human to live on."

Calysto squinted at the word *human,* but didn't entertain it.

"Concerned about me, are you?"

"Fuck you." Python tossed the chips onto the counter. "Come on let's go."

"Go... where..."

Calysto didn't like the sound of whatever it was that involved leaving his house. And Python definitely intended for him to do just that.

"To get food, fucking idiot! Come on, put on your fucking old man sandals."

"No." Calysto crossed his arms.

"Are you serious?" Python barked a laugh. His sharp fangs glistened in the overhead flicker of a dying bulb. "Fine then, die for all I care."

"... Wait." Calysto sighed, hesitating a long breath before asking. "I am... I'm a little hungry... how far do we have to go?"

"Not far," Python grinned. "Turns out, if I would've gone the other direction when leaving the other day, I would've easily found a town."

Calysto sniffed, wrinkling his nose. "So, what you mean to say is —you found a place to stay, yet you choose to stay here?"

"Yep!" Python turned on his heel, kicking trash out of the way as he did. "It's free real estate, baby! Coming or not?"

"Hold on, hold on. I'm fucking coming," Calysto grumbled and reluctantly followed behind.

FIVE

Python's legs were killing him. Not from exhaustion or exertion, but from walking so fucking slow waiting on this guy. He forgot just how irritatingly sluggish everything is when you're human. Every action took so much time and effort. For Calysto it seemed it was even harder as if beneath his youthful shell he carried the bones and heart of a man a hundred years older.

Python kind of liked this weird hermit. Granted, he was grouchy as hell and snapped back at nearly everything Python said and well, Python had to admit he did find some amusement in getting a rise out of him. But Calysto had discovered he was a vampire—almost instantly, due to his own negligence—and instead of cowering in fear or running away screaming or trying to kill him like anyone else did, he'd shrugged and embraced it. As if there weren't anything stranger in this world. He'd even had the audacity to approach Python immediately after and demand to see his teeth. It was strange, intriguing, bizarre.

So yeah, maybe he did choose to keep crashing in Calysto's living room instead of finding a trucker to give him a bunk and a ride in exchange for a fuck and a bite. At least he didn't need to worry about waking up with a knife to his throat or a stake near his heart. Which had happened maybe a few more times than he'd like to admit.

Therefore, he might've slowed down a little bit to let the crotchety human keep up. Just a little. Though don't mistake Python for any kind of altruistic, he still had the mind of using Calysto up for all he was worth, and the scrape of Calysto's sandals on the blacktop was starting to get directly on his nerves.

Python was already at the limits of his already limited patience.

"Can you hurry up!" he called back.

"How fucking far is it, Python?" Calysto panted softly.

Python peered back at him through the dark and saw small beads of sweat glistening on his brow. Calysto's hands were shoved deep in his sweater pockets, and he sniffled loudly as he approached. Python paused, waiting for him to catch up.

"Uh, I don't know."

"I thought you said it was close." Calysto frowned.

Python laughed lightly. "To be honest um, I was running so. It could be farther than I thought. For your little human legs."

Calysto glared at him but didn't speak. His heartbeat beneath his chest was pounding fairly evenly for having speed-walked two miles in the middle of the night. Python peered at him closer, curious. The golden-brown stubble on his cheeks had grown longer in the past few days, and the dark circles that were permanently etched under his eyes didn't look any better. Come to think of it, Python had never seen him sleep. Any normal person would be asleep whenever he was up prowling around in the night. But Calysto was always awake, always answering him with a slightly irritated sigh—but answering nonetheless.

"How are you alive?" Python asked, blurting it without thinking.

"Easy," Calysto answered, giving him a pointed look. "Keep breathing."

"Ha. Ha. So funny," Python deadpanned. "Seriously, I never see you sleep, and you never eat. So what gives."

"You want to see me sleep?" Calysto bit back. "Can we just go?"

"You know that's not what I meant," Python grumbled. "Fine come on, I can see lights ahead."

Calysto shuffled up behind him. "Really?"

"Yep." Python pointed. "Another mile."

Calysto just groaned.

"MOTHERFUCKER," Python cursed while standing in front of the sliding glass doors of the gas station entrance.

"What?" Calysto called.

Python didn't answer him and started prying the doors open from the center seam.

"It'll open on its own," Calysto grumbled as he approached. "Just fucking wait."

"No it won't." Python righted himself as the doors flung open. "Vampire problems."

"Wow, not even motion sensors, huh?" Calysto looked up at the blinking light above the door. "Ask next time, then."

"Yeah, yeah." Python waved him off as they entered.

The cashier, dressed in a red polyester nightmare that constituted the degrading costume of a shit hole masquerading as classy, was staring out at them from her position behind the counter and the rim of what was likely her fourth or fifth cup of coffee. It was the grave-yard shift—though neither warlock nor vampire paid attention to such things—and she had to not only stay awake for it, but she also had to put up with the weird assholes such hours tended to attract.

"It'll open on its own," she said blankly, her tone clearly indicating she'd seen it all before. "You don't gotta pull it."

Calysto nodded to her then shot Python a solid glare. "See?"

Python growled. "Just get your shit will you."

THE CASHIER TURNED BACK to her coffee, nursing cold hands around the sticky red styrofoam. From over the edge her eyes carefully watched the two men traipse around the store. But then, she looked up into the large bubble mirror that gave her a bird's eye view of the aisles, and only saw one of them—the haggard-looking man with cracked glasses was holding a sack of donuts between his teeth while rifling in the back of a shelf for a very specific can of Spam. But the other man was nowhere to be found. Then she saw something even stranger—a bag of ranch potato skins hanging, suspended in midair. She startled, nearly dropping her coffee, before looking out into the aisles. What met her stare was the tall grey-haired man, shoving chips into his mouth with a mischievous grin. Her face must have betrayed her shock as he simply said,

"Don't worry, I'm gonna pay for them."

She forced a nod, then as soon as he looked away, she checked the mirror again. Sure enough, that bag of chips was simply floating there with no man attached. No face, no hands, only a leather jacket that moved on its own. She blinked and rubbed her eyes. Maybe she needed to take a weekend off, or switch to some daytime shifts once in a while. This was next level tired, even by her terms.

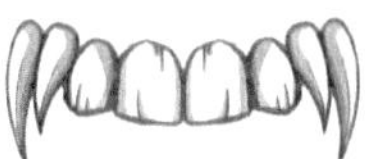

"WILL YOU HURRY UP," Python said between loud open-mouthed crunches.

"I will if you stop bugging me," Calysto responded. Then he seemed to realize something. He shoved his arm full of snacks into Python's hands. "Hold this."

"Wh— okay... what, what're you doing?"

He followed behind Calysto as he made a beeline for the refrigerated cases in the back. Calysto didn't answer and began scooping out energy drinks from the frosted shelves by the armful.

"I need a basket," he said finally.

Python waited, leaning against the foggy glass door and trying to decide between impatience or resignation as he watched Calysto acquire the most unhealthy assortment of gas station food he could find. Python hadn't been human in a long time, but he was fairly sure they needed a vegetable or at least a glass of water every now and then. Once a week or so, right? Ah, he couldn't remember.

Calysto returned with a handbasket, grabbed all the food from Python's hands, then turned to the refrigerator and began to fill the basket to the brim with cans.

"Gross." Python sniffed. "You like those?"

"Like? No. Want? Yes. Well... this one's not too bad." Calysto shrugged, holding up a silver and red can splattered with a graffiti-esque logo of cherries and shotgun shells. Python made no comment except to wrinkle his nose at it.

Calysto hauled the basket up with a soft groan. "Come on."

"Cal."

"What."

Python dropped his voice, "You know I don't have money right."

"Yeah? Neither do I," Calysto answered, matter of fact. "Let's go."

"Oh yeah." Python grinned devilishly, throwing the empty bag of potato skins on the floor. "I like that."

PYTHON TOOK a long drag from one of the cigarettes he'd dashed behind the counter to steal and exhaled the smoke into the air where it mingled with a cloud of cool early morning frost. Calysto walked beside him, waddling slightly under the weight of the stolen basket of goods.

"Did you even get one real thing to eat?" Python scoffed, flicking ash behind him. "How can you live off this junk?"

"Says the guy with a cigarette in his mouth," Calysto panted between words, his face scrunched in discomfort.

Python snickered at the sight.

"Yeah, well, I'm dead remember? Shit doesn't hurt me."

"Are you really?"

"What."

"Dead?" Calysto asked. "You really died? How?"

Python scowled, teeth digging slightly into the filter dangling from his lips. "That's none of your business."

"But you did die, right?" Calysto continued on seeming unfazed.

"I just said I did," Python snapped, taking an aggressive puff and burning up half the cigarette in the process.

"So, there's others like you then?"

Calysto's glasses were slipping down his slightly sweaty nose as he peered up at Python in the dim moonlight, awkwardly craning his neck to study him.

"Sure," Python answered, his tone clipped.

He was getting real tired of this guy's invasive fucking questions. It was like he didn't know what not to ask or when, or he just didn't care. Couldn't he act impressed or ask Python to do something cool like climb a tree in three seconds or lift a car? Why'd he have to get so fucking personal about it?

Some scientist.

"Why don't you..."

"What, live with them? Be buddies? Hang out in some big vampire orgy coven like the movies?" Python bit back.

"Well, yes," Calysto answered seriously. "I was unsure if that was a stereotype. You are the first real vampire I've met after all."

"That you know of."

Python threw the cigarette into a pothole disguised as a puddle and listened to the sharp hiss of its death before continuing.

"If you really want to know, I don't hang out with other vampires 'cause I don't fucking like them."

"All of them?" Calysto wheezed, setting the basket down in the grass on the side of the crumbling concrete back road. "Hold... hold on a second."

"You need to get out more," Python observed as Calysto held his side with one hand and winced.

"You could carry it for me, Mister Super Strength."

"Nah, I like to watch you struggle." He flashed his teeth and Calysto sighed.

"And to answer your question," Python continued. "Yes, all of them."

"That's odd." Calysto frowned.

"Says the most asocial hermit human I've ever fucking met."

Calysto didn't answer, and stared down at the handbasket as if it were full of a mystery more intriguing than Python, the vampire, standing right there.

Hellooooo.

"Can we go, now," Python huffed. "What, are you mad I called you a hermit? It's true."

Calysto still didn't speak and scooped up the basket, continuing down the road without another word.

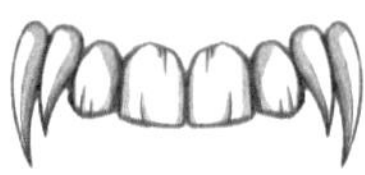

HUMAN. That's what Python kept calling him. Fucking human. He had no idea of course and Calysto wasn't about to tell him. Yet it bothered him. For another person to assume him weak, incapable, without value. Calysto *wished* he was human. Then maybe he could have died a long time ago and wouldn't have to live this miserably long existence full of nothingness and loneliness and pain. Trudging through each day with only his stupid ideas and stubborn as fuck attitude to keep him going.

He was alone. And he'd been alone for so long he was more than used to it. But the reason he was alone would never cease to dig at his mind, and tear at a wound so deep that no time had even come close to healing it.

No, No, No. We're not going there. This is now, that was then. It's better to be alone, it's best to be left alone. No one knows me here, I'm safe, I'm fine, it's okay, it's okay.

"Hey!"

He heard a voice but didn't pay it much mind, keeping his eyes on the road right in front of him and focusing on the way his toe stuck awkwardly out of the front of his shoes. They really were getting old, weren't they?

"HEY!" It was Python. *"GET OUT OF THE FUCKING ROAD!"*

With those words Calysto found himself being tackled and flung into the ditch. Mud splashed over him from head to toe, getting in his mouth, eyes, and hair. He barely caught himself from slamming face-first into the foot-deep muck with a hand that twinged painfully at the impact. The basket of illegally acquired treats flew out of his grasp and the items spilled into the far reaches of the night. He heard one can explode as a passing car squashed it flat, spraying its precious contents high into the air.

Mud-covered and soaking wet he sat up to the sound of Python calling out, "Still alive?"

"Mhm."

He groaned and removed his completely ruined glasses, trying to wipe them on a part of his shirt that wasn't dirty. No luck there.

"Where's my stuff."

"Mostly all over the road," Python answered, his voice coming closer. Calysto blinked but couldn't see more than blurry darkness. He could somewhat make out Python's outline squatting in front of him, but no details were clear. "You almost got flattened with it, idiot."

Calysto didn't immediately answer as he had turned back to furiously trying to scrub his glasses clean.

"... Thanks for saving me I guess."

Python exhaled loudly. "I guess you're welcome. Where's your fucking head?"

"Just thinking."

Calysto slipped his glasses back on. He wasn't too keen on Python reading into him too much. No doubt if he caught wind that Calysto had any kind of inner turmoil he'd pick it apart and exploit it to the fullest. The vampire was intrusive that way, seeming to be unendingly fascinated by him. But Calysto was the studier not the studied, and he intended to keep it that way. There wasn't much interesting about him anyway.

"Can..."

"What."

"Can you get the stuff," he mumbled meekly.

"Why can't you."

"I can't see," he sighed.

It probably wasn't a good idea to admit that to someone like this. A weakness. But in this moment, he didn't really have a choice.

"You really need those things that bad?"

Calysto sighed again, wiping the mud from his hands and smearing his pants with streaks of black. He pushed himself up, mud squelching around his fingers and undoing the half-assed clean-up he had tried to accomplish a moment ago. He stood shakily and began to crawl up the side of the ditch onto the road. Python simply breezed by him and blinked up the incline.

"Fuck..." Calysto hissed. "I lost a shoe."

"Honestly, that's for the best." Python shrugged and looked down at him, still not offering a hand. "How long have you had those anyway?"

"Can we just fucking go."

Calysto reached the edge of the road and squinted, trying to spot his scattered belongings in the dark. He shuffled ahead—a bit unevenly since the loss of his shoe—leaving a muddy trail behind him. A can rolled away from him as he kicked it blindly, and he reached to get it again but it traveled out of his grasp.

"Damnit," he grumbled.

"Oh my god, fine! I can't watch this!" Python exclaimed from behind him. "I'll get your shit, goddamnit! This is too pathetic."

THEY FINALLY MADE it back to Calysto's cabin as the sun was threatening to peek over the horizon slipping hazy orange streaks through the early morning fog. Python ran ahead with Calysto's shitty snacks and caffeine bundled in his sweatshirt—the basket had also been broken in the shove-to-the-ditch debacle. Calysto trailed behind, exhausted, wet, cold, and muddy. He entered the house without a word and tiredly made his way up the stairs and across the long hallway into a room he rarely frequented—the bedroom. On the opposite side from a bed covered mostly in books and bits with not enough room for a person to really fit, was the entrance to a small bathroom. Calysto went inside and closed the door.

Completely isolated, Calysto sagged against the door, letting himself slowly sink to the floor. He took a deep breath and made a small sign in the air with his left hand. The trail that followed his finger was bright red, sparking in the air like a suspended line creating a symbol. Calysto carefully cupped the sign in his palm and pushed it gently toward the direction of the very dirty shower stall. It floated behind the moldy plastic curtain and exploded into a spray of steaming water.

Calysto let the magical shower run while slowly peeling his damp sweater and shirt over his head. He kicked off his sweatpants and finally undid the length of string in his hair that held it all together. Slowly and without getting up Calysto half-crawled half-scooted across the floor and into the shower. He didn't even bother closing the curtain and simply curled up underneath the scalding hot stream. .

He lie there, letting the water melt away the layers of dried mud on his face and arms. With achingly slow movements he sat up and reached for a nearly-melted-to-mush bar of soap. As he began to lather himself he realized he couldn't remember the last time he'd done this. He ran his tongue over his teeth and grimaced. When had he become such a mess? Such a fucking disgusting sight. No wonder Python was always sneering at him and his appearance.

Finally, after a thorough scrub, Calysto climbed up out of the shower, and with a wave of his hand, the water stopped. He toweled himself off and even scrounged up a comb to yank the knots out of his hair. Then, he padded from the bathroom into his room and over to a very under-used closet. He dropped the towel and slipped into a pair of dark blue jeans that he couldn't remember ever buying, and as he reached in the closet to scrounge for another sweater Python burst through the door.

"You got a fucking shower in the—!"

Python slung the bedroom door open to be met with the sight of a half-clothed Calysto spinning around with a furious expression. Python's shout caught in his throat at the sight. It was Calysto. But clean. His golden-brown skin blushing slightly pink from the heat of a shower, and his hair which was usually tangled in some abomination of a hairstyle flowed in long gold curls across his shoulders. But what caught Python's attention the most wasn't any of that, but the presence of a scar.

When Python could get a good look at his face—which wasn't often as Calysto tended to be constantly looking down at something, or intentionally not meeting his eyes—he could see a thick ribbon of gnarled flesh that crept up from under his neckline, up his jaw, and came to rest below his right cheekbone. But Python hadn't thought about how far it actually went.

All down the right side of Calysto's neck and torso, it spread, extending wider as it went. It covered his chest and part of his shoulder, down to his ribs and stomach, and ended slightly before the waistline of his jeans. The flesh was stretched taught and thick, white and mottled pink and jagged on the edges.

"Oh shit," Python breathed. "What the hell is that?"

"Get out," Calysto answered, his voice tight. Controlled.

Python looked up to see his cheeks, like his chest, were flushed, and his dark gold eyes sparked hot with anger.

"Just looking for the —"

"Get *OUT*, Python!" Calysto raised his voice.

"Okay okay!" Python swung the door closed and leaned against the wall outside.

He thought about what he just saw and for a second he let slip a laugh, before instantly muffling it under his hand. That scar was really unlike any he had seen before, he couldn't help but stare. What had happened? He *had* to know.

Maybe Calysto wasn't so boring after all.

And well, he might be a fucking ass, but he was also kind of fucking hot. Python had no idea how Calysto maintained any sort of physique with his atrocious lifestyle and diet, but it didn't matter in the face of a sight like that.

Calysto had even more to offer him than he'd initially thought.

Python licked his lips and tipped his head back against the wall. His teeth glimmered in a mischievous smile. He decided then and there that he was going to get a taste.

Whatever kind.

CHAPTER

SIX

Aeris placed a piece of paper back onto the lotto scratch-off ticket-covered counter and slid it over to the gas station clerk. It hadn't taken her long to catch wind of another strange occurrence less than a two-day ride from the shitty town she'd tracked Python to last. The black and white laser printer-streaked poster taped to the door had been an indication she was on the right track. Something about an invisible shoplifter and accomplice stealing an unacceptably high value amount of caffeine.

"There's nothing here," Aeris said flatly. "I want to see the tapes."

"I... well I don't know if I can do that," the girl behind the counter spoke carefully, too used to dealing with late-night customers with strange demands. "Even if you are a cop, don't you gotta have a warrant or something?"

"Listen," Aeris sighed, tucking her fake badge away into her breast pocket. "I've been tracking this asshole all over for years. He's committed a list of crimes I couldn't even begin to name. You would very much be serving a noble cause by helping me catch him. Now," Aeris plastered on a fake and impatient smile. "Wouldn't you like to be a part of something like that?"

"I don't care," the clerk shrugged. "I just don't want to get fired."

"No one has to know. Say you misplaced the keys. Lay them on the counter here, then turn around to stock the shelf. I went in when you didn't see me."

Aeris and the girl locked eyes and for a long moment it was silent between them. But finally the clerk sighed.

"Well... alright," the girl agreed. "Just be quick, please."

Aeris snatched the keys up from the marred plastic tabletop and crossed behind the grimy half-door marked with EMPLOYEES ONLY in fading stenciled letters. It squeaked with resistance and age and swung back hard, barely missing the edge of her coat as she passed. She also grabbed a giant stick of beef jerky, tearing it open with her teeth on her way.

Inside the dingy backroom, it reeked of mold and the smell hit her nose with a wave of stale heat and body odor. The office chair was sunken nearly all the way to the floor, its hydraulic exuberance worn down like the rest of the place. An arm was missing and the once-tan fabric surface was now dyed brown with stains and dirt. A very clear ass-imprint in the cushion was leaking foam from frayed seams like too much peanut butter in between slices of overly-toasted white bread.

Aeris grimaced slightly as she sat, tentatively testing it to hold her weight. She didn't have much to worry about since the manager no doubt used this room as his impromptu spank bank spy cam on the daily and the poor chair was still standing.

In front of her were three monitors that weren't even good when they were relevant, all buzzing loudly and contributing heavily through their giant backsides to the thick heated dampness of the closet. On their screens flickered the fuzzy black and white view into the strange 24/7 life of the gas station grounds.

One camera showed an overview of the front and outside of the shop. Knee-high pixelated weeds slapped against the only two gas pumps left standing with a gust of hot afternoon wind. The few cars parked around were as old as those who piloted them, with rusting hinges, missing tailgates, and exhaust clouds big enough to temporarily suffocate anyone in the immediate vicinity. The camera left plenty of blind spots that couldn't be seen, but the view of the entrance was still clear.

Aeris hit the rewind button and sat back, chewing on her snack as the tape ran itself raw in a frenzy, whining loud as the blocky white date in the top corner clicked back and back to a few nights before. Finally, it hit 3am and she played the tape.

Sure enough, the outdated outline of someone dressed like a flamboyant front singer floated up to the door. There was no face or skin, but the clothing was indication enough.

"There you fucking are," she sneered at the screen. She watched as invisible hands flung the door open and another rather unkempt man followed Python inside. Aeris slammed her fist down on the keyboard, turning her attention to the camera positioned inside of the store.

There it was. Exactly as the poor, tired, probably-thought-she-was-hallucinating clerk had said. A fucking black leather outfit, complete with a burgundy velvet scarf, faux silver cuffs, and even an ear lined in earrings, floating there in the aisle and holding a bag of chips with a nonexistent hand.

Aeris almost bolted from her seat. Python had *just* been here. She was so close. But what she saw next made her double-take. The man beside him. While she hadn't paid him much attention before—his presence seeming no more relevant than a late-night stoner looking for a variety of munchies to skitter back home with—it was when he turned his face to the camera that she nearly fell out of the chair.

Unsure of what she saw, she backed the tape up. Played it again. Leaned closer. No, there was no mistaking it. It was him, it was him. It can't be him. How was he here? And most of all, that fucker was in the company of a vampire. She should have expected it, seen it coming. But both of them at once? It was too good to be true. Oh, this was too good. This was *too* fucking good.

Aeris felt as if she'd picked the only winning ticket from the front counter filled with frauds. Like life had finally given her everything she had wanted, all at once.

She swore a string of curses as she stood, nearly shaking with anticipation. Her long coat trailed out behind her as she slammed the office door, threw the keys onto the counter, and vanished before anyone would even remember she was there.

"*CAL!*"

Python took the stairs three at a time, so fast that his feet might not have touched the ground. He burst into Calysto's workshop to find him sitting on the floor, bent over a crystal and sneering at it. He turned that look on Python as soon as he entered.

"What."

"We gotta go," Python was frantic and his babbling successfully betrayed his panic. "Look, it's a lot to get into right now but there's this lady who wants me dead—I didn't even do anything I swear!" He lifted his hands in defense as Calysto raised an eyebrow, but continued pacing erratically back and forth. "Listen, I'll explain but just, see the thing is I need you to... Can you move the house like you did before?"

Calysto watched him from his place on the floor, legs splayed out on either side of a large shimmering stone structure between his thighs.

But his impassive expression didn't faze Python in the slightest, because he was feeling something he didn't often feel—fear. He reached down and grabbed Calysto's arm trying to pull him to his feet, and he was easily successful.

"Hey! Fuck!" Calysto yelped as he was hoisted into the air, and then dragged by the arm and out the door. "Python, slow down! What's happening?"

"Move the house, okay!" Python spun around. "Come on, will

you? Just or... just tell me how to do it! I'll do it! You made that location thing, right? You can take me back, just do that! Just do me this one thing and I'll be out of your hair forever, promise, okay?"

"What?" Calysto pinched his lips together.

Python could see the stress lines appearing around his brow. He had quickly learned that Calysto didn't like to be pressured into making any kind of decision and was methodical and slow when making a choice. He didn't have time for that right now.

Surely the promise to leave him alone would have to work. But it didn't.

"I can't." Calysto shook his head.

"What! Why not?!" Python's voice was edged with a hint of hysteria, but he didn't even care what he revealed at the moment. Aeris had found him and he was fucked. *Fucked.* "Look. Please? Do I have to do something? Say I'm sorry or grovel or some shit? Come on, Cal, I'm sorry, I'm sorry I'm such a fucking freeloader, bother, a thorn in your goddamn side, but I'm fucking begging you to move this fucking house!"

Calysto only frowned further the longer Python rambled on and he shook his head again.

"I don't know what's got you so upset, but if I could take you back, I would."

"Why can't you!" Python viciously shook Calysto by the arm, jostling the man back and forth.

Calysto snatched it away. "Well, if you happen to recall, you barged into the room the other night and knocked over the fucking table. Which is what I happen to be trying to fix now. The house won't move without it."

"Can't you just tr—"

Python was interrupted by a loud bang and beside him Calysto jumped. It was followed by a series of knocks, circling around the outside of the house. It sounded like someone hitting the walls with a club. *Thump. Thump. Thump.*

"She's here," he lowered his voice.

He looked over and Calysto's face had turned from frustration to concern.

"Who is she?" Calysto whispered. "What did you do to piss her off?"

"It's a long story, Cal, but to make it short she kills creatures like me." Python stayed frozen, listening as the slamming continued to circle the house. "What the fuck is she doing?"

"A vampire hunter?" Calysto suddenly had that curious-when-he-shouldn't-be tone again. "I didn't think about the possibility of those, though I suppose that must make sense. If there is you, there is anti-you. Is this who was chasing you before? She found you again very quickly. Did you wrong her somehow or something? She's determined to find you then... what is it, scorned lover? Kill someone she cared about? Is she after only you, or is it all vampires? I haven't seen you like this before, has she caught you befo—"

"Will you shut up!" Python hissed.

Calysto did for a breath. Then he spoke again, "She's probably looking for a way in."

"Why not just use the front door then," Python grumbled back.

"I hid it," Calysto answered. "After you showed up, I figured it was best to make sure people couldn't find a way in so easily."

"No you didn't, I saw it when I came in. And what do you mean, hid it?"

"I did, just not from you," is all Calysto said.

Python didn't exactly know how to answer that so he stayed quiet.

Down below there was the sound of splintering wood. She had found the door or something else similarly weak-walled. Another crack.

"Calysto." Python grabbed his arm again in a crushing grip. "Look, do me this one last thing. Fuck, are you gonna make me beg you?"

"She's really going to kill you if she finds you here, huh?" He pushed his glasses up with a wrinkle of his nose.

"Yes!" he whispered sharply. "And you too probably, she doesn't exactly care what gets in her way!"

Calysto sighed and rubbed his temples. "Okay, okay, I really can't promise anything. I have no idea if it's going to work."

"Yes!" he exclaimed softly. "Okay, go go go! Hurry!"

Calysto didn't respond but he turned and bolted into his workshop, reappearing with the large crystal in hand and a couple of tools in the other. He brushed past Python without a word and went into the tiny control room that apparently moved the house. Python followed anxiously behind him to the sound of wood scattering on the floor below.

"*PYTHON!*" A voice rang out, loud and clear. And angry. "*I KNOW YOU'RE IN HERE.*"

"*SHIT!*" Python ran to join Calysto in the room but Calysto had already turned, shutting him out. "Cal, let me in, what the fuck!"

"No," Calysto said simply, muffled through the wooden door. The sound of heavy footsteps came from the stairwell and the vampire and the hunter locked eyes.

"It's private," Calysto said.

"She's gonna fucking kill me if you don't let me in right the fuck now!"

He pushed the door open and Calysto stumbled back a few steps. "No!"

"What's the big fucking deal!" Python gripped the door harder, shoving Calysto further back.

"*PYTHON, COME OUT YOU COWARD!*"

The sound of the cocking of a no-doubt silver-loaded shotgun reverberated down the hall.

"Cal, I swear if you don't move this fucking house right now…"

Calysto came to a decision and let go of the door. He quickly shuffled over to the coffee table and dropped the crystal on top. A shot rang out. Something hanging in the hallway fell, shattering as it hit the ground.

Python slammed the door shut and grabbed the lone chair in the room, shoving it against the doorknob. Calysto leaned over the table doing who knows what to the crystal. A strange glow emanated from around him but his back was facing Python, and it blocked the view into his actions. A low hum vibrated from the table and Calysto mumbled unintelligibly to himself.

"Come on come on come on," Python chanted, leaning against the chair while squatting on the ground, head ducked down.

"Oh honey." The voice was right outside the door, and it crooned in a pseudo-sweet song laced with venom. "Why don't you come out and we'll talk, huh?"

"Even if I move the house now," Calysto spoke up. "She's coming with us. You have to get her outside."

"What!" Python hissed from his position on the floor. "She's got a gun!"

Calysto just shrugged. Python cursed in at least two languages and grit his teeth.

"Okay, I have an idea. But it's only gonna slow her down so don't fucking stop what you're doing. When I open this door you better fucking duck."

Calysto nodded once, not turning away from his work.

Python listened closely and waited for the moment when she was reloading to strike. He slung the door open in a rush and charged into her chest, wrapping his arms around her waist. She yelped in surprise and nearly dropped her shotgun. But Python didn't stop. He ran straight across the hall and broke through a closed door. Fast as lightning with Aeris in tow, he flew through an empty room towards the furthest wall and shoved her right out the window. Razors of glass shattered onto the ground as he released her and jumped back.

The cabin wasn't exactly a mansion nor much of a proper house, and the fall was barely one story and only enough to wind her. She hit the ground with a shout but quickly stood, meeting his wide eyes with a glare.

"*CAL, GO NOW!*" Python shouted.

"IT WON'T GO!" He heard Calysto answer. *"IT'S BROKEN IT'S—"*

Whatever he was saying cut off and Python backed away from the window to return and join him. But his feet met air as the floor slid out from under him and the house began to tremble.

Yes! He did it!

Python's celebration was short-lived.

It was instantly evident this wasn't at all like the last time the house moved. This time the shaking was less like a bad thunderstorm and more akin to the ground opening up beneath him, cracking wide and swallowing the cabin whole.

Python's vision filled with white and sparks like fireworks shot out through the air. Ringing, ringing so loud he was sure if his ears could bleed they would. He grasped around to find a handhold, but he was violently dragged across the floor by the power of the vibrations, as was any furniture and untethered items as they crashed down off shelves around him. The screaming whine grew louder and louder torturing his sensitive hearing.

Python squeezed his eyes shut as they began to sting and blood-red tears dripped down his cheeks from the sheer effort he'd maintained trying to keep them open. He couldn't tell where he was—if he were on the floor or suspended in the air—as his senses were entirely overwhelmed to the brink of disorienting madness.

"CALYSTO!"

He finally managed to shout, but the words landed on nothing. They were sucked up into the screeching white-hot air around him and didn't even reach his own ears. Then an eruption of sound, like an explosion. Maybe that's what this was. Maybe Calysto had planted them straight onto a volcano and it was underneath their feet.

BOOM. Another one.

Python tried to curl in on himself covering his head with his hands. He prepared himself for anything to happen—the ground to turn to lava, debris to smash him flat, the whole house to collapse. But then.

Silence.

Everything was completely still. The light that had blinded him vanished and Python found himself lying in the hallway of Calysto's shitty little cabin. He pushed himself up on unstable arms and blinked the bloody tears from his eyes.

What the fuck just happened?

As his vision cleared he could see smoke coming from the room that moved the house. He tried to stand, stumbling forward and gripping the wall for support.

"Cal!" he called. His voice was hoarse.

Python waved the smoke away with his hands, trying to disperse the air in the room. Finally, as he entered he got a good look.

There in the middle of the small space, with his back still turned, was Calysto. Standing with his head bent down, staring at the crystal on the coffee table in front of him. His clothes were smoking and small sparks flickered around him in the dark, crackling bright then fizzling out, disappearing into the air.

"Cal?" Python asked, approaching him cautiously.

Calysto was frozen stiff and didn't respond to his calls. Maybe he couldn't hear, either. Python approached and over Calysto's shoulder he could see the table had cracked, and what once was a beautiful lavender crystal of magnificent size, was now a charred hole in the center. The wood smoldered with hot embers around the shape of a stone that was no longer there.

"Calysto!" Python reached out and grabbed his shoulder, spinning him around.

Calysto's amber eyes were bloodshot, glassy and far away, not really seeing as he looked up towards Python. His glasses were gone and his hair was wild, torn from its rubber band and sticking with sweat to his forehead. Soot, in black and grey spatters of dirt and smoke, smeared across his golden-brown skin. The arms of his sweater were singed off up to the elbows, fibers on the edges dying out in a twisting orange glow. Python's gaze moved down and he realized Calysto's forearms were burnt dark as night.

Python had gotten used to Calysto ignoring him—not always answering right away, or not at all—and often not explaining himself, choosing to act first and speak later. So the neurotic little human's silence wasn't exactly strange, even considering whatever the hell he'd done.

No, that in itself wasn't exactly unnerving. But what he set eyes on next, was. For as Python looked down, following Calysto's trembling arms to the charred surface of his hands, he saw. In the middle of both of Calysto's upturned palms a soft crimson light pulsed gently from beneath the skin.

His hands were glowing.

CHAPTER

SEVEN

Everything was muffled and slow, padded in a bubble of cotton, coming to him in rippling waves as if he were submerged underwater. He wasn't even sure what had happened. His hands shook as a level of power he rarely ever tried to use rattled him to his core. The air smelled of campfire and something like cinnamon. It was rather pleasant, in a way. Where was it coming from? Smoke surrounded him, curling around his body in a slowly asphyxiating cloud. Then there was a strange gust of clean air and a deep muffled sound. He couldn't feel his fingertips.

Where am I?

"Calysto!"

An ice-cold hand gripped his shoulder, swinging him wildly off of his axis. He looked to see what it was and was met with the pale white face of Python. But Python wasn't looking at him anymore, but down at his palms. Calysto followed his gaze and saw—the power he'd called upon still simmering hot and bright beneath his skin.

Oh, that's why he was shaking.

"Uh..." He tried to clear his throat and found it dry as bone. "What... what happened."

"Wh— what do you mean what happened?" Python's retort sounded hoarse, too. "What... what is this?! What did you do?!"

"I'm not..." Calysto swallowed thickly. It tasted of coal. "I don't know."

Python's hand on his shoulder loosened and he stepped back, his crimson eyes wide. "Calysto... what is all this? What are you?"

"It's nothing." Calysto watched his palms with detached interest as the burning glow began to fade. "It's nothing to worry about Python."

"Yes... you..." Python's mouth moved with no sound escaping his lips. "You... Cal, I..."

"It's just magic," Calysto sighed and rubbed his forehead. Soot smeared through sweat and left a long black line. "Have you seen my glasses?"

"What? Magic?! What the fuck are you—" Python paused to cough, then spat black onto the ground, glaring down at it before continuing. "Magic's real?"

Cal grimaced, this really wasn't something he wanted to talk about with anyone. Much less Python.

"... Yes."

"Hold on, hold on." Python held up a hand. "So, what *are* you then?"

"I'm not anything." Calysto scowled. "Really, I... I need my glasses."

"Oh, fuck your glasses!" Python exclaimed. "Seriously? Fucking answer me, Calysto! You... you've known what I am this entire time and asking all these fucking questions when you've got a huge secret of your own?"

"It's not a secret," Calysto mumbled. He was way, way too tired for this. "I wasn't hiding it. You just didn't notice."

"Yeah, but hiding what exactly?"

Calysto didn't answer. Instead, he bent down to search around with his hands in the rubble of the table and all his instruments until finally he stopped and emerged with his glasses. He squinted furiously while trying to clean them on the edge of his soot-soaked sweater.

"Give me that."

Python held out his hand, scowl still visible even with Calysto's limited vision.

Calysto paused and blinked up at him. "Are you going to break them?"

"No, asshole. It may come as a surprise, but my shirt is cleaner than yours."

Calysto hesitated a beat longer, then passed them over. Python snatched the thin wire frames, scrubbed them between the tail of his shirt, and shoved them back.

"Here, now that you can see, how about you do some explaining." Python leaned back against the door with arms crossed then added, "Not that you need your glasses to use your fucking mouth."

Calysto slowly put his glasses back on and stood, leaning on his knees for leverage.

The room was a disaster, and everything was either knocked to the floor, broken, or burnt to a crisp. His tools were scattered, shattered glass had slid into every crevice of the floorboards, and the copper boiler was spewing steam into the air with a soft hiss. Pipes and wires were disconnected, and small showers of sparks periodically sprayed into the air.

Calysto didn't even feel the slightest bit fazed. Or maybe he just accepted it, that things like this would happen. That the worst outcome was always the most likely one, that anything he tried to accomplish would somehow turn to ruin when he touched it.

"What do you want to know?" he said, resigned.

"What are you?" Python demanded, breaking Calysto out of his melancholy thoughts.

"A warlock, is what I'm typically called. By human folklore."

Calysto's voice sounded strange in his ears. He heard himself speak the words but he didn't exactly feel himself doing it.

Some warlock. Some fucking warlock. His magic was shit, his

powers were shit, his knowledge was useless, and he'd never find a way to... He'd never—

"Warlock..." Python repeated, his voice barely above a whisper. "Wait... wait... magic is *real*? That was *real* magic?!"

"You just asked me that. Are you surprised?"

"I could ask you the same," Python shot back. "You're a fucking wizard—"

"Warlock."

"Warlock. And you're surprised that other things besides humans exist?"

"As are you it seems, vampire."

Python sighed impatiently. "You know what I mean. Wait so... if you're not human, do you... how old *are* you?"

"You first." Calysto sniffed. This was getting off-topic.

Good.

"What year is it?" Python pushed his hair back, scratching at his scalp as he did.

"Somewhere in the early second millennia," Calysto hummed. "First or second decade, I think."

"So I'm..." Python was counting on his fingers as Calysto watched him quietly. "Uh, somewhere around one hundred and seventy-ish. Maybe eighty?"

Calysto nodded slowly. "As am I. Ish."

"Yeah?" Python grinned, and Calysto could see his teeth shining bright against the blackened walls around them. "We're practically spring chickens."

"I don't think people say that anymore." Calysto sniffled again and shuffled his feet on the dirty floor. "Don't you keep up? You have to keep up, otherwise, people get suspicious."

"That they do," Python laughed. "Damn, Cal I have so many questions!"

"That's not surprising," Calysto sighed.

"Well... Hey so, when you move the house the first time, you thought someone was after you, that's why you moved? Who?"

Python bit his lip, thinking hard. "People don't like warlocks? I mean I get me. I do. But you? You don't like, eat children or something do you?"

Calysto shot him a look. "No."

"Okay, just checking."

"Do you?"

"No!"

"Just checking."

Python leaned up off of the door. "So, that was different, right? What'd you do?"

"I might've..." Calysto suddenly felt awkward, scrunching his nose and rubbing it with the back of his sleeve. "Well, I don't hear your friend so I'm assuming I made the house move, anyway."

"I knew you could do it!" Python exclaimed. "I'm gonna go see where we are!"

He kicked some debris out of the way and slung the now-half-off-it's-hinges door open and disappeared down the stairs, leaving Calysto dazed and wondering in confusion as to what the fuck just happened between them.

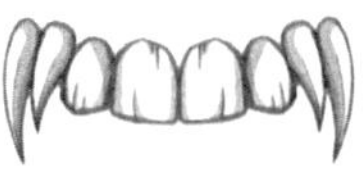

Calysto was numb.

His hands tingled but the rest of him felt like he'd lost all control. He wasn't sure how he'd managed to form the words to speak through lips that touched each other without sensation. He knew the nothingness wouldn't last long though, it never did when he overdid his use of magic like this.

Thankfully, Python had left the room in time to miss Calysto's knees give out as he fell to the floor. He might not have felt anything on the surface, but underneath his thoughts were racing and his heart was nearly pounding out of his chest.

Just what *had* he done? His arms began to prickle with pins and needles as they trembled against his thighs where he sat half slumped against the broken table. Python had asked him to move the house and so he did. But he had no idea *how* he did. And if the charred crystal and the hole in the table were any indication, he had no idea if he ever could again. He only hoped they were somewhere good, somewhere that could last until he could figure out what to do next.

To compound Calysto's problems the fucking vampire knew about him now. No one had known about him for decades, a lifetime or two, even. He had learned since he was young that what he was, was best to be kept a secret.

Better than being found out and exposed to danger at the worst. Better than being surrounded by people who'd never know him, much less like him, at the least.

This facade of a human skin was something he'd always kept up, and eventually when the effort of pretending and the ache of two lifetimes of loneliness set in, he'd retreated. Now he'd been a recluse for almost longer than he could remember.

He was a warlock and not even a good one at that.

The magic he carried beneath his skin, which had bloomed in his being since birth, was simply never that remarkable. He could never make it perform the way that others of his kind once could. But that had never mattered to those who were supposed to care for him most. Through no fault of his own he was weak, and he'd spent his life trying to make up for it, to apologize for it, even when no one had asked him to for many, many years.

Sometimes, oh, sometimes he hated it. That deep sense of isolation. Otherness. Of no one wanting to know him enough to understand. Judging him for his lack and seeing him for nothing else.

No matter. All those people were long gone now. Long dead. Calysto was the only one left. The only one not burned for the mistake of the gift of their birth. Perhaps because he was so weak, he passed right below their eyes and what they'd expect him to be. Granted mercy—a hall pass by order of seeming just normal enough. Was it mercy? Was it right that the legacy of generations upon generations of witches and warlocks was laid upon his inca-pable shoulders by the simple fact of his lack? He certainly didn't think so.

He'd carried that coward's badge with him his entire life. The knowledge that he could've died along with them all but was spared by the simple fact that he could blend in.

So he tried not to, blend in, that is. By virtue of not integrating himself with people at all. If anyone knew what he really was it would be his end, he'd thought.

But now, Python knew. Python had seen him and he'd almost acted normal about it. Well, if Calysto ignored how he was a bit too fascinated, really. Granted, Python didn't strike him as the sharpest tool in the box. Maybe he didn't even understand what he'd learned. There was a chance of that. Maybe he'd forget? Nah, he might be dense but Calysto could also tell he was a shark, latching onto anything and anyone who might benefit him. A shitty warlock was probably a benefit. Somehow.

Terror from the simple fact that his deepest secret had been revealed coursed cold through his veins. Veins that were beginning to ache with the shock of a burst of magic unlike anything he'd used in ages, stretching to fit and fill with it, flexing and pulsing against it. And it hurt. Suddenly it ached all over.

Calysto groaned and curled in on himself in the middle of the soot-covered floor. He felt a bit sick, his throat hot and his head pounding. Even in the darkness, the smallest of light from smoldering embers and moonlight off the copper boiler felt like penlights directly into his eyes. He clenched his stomach and tried to breathe as his body shook against the strain. It was good he hadn't eaten anything, for there was nothing to heave up when he inevitably did.

Finally, with limbs that screamed with exhaustion, he pushed himself up off the floor, rocking slightly as he stood. He should defi-nitely not use his powers again to that extent. Not for a long while. He wouldn't be surprised if he'd stripped himself of it forever now.

The house had fallen into an eerie silence. Soot smoke hung light in the air, curls sparkling as it passed by the moonlit window. It dissipated into the room, swirling sharp into his lungs.

Hit with a bout of dizziness, Calysto caught himself on the wall and leaned heavily against it. Maybe he needed something to eat. Yeah, he just, needed to stop forgetting to eat. That would help. Running his tender palm against the rough wooden wall, he carefully made his way down the stairwell one aching step at a time, across the messy living area that made up Python's room, and into the kitchen.

He hadn't been in there since their little late-night escapade so the scene that met him caught him by surprise. One counter was cleaned. Well, all the shit had just been shoved off onto the floor but it was empty nonetheless. That is except for the five plastic pouches of donuts, three bags of potato chips, two packs of gum, six satchels of sour gummy worms, and ten small bags of hot fries that had somehow survived the trip into the ditch and being scattered all over the road.

Calysto rested on the refrigerator door and felt that it was slightly cool. It had been plugged in and hummed softly against his skin. With a shaking hand, he pulled the door open to find every variety of energy drink and iced coffee he'd so shamelessly stolen lined up neatly on the shelves.

Why can't he organize his fucking clothes like this?

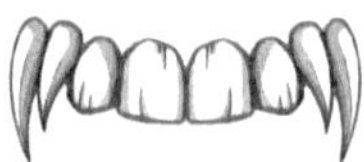

HE WAS SITTING down in the once-part-of-a-set wooden chair at the plastic fold out table slowly chewing on a gummy worm when Python burst back in through the door.

"Calysto!" he shouted, stopping as he caught sight of the warlock in the kitchen. "Oh there you..."

Calysto could see the glimmer of his strange cat-like eyes in the dimly lit living room. As he got closer, Calysto could also make out his expression, and it was furious.

"What," he responded, taking a huge gulp out of a red and white can labeled 'Fast-N-EnergiZd' that touted the ability to make one '*supercharge their brainpower*'. The warning label on the side cautioned the legal-high-chasing consumer that the can contained the recommended daily limit of caffeine for an adult human being. But Calysto wasn't human, nor did his caffeine tolerance have anything close to a limit. He used the butt of it to kick another empty can onto the floor. Might as well continue the Python-induced trash pile that he started there.

"What do you mean, *WHAT!*" Python charged forward, slamming his hands on the table. "Do you think this is some kind of joke? Are you just fucking with me cause I begged you? I should have fucking known you wouldn't do anything nice for free. You have no fucking idea how to be decent, do you? If this is how all your kind are, well I'm glad I've never fucking met any. You're as bad as the vampires and all the rest. Well, you can't fucking play bullshit games with me, warlock, I'm not going to let you."

Python was seething, his blood-red eyes burning around the rims. Long fingernails were digging deep into the soft plastic of the table-top, and Calysto looked down at them with detached interest. He wasn't sure if Python had realized he had done it.

"Two things," Calysto answered calmly. "One, there are no others, all my kind are dead. And two, what the fuck are you talking about."

"Two things," Python shot back in a petulant tone. "*Good.* And you know damn well what I'm talking about!"

"No, I fucking don't." Calysto slammed his drink down a bit too hard and a droplet splashed onto his soot-covered skin, running down the back of his hand and leaving a single clean line. Whereas before a sensation that neared his version of relaxation had begun to wash over him, now his scowl had returned full force.

Python seemed stumped and he slowly stood, releasing his fingers from the claw-marked trails he'd left in the table.

"Why don't you tell me," Calysto snapped impatiently.

"Calysto, where are we," Python said. No question, no more

accusation, only a simple statement with a soft demand for an answer.

"I don't know, I told you it doesn't work like that."

"Oh." Python looked stunned, then his expression fell blank. He looked unsure of what to do or what to say. "Um, listen this is weird but... When I went out I... Well, for one we're not that far from a town. But it's... the thing is, it's unlike any town I've seen in..."

Calysto leaned forward in his chair, his elbows crinkling the layer of trash underneath them.

"What do you mean."

"I... I can't explain it." Python shoved his hair back. "Won't you just come?"

"How far is it?"

"Not far."

"Not far or not Python far."

Python seemed to try to suppress a grin. "Not far."

Calysto pinched his lips, whatever this was about to be was surely about to make his night at least a little bit worse. A whole lot worse, knowing his luck.

"Let me get my shoes."

He stood, took a few long gulps from his drink, threw the can on the floor, and shoved a handful of gummy worms in his mouth, before shuffling around to locate his shoes and haphazardly shoving his feet inside. Python wrinkled his nose but didn't comment. Calysto opened the door wide, letting the cool evening air inside.

"Lead the way."

Python walked past him in the doorway then as he went by said, "You look like shit you know."

Calysto didn't answer.

EIGHT

Python once again found himself on the waiting end of Calysto's achingly slow walk and circled around him again and again as they went. Whatever he had witnessed had made him anxious, so much so he had turned around and high-tailed it straight back to the house. Much to his chagrin he was dependent on Calysto for wherever they had ended up. Just until he could get on his feet, that is.

He kind of liked living under a consistent roof, but not with a consistent annoyance. Mystical warlock or not. Besides, Calysto was the opposite of anything he really would ever have imagined a warlock to be. Warlocks, wizards, witches. They were supposed to be these ancient magical beings with deep wells of knowledge and altruistic intentions. Full of power and goodwill, dressed in a purple robe, he didn't know. Not like... not like whatever Calysto was.

But then again, vampires were supposed to be something, too. Weren't they? And he knew from experience that what they actually were wasn't anything close to the glamorous portrayal that people so often painted. Everything negative you've ever heard about a vampire? True. Good things? False.

Okay, maybe he was biased in that regard. He couldn't help it. He might be a little bit of a scoundrel, he might steal and cheat and lie to get his way, and he might use others for his own gain, but he didn't think himself *that* much of an asshole. Not like the rest of them. You haven't met asshole until you've met the vampires Python knew. Especially the one who turned him.

Python growled deep in his throat at the thought and Calysto gave him a surprised glance. He hadn't realized he did that out loud and frowned, biting down hard on his lip. He hated thinking of that man, the one who did this to him. Python had made his peace with his fate a long time ago, embracing the night and the need for blood and the generally inescapable eternity of it. He had been born into a world that already didn't accept who he was when he was human, it wasn't so hard for him to become something they hated even in their nightmares.

But, what he hadn't made peace with was the way that it happened. He had been so young then, so trusting, so naive. So hopeful, yet so afraid. He rubbed absently at the only scar he carried, right on the crook of his neck. That jagged bite mark that would never leave him, and always remind him. He wished he carried more scars, so then at least it'd feel fair, it'd feel even. Like being turned wasn't the only thing that ever happened to him that mattered.

"What're you thinking about so hard?" Calysto asked.

Python nearly jumped out of his skin. The warlock had been so quiet beside him and himself so lost in thought, Python nearly forgot he was there.

"Nothing," he answered, a bit harsher than he intended. Calysto's face that a second ago was genuinely curious instantly hardened. Was that remorse Python felt at the sight? As if.

"Why?"

"Never mind."

Calysto turned away and looked back at the worn tire-tracks trail in front of them.

"Almost there," Python said a bit softer, the tone a half-hearted peace offering between them. One he was fairly sure Calysto wouldn't accept.

WELL, he tried.

Calysto looked down at his feet and watched them with rapt interest as they followed the trail through the woods. Maybe that was too forward, was it too nosey? It was too hard, this socializing thing. He'd never been good at it, even when he was younger and more accustomed to being around people. Now, he could hardly stand to leave his house to go to the fucking gas station under the barely scrutinizing eye of a clerk who was an infant in comparison to his age.

Still, he hadn't had to come face to face with how awful he was at it in quite some time. Not until Python came along and ran circles around him with his conversation and attention, that is.

Sure, he didn't have to be lonely, but it was better that way. Every time he reached out it was like the expected pain of a hot stovetop. He had kept trying—albeit more cautiously—each time, until he gave up on getting burnt altogether.

Python had been living with him for over a week now, and what was a week in Calysto's time? Nothing significant, really.

But he found himself curious, and one could say he had almost started to like the company. A little bit. Yet he couldn't open himself to it and responded to every perceived slight, every change in tone, as an indication of an attack. It certainly didn't help that Python was the argumentative type and loved to challenge everything he said. Not including the fact that Python probably yelled at him about something at least once a day. *And* not to mention that the vampire was the definition of just that—absolutely going to use him up and hang him out to dry and catch the next bus to freedom without so much as a backward glance.

Despite this Calysto still, deep in his icy closed-off heart, kind of liked having him around. At first, the annoyance at his presence was true, and don't get him wrong, it still was. But Calysto found himself almost... *almost* enjoying hearing someone else's thoughts beside his own for once. Someone who clearly had no problem sharing them.

All of them, all the time.

Yeah, it was definitely still fucking annoying.

Calysto had stayed his tight-lipped self, not revealing anything about himself without Python's excessive digging or prompting. Of course, the warlock thing was by accident. He would've made up a lie if he'd had the wherewithal to think of a good one. But the truth had slipped out.

Calysto had to not look at that one too directly, for each time he remembered that Python knew who he was, the fear of his life being held in another's hands struck him like a lightning bolt to the gut.

He stumbled just thinking about it now. Python knew. Python—this scoundrel and drifter of a man. This creature that he didn't even know existed until a week ago. One who walked through the world with the confidence of a man who has broken every rule and law and lived to tell the tale of getting away with it. A vampire, who took what he pleased and destroyed the rest, drinking the blood of anyone who came his way. This vampire knew who he was, no... no he didn't know that. But he did know what.

Calysto cautioned a quick glance over at Python and found him already staring back. Python blinked, then looked away. As did he.

Is he thinking about how he can use this against me? Is he—what is he thinking?

This is the same train of thought he'd had that brought him to blurt out that question in the first place. He should have known Python wouldn't respond well, and if he had taken more than a second to think about it, he would have kept his fucking mouth shut. Of course Python wasn't going to trust someone like him, a stranger, with what he was really thinking. He obviously wasn't the type to make friends or even make peace.

What did you expect? That he would stay and irritate the shit out of you forever? It's only been a week, don't be so fucking clingy. He doesn't like you, he's just using you and you're letting him and now you're in too deep to back out or say no so you have to suck it up and see it through to the end.

Calysto found himself hoping whatever town they were headed towards would catch Python's interest enough to where he'd hurry up and get the fuck out. Let him go back to his work in peace. His endless, fruitless, lonely work. Yeah, that was fine.

That's fine by me.

Besides, the constant attention made him feel itchy, watched, self-conscious. Especially by the red-hot eyes of a creature with sight that could certainly see more than the norm.

Python's eyes glimmered in the dark, like two fluorescent candles flickering back and forth and they found Calysto's face as easily as if it were daytime. They were doing that now, as Python kept looking over at him, likely to check to see if he was about fall face down in the dirt. While Calysto didn't have night vision, his years of scuffling around like a rat in his own house had made him plenty accustomed to navigating in the dark, and he was having no trouble keeping up.

Calysto continued to gaze at his feet though, the suffocating ball of shame at his own actions that truly deserved none still clenched in his chest. But then, he decided to try again.

Fuck it.

"How much farther, Python."

His voice came out quiet and flat. Dead of life and void of emotion. Exactly as he wished he felt. Exactly in the way that would keep him as detached for as long as he could. Oh, and he could.

"It's coming up."

Then Python's hand was on his shoulder, and Calysto instinctively recoiled. He shot Python a vicious glare only to realize Python wasn't paying attention to him but instead was focused on a spot through the tree line. The hand guided Calysto off of the road and into the brush.

"Look." Python motioned ahead.

"I can't see anything," Calysto answered. "We're too far, still."

"Oh shit," Python huffed a small half-laugh. "Alright come on then. Stay down."

As Calysto followed Python further, he could see the beginning of a paved limestone road with deep, thin tire tracks dug into the soft and rocky earth. Buildings of a city loomed tall and black in the distant night sky, and pointed roofs spewed grey and white smoke into the air from billowing chimneys. The sound of voices, drunken and singing, carried over through the air, bringing with it the stench of sewage, beer, and rot.

At first the two of them stayed close to the edge of the trees but then Calysto stepped out onto the road. In front of him was a wooden sign with hand painted words in big white letters. He squinted up at it, unable to read the backlit face.

"What does it say?" he called back.

Python emerged from the trees and walked up to his side. "Welcome to Purvel."

"Welcome to Purvel," Python answered. "Huh."

Something about it felt familiar. But Python was distracted by the sound of Calysto's breath picking up and his heart beating hard in his throat.

"What?" he asked.

"No. no. no. That's impossible. It's *impossible*." Calysto was muttering to himself frantically. All while backing away.

"Cal?" Python turned to face him and saw. His eyes were wide open with shock and he was shaking his head, murmuring low words that Python could hear but couldn't make out.

"Calysto!" he barked.

That got the warlock's attention. He met Python with a face nearing the expression of sheer panic.

"What's wrong with you!"

"I uh... Py... Python, what..." Calysto stammered and tried to clear his throat. "Does the sign have, have a year? On it?"

"Why?"

"Just look, please." Calysto looked so tense he was on the verge of snapping in half, so Python humored him and craned his neck over towards the sign.

"Uh, let's see. It says welcome to Purvel. Established 1813."

Behind him, he heard Calysto let out a pained wheeze.

"Why, what's the big deal?" He turned to meet Calysto's gaze again. "I told you it's a weird old town."

"It's not ..." Calysto took a step back, and then another, slowly inching away from the town at Python's back. "It's... Oh shit, I... It's not possible..."

Python shot forward in an instant, catching Calysto by the arms. He shook the warlock slightly demanding, "What the fuck is going on?"

"I'm... I don't know."

"Okay well, what's got you freaked out?"

"Purvel," Calysto said simply. "I grew up near there."

"Oh?" Python asked. "Don't care to revisit it?"

"No, Python..." Calysto's breath was hot in between them, fogging the cool night air with frantic puffs between his words. "That's... that's the thing... Purvel was abandoned and ultimately rebuilt and renamed in the twentieth century. Nineteen fifty-eight. Purvel doesn't exist any more."

"Okay..." Python pinched his lips, not grasping what the fuck Calysto was on about and getting frustrated with the dramatics. "So, maybe you were wrong?"

"No. No," Cal shook his head again. "It's... I think. Python I think we..."

"Will you spit it out!" An edge of anxiety was creeping up Python's spine and frankly, it was getting irritating.

"I think we went back in time."

Python laughed and released Calysto's arms, suddenly overtaken by the absurdity of this whole situation. "You really *are* fucking with me, aren't you?"

"I'm not joking."

Python frowned then. "Well, maybe you're not but there's just no way. Time travel is impossible."

"So is the existence of warlocks and vampires," Calysto shot back.

Python could hear the tension in his voice as he spoke, the vocal cords pulled tight with stress, the blood pumping much too fast around his body and through his veins, his rapid blinking and the clench of his fists at his sides.

He was serious.

"... You're serious?" Python suddenly sobered. "How?"

"I don't know," Calysto took another step back. "But I don't care, I'm going back home."

"Wait!" Python grabbed him again.

"Let go of me."

Calysto tried to pull away, but he was no match for even an ounce of a vampire's might.

"You're running back to your house?" Python scoffed. "You just surmised we moved *back* in time somehow, and you're going to run away?"

"I'm not running away!" Calysto yelped. "I'm going to figure out how the fuck to get us home. Or do you want to be in the past all over again, Python? I can't imagine that was much fun for you either."

"You're running away," Python shot back. "And you don't even know for sure that's what this is!"

"I am *not,*" Calysto bit out. He jerked his arm out of Python's grip, and this time Python let him go. Before he followed behind, he watched with smug satisfaction at how Calysto most definitely *was* running away.

Calysto was going to panic. His skin was too hot and tight and clammy and itchy. He couldn't get away fast enough. Away from whatever this fucked up illusion was. Maybe he really did have too much caffeine, or maybe he was still knocked out from moving the house and all of this was happening in his head while he was unconscious on the floor.

Maybe Python's arrival and everything since then was a nightmare. Maybe he was slumped over on his desk, having some deeply elaborate and lonely dream about going on adventures with a mythical creature. Maybe he'd wake up and find a project resting under his hands, scrub his face hard against the lines of the table etched into his cheek, and stand to turn on the TV and wipe this weird trip from his mind. Maybe he'd made it all up, finally losing the grip on the edges of his already fragile sanity. He'd created Python from his deeply buried desire to have a friend. Someone who knew who he was, someone who could understand. Someone who could last, as long as he. For surely, there was no one else. There was no one who actually existed like that. He was alone and he'd always be.

Yes, yes, that's definitely it.

Calysto stormed up to his house and slung the door open, not even bothering to check if Python was following. He ran up the stairs, nearly tripping over the last step in his hurry, went into his lab, and slammed the door shut. Scurrying to the corner he leaned against the wall, and let himself slide to the floor. He'd really lost it, huh? He'd completely lost his mind. A defeated sigh into his hands turned into a single, silent sob. How long had he been alone now? Was it a hundred years? More?

He nearly jumped from his skin when a knock came at the door. Certainly that sounded real. But Python didn't knock. Why would the personality of this made-up irritant change now?

"Cal?" Python's voice carried low through the door. "I'm coming in."

"Don't," Calysto answered, but it barely carried above a whisper.

The door opened and Calysto shut his eyes, pulling his knees to his chest. He didn't want to see.

"Where are yo— what the fuck are you doing?" Footsteps carried out across the floor and stopped in front of him. "Calysto."

Calysto shook his head. He felt childish, curled up in this corner, afraid of his own delusions. But what else was there to do? Face them? Confront them? Accept the fact that a Python, who felt and appeared as real as him, was only an elaborate coping mechanism he'd picked up without even realizing? No, no. He wasn't ready.

"What's wrong with you?"

Python's voice was closer now, deep and bordering on soft. Calysto looked up without meaning to, head jerking alert to meet Python's eyes.

"Don't you already know," Calysto managed, his voice cracking.

"Uh, that we went back in time?" Python asked. "Yeah, I still don't get that one. I don't see how that's possible, you've never done that with your magic before, right?"

"No..." Calysto shook his head. It felt fuzzy and hot. His thoughts were moving through a haze and he wasn't even quite sure of what he was saying. "It's all made up. You, this, all that, the... thing..."

Python huffed a short laugh then searched Calysto's face. "You're serious? What, are you crazy?"

Calysto shrugged weakly and didn't meet his eyes.

"It makes sense," he said. "More than traveling through time back to my childhood. In eighteen fucking whatever. And you being a vampire. And any of this."

"Does it? Or do you just need to go the fuck outside more?" Python scoffed, his long slender hands rested on his knees. Calysto looked at the sharp nails, noting something.

"Ha," he laughed once, without humor. "See? Your hands! After that explosion, there's no way they'd be that clean. You couldn't be."

"I was in the other room, Cal." Python's tone held an edge of concern. "Seriously, what's wrong with you?"

"Nothing." Cal rubbed his still soot-covered-face and sighed.

"Nothing at all, Python. I just made you up out of my imagination because I'm so lonely I'd rather die than go on another day by myself. It's fine!" he laughed again, a flat and empty sound. "But hey, who cares if you're fake? You certainly don't act fake."

"What the fuck are you talking about?" Python frowned and gave Calysto's curled-up legs a shove. "You think I'm a figment of your imagination? Seriously?"

Calysto didn't respond, and Python sighed.

"Okay, so if I'm fake, then what about the woman who's after me, did you make that up too?"

Calysto shrugged once.

"What about moving the house? That happened, right?"

Calysto nodded once.

"Those things really happened, and they couldn't have happened if I wasn't really here."

"No, they could have. I've seen enough TV to make up a few stories," Calysto said, resting his head back on the wall.

Python growled in his throat, clearly losing patience. Suddenly, Calysto felt a sharp pain.

"*HEY!*"

"That real enough?" Python leered up at Calysto from the bite he'd carved into the back of the warlock's hand. Two near-black puncture wounds slowly oozed hot blood down his wrist and he quickly covered them as pain began to bloom.

"You bit me!"

"Yes," Python agreed without remorse. "And it's a real bite. Check and see, you're still bleeding."

Calysto met Python's eyes, then looked down at his hand. He uncovered it and sure enough. Two symmetrical holes like that of a snake bite were slowly seeping with blood. And it *hurt*.

"I'm beginning to see how your name makes sense," he mumbled, and Python grinned wide, flashing his double set of razor-sharp teeth.

"Believe me now?" he asked.

"Uh…" Calysto still felt lightheaded, it was all too much to process. "I think I need a… another shower."

"That you do."

Python grabbed his hand, but this time it was only to pull him to his feet. Calysto swayed in place and caught himself with a palm to Python's chest.

It was strange how cold he was. He really was a living corpse. Calysto wondered if since his heart didn't pump if all his organs lay dead, suspended inside his body. Maybe they had withered away? Maybe he'd really thrown them up the other day. How did drinking blood actually work? Were all his limbs this cold? Did he even have a heart anymore? *Huh, I wonder if he can get an erec—*

Calysto caught himself and jerked his hand away from Python's skin. That was quite enough curiosity for one day. He glanced up to see Python observing him with a curious expression.

"Need some help?" Python offered in a mocking tone void of altruism.

"No. No, I've got it," Calysto straightened. "When I… When I get out we have to figure out what's going on, Python. Really."

"I'll be waiting," Python said.

Calysto turned to exit the room, taking his steps carefully one at a time. He paused and almost looked back, but then decided it'd be easier to speak instead to the empty hallway.

"Python?"

"Huh?"

"I like it better when you're real."

NINE

Python waited until he heard the sound of a shower running before wandering back downstairs. He snatched one of Calysto's drinks and bags of chips and slunk over to the couch, flinging himself half on and half off of it.

Then, there was a strange smell. Like old meat, and dirt, and grime. He looked down, and taking in the state of his clothes, realized it was him.

Python shot up, set the can of disgustingly sweet cherry-flavored caffeine near the edge of the couch, and proceeded to strip. He threw the clothes into a dark corner—of which there were a few more filled with other dirty clothes of his—and scrounged around in a pile for something to wear.

Finally, he settled on a billowing black button-down shirt made of excessive amounts of soft silk that tied off neatly at the wrists and fell open at the neck, exposing the middle of his chest. He slipped on a stretchy pair of leggings that were also jeans—a more modern revelation that he adored—and a pair of black leather ankle boots with an inch-thick sole. He didn't need to be any taller than he already was, but he kind of had a thing for being the tallest person in the room. He made sure he was never in a position of having to look up at anyone.

His head brushed the low ceiling as he stood and ran a hogs-hair brush through his thick silver-grey hair. From the end table, he utilized a stick of deodorant, a moisturizing makeup-remover face wipe, and a stick of chapstick. Then he dug out a small handheld case from his jacket hanging on the banister near the door, and wiped his eyelids smooth with a deep red shadow.

He didn't need to be able to see himself in a mirror to know he looked damn fucking good.

Finally satisfied, he plopped down on the couch and resumed eating Calysto's chips.

He hadn't taken the time yet to think about what transpired upstairs, a bit too busy with his own appearance to let it sink in. But now it did and as he chewed the scene played out in his head. Calysto really thought Python was a figment of his imagination?

Flattering himself don't you think, Python scoffed as he thought about it. *That he could make all of ME up. Really. Wait, does that mean he's fantasized about me?*

Python laughed to himself and took a sip of his drink.

Eugh, how does he drink this shit?

But what was it Calysto had said? *I'm so lonely I'd rather die than go on another day by myself.*

Python paused and set the can between his thighs, letting his neck drape over the back of the couch. Python felt he knew Calysto well enough to know that he wouldn't just admit that. Not to anyone and not to someone he thought was really there, actually listening to him. Calysto kept himself so under wraps that Python was surprised he wasn't already mad when they met.

But still, this was something that Python didn't quite understand.

He *wasn't* lonely, he was just fine. He liked being nomadic, he liked carrying on from one place to the other with relative ease and no attachments. No one knew him and he didn't know them and he liked it that way. Besides, it's damn difficult to make any meaningful or lasting connections with humans when they don't know who you really are, and all you can see them as is lunch.

But Calysto was different. He was also immortal. Or something like it. The man was damn well one-hundred-and-eighty-(ish) years old and he looked like he was thirty. If it weren't for the way he walked like he should have an aid simply to support the weight of his thoughts alone, you could never tell he wasn't.

Python *wasn't* lonely. Not like that. Not enough to even think he could make up an entire fake person just to get by. He had plenty of people to be around, all the time. Whenever he wanted, should he so choose. He was great at making friends, weaseling his way into another's life, fitting in where he didn't belong, and making a place for himself. For a while, anyway. It's not like he wanted to stick around any longer than that.

It was none of anyone's goddamned business how he spent his eternity of time, and he would spend it how he pleased. Who's asking? Fuck off, thanks.

Yeah, he clearly wasn't running from anything.

But still, he knew what he had learned from the admittedly emotionally compromised Calysto rang true for that weirdo, and for once in a long time, Python felt a *tiny bit* bad. A *bit* sorry for someone else. A small whisper of the warlock's voice was still gnawing inside him, as if asking him to pay attention. He scoffed at the thought and tipped the crinkly aluminum bag of spicy chips into his mouth. But try as he might to deny that he *might* care, his eyes kept drifting to the stairs, and his ears were keenly tuned to the sound of the shower from far behind the walls.

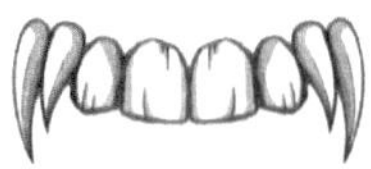

CALYSTO SIGHED and sat down on the cushioned couch edge, still drying his hair with a towel. Python was once again struck with how pretty he was, when he wasn't scowling or covered in dirt that is. It was the second time now he had seen a golden and blushing shower-fresh Calysto and frankly the short look he'd gotten the first time was way too quick for his greedy eyes.

But there was a problem. It was one thing to get turned on, to eat up a sight all for himself but, something about Calysto was different. Python looked away, irritated at himself now for the slight flutter he felt in his stomach at the sight of the wet-haired warlock.

He shoved down any thoughts he might've had outside of purely carnal desires and took a long gulp from his drink. Calysto was *annoyingly* pretty, that's all it was. Python didn't care one way or the other who someone was, as long as they were good-looking, and Calysto just happened to check that box, is all.

Not the amiable-and-wants-me-back box, though.

Python didn't care. What he did care about is how he kept finding himself thinking about the way Calysto's lips might feel under his own, how his hair might feel, how his hands might fee—

This fucking wizard was getting under his skin.

He cursed under his breath and stared at the ceiling.

"What?" Calysto asked.

"Nothing."

He's just so fucking annoying I want to shut him up with my mouth.

Sure, Python. We'll let him have that, for now.

"As I was saying, I can't just take us back," Calysto said.

Calysto had calmed down significantly. Though if Python had actually decided to look at his face he would have seen the hot red rims of his eyes. Which was likely only from the shower and not from any quiet emotional breakdown he muffled under the spray of scalding water onto his face. But regardless, he appeared much more in control of his faculties than earlier.

"You saw the room in there. The place is fucking toasted. The crystal is destroyed. There's no going anywhere until I can get another one, and they aren't easy to come by," Calysto continued.

"Why not? What's so special about it?"

"It's…"

Calysto cleared his throat, and when Python chanced another look at him he saw the hesitance written all over it.

"I'm not gonna tell your little wizard secrets," he scoffed.

"Warlock."

"Yeah, whatever." Python shoved him with his foot. "Who's gonna believe me anyway?"

"… Okay…" Calysto swallowed hard. "Well, it's ancient. I… there's only two like it in the world. That I know of."

"Well, where'd you get the first one?"

"I stole it." Calysto frowned. "The other one is gone. I don't know."

"Shit."

Python sat up, using his feet on Calysto's side as leverage against the slow-consuming squish of the couch. He could see Calysto's scowl without even looking at him and snickered, but didn't remove his feet.

"Shit, indeed," Calysto agreed in a tight voice. "There is— " he began again then stopped.

"There's what."

"Nothing…"

"Cal, if there's a way to get back home that you're not fucking telling me, you'd better fucking tell me." Python kicked him again, none too lightly.

"Stop kicking me," Calysto snapped, then sat forward and leaned into his hands with a heavy sigh. "If I'm right about where we are, and what time. It's possible that there's one here. Now."

"Really?" Python sat up fully. "Well fuck, let's go get it!"

"It's really not that simple," Calysto mumbled. "It's… it's extremely hard to get to."

"Why?"

"Python, can you trust me on this," Calysto's voice took on an edge of pleading.

"Ughhh, I don't feel like arguing right now," Python groaned.

"Listen. I know you're fine nibbling on your fucking candy and all that but I need to eat to survive. So I'm going to go back before the dawn comes. Coming?"

"Oh like... blood?"

"Duh."

"I don't... I think I'll stay here."

"Huh, figures, " Python scoffed. "Alright well... I'll go and find out if we're really in the past or this is some fucked up illusion or I don't know, maybe they're re-enactors or something right? Like one of those fake-tourist-town things. That's a possibility."

Calysto raised his eyebrows. "I hadn't thought of that."

"Ha!" Python puffed up and jumped to his feet. "See! It's probably fine!"

"I hope you're right." Calysto still didn't look too happy. But when did he ever?

Python slung on an overcoat and was out the door with a slam.

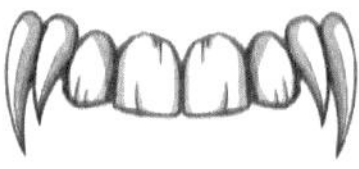

PYTHON RAN the empty road through the short trail in the woods and into town. He slowed before he reached the edge, walking as close to normal speed as he could manage. He'd gotten better at that since spending so much time with Calysto.

The moon was descending slowly in the sky, therefore reaching evening in Python time. The first buildings he approached were lit only on the exterior by oil lanterns dangling from wrought iron poles. The wooden panel buildings were lined up neatly side by side, all with tall shingled roofs. A wide center road weaved between them, lined with potholes, footprints and mud puddles. The whole place smelled of actual shit. There was a distinct lack of people and most of the windows were dark. If this actually were a tourist town, then all the actors had gone on home for the night.

But lining the edges of the road weren't cars or bikes or anything modern, instead there were horses. A few were hitched outside one particular building that Python would recognize anywhere—a saloon.

As he walked closer he could hear voices and see motion warbling inside through the window. Hand-painted letters on the glass spelled out *"LIBATIONS"* in a steady hand. Python hopped up out of the mud covered street and onto the wooden porch before making his way inside.

The bell on the door jingled and a few heads turned. Then more. Then he quickly realized he was being stared at by everyone present.

"Eerie."

What the fuck is their problem? He scowled at someone, who quickly looked away.

"Can I help ya stranger?"

A well-dressed gentleman who looked like he stepped straight out of a Victorian fashion magazine was leaning back in his chair, thumbs in his waistcoat pocket, large cigar clenched in his teeth, and puffing smoke enough to block out the features of his face.

"Just trying to get a drink," Python flashed his most mock-polite smile at the man. He slid between two chairs and up to the bar. "Do I need your permission? What is this, an after-hours cast party?"

The man didn't respond.

"Whiskey," Python addressed the bartender, who nodded at his request. As he served the drink he looked Python over with a curious gaze.

"Sir," he finally said, unable to bite back whatever was pressing on him. "May I ask where yer from?"

"Not around here," Python answered dismissively. "Why?"

"Mean no disrespect, sir." The bartender fidgeted, a nervous bean pole of a man with greying dark hair and a beard to match. "I don't want trouble, you're only dressed different, is all."

"Different how? Wow, you re-enactors really take this shit seriously, huh?"

"Reen-acter?" The bartender shook his head. "I don't know what ya mean, sir. Just can tell yer not from here."

Something about the way he spoke suddenly struck Python as oddly reminiscent, like a tone or lilt he'd heard once before. Well, of course he had. If this were the eighteen hundreds he had been alive then, albeit very young. But alive. He remembered this kind of tongue, the simple twang accompanied by outdated slang. These people had really done their research. The whole place had been transformed, it was actually quite impressive. If only Python could get one of them to break character for a minute.

"Okay, okay," Python played along for the time being. "What's the nearest town over then? Where can a guy catch a taxi?"

"Industry."

Python froze. He cleared his throat. "Tell me... is Industry, uh... which direction?"

"North. Up there through the mountain pass! Town here's all headed up that a way at dawn for the big execution. If ya need a ride along there'll be plenty of wagons going thata way."

Python downed his drink and barely felt it. "Another if you would."

The bartender nodded and served him.

"So, you all live here?" Python said, half-dreading the answer.

The bartender eyed him quizzically. "Well, yessir. Where else?"

"One more thing," Python met the man's watery, alcohol-stained eyes. "Execution of who?"

"Oh, all them witches and warlocks!"

Python felt a bone-deep chill sink into his skin.

He looked around at the lounge. People were milling about, drinking, congregating, playing cards, and loudly swapping stories. Some were passed out in their chairs or were more than halfway there, sliding dangerously towards the floor. A man a few seats down at the bar peered over at Python through a glassy gaze and lazily lifted his drink in greeting, but Python didn't even register it.

The whole thing was too familiar and it tickled at a corner of memories that he hadn't touched for ages past. It reeked of a time and a place he used to call home. Not to mention he could tell this wasn't a late-night green room hangout of modern folk who played pretend for a living.

Suddenly he knew, he knew where he was. *When* this was. He knew it was real.

His hunger for blood forgotten, Python backed away from the counter a step, swallowed down the lump in his throat, and ran.

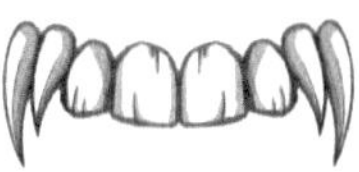

"CALYSTO! CAL! CAL!!"

Calysto was bent over, hands resting on his knees, watching something spin round and round in the microwave, something that probably—no, definitely—shouldn't be microwaved. For all that could be seen through the small yellowed plexiglass window were sparks and smoke. He looked up over his glasses as Python entered, slammed the door, and traveled the distance between them in a blink.

"Must you yell," he said, turning his attention back to the microwave.

He had regained his calm while Python was gone, letting the comforting silence of his home lull him back to whatever his version of normal was.

Python huffed hard enough that Calysto could smell the alcohol on him. Suddenly, the microwave stopped.

"Excuse me. I was doing something." Calysto clenched his jaw and straightened up.

"We need to talk," Python said, before walking over and sitting down stiffly on the edge of the table-turned-laboratory in the center of the room.

The overhead bluish-white light flickered, buzzing with the static of bugs relentlessly trying to meet their end inside of it. Despite the bugs constantly bouncing and swirling around Python's head, which was tall enough to nearly brush the bulbs, and despite his usually loud and constant bellowing of hatred towards them, he didn't even move to swat a single one away.

"What happened," Calysto demanded then, crossing his arms. Expecting full well that Python had gotten them into trouble again. "Get discovered?"

"No." Python frowned. "But I did discover something else."

Calysto raised his brows, waiting for an explanation.

"You were right."

Calysto ceased to breathe. "What?"

"We... I think we really did go back in time," Python admitted.

"Don't fuck with me right now, Python," Calysto managed to squeeze out, even though he really wished in this moment that Python most certainly was. He'd spent the last hour convincing himself not to worry. That Python would come back to tell him he was a whole idiot. This was not what Calysto wanted to hear, at all. "Tell me the truth."

"I am!" Python exclaimed. "I... I've been here before!"

"You have?" Calysto's eyes widened in surprise. "Where?"

"Industry," he said simply. "I... it's the town I grew up in. I thought Purvel looked familiar, and that's cause it's their neighbor."

"You grew up in Industry?" Calysto repeated, making sure he'd definitely heard what he thought he heard. "In the eighteen hundreds?"

"Mhm."

"I..." Calysto felt ungrounded and retreated unevenly until his back met the counter. He caught himself against it, barely holding himself up with his hands. "I don't believe it. What the fuck is going on..."

"What?" Python crossed his arms over his chest, clenching his fists tight.

Calysto's eyes moved so slowly to meet him it was as if they were glued to the floor. When he spoke, his voice nearly stuck in his throat.

"So did I."

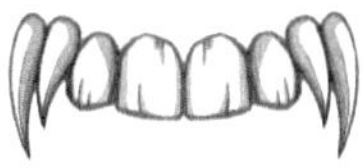

PYTHON STOOD up so fast the table tipped over, crashing sideways onto the floor and taking all the trash with it. The slam of the furniture and subsequent cacophony of noise as things fell, broke, or rolled away, was the only sound between them. Calysto stared at him and neither of them broke eye contact as Python instantly closed the distance between them.

"Calysto, tell me what you mean."

"What more is there to say?" he said quietly. "We're in our own past and we're stuck here."

"Cal," Python's voice trembled and he quickly cleared his throat before continuing. "Whatever you have to do to get us back, do it. Tell me what I need to do, and I'll do it. Do you hear me? I can't be here. I can't fucking be here."

He loomed in so closely Calysto was leaning near horizontally back over the countertop to get away from him.

"Get off of me," Calysto said, a bit desperately. "I need to think."

Python backed away and nearly collapsed into the trusty wooden chair. Calysto instead slid down the back of the kitchen cabinets and onto the floor. Slowly he removed his glasses, folding the arms against the cracked circular frames and setting them aside. Then he massaged the bridge of his nose and closed his eyes. A long, quiet sigh escaped his lips. His hair was still loose, falling in waves around his shoulders. He ducked his head into his knees and it covered his face like a shroud.

Python stared slightly through him, without so much as a sound. He could be quiet when he wanted to be, or needed to be, or when he simply couldn't think of anything else to say.

Like right now.

"Did you learn anything else while you were there?" Calysto's voice emerged muffled from between his knees.

Python thought about what the bartender had said and paused. Should he say it—

"Why are you hesitating," Calysto's voice cut through his thoughts. "I can feel you doing it."

"What is that some warlock power?" Python shot back, nerves making him raw and irritable.

"No, you're just really obvious about it."

Python heaved a weary sigh. "He told me there's an execution tomorrow." He heard Calysto's pulse quicken. "Witches, and... such."

"Oh," Calysto said simply. But the strain of his voice and the pace of his shortened breath were evident.

"Did you..." Python hesitated.

"Ask whatever you want Python," Calysto answered, his voice empty. "When has propriety stopped you yet."

"You remember it?"

"A couple of them, yeah."

"Shit."

"We should go."

"Huh?" Python was not expecting that.

"To Industry." Calysto looked up. "I do remember the execution. But I also remember when the last one happened, and the thing I need to move the house may yet still exist, if we hurry."

"Okay, cryptic much." Python sat forward, elbows on his knees with hands clasped. "Lead the way then."

"Do you not remember your way around?"

"Fuck no," Python shook his head. "I did my best to bury the memory of this godless land a long time ago, I'm surprised you haven't."

"I tried." Calysto shrugged but didn't elaborate. He began to stand and put his glasses back on. "Sun's almost up, I'll have to go alone."

"Are you sure that's a good idea?" Python stood as well. "What if something happens?"

"What's going to happen?"

"Oh, I don't know, you also get executed."

"That won't happen." Calysto ran his fingers through his hair.

"How do you know? What if they find out what you are? Maybe this is how you die, in some twisted time warped way."

"Since when do you care," Calysto snapped, suddenly angry. "And they won't find out. Because I'm not going to *get* found out, alright?"

"Shit, geez, fine, okay." Python raised his hands in defense. "Chill out will you."

Calysto took a shaky breath. "I'm not going to fucking chill out, Python. I'm in the past, my own goddamned past. And so are you. And somehow you and I grew up in the same place, which is weird enough, but besides that, as much as I wanted you to come back here and tell me this was some elaborate prank. It's not? It's not. I'm... I'm lucid, and everything is very much real, and this isn't some wishful fever dream or sci-fi TV show where we can just go back and right our wrongs and change the future for the better with no conse-quences. This is a dangerous fucking situation, and we have one damn shot of getting out of it."

"Okay, okay," Python softened his tone. "Well, here, they were giving me fucking weird looks when I went. So, let me at least help you dress the part. As close as we can get."

If Calysto could scowl further, he did. "What do you have in mind."

PART TWO
REMEMBRANCE

CHAPTER

TEN

Calysto left his house dressed like a proper old-fashioned gentleman. From head to toe, Python had done his best with his extensive and varied wardrobe to deck him out as accurately as possible.

He wore a flouncy white shirt with billowing sleeves and ruffled collar—a very stereotypically vampiric thing for Python to own, he noted—and a forest green waistcoat over top. All of Python's pants were too tall, and too full of 'stylish' holes for Calysto to wear, so they made do with a pair of Calysto's black sweatpants tucked into knee-length leather boots, which were also much too big. Overtop he wore a long dark red peacoat and a silk scarf. Python had even pulled Calysto's hair back with a small black ribbon, tying it off into a pony-tail at the base of his neck. He looked as close to the part of an everyday middle-class man as they could make him.

Good thing Python was a sucker for all things fashion and had sticky fingers to boot.

"You'll need to get rid of those, won't you." Python motioned to his glasses. "They're pretty modern."

"I can't see without them." Calysto fended Python off from grabbing them, but Python got ahold of them anyway.

"What kind of warlock are you?" Python scoffed, holding them up to the light. "You can't like, fix your eyesight, or make magical invisible lenses, or come to think of it, why don't you just have contacts?"

"You have very strange ideas of what a warlock is," Calysto said in return.

"Well then, why don't you tell me, huh?"

Calysto snatched his glasses back without another word.

"They'll be fine. People have worn glasses for hundred of years, even at this point," he grumbled.

Python just rolled his eyes and moved close to right Calysto's collar.

"Let's go over it again," he said quietly, not looking at the scar on Calysto's cheek or the spattering of freckles that traveled beneath the hem of his shirt with it.

"If I'm not back by sundown, you're coming to find me. And we meet at the tavern."

"And you're going to find the crystal and get out."

Calysto nodded once.

"I really think you should wait for me," Python muttered while stepping back to admire his handiwork.

"Well, I really don't want to wait," Calysto answered, then shifted his weight awkwardly in his too-big boots. "How is it?"

"You definitely pass for the part in my eyes," Python shrugged, hands shoved into his pockets. "But it's been a fuckin' hundred years since I've had to think about it. It'll do."

"Okay." Calysto coughed. "Stay out of sight. If people come knocking just let them knock. I've warded the house against entries outside of you or I."

"Really? Oh, that's cool." Python looked up and around.

"It's invisible."

"Oh, so you *can* do that then." Python grinned. "You're holding out on me, warlock."

"Don't call me that," Calysto retorted. "Especially not here." He seemed to hesitate, digging his hand into the thick wooden fabric of his coat. "Please."

"Alright, sorry," Python lowered his voice. "I'll be careful."

Then as Calysto went to leave, Python spoke up again, "You be careful, too."

Industry.

An aptly named city, if not one severely lacking in creativity. A booming epicenter of modernity and technology, and the last place on this green earth that Calysto wanted to be, or ever thought he'd be, again.

He had rejoiced when it had fallen. The city-wide fire that had spread from the upper district burned it to the ground and forced nearly half the town to be abandoned. It never quite recovered from such devastation, and as quickly as it had grown it had died. People and business and wealth bled from the place like an open wound and it didn't take long for the once busy streets and well-kept manor houses to become the ominous stage dressing for a ghost town. In Calysto's opinion, it had done the world a favor by crumbling to dust.

He climbed the pathway in boots that were beginning to chafe, feeling the heavy weight of a place all too eerie and familiar. It was as if he were yet again a child, just a boy in tattered clothes, making his way home from the market carrying his mother's wares.

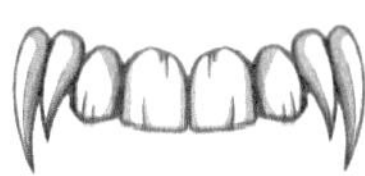

The past.

· · ·

"BOY!" A demanding voice scratched down the walls and sent his heart racing. A child of no more than ten, Calysto climbed up from the floor where he sat and ran towards the call.

"Yes, mama?"

"Don't you *yes mama* me," came the harsh reply. "Make yourself useful and fetch your sister's apron."

Calysto nodded and pattered barefoot across the dirt floor, standing on tiptoes to pull the brown leather apron from the rung. He carefully made his way over to where his sister Essi sat with her nose somehow upturned but also shoved in a book.

"Here."

He held it out in one hand, keeping the rest of him as far a distance away as he could. She didn't even look up, beckoning him until he scooted close enough for her to snatch it up.

He yelped as she yanked him close by one thin arm instead and hissed, "Afraid of me are you? Well, you should be. Had you been what was promised you and I would've been great friends, and yet here you're just a talentless waste of space."

Calysto shuddered at the smell of her garlic laced breath and the weight of her words.

He was supposed to be powerful, the most skilled warlock the likes the world had never seen. His mother's coven had predicted it.

But he came out wrong, powerless. And now he was simply a burden and a nuisance. He was basically only a human boy with a broken, twisted, tainted connection to the raw and mighty abilities that others like him were able to access so easily.

He did not know his father, except to barely know of him. A weak man, incapable of producing worthy seed, a hunter of some kind, there one day and gone the next. Like the man he never knew, Calysto was born with the curse of weakness and he would never be allowed to forget it. Not by his family, not by the coven, and not by the feeble excuse for power that barely bloomed in his hands.

Poor little Calysto.

They never called him by his name, it was simply 'boy' or 'child' but never 'Calysto'. Sometimes he wanted to speak up, to say, *I have a name! I am a person and I have a name!* But he never dared. For even for the smallest slights would he be punished, and he didn't know what would happen to him if he did.

His mother never looked at him, except to sneer in disgust, impatience, and anger. He used to want her to look, to see love in her eyes directed at him. Like the way she looked at his sister.

But now, he knew better. And he knew it was best that she never saw him at all. So, he would hide. When he wasn't wanted for some kind of errand or chore or outlet for his mother's frustrations, he would scurry away where he could be alone. Up in a tree, in the small broom closet he called his room, out in the tall grass fields between the reeds that were as thin as he.

Once he snuck into his mother's room while she wasn't there, busy with her friends and playing nice with her sisters in the coven. He dug in her closet for her makeup and clothes, tying his hair up on top of his head, and sticking a multitude of pins in it to try and make it stay in some semblance of the fancy coifs and buns she wore. He smeared on her lipstick and rouge, wrapping himself twice over in a dress that dragged under his feet onto the floor.

She had found him like this and he had rejoiced, turning to her with a huge painted grin.

"Mama! Mama, see I'm like Essi now, I'm powerful, too!" he had exclaimed, proud of himself and his transformation. But from her came not approval but hate, and a face that turned dark with rage. She stormed over and grabbed his arm tight, yanking the dress off with the other.

"What in the world are you doing? Touching my things!" She turned him roughly and held the back of his head, using the corner of her apron to viciously scrub his face. He stood shivering in only his knickers as she yanked his hair, pulling the pins out one by one and taking bits of hair with it.

"You will never be like your sister, do you hear me? Never! Goddess above I wish you would be. You would save me a lot of grief!"

Hot silent tears slipped down his cheeks that bloomed with shame.

"What're you doing crying, child! I am the one who should cry, for I birthed you! A failure! A wretched useless thing!" She pulled him closer and he staggered toward her, suddenly afraid of their closeness. Her body had never offered him a motherly comfort, and he knew better than to indulge in wanting it now.

In her hand, she held one of the long needle-like hair pins, and she slammed his tiny arm on her dresser and held it there. He tried to pull away—but a child is no match for an angry mother's might. She brought the pin down, pricking the soft flesh on the back of his hand, and a thin streak of blood rolled down his knuckles as he whimpered.

"Mamaaa!..."

"Silence, boy," she snapped, and pricked him again, her voice rising dangerously in pitch and fervor. "You will never be like your sister. Do you hear me?" The needle jabbed his skin. "The best you can do for this family is be of *some* use! You will not waste time wishing for what will not be!" And again.

He gave up trying to struggle, his hand was aching, and the blood had turned into a small river.

"I said," she growled, jolting him to her attention. "Do you understand me!"

"Yes, mama!" he finally wailed, his little throat thick with anguish and tears. "Yes, mama!" He sobbed and fell to the floor as she released him with a shove.

When she spoke again she was calmer, her voice was even. Gentle almost. As if nothing had happened between them. As if she weren't a bitter tyrant releasing her vitriol on an undeserving child. A child borne of a promise unfulfilled by no doing of his own, a child desperate for her love yet already so resigned to receiving her hate, instead.

"Now listen, I don't want to hurt you, but you force me! You leave me no choice. You must learn your place, you hear me?" She stroked his hair, petting him with a hand that held no warmth.

He cradled his hand against his chest and knew better than to be slow to answer again.

"Yes, mama," he responded in a warbling whisper.

"Good." She stood, dropping the pin onto the dresser. "Now clean up this mess, and don't make me have to see this again."

Calysto's mother then turned and left her bleeding son on the floor without another word.

Calysto rubbed the back of his hand, absentmindedly palming at the long-faded pain as he continued to climb the cobblestone incline that led out of Purvel and into the outskirts of Industry. It had taken him hours to travel the road from where his house had landed to where he was now. And the whole time all he had to do was think, and think, and remember, and think some more.

He had never really wanted to be like his mean and sour sister. He had only wanted his mother to love him, and was that such a bad thing to ask? He had never felt that warmth, and the absence of it always left him guessing.

What would I be like, if I'd had that? Who would I be, if she'd done that?

The weight of these thoughts had plagued him his whole life. Even after she was long gone, he still wondered. Would he have a family? Friends? Would he then, himself, be able to love someone back? If only she had loved him. *What then, what then?*

Well, if she had loved him he would have died alongside her. This one thing is for sure.

He had lived with his mother and sister further towards the outskirts of Industry in a rickety old cabin. The slums. The place where washerwomen and fishermen and hunters and blacksmiths made their homes. Far enough away not to disturb the wealthy, but close enough to be at their beck and call.

His mother was a witch, and her coven met in secret with their magic muffled beneath their hands. Hands of cooks and launders and tailors and nannies. Hands with a deep connection to a magic only known by them. Something lost to modern time and turned near mythic, not a thing believed in reality, but still feared. And as such, magic was a real threat and the simple idea of a witch even more so.

But whether they were truly witches or simply misunderstood humans, still, the fear of the other was fear enough. So despite their power and might, a real witch would keep such things hidden away. But even as they were subservient to the rich and their true nature shunned by a fearful world, Calysto was even more so shunned by them.

He was a lackey. A servant to servants. And more so, a stain on their coven, the shit under their shoes, and another mouth to reluctantly feed. A basic task they more than often neglected to do.

In fact, much of Calysto's young life could be defined by that one word: neglect. Lonely and ragged, he would wander the wet and mud-covered cobblestone streets on cold bare feet. Many thought him a beggar, an orphan. A child with no place to call home and no one to claim him. No one to want him and show him comfort. At least most of that was the truth.

Sometimes, a passerby would slip a coin into his grubby hands as he sat at the street corner counting down the dreaded minutes until he had to return. For he did have a home, but in some ways, wouldn't it be better if he didn't?

Little Calysto would twist the copper in his fingers, admiring the shiny rubbed-smooth surface in the fading sunlight. Above his head, putrid black smoke poured into the sky from chimneys at every building, factory, and business, filling the air with smog. Thus the small glimmer of a coin captivated him as he turned it this way and that.

It was a treasure not only for what it could provide but what it represented on its own—a bit of regular everyday magic.

For magic was just that—simple.

Magic wasn't the power that came from the cruel hands of his mother, magic wasn't the horrible gift they had to hide, and it certainly wasn't that dreaded thing he lacked. It was these small moments of beauty and wonder he found in dirty corners of this wretched town. It was the little act of kindness clenched in his small hands.

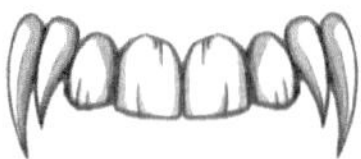

Morning had dawned behind him when Calysto finally made it into Industry.

The sun crept up slow and hazy from behind the height of houses that grew taller and more frequent around him. He shoved his hands deep in the pockets of Python's peacoat to thaw them against the cold. Something was in the left pocket and he pulled it out to inspect.

A pack of smokes with a flimsy cardboard lid held three crushed cigarettes and a tie-dye patterned plastic lighter. Smooshed behind the lighter, folded carefully along worn creases, was a piece of tobacco-and-dirt-stained paper. Calysto's curiosity got the best of him, and with his task momentarily forgotten he veered off the side of the road and squatted down on a picket between a couple of tethered horses. They didn't seem to mind his presence as he squeezed in beside them.

Calysto opened the paper carefully, smoothing it out to find a chaotic mess of notes in scrawled elaborate cursive.

I'm glad that motherfucker is dead, but it didn't do any good. He couldn't take it back, and there's no one else.

Get more smokes.

How many has it been again?

Richter

Aeris ???

Gabriel

And at the bottom, in a newer hand with fresher ink;

Calysto

Clearly, they were notes from Python. Private notes, he realized. Calysto carefully folded it back along the fraying creases and slipped it back into the pack. He stood, and tried not to think about why his name was on that list. Or who that 'motherfucker' was that Python wrote about.

Did Python hate being alone, too? Was he even lonely? Did he dread the rising of the sun not just for what it could do to him, but because of the way that regular life passed him by as he was forced to linger on the sidelines? Did he too face each day with a sense of resignation and emptiness? Every one the same in event and yet unique in whatever disparaging thought spiral might strike him, tunneling his thoughts down into a bleak and hazy pinpoint that blocked out all possibility of hope and optimism? Yeah, maybe that one was *a little too* specific.

Calysto realized he really wanted to know, yet he didn't know how to ask such things. And who would? It was as revealing of a question as the answer it would bring.

So Calysto shook his head and tucked the pack of cigarettes away, placing himself firmly back into a reality he wanted to be in now even less so than usual, pat one of the horses gently on the nose, and headed back down the road.

CHAPTER

ELEVEN

The past.

Han was carrying out his work since before dawn and was making his rounds when he came upon the main square full of people. The shouts could be heard from blocks away, and everyone had been streaming in that direction already. Han had assumed it was a fight carrying on—between beggars over a piece of bread, or shopkeeper and shoplifter—that attracted a scene and some kind of entertainment for mid-afternoon pedestrians.

What he came upon was not at all what he expected. In the square were pyres. Rows and rows of them. They must have been erected overnight and he lived far enough in the slums away from the center of town that he hadn't heard it. But what was even more shocking was those who were upon it. People shackled in a line from young to old. Their wailing and cries carried out into a jeering crowd, falling on deaf and merciless ears. Some threw mud, some handfuls of horse shit, some rotten fruit, some stones.

Witch hunts were common and he'd heard of their punishments, but he'd never witnessed an execution before. He paused on the outside of the crowd and watched in muted horror as the condemned endured such vitriol at the hands of these people who were likely once their neighbors.

Then an elderly man dressed in white lace and a satin coat complete with a pompous air climbed the wooden staircase that led up the side of the scaffolding pyre. He raised one hand to signal for quiet, and in the other, he held a small notebook.

The crowd fell silent as he cleared his throat and began to read.

"I, Magistrate Cadwell, hereby decree that those convicted have been found guilty of witchcraft and associated practices of devil worship, sodomy, ritualistic demonic rites, and spellcasting! Tried through the noble courts that uphold law and purity in this land, they are sentenced to death by fire before the eyes of all righteous people who constitute the great and prosperous city of Industry!"

As he finished his speech with a flourish of his lace-frilled wrists, the crowd erupted into cheers.

Han did not join in, standing stiff with disbelief as events continued to unfold. Then before his eyes, living human beings were turned to ash.

The pyres were already standing high above the crowd and Han had to crane his neck upward to view them. Once they were set alight, the flames quickly climbed up to the height of the tallest roofs.

At first there was silence, only the crackle of tinder and branches catching could be heard. But then came the sound. Moans against the beginning of pain they quickly turned to shouts, then wails, screams, howls. Cries that rung out as inhuman as the method of their deaths.

Han watched, unable to tear his eyes away from the grotesque display in front of him. For a second, he thought he saw a flash of light, a flame turn blue, then flicker back to raging orange again. But no, probably not.

Soon, as nerves died and the smoke was inhaled, the shouts died out only to be replaced by those of the crowd. All of the so-called witches stood, chained to their still smoldering pyres, the fiery light replacing that of the sun as it began to wane and set. But Han couldn't stop staring. He was frozen to the spot.

Witches weren't real, of course they weren't. Witches weren't more real than any other mythical creature created by humanity to instill undue fear in the hearts of those who would stray without them. Fear created to keep one in line, force one into place.

Han had heard the list of what they'd been accused of. He swallowed hard, and thought about how he too, would then be guilty. He lived with the shadow of that every day. The knowledge that he co-existed and served a city that would also gladly burn his body to ash than to see it with another man. How does one trust and care for their neighbor when if their neighbor knew who they were, they'd betray them on the spot? Without question. Without hesitation. With a sense of righteousness and duty.

His fear twisted to rage in the face of those flames and it seared a hatred in the young man named Han. He would never belong here, he wasn't wanted, wasn't accepted, and was one simple mistake away from a similar fate. Accused of some corruption that would bring the population of the mindless and fearful together against a common enemy. One easier to vilify and destroy than their true foe, who stood watching from gold-framed opera glasses on high balconies with handkerchiefs pressed to their faces. As if perfume in their noses could numb them from the reality that the streets were coated in the refuse of the poor and starving who outnumbered them tenfold.

No, someone like Han—someone like those dying in front of him—was a much easier target, when everyone who wallowed below secretly wanted to be the one standing above. They quietly craved that power, that ability to determine life and death, that privilege of a clean shoe and an even cleaner conscience. Who wouldn't want that blissful unawareness, that reckless opulence? That simple pleasure of eating when one was hungry, and resting when one was tired. With nothing and no one to demand otherwise. Why turn against that which they each truly coveted the most?

So they placed their blame on the innocent and the weak, the different or the unique, anyone to let them misdirect their hate and stoke its flames with self-righteous fire. For not one soul in the crowd could say they were truly innocent of all the same of which they so boldly condemned others.

Young Han stood slumped against his cart of tools for a few long hours. He had certainly neglected all of his duties, which he would hear an earful for upon his return. But for now he couldn't move, as waves of anger and hatred and shame and fear wafted over him. Each person who eventually left the square earned a glare, and those who passed close by to him earned a special expression of disgust. He stayed in the square, long after the sun went down and the crowd had cleared. He stayed until nearly all the embers had died, and the only smoke left traveled in subtle wafts with the cooling wind.

Then behind him he heard a small patter of footsteps on the stone and someone stopped beside him. Han looked over through his shaggy black hair, expecting some kind of authority to tell him to get lost.

But no. It was just a small boy in dirty clothes.

"Hey," Han called over to him. "You shouldn't look at this, why don't you go on home."

The boy didn't respond, and fisted his small hands into a tattered shirt. He didn't take his eyes off the pyres. Han looked around, but there was no one else there. No one who looked they might care where this child had gone.

"Hey..." Han called again, softer this time. He crouched down, and the sudden movement made the boy flinch. "I'm not gonna hurt you."

"That's my mama," the boy said. His small voice was calm and he stared straight ahead.

"What?"

"That's my mama," he said again and turned to look at Han. Only then in the dim streetlamp light did Han see his face. A bruise had swollen part of his cheek and his lip was split, but his eyes were clear. No tears, no sadness. If anything, they were extremely cold.

"That's my mama. And my gramma. And my sister. And my coven," he said, then pinched his little mouth shut.

"Y—" Han looked back up at the burning pyres. "Oh... I... Oh shit, I'm sorry. Do you have somewhere to go?"

The little boy nodded, his golden hair was clumped with dirt and tangled in knots around his cheeks.

"I don't live with mama no more," he said. "She sold me to the science man 'while ago."

"Science man?"

Han grimaced at the word 'sold' and wondered if the boy made a mistake. Maybe this man was a family friend and his mother had known there was danger.

The boy nodded, meeting Han's eyes. "The science man who makes the medicines."

Ah, not a friend. But Merik. Everyone knew of him. A chemist of some kind and an absolute narcissist, but a successful creator of all things remedy. A mean man, without an ounce of mercy in his heart if you didn't have the coin.

Folk had been known to die on his pristinely paved doorstep—keeling over into a rosebush and tossed into a barrel to become compost—if they couldn't afford his services. Merik looked down on everyone from the tip of his nose, from peasant to noble alike.

Han found himself a bit sorry for this boy who had somehow come under Merik's care. Had his mother really sold him? Only an idiot would willingly put someone they loved under the eye of such a man. An idiot, or one who held no love for their child. From the look on the boy's face at the sight of his own mother's corpse, Han was betting the latter.

He didn't know what to say.

Everyone had it hard here. There was no use in being a bleeding heart for anyone who happened upon misfortune, for misfortune was as common as sickness, as ripe as the sticky smashed fruit on the scaffold behind him, as plentiful as the rain that threatened to come down with a crack of thunder overhead. Still as pitiful as the boy looked, he didn't seem to be asking for sympathy. And something about that made it much worse.

A coldness had already set in, the heart of this child had too soon hardened on the edges, closed off from even the most vulnerable of hurts. He peered up at the bodies of his family and appeared blank. Empty. Listless. Lost. As if in the space which grief was supposed to fill there came up nothing.

Rain started to fall, splattering onto the charred and smoldering shapes where people once were. Soft sounds melded with one another into a long drawn-out hissing decrescendo as the remains of any fire were slowly put out. The boy still didn't move—it was as if he'd forgotten Han was there.

"Hey..." Han finally spoke. "You should get on home."

The boy shook his head.

"It's raining. You'll get sick."

The boy shook his head again, gripping the hem of his shirt tighter. Han sighed.

"You don't want to go back to the science man?"

The boy hesitated, then nodded.

"Well..." Han thought for a moment. "Look. You have to go somewhere. And it's better than nothing, right? Will you stay out in the rain?"

The boy still didn't answer. Han leaned forward onto his knees, reaching deep into his pants pocket. He pulled something out, holding it carefully.

"Here, look at this," Han said softly as he opened his hand.

The boy looked.

In Han's palm was a small pewter deer, intricately detailed from hooves to horns. Its front leg was lifted as was its head, and the small mouth was open as it bellowed up towards the sky.

"This is a good luck charm, you know what that is?"

"Yeah." The boy didn't take his gaze off it.

"I want you to have it, okay? It'll be your friend. It'll help."

"It will?" The boy's voice was hushed.

"Yeah," Han smiled. "Take it, it's yours now."

"Okay."

The boy slowly reached out, and his fingers trembled as they brushed Han's palm. This time when he looked up, the statuette clenched in his fist, his big amber eyes were glistening with tears.

A CART ROLLED PAST, shuddering against the uneven street and clattering its contents back and forth. It broke Calysto out of his reverie and the way he had been studying the interesting pattern his boots made when they sank into the mud. He looked up and realized it was approaching mid-afternoon, and there were people out and about all around. He had been completely lost in thought, remembering again the events of so long ago typically kept hidden within him. He tried to shake them loose and, as much as he didn't want to, focus on his surroundings and where he was slowly headed.

Then, Calysto noticed that everyone was traveling in the same direction as he, and the dread hit him like a punch to the gut. They were going *there*. The spectacle that was his life, on full display for the world to see as it burned to the ground.

This wasn't the same pyre from his memories, not the one that he'd seen as a small and dirty child, nor the one that killed the semblance of a family he'd once had. But one he'd only heard of in passing. He'd be older around this time, he figured. A teenage boy with his face buried in a book, tucked away in a dark corner of Merik's estate.

Calysto halted at the edge of the square. The smells and sounds hit him full force with the weight of what he was about to witness. In the pocket of Python's coat he gripped tight to the worn figurine of a deer.

He had brought it along for luck, taking the chance to swipe it out of his nightstand drawer where he'd kept it safe in a small wooden box for countless lonely years. It had never actually brought him luck, but that didn't matter. It was more about the idea of the thing, and certainly a token of comfort he needed now.

The smell of smoke like that from charred meat hit him full force with a gust of wind and he halted short. In front of him were the scaffolds, the people, the jeers and the screams. All of it a near exact reflection of that which he had remembered but ultimately chose to try and forget. He clenched his hands tight, crushing the deer's worn antlers into the soft flesh of his palm, and the poor abused cigarette pack in the other. He stayed near the edge, barely able to catch his breath against the overwhelming reality of it all. As the screams began to die he stumbled, retreating in a haze until his back hit a wall, and there he stayed. Dazed and alone.

He thought he would be fine, that he could see this, face this part of himself, and it would not touch him. Just as if he were that cold and angry child again. But he was wrong, and time had softened some part of him. Turning the hate into anguish to guilt to regret. The youthful fury at the cruelty he'd endured had aged into sorrow and his broken heart that lie buried had never truly stopped its incessant yearning. Smoke stung his eyes and he dipped his head, closing his eyes as a silent tear trickled down his cheek.

Calysto held his breath on and off in shallow gasps as he looked out to the cobbled plaza where the afternoon waned. The crowd slowly turned their attention from the dwindling spectacle to the more pressing matters of duty and commerce. Moving on from senseless murder with barely a second glance.

Yet in the midst of all the pain, this sight reminded him of another memory that instead, was golden. Tucked between so much hurt it was almost forgotten, but juxtaposed against this smoldering backdrop of senseless murder was a shining beacon of light.

Calysto stood in his place in the shadows as he remembered the state of his youth in the place of his birth. That pitiful existence of his only just beginning, yet already filled with so much longing for it to be over. But once, in this very place, there had been a boy. Gently he had spoken, looking upon Calysto with a kindness he'd yet to ever experience. And one he'd rarely known since.

His heart ached at the thought of the dark-haired boy not much older than him, who had knelt down and held out his hand. At the same time Calysto recalled how he'd taken that symbol of luck, he gripped the very same one in his palm.

At times he'd looked upon the small deer and had wondered what happened to that boy, probably lost in the sprawl of the city and fallen victim to its cruelty in one of its many forms. A life ending much too short, a life reduced to dust beneath the heel of the monster it was born to serve, a life forgotten by most. Not a life wasted, not forgotten by him, not entirely.

Because even now in Calysto's memory, he was here, he was alive, and he was kind. That boy had never died, not in the depths of Calysto's heart at least. For it was this simple act from a boy who chose to see him that made him decide to keep on living.

In the face of those burning flames had young Calysto considered his own death. He had looked upon the scaffold and considered making the climb. For he didn't want this life, and who would? He would find no fulfillment here, no purpose or place. No one else would speak to him with such a smile and worry if he had a home. Nor would he expect it ever again. To be overlooked was the norm and to want more was the wishful fancy of a fool. This was simply the way of the world, and why should he expect any different? And so he never did. But he also never let go, not of that deer or of his desires. Though both had lain stored away in boxes, hidden from sight and memory and feeling alike, they had carried on. As part of him as anything else, and more a part of him now than ever before.

The two boys had parted, the briefness of their time together a mere breath in comparison to the length of life that one like Calysto had lived. Yet here it remained, shut away in his heart, tucked away in his pocket. A tangible reminder that goodness begot goodness, and that goodness had happened. Once. Even to him.

The memory Calysto saw in his mind, while standing in his past, came to an end.

Python couldn't sleep. He had paced around the small living room in an even smaller circle over and over, waiting like a caged animal for the sliver of light under the door to disappear. He had long since dressed, and as soon as darkness fell he bolted out the door. It didn't take him long at all to reach Industry, and when he arrived he was barely wet despite the downpour that had begun on his way. Perks of being a vampire.

Speaking of being a vampire. He hadn't eaten in quite a few days now and had even less rest. This was the last run he was going to do for a while unless he happened upon a tasty townsman in the midst of Industry's sprawling streets. Not really a difficult feat if he didn't care about getting caught.

Python had lived long enough to learn a few things, two of those being that getting someone alone either took a whole lot of effort or a good amount of luck and to never, ever go hungry. He made stupid decisions when he didn't eat, and had less than half the energy he normally would to see those fuck ups through in any way that didn't end in desperate escape or senseless slaughter.

Also, it made his skin itchy. He really didn't like to be itchy.

Though right now he wasn't in the mood to lure someone into his clutches, and he briefly considered charging at Calysto the moment he saw the glint off the rim of his glasses. But as he neared the town square of Industry intent on finding the tavern and a grouchy warlock in the same vicinity, he halted. Calysto was there in a faraway dark corner, soaked to the bone and unmoving. It wasn't exactly unlike the guy to look pensive and sulky, but the sight temporarily killed Python's appetite for some unknown and very bothersome reason.

"What the fuck are you doing out here?" Python called out as he approached. "Did you get it? Why aren't you at the bar?"

Calysto didn't answer.

"Did something happen?"

"I didn't think I'd care." Calysto's voice came out quiet. If Python weren't a vampire he might not have heard.

"About what?" Python followed Calysto's empty gaze up to the smoldering parapet. "Oh, uh, did you know them?"

"You could say that," Calysto said, his expression blank. "I... uh, didn't... didn't get it yet."

"You've been here the whole time?" Python scoffed. He'd really spent all day worrying for nothing. "Fucking hell, Calysto, useless much."

Python expected him to retort or snap, to say something equally as callous and short. But he didn't. He looked down at his feet, hands deep in his pockets, his glasses fogged with cold and rain, and what he said next made Python feel terrible.

Something that Calysto was apparently good at making him feel.

How inconvenient.

"I'm sorry," he said with a rasp. "I... I'll go do it now... You don't have to come."

Python was taken aback by the apology and stepped closer into Calysto's space.

"No... It's fine, it's just one day. Look, why don't we just get a drink and try again tomorrow? Don't worry about it."

"I want to leave." Calysto shrugged as if trying to weakly protest.

"I do too," Python agreed. "But like I said it's just one day so. It's not a big deal."

"Are you sure?"

Python caught Calysto's hesitant gaze flicker up at him, and in that moment the depth of his dark gold eyes shook Python to the core. He was struck with the thought that Calysto could see straight into his mind and anticipate the possibilities of what he could say next. His stare was endless, overwhelming, full to the watery brim with a multitude of words he wouldn't say. The feeling came over him without explanation, and it occurred to him that he could know Calysto better than anyone he'd ever met, and Calysto could know him in return. Like they'd spent a lifetime together in these short weeks, an amount of time that barely meant anything to either of them anymore. Potential snagged on the sharpened fragments of his heart, pulled taut where it tangled around the sight of a warlock standing in the rain.

Who was he fooling? Python knew nothing about him at all. Calysto was a stranger, a puzzle as complicated and twisted with mystery as himself, and Python had no idea who he was. He was already lucky enough that Calysto hadn't tried to drive a stake into his chest while he slept, and only treated him with mild disdain and a cool level of tolerance. Whatever Calysto was going through right now was none of his business, nor did he even want to assume to ask.

Not that Calysto would tell him.

Not that Python cared.

"Uh... Yeah, yeah." Python feigned irritation at the rain and vigorously rubbed his face, pushing his hair back from off his forehead and the feeling of vulnerable unease down with it. "Come on, you at least owe me a drink."

Calysto nodded and pushed himself up off the slimy stone wall.

"I think I got your coat dirty," he mumbled apologetically as he fell into step beside Python.

Python chuckled. "At this point Cal, I wouldn't expect any less from you."

"Whiskey," Python said to the bartender, then turned to Calysto. "What do you want?"

"I don't know." Calysto still seemed dazed, attempting to clean his glasses with the tail of his wet shirt and failing spectacularly.

Python sighed and said, "Make that two, and give me those."

Calysto stopped and slowly handed his glasses over. Python pulled out a handkerchief, cleaned the cracked lenses, and gave them back. Calysto slipped them on then looked at Python under the warm evening lamplight.

"What?" Python snickered, leaning his elbows on the bar behind them.

Calysto shook his head as if to dismiss him, but then said, "You... look nice."

"Oh?" Python perked up. Determined to make sure that was exactly what he'd just heard, he leaned in a hair closer. "What's that? Is that a compliment from the world's most stoic man? Why Calysto, I'm positively flattered!"

And he was. It was in this moment as he saw Calysto's cheeks redden that he was glad he could no longer do the same—unless he'd recently eaten. He might tease, but he didn't want Calysto to know how much he liked hearing that. He did put some effort into this very period-appropriate outfit and it needed to be appreciated by *someone*, at least. Even if it only came from the most fashion-averse man he'd ever met. And that was saying a lot, considering most men.

Python cleared his throat, stopping himself before he overthought Calysto's comment to death and ruined it for himself.

"Here," Python slid one of the glasses over and picked up his own, nodding in Calysto's direction. "To getting the hell out of here."

Calysto silently lifted his glass and downed his drink in one go.

A few drinks later they were both reclining on the edge of the bar but still barely talking. Python tried his usual techniques of getting someone to engage in conversation with him—before he'd flirt his way down to their pants or up to their neck.

But nothing was working.

Calysto was a closed book, locked tight with a hidden key that Python couldn't seem to find. He was getting bored of people watching and hungrier by the minute, too. As he scanned the tavern populace for his next meal he decided to try with Calysto one more time.

"Cal, just answer me this," he said, nudging the slightly bleary-eyed warlock with his elbow. "How long have you lived alone in that house? You've never had other roommates?"

"No, I haven't. And it's been since I left this hell hole," Calysto answered with a subtle slur. "I built that house and then... I got away."

"You built it? Really? How?"

Calysto slid over on the polished edge of the bar and leaned in towards him, so close that their cheeks brushed as he whispered in Python's ear, "Magic."

Python laughed. "I should have guessed as much."

Maybe it was the result of the drinks or the way his ability to see in the dark warped the air into rippling shapes around the lamplight, but Python thought the corner of Calysto's lips might've lifted, just a tiny bit.

"Well, Cal my friend," Python reached over and slapped him hard on the back, erasing any semblance of mirth that might've been on Calysto's face. "I gotta eat, so... uh, bear with me, huh? We can head back in an hour."

Calysto shrugged and didn't seem to have any intention of moving from his spot at the bar. Python took that as assurance enough that he wouldn't go anywhere and slipped off his stool into the unsuspecting crowd.

CHAPTER

TWELVE

Calysto was absentmindedly swirling the last drops of his drink around in the bottom of the glass, and the whiskey had gone much too quickly to his head and empty, churning stomach.

He grimaced. Alcohol wasn't typically his *thing*, but having an object in his hands to fuss over was. So the glass made a nice temporary replacement for something he could study or fix. So the glass kept getting refilled and he kept drinking from it. So the glass was its own kind of distraction from his thoughts, like a project or idea or invention could be. He remembered the appeal of liquor, now.

The events of the afternoon had hit a bit harder than he'd expected, and he'd wasted his whole chance to get the crystal. Time was ticking down for a reason he wouldn't say, and he knew he'd just squandered over half of it. But he really wished Python hadn't called him that. What did he say? Useless.

That word stung worse than the burn of liquor sliding down his throat. He signaled the bartender for another drink and certainly didn't think too much about how close he had gotten to Python's face a moment ago.

Python had slunk off into the night to find a meal, and he hoped to be left in peace until the vampire returned. But he wouldn't be so lucky.

"Hey, sweetheart."

The low singsong voice of a woman traveled up from behind Calysto at the bar. He ignored it.

The voice from over his shoulder got closer and spoke again.

"Calysto."

That made him jump. That wasn't Python.

"Do I know you?" He twisted his neck to face the sound.

"No, but I know you." A woman with long dark curls and matching black eyes was smiling at him. "Though... you're a bit more unkempt than I would have imagined. But I'd know that pretty face anywhere. I've heard of your work, and I'm here to offer my assistance."

Calysto squirmed slightly at the compliment. "I think you have me confused with someone else."

"Oh no, certainly not." She smiled again, scooting up closer to him. "You are Calysto are you not?"

"Yes..."

"Famed vampire hunter?"

"... No?"

"Don't be shy." She slid onto the stool next to him and leaned over, so their shoulders were nearly touching. "You can tell me, I won't give you away. What, are you here on a hunt? Are there vampires here?"

Calysto shot her a look. "Well, if there were, you surely already gave me away by talking so loud, don't you think."

She gasped, slapping a hand over her mouth, then after a moment she sheepishly spoke again, "I'm... I'm sorry I wasn't thinking. I swear I'm usually more careful than this, I just... I'm so excited to meet you."

"I told you I'm not who you think I am," he said again.

"Okay, don't tell me then." Her smile returned. "I get it."

Calysto sighed and looked down to realize his glass was full again.

"What is it you want?" he asked, before finishing it in one gulp.

"I want to learn from you!" She waved her hand like it was obvious.

"I have nothing to teach you." He coughed lightly.

"Oh but I'm sure you do." She leaned in again, much too close for Calysto's comfort. "Teach me to hunt vampires, to track them, to kill them!"

"Why?" He rubbed his temples. "Why do you want that? What have they done to you?"

She frowned then, the first one Calysto had seen on her yet. "Well, it would be interesting is all."

"Interesting?" Calysto scoffed. "You want to hunt an extremely dangerous and evolved form of humanity because it'd be interesting? You'll get yourself killed."

She grinned again and brushed against his arm, seemingly unaware that she was touching him. "Well sure. Isn't that why you do it?"

Calysto was no vampire hunter, he knew that much. He hadn't even known they existed until a few weeks ago. But he had seen only a bit of what Python could do and it wasn't anything to laugh at. The vampire was extremely fast with the strength of ten men or more, his eyes surely had the ability to hypnotize, his teeth were razor sharp and accurate, and he had claimed to be able to turn to mist. Calysto hadn't actually seen that last one, but Python had said as much. And sometimes it was hard to tell when Python was lying.

Regardless of that, vampires were certainly not a thing to be fucked with. Calysto only felt grateful that Python hadn't drained him dry in his sleep, or broken him in half for pissing him off. He was able to tolerate the barely tolerable with a cheeky smile and an equally vicious jab or light-hearted quip.

Calysto had no idea what compelled that vampire to put up with him. No one else had ever voluntarily stuck around Calysto's difficult attitude and peculiar habits for so long, if at all. But Python said he chose to stay there, with him, in his house, even when he had elsewhere to go. Sure, he was probably just freeloading in a place that gave him consistent shelter from the sun when he needed it. Yet Calysto still found it strange. Uncomfortable even. It didn't make sense. And now he'd gotten them fucking stuck in a horrible situation that was only quickly getting worse.

He wished he had another drink. He wished Python would come back.

He chanced a look at the woman to his left and he knew he couldn't blame her for simply finding something interesting and running after it full force, no matter the consequences. He had certainly done the same thing a few times before. This was different though—this was vampires. Not only were there more of them, there were enough that there were also famous hunters of them. And apparently he was one of them?

How did she know his name?

What is going on?

He knew he should try to find out, but his thoughts were racing too hard for him to find the words to the questions that would get him the right answers. He was also becoming uncomfortably drunk.

What if Python comes back right now?

Python, with his glimmering cat eyes and his lips a deep red, reinvigorated with life from someone's fresh blood. If this woman knew about vampires, it was likely she knew about traits such as that, as well. Suddenly his heart was in his throat and he abruptly stood.

"I have to go," he blurted.

"But, wait!" She leaped off her stool and grabbed his arm.

"Don't touch me." He pulled away and met her with a glare.

"You're just going to leave?" She continued unperturbed. "I came all this way to find you."

"I'm busy," he said plainly. "I don't have time for this right now, alright? Just hear me on this, you shouldn't meddle in this kind of thing no matter how fascinating you might find it, okay? You don't know what you're asking."

Much to his dismay she didn't look discouraged at all. Instead she seemed to glean some kind of reassurance from what he'd said.

She winked and lowered her voice to say, "I see, I understand completely, mister Calysto. Absolutely."

He groaned quietly in his throat. She was as determined to latch on to him as he was to shake her off.

"No," He wiped his mouth with the back of his coat sleeve and tried to make himself seem as serious as possible. "I'm not suggesting anything, and I'm not speaking in code. I'm telling you not to do this."

"But you do it!" she exclaimed, seeming offended.

"No, I don't!"

"It's cause I'm young isn't it?" She crossed her arms, a pout pursing on her lips. Calysto went to protest but she continued talking right over him. "Well, I'll prove it! I'll prove it to you that I can do it!"

"Please!" he raised his voice slightly and nervously shot a glance around the room. "Please stop."

But she was much too far in her own ideas now to listen. She scowled at him, her eyes turning dark with a mixture of annoyance and determination. Before she turned to leave, she said, "You'll see. I'll show you."

She marched away from the bar and Calysto watched on in confused dismay as she disappeared out the door.

Whatever that just was, it's bad.

He decided to hurry up and find Python and the crystal and get the fuck out of there before things had a chance to get any worse. And if there happened to be more vampires around, well, Calysto had enough of one and didn't need the trouble of more.

Calysto stepped outside, having told the bartender to put their drinks on a tab he definitely wasn't coming back to pay. Maybe he did that. He wasn't sure at this point. The alcohol was entering his bloodstream with an alarming intensity and he had to grab the doorframe to keep himself from stumbling. If there was something else he remembered about this place, it was that one could quickly find themselves locked up in a damp overnight cell for public intoxication. He wasn't about to attract any more attention to himself than the sight of his fucking face already did. He needed to tell Python about this.

Where is he?

The night was humid and thick from the passing storm and offered little relief from the warm interior of the tavern. Calysto leaned on the wooden railing and slowly made his way, step by step, down the narrow stairs and into the street. He wasn't even sure where to go, or where to look. Where *did* a vampire go to find people to eat? Where did they *go to* eat?

"... Let me get a cheeseburger with fries, extra ketchup, and a large side of O-Negative please?"

Calysto swayed in place and thought of Python's previous quip. A small chuckle tickled his throat. He had to admit that was kind of funny, now that he wasn't entirely annoyed by it.

Maybe vampire taverns will be a thing one day, and he can have a Bloody Mary... extra bloody.

Calysto chuckled again, entirely amused by the thought of Python sipping on blood from a fancy glass. At least he was until the slam of the tavern door behind him planted him firmly back into reality.

"Python...?" he mumbled in a weak attempt to call out.

His words landed on empty air, and he continued forward keeping his hand on the long wooden railing for support. He hadn't drunk this much in an unknowable amount of time, and probably shouldn't have now.

Stomach churning, he pinched his lips together in defiance

against it and continued down the road still not exactly sure where he was headed. The smell of smoke from the pyres wafted past him in the dark. The bodies of his family, his coven, his previous life, had once been left in the square to crumble to dust for days after their execution, and so these would be their own lingering reminder. Suddenly nothing was funny and he was beginning to sink back into that familiar feeling of misery.

"Python... !" he called again, this time a bit louder. He was still met with silence. Python could be anywh—

"Oh, there you are," the familiar low voice came from behind him. "You were supposed to wait for me."

"Hey!" Calysto stumbled as he spun around. Python caught him by his shoulders before he fell, and Calysto found at this moment he didn't mind being touched. Not by him.

I'mmmm... really drunk. Focus... what was I supposed to tell him...

"We have to go!" is all he managed.

"Did something happen?" Python looked down at him, blood-red eyes bright against the backlit shadow of his face. Calysto's voice caught in his throat.

Incredible.

"I... just... sun's coming up, isn't it?" he mumbled, unable to collect his thoughts.

Python snickered and licked the corner of his lip. "Wow, you're really drunk. Come on, there's an inn near here. I got some coin and blood off the same guy, let's just stay there for the day."

"Got some?" Calysto slurred.

"Stole. Whatever." Python shrugged. "He won't miss it. Come on."

"Can you..."

"Yeah, follow me."

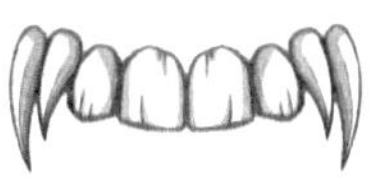

"I'm sorry, sirs," the innkeeper said with a tired sigh that clearly indicated he hadn't expected anyone else this time of night was nearly about to lock the doors. "Rooms are all filled up."

"I'll pay for a whole day," Python was saying. "Two, even."

"I'm sorry." The innkeeper shook his head. "I ain't got the beds for the two of ya, just the single room."

"Python let's just—"

"We'll take it," Python agreed and in the same moment gave Calysto a wink. Calysto scowled, which only made Python's grin curve wider.

The innkeeper looked them both up and down and Calysto tried to create some semblance of distance between him and the vampire in the tight foyer. He certainly didn't want any undue assumptions thrust upon them when it could lead to actual unacceptable and unwanted truths.

Calysto watched in a haze as Python paid the man and received their keys. He felt the innkeeper's gaze on their backs and they ascended the stairs until they were out of sight.

"I think he thinks we're...." Calysto whispered. "Y'know...."

"What, together?" Python said at full volume.

"*SHH!*" Calysto shoved Python's back as he opened the door, pushing them into the room. "Do you not know what they'd do here if they thought we were?"

Python flopped on the bed and kicked off his shoes. "Of course I know. I'd like to see them try to do anything to me now." His brows were pinched and a scowl crossed his face, but he didn't elaborate. Calysto locked the door, went to the small window, released the cord, and pulled the curtain closed shut, tucking the corners into the windowsill.

"No sunlight," he murmured to himself. "S'bad."

He stood near the window for a moment before wandering over and plopping onto the edge of the mattress.

"Hey, get off the fucking bed!" Python snapped.

"Why?"

Calysto was very much thinking of sinking into it and not getting up. He was bone-deep exhausted and way too drunk to be healthily conscious. A small fireplace crackled with warmth, stretching light out across the space and illuminating the room in a comfortable glow. It made him tired. A deep, I'm-almost-two-hundred-years-old, tired.

"Your clothes are still wet!" Python shoved him until he stood. "Lay them out while you sleep at least. Fucking nasty!"

Calysto took off the crimson peacoat and placed it neatly in front of the fireplace, then his boots and vest. Then he stopped. He turned around to see Python watching his back, very intently.

"Don't look."

"I'm not," he said, while still very much looking.

"I'm serious." Calysto frowned.

"Yeah, yeah," Python waved his hand dismissively. "When are you not, huh? What's there to see that I haven't already?"

Calysto's face burned and he turned to the fire, but made no move to undress.

Python sighed. "Okay, fine I'm not looking."

"Are you lying?"

"No," Python sounded amused. "I'm not, look you can check, I'll get under the covers."

"What?! No! I'm not sharing the bed with you!" Calysto spun around.

"Well, then sleep naked on the floor, princess."

Python smirked, and in a blur that Calysto could barely register, went from sitting on the edge of the bed to being buried within it. True to his word, his head was under the blankets as well. Calysto sighed long and hard before slowly peeling away his remaining layers of clothes until he was in his undershorts. He wasn't taking *those* off.

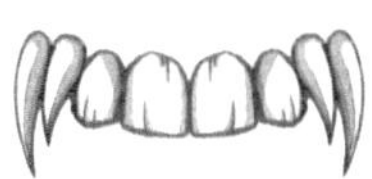

Python felt Calysto climb gingerly into the bed beside him and lie down stiff as a board. He laughed into the blankets and shook his head.

"There's no way you're sleeping like that."

"Why not."

Calysto was trying to seem stern, but the alcohol had worn away his usual edge. He just sounded like he was pouting. Python grinned to himself and flipped over to face him.

"Don't turn this way!" Calysto exclaimed as Python met his eyes.

"Why not?"

Whatever he was about to say next died in his throat as he caught sight of Calysto's exposed shoulder. He hadn't seen the scar up close before, but now only inches away he could see just how bad it really was. It was raised in some areas, thick and gnarled, but in others it looked like the skin was eaten away, having healed with only a thin layer of tissue stitching it all back together. Calysto yanked the blanket up over him to his chin.

"Stop looking," he said weakly.

"What happened?" Python blurted.

"I don't want to talk about it," Calysto said with finality.

"Alright whatever," Python gave up, but then added one more thing. "If only that innkeeper could see us now."

"Want him to?" Calysto scowled, but it was lopsided and noncommittal and tired.

"Why not? What're they gonna do? Between the two of us, none of these assholes stand a chance."

Python was smirking, but he felt the air turn serious as Calysto murmured, "... Are you...?"

"What?"

"I dunno... gay." Calysto was watching him carefully now, he realized.

"Would it bother you if I was?"

"No."

"I like all types," Python shrugged. "And I'm not particularly choosy."

Calysto nodded into his pillow. "I see."

"What about you?" Python poked Calysto as his eyes started to drift shut.

"Mmm. That too…"

"What, like what I said?"

"Mhm." Calysto was sounding sleepier.

"No way!" Python exclaimed, excitedly shuffling around in the blankets. "I would've never guessed, I totally pegged you as straight!"

"Why're you even thinking about that," Calysto mumbled.

"Cause I think you're pretty," Python said lightly, shrugging in the direction of the sleepy lump that was the top of Calysto's head. Calysto's eyes snapped open and his typical glare was glassy, softened by drink and exhaustion. But that scowl was as vicious as ever.

"Don't tease me."

"I'm not!"

Calysto blinked and turned himself over, showing Python his back. "As if I'd believe you."

"Cal, come on, I'm serious! What's wrong with that?"

"Goodnight, Python."

Python groaned and rolled onto his back, staring at the ceiling in defeat. What had he said that was so wrong? He wasn't making a fucking love confession. He scoffed at the thought. As if. He was just bored and horny, and Calysto wasn't half bad looking.

It would be fun, right? Just fun. He should've known that Calysto would be against anything to do with the idea of *fun*. The warlock had a limited range of moods—from irritated to impatient to some kind of sulky—and none of them involved even cracking a smile.

This whole getting-into-Cal's-pants endeavor was going to be a bit harder than he thought.

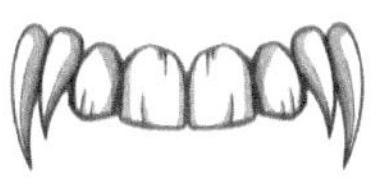

HAN GRUNTED low as he released his foot from the interior of the chimney wall and slid down, landing in the fireplace full of ash with a soft thump. Ducking his head he crawled in a slight crouch until he emerged fully from the hearth, his sharp bristled broom in hand. He threw it to the floor and sneezed once, twice, three times. This was followed by a harsh cough that he tried to muffle into his dusty sleeve. It wasn't for the folk of the manor to be reminded of the help in the house. His job was to get in, clean up, and disappear. All while making as little ruckus and drawing as little attention as possible.

His cough had been getting worse by the day though, and he was hacking up thick wads of black spit that tasted of ash and coal. When he was finally able to go outside, his chest would hitch painfully when breathing the fresher air. Not that the outside air in this thick smog-covered city was that much better. It was still an improvement from being inside the belly of the beasts that produced it. Which is where Han—no longer the boy from Calysto's memories, but now a young man of maybe twenty—spent the majority of his time since he was old enough to hold the broom upright.

Han finished up his work in the fireplace in the living area—a space larger than any place he'd ever had the privilege to call home—and slipped his tired leather boots on. He carefully brushed himself with the broom so as not to track his footprints on the pristine cream-colored carpet that lined the entire room and the path to the door.

Slinging the sack of soot over his shoulder, he clutched his tools and overcoat in hand, and slipped out of the door without a sound. Outside, Han tried to take in a deep breath and found it hard. He had tried to tell his master about it years ago but 'occupational hazard' is the only response he was given. Occupational hazard, life hazard. Life expectancy: short.

Han had already lived much longer than most the boys he had apprenticed alongside, due to his nimble frame and apparently double-jointed limbs. Where others would die from becoming stuck in with their knees pressed to their chests, Han had been able to slip out of such predicaments with relative ease. Even now as a young adult, he still climbed the precarious chimneys, his flexibility and long thin limbs a perfect size and shape for getting in and around tight corners.

The problem was he was also a walking health example of what happens when one of these boys doesn't die young. His skin was constantly caked with soot, washed clean only by the rain or an occasional luxury of a small piece of lye soap and a bucket of ice water over the head.

The cough that settled in his chest made his whole torso cramp, leaving him softly gasping and sometimes wiping his lips of blood. His skin had lesions, a type of 'chimney rot' as if his body was trying to expel the poison in any way it could.

Black scabs ranging from the size of a shilling to the concerningly large one on his thigh, itched and cracked and oozed continuously, with no sign of ever healing. Han would try to wipe them clean but to no avail.

What was clean, anyway?

His shoulder-length hair might have been naturally black, but at this point it was too hard to tell. He kept it pulled away from his face, tied at the base of his dirty neck to avoid getting it in his eyes, or worse—catching it on fire.

His clothes, hand-me-downs from his master, were riding up his shins and ragged in all the wrong places. His once sweat-stained-yellow shirt was now simply grey and black and brown. The coat he wore to try to keep out the cold was woolen and worn, patched at the elbows and missing all the buttons. Still, he carried with him wherever he went. It was his nicest possession after all, and he didn't want it getting stolen by another boy back at the house.

The same house that he returned to now was where he placed his tools and delivered his sacked collection of soot. A place not fit to call a home, though it had been that for him nearly all his life. He had graduated from sleeping on the floors covered only by an empty sack, to a small cot with a ragged and soot-stained blanket instead. Perks of the promotion his master had said, with rotten teeth that laughed at

Han's misfortune and the lack of say he had over his own life. An eternal apprentice, Han would never be a master, not unless that lazy bastard died. Han didn't want that, regardless. He wanted out.

Han flopped down on his wobbly cot and let out a breath. He was alone in the cramped room that all ten boys shared with one another but he still liked to be sure he was alone before making his move. After waiting a long moment, he dug something out of his pants pocket and slunk to the corner. There near the floor, he pried back one of the wooden slats of the wall and pulled out a small bag made of scraps and a piece of twine. It jingled softly as he tugged it free and slipped a single copper coin inside before stuffing it back into the wall to the sound of the side door opening.

Other boys, half his age and younger came filing inside, their days work likely over or just beginning depending on what shift they were on. For sweeping was a full-time job, with one day of rest a year and nothing more. The wealthy side of town—the ones with enough money for a fireplace and a chimney and often an abundance of them —never slept, so therefore neither did they.

Han sat on his cot and used a rag to try and scrub his face, ears, and neck. He might be finished with his work, but not with his day. Not today, anyway. Because he had heard of a place, a secret place. For people like him to gather in the dark. Out of the watchful and judgmental eyes of a society who hated any deviation from a comfortable norm. Even if that norm harmed more than it helped. Even if that norm meant most people lived their lives squashed into roles not of their own choosing, pretending to be exactly as they were supposed to be. Not knowing that should everyone take off those hideously rigid masks, they would find similarities to one another in a much more meaningful way. But their society did not thrive on harmony, nor love, nor acceptance. It survived on strife.

The older he got and the more hopeless and narrow his future felt, the more he only wanted to feel less alone. Not surrounded by little boys who wouldn't live out the winter. Not ruled by some master who fed himself first and gave the rest of them not much more than his fists to feast upon.

So Han waited. Until all who were present were huddled with empty stomachs underneath their coal-covered sacks. Until the silence of sleep had fallen, save for the rasped breathing of lungs much too tired for their age. Until all was still, except for the racing of his heart beneath his rough cotton shirt. And then when it was finally time, he tiptoed between bodies and barrels and out into the night.

The streets were quiet in this part of town. Anyone not out working some late-night task that made the lives of the rich more convenient was asleep—collapsed exhausted until the dawning of a new and equally grueling day ahead. Han was still cautious though, careful to keep to the shadows and out of sight of a patrolling night guard or drunk passerby looking for trouble. The place he was headed did not want to be found, and nor should it be by someone suspicious of a young man's late-night escapades into the city's underbelly.

He was given vague directions by a milkman. Someone he saw nearly every day at the start of his morning as they both made their long and arduous routes around town. The man was polite to him at first, a wave here, a nod there. Then soon, if either could spare the time, a small exchange of words, a friendly, perhaps more-than-friendly glance. A free bottle of milk but 'not because he looked like he needed it' but as a gift, a gesture of goodwill. Or something more. Neither would break the barrier to say otherwise. Not yet. Not here. But there. There they could.

Then, they could.

Han was going to find it, come what may. He was determined and driven with the purpose of belonging, and a maybe with a certain man in a crisp white uniform, on his mind. Finally, after a series of twists and turns, he arrived. It was an unassuming house from the outside, with a light in the window made to glow a pale lavender with a colored glass lampshade. Once he squeezed into the small causeway and around to the back, he saw the cellar door. Closed and quiet it appeared to be as unremarkable as all the other homes around.

After one last look around he knelt, knocked twice hard then twice soft, and the door burst open. He was yanked inside by the ratty scruff of his neck by someone who quickly disappeared.

He stumbled down the stairs and what he found before him was unlike anything he'd ever seen. On the rickety wooden staircase that he slowly descended, two women were locked in an embrace from legs to lips. They barely moved to let him by but the one facing him looked up to give him a quick friendly smile as he passed. His feet landed at the bottom and came to a halt.

As he took in the room of people he suddenly felt incredibly out of place. What was he doing here? He was underdressed and awkward, and certainly this wasn't what he had been looking for, was it?

But then, he saw him. Not in his milkman uniform. Of course he wasn't.

It's not like he wears it all the time.

For some reason, Han was a bit disappointed by this revelation. Regardless, the man caught his eye, noticing him from across the room. He nearly leapt from his chair, pushing his way through the crowd towards Han, and only Han.

Suddenly, Han felt nervous, dirty, silly, self-conscious.

"You came!" The man exclaimed, smiling at Han as if he'd been anticipating his arrival. "I knew it. I just had a feeling about you."

"About... about what?" Han stammered, scrubbing the back of his neck.

The man laughed heartily then waved his hand across the small expanse of the cellar. "Well, that you'd belong here, too!"

Han smiled back, and in the same moment realized he didn't even know this man's name. Before he got a chance to ask, he was being tugged by the arm up to the bar. Or rather, a rickety wooden picnic table covered in beers and various assortments of booze. It was guarded by a bored-looking woman in trousers and a vest sitting atop it with a long filtered cigarette hanging out of her mouth.

"Rosa," the man called out, and she looked up, giving him a nod. "Please get my friend here whatever he'd like."

Her dark eyes traveled over to Han from underneath her newsboy cap and she pursed her lips in amusement. "Ah, a new fella huh? What'll it be?"

"I..." Han cleared his throat. "What do you have, ma'am."

"Now, don't go ma'am-ing me," she said, hopping off the tabletop. "You'll go makin' the ladies think I'm like their mama when I'm tryna be their daddy."

"... Pardon?"

Han was feeling way out of his depth. But then she turned, a full shot glass in one hand and a beer bottle in the other.

"Don't you worry bout it, you'll find one who's the right type for you, too." She gave him a wink from behind a cloud of cigarette smoke and shoved the drinks into his hand. "Seems like he just might be one."

Han twisted his neck around and startled. He hadn't realized the man was still behind him.

"Come on," he said. "I'll show you around."

Han nodded slightly and clearing his throat asked, "Uh... by the way... what's your name?"

The milkman grinned and met Han with a pair of soft hazel eyes that nearly made him weak at the knees.

"Gabriel. Gabriel Lawrence. Nice to finally meet you."

CHAPTER

THIRTEEN

*F*ire.

And light. Red and orange. Yellow and white. Blue.

Heat, unnatural heat. Too hot. Charcoal and ash and the crash of weakened timbers. Smoke driving into every corner, consuming any breathable air, feasting on oxygen, and the inhalation of continuous screams. Flames licking across any viable thing, creeping up the trails of spilled jars. Chemicals sparking, smoking, burning. Feeding it. Growing higher and higher as deadly tendrils tickled the ceiling, scaring the surface with black stripes of searing heat. Glass, cracking, exploding, shattering across the molten floor and scattering in vicious pieces flying at deadly speeds, slamming jagged shards into the walls and anything in its path. Something hissing, loud like a whine, under pressure and hot, boiling, getting hotter. Then a pop, louder than the roar of the flames that covered everything with its destructive blaze. Shelves falling, delicate limbs crumbling to ash and taking more bottles, jars, flammable liquids, to the floor. Another scream, desperate and afraid, anguished and crying.

Suddenly, a burst of cool air, a door slung open. A string of loud curses followed by an even louder shout. A burst of something white and blue, silver at the edges. Not hot. Cool, like ice. Like the gaze of a cat, or a brisk autumn walk. Calm, like a tranquil river, creeping in and extinguishing all misery along with the flames. A sharp and slender hand, reaching through the dust and the sparks and the smoke. A small, golden-brown hand, reaching back.

Fire. Fire again. But this time someone else's flesh was burning. Mama. Mama. Mama. He watched, he saw it, his eyes stung with the remnants of it. Of them. Of a family who sold him away as easily as they would trade a bag of grain. Disposable. Worth no more than the few coins exchanged over his head as his life was changed from bad to worse without a second thought. The ash clung to his clothes, his hair, his skin. Washed away with a rough hand that cared not for his cleanliness, but the presentation of what he appeared to be. Cleansed, but never from his heart, the blackened stain spread further with each day, with each cruelty, with each time he was looking upon with disdain.

The sting of a slap. By a hand much stronger than hers. A hand that cared not even for his name, like all the rest. A lump of iron, ice cold and stuck to sweaty skin. Meat met metal. Turn it to gold. Turn it to gold. Useless thing. He couldn't do it. Nor would he, should he actually try. Not for them, not for this man, not for anyone. He wouldn't do it.

Magic, seeping through his skin. Brewed to boiling with a rage indescribable in words by someone his age, but who felt it nonetheless. Magic, lacking in his hands, slipping away. Just out of reach. The taste of its comfort a phantom on his tongue. The ache for its presence a silent prayer on his young lips. If only it would come. If only he could. Find it. Why didn't he have it? Where was it? Please, please, please, let me have it.

Nature. Nature had done this. He was cursed and shunned. No good at magic, even worse at alchemy, and no combination thereof brought any reprieve. Only spite. Hate. At them, at all of them. At anyone. At himself. Mostly himself.

A little pewter statue. A little pewter statue clenched in an aching fist. A small silver reminder, a shining star of hope that kept him living. A tiny thing, like a copper coin in his hand, the magic that he loved, that he craved even more than the other. A gift. A gift. He had been given a gift. Nothing expected in return. There was nothing like it, nothing more precious in his bleak world, than that. Than love, than kindness, than the absence of pain. Even the lack of it was enough. He wouldn't dare to ask for more.

Fire. There was fire again. Eating away at his skin, down to the muscle and bone. He screamed until his throat calcified like the inside of an overused chimney, with no one willing to reach in and clean it out. Clean him out. Give him the right to live. The space. The will. He screamed until he couldn't feel it, nerves melting away with the loss of his flesh. He didn't try to fight it. He wondered if this is what they had felt. All this pain, and then nothing. That's all they had been to him in his life. Pain. And then nothing.

But even still in this moment on the precipice of dying he hoped it hadn't been this bad. Not for them, not for anyone like them. Or him. They deserved their deaths but not for this. Not for something born within them since birth and passed on in a linage not of one's choosing. Where was the justice, the fairness, the ones who would stand up and say no more? No more. No more!

Silent screams on bleeding lips. A horrific howl muffled by smoke and a hardened heart. He wouldn't let them see he would rather die here than let him see. See anything of who he really was. His pain. His heart. He had lost understanding of the usefulness of it quite a long time ago, and the bit he still kept close was undeserved by every evil, spiteful eye that looked his way.

Nothing. He was nothing to them, and he began to like it that way. Let them think what they will. Angry child, stubborn son, obstinate boy. Never listens, never remembers, never learns.

But they were wrong. For he remembered it all.

He read the texts with hungry eyes. He touched the rippling river of magic and mystery and he knew. He knew he would make it his own. If it would take him the entirety of his long and endless life. They wouldn't take this away from him. They couldn't. Not *with pain or fire, not with a callous barter of his life and soul, not with useless tricks meant to garner wealth from a source more sacred, more divine, more eternal, than something as fickle as money.*

No. That power was his and he would have it if he had to drag it from the ground. Clawing till his hands were raw, till his nails peeled back and bled his magic-starved blood into the selfish earth. He wanted it. He would take it. It would be his again.

Fading, fading away. Screams and howls, struggles and feeble attempts to quell the flames were put out alongside them. With that cool, cold air. That hand again. So unlike his own, reaching down. Saving him, carrying him, healing him. Placing him gently at the doorstep of what would become his future and a destiny of his own choosing.

The flames, the burn. The burn that would never fade, a reminder of from where he came. A permanent brand of everything he had felt, and the ways in which it had been cut away.

Magic. Magic. A little statue and fire. So much fire. He hated it, he ran from it. He still couldn't look straight at it. It hurt it hurt it hurt. It didn't hurt at all. That little token of love. That handheld shrine of kindness. That hand. That hand reaching down...

Who are you? Who are you?

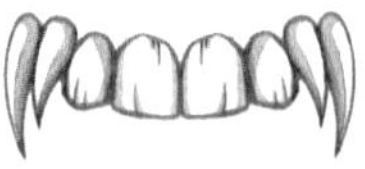

"Calysto! Cal!" Python was shaking his shoulder.

Where am I?

Their legs were touching under the covers and Calysto scooted his away, hoping it wasn't too noticeable. His head was aching. A phantom burn pierced his shoulder blade. He curled in on himself.

"What," he mumbled into the blanket wrapped around the lower half of his face.

"You were moaning in your sleep," Python responded, with that predictable teasing edge of his voice that was much too close to his ear. "Having a nice dream, were you?"

"Is everything always about sex with you?" Calysto sighed, weary of his antics already, and it'd only been ten seconds since he woke up. He really wasn't in the mood.

"It's not for you?" Python snickered. "Oh no, wait, I forgot. You haven't touched another person in like, a hundred years? More? Do you even like sex..." Then Python gasped and sat upright exclaiming, "Have you even *had* sex?"

That was it. Calysto slung his legs out of the bed and marched over to grab his still semi-damp clothes off of the floor.

"Have you!" Python called out, not giving up.

"Shut up, will you!" Calysto's face was burning. "Of course I have!"

"You don't act like it." Python flopped back onto the pillows and rolled to face him.

"And what," Calysto bit out between slipping Python's borrowed shirt over his head. "Does acting like it mean, exactly? Acting like you? Someone with their dick practically half out at all times?"

Python grinned, smushing a pillow underneath his chest and swinging his legs behind him.

"Better than acting like a stuck-up prude, with the only thing up my ass being a stick, firmly lodged."

"Shut. *UP.*"

Python laughed and sat up, throwing the pillow somewhere behind him. "Relax will you, I'm just messing with you."

"I wish you wouldn't," Calysto snapped back. "I just woke up. And it wasn't a sex dream if you must know."

"Oh?" Python scooted off the edge of the bed, sitting on the side closest to him. Calysto didn't want to answer but he had a feeling if he didn't that Python would nag him to no end. He rubbed his temples and sighed, long and weary. But then after biting down hard on his lip he managed to speak.

"I just think this place is getting to me."

"Already?"

"How're you so calm about it, Python?" Calysto turned to him then, his expression vulnerable and open. Worried. Sad. "Doesn't it bother you... being here?"

"I guess," Python shrugged. "It's weird, but honestly, I don't remember much, it's been so long."

Calysto scoffed quietly. "That must be nice."

"What, and you do?"

"Of course," Calysto hopped on one foot trying to cram a boot on before continuing. "I grew up here. It's hard to forget, even though I want to."

"That bad, huh?"

"And it wasn't for you?" Calysto responded, shooting him a glance. "I don't know a whole lot about you, but I do know you don't act like you've always been well off, that's for sure."

Python pushed his hair out of his face then solemnly said, "Yeah, no. I wasn't."

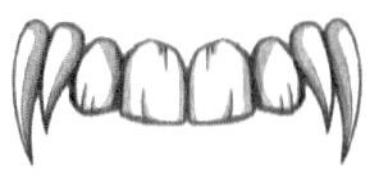

HAN COUGHED AGAIN. He coughed so hard he nearly doubled over, the vice in his lungs grasping at every surrounding organ. Gabriel had said hello and Han had waved and ran. Not because of what they had maybe done together that night in the cellar, and not because he wanted to pretend he wouldn't run straight into Gabriel's arms if only no one could see. But because he couldn't breathe.

He slumped around the corner, clutching his chest and heaving, eyes watering against the strain. He dropped his supplies in the street, the sack of soot falling open and spilling its precious contents into the mud—he would have to work an extra few houses to make up for the loss, or never hear the end of it. But an extra few houses was the last thing he needed right now. He needed to stop. Hundreds of thousands of chimneys ago. He should have never started. None of them should. The slow death crept in, killing them all one by one, he had just outrun it a bit faster than most. There was only one end, and now it was gripping him by the throat.

"Han?"

He startled, inhaling against an impossible clog in his throat. As if he were a chimney himself, full of soot and ash and tar. Would if he could turn himself inside out and use that broom in his chest—put a child down his throat and let them clean him out. But that child was stuck. Knees pinned to chest on the sticky lined walls of his esophagus, slowly suffocating with the lack of air, and taking Han down with them.

Someone was calling his name and he tried to gather himself. It was Gabriel. Oh, oh no, he hadn't wanted him to see this.

All he could manage as he righted himself was, "Hi."

"Are you alright?" Gabriel stepped back to give him space. To give *them* space, in the center of the wooden-planked sidewalk, in the middle of the day.

"Yeah…" He wiped his lips and found himself hoping he didn't look too dirty. Too bad. "I'm… I've had this for a while, it's nothing."

"It doesn't sound like nothing." Gabriel looked concerned. "Have you seen someone about this?"

"Seen who?" Han leaned against the cold stone wall behind him, and a dry smile twisted his lips as he said, "There's nothing to do, Gabe. I've only lived this long out of an abundance of bad luck."

Gabriel didn't seem to find that even a bit amusing.

"Han," he said firmly. "What about Merik? It's said he has a cure for most ails."

"I don't know what gave you the impression I have money, Gabriel, and I hate to break it to you, but you'll never be a kept man."

"Will you stop joking around!" Gabriel raised his voice slightly, then glanced at their surroundings and lowered it again. "Han, seriously. Will you just go? For me? Please. You sound terrible."

Han sighed hard. As much as he could before that familiar grip stopped him and he coughed again.

"Okay, okay," he agreed finally, his weight sagging against the wall. "I'll go I promise."

"Today?" Gabriel took a small step closer.

Han met his eyes. Beautiful dark eyes filled with concern, framed by a handsome young face with a thick and closely groomed beard that outlined the contour of his lips. Lips he had, since that night months ago, kissed many times. In secret, in silence, in the even more hidden corners of an already hidden underground club. How he would kiss them in this moment if he could.

"Only if you promise I'll see you tonight," he said in return, trying to focus his attention somewhere less tempting.

Gabriel smiled knowingly. "I wouldn't miss it."

A young boy in his early teens answered Han's rapid knock without a word and quietly let him in. Behind him, a stern bark traveled from far beyond the stairwell.

"Who is it, boy?"

The boy didn't speak to answer that voice either and didn't meet Han's eyes as he motioned for him to follow. Han stayed a step behind, afraid to get lost in such a large place. He had been in homes like it many times but never gone further than the threshold of their fireplaces.

Now, he took a moment to look around, at the high arching ceilings—a sign of wealth simply because of the expense it took to heat such rooms—the soft plush dark blue carpet underneath his much-too-dirty-for-this-place boots. The long banisters lining the staircase they climbed were polished, oiled and cleaned. Sturdy, even. Likely built so well that they had not needed repairs, and if they did, they would be taken care of. Not left to rot and fall and break. As if the life inside these walls had value. As if the lives were worth preserving and paying for.

Nothing here was neglected. Not the furnishings, or the perfectly warm temperature that slowly thawed his frozen bones. Not the gentle aroma of a meal cooking, or the strange herbal scents that mixed with it. Everything was pristine from top to bottom. Han could see how, contained in this opulent box, one could easily forget about the squalor of others. The way in which they all lived, outside a cocoon of wealth such as this.

Then, Han's awe was slowly replaced by a bitter hollow ache. He stared at the back of the boy in front of him, silently cursing him for the life he lived and the privilege he'd been given. What made him so special?

What gives him the right?

Han had a fleeting phantom of a fantasy of yanking that boy by the collar and flinging him down the stairs, if just to make him feel some type of meaningful pain. It was only fair. That he had a taste, an idea, of what it was like for the rest of them. Let him live with an ill-healed bone, a twisted tendon, a pinched nerve. Something to dig into his unruffled psyche and undeserved confidence. Anything to make his pretty life a little less so.

By the time they'd tracked across the foyer, down the hall, up the stairs, and to a half-opened door, Han's jaw and fists were clenched so tight he bordered on tremoring. The boy leading him reached out a hand and slowly pushed a large carved wooden door, it opened wide and the boy stepped aside to let Han through.

The room was uncomfortably warm, unlike the rest of the temperate house. A roaring fire was ablaze in the fireplace, crackling loudly and illuminating the interior in bright contrast. To his right was an exam table covered in a crisp long sheet of white parchment. A small stool was placed in front of it, next to a table lined neatly with metallic instruments that had no meaning to Han in their purpose. At a desk at the far window sat a middle-aged man, hair streaked with grey and a closely cropped beard to match. Dressed in all the finery of a gentleman of his status, he sat in a large leather armchair with his emerald green quill in hand. Behind him were rows of glass-laden shelves, and a tall copper contraption that billowed puffs of steam smelling of a sickly sweet caramel and camphor.

Han approached, but the man didn't immediately look up, rather choosing to continue his writing as if Han wasn't there.

That must be Merik.

Finally the man paused and placed the quill down, aligning it beside his papers in perfect symmetry with one another. When he did eventually acknowledge Han's presence, it was through two ice-blue eyes, one monocled and both incredibly stern.

"What is it," he said, voice clipped and to the point.

"I need medicine."

"Do you now," the man said.

"Yes, sir. I have a cough…"

"Something you are aware of is commonplace in your line of work, no doubt," the man cut him off. Han watched as Merik's eyes scanned over his appearance in a scrutinizing manner.

Han bit back his building annoyance and nodded.

"Yes, sir. Can you help?"

Merik hummed and leaned back slightly in his chair. "Sit upon the table. And don't touch anything else, should you dirty it."

Han complied, taking care to jump up onto the table using only his hands. He landed with a loud crinkle on the white paper, immediately marring it black with his soiled clothes. He was starting to feel like one big stain in comparison to this place.

The doctor stood and after readjusting his chair in the just right place, he approached Han on the bench.

"Boy."

Han realized he had completely forgotten that someone else was in the room. Standing with his hands clasped in front of him and quietly tucked into the space by the door, the boy barely moved except to look at Merik when he was called.

"Fetch my stethoscope…" Merik said, not even looking in the boy's direction. Then, Han saw a slight smirk cross Merik's lips before he said, "And, stoke the fire while you're at it."

Han heard a small inhale come from the boy who hesitated, before ultimately obeying. He was distracted from anything further concerning the boy by Merik grabbing his chin with a gloved hand.

"Open your mouth."

Han too, did as he was told.

It was a quick series of exams. Breathe in, breathe out, cough, no, *really* cough. Listen. Let me see your tongue. Hmm.

Merik pulled off his gloves with a snap and placed them one by one on the small table.

"Your condition is severe," he said without sympathy or tact. "You will need to follow a strict regimen for four weeks. And if you truly wish to overcome this, find a new profession."

Han ignored that last part and the impossibility of it, latching himself to the tiny spark of hope he could see. "So you're saying I'll live?"

"Well no," Merik answered, sounding much too cavalier. "You will soon die, like most all in your class. But, if you wish, it will not be from this."

As much as Han hated to admit it, he needed what Merik had to offer. As he was running through this myriad of conflicting thoughts, the doctor walked back to his desk.

"In any case. Should you wish to hire my services, that will be fifteen silver to start. And ten for each dose after."

"What?!" Han exclaimed. "That's outrageous! I can't pay that much!"

"Then," Merik placed himself back in his armchair, righting his tightly tailored vest. "You should not have come here. This is not a doctoral service, nor is it a charity. It is a cure, the result of hard work and years of research. I have no obligation to help you, not unless you can pay."

"You've lost your mind!" Han jumped down off the table and marched over to the desk. "Who can afford that?"

"The type of people who are my patients, sweep," Merik said, thick grey brow clamping down hard over that obnoxious monocle.

"You can't be serious!" Han shouted.

"I am very serious," he responded, as cool and detached as if discussing the weather. "Pay. Or get out."

Han was stuck with his mouth hanging half open, he couldn't believe he'd come all this way and had even been given a semblance of hope all for it to be snatched away as if it meant nothing. As if his life meant nothing.

But he gathered himself enough to spit, "Fuck you."

This outburst made Merik's eyes turn cold.

"Boy," he snapped, not taking his steely stare off of Han. "Show our guest out."

"No need," Han snapped back. "I know the way."

He spun on his heel, storming out of the room—but not before pausing to kick over the small exam tray, spilling its contents all over the floor. Then he slung the door open and shut it with a slam.

"Wait!"

Han was livid. He stalked down the street fast-paced and furious, with hands shoved deep in his coat pockets, cursing the name of every person with wealth he had ever met. He was halfway down the block before he finally acknowledged the calls that continued from behind him.

"Sir, please! Wait!"

Han turned around to see the boy from Merik's house running after him, his shaggy golden hair flying in the icy autumn wind.

"Fuck off," he growled.

The boy stopped short, his eyes wide.

"I..." He was panting as he spoke, pulling something out of his pocket. "Here."

The boy reached out, and in his hand was a blue glass bottle with a small tag on the seal. Han hesitated and didn't take it, eyeing it skeptically.

"What is it."

"Medicine," the boy said between breaths, pushing it towards him. "It's not laudanum. It's... it's special. It'll help."

"I told your master I don't have any money."

"I know." The boy didn't retract his outstretched hand. "I stole it."

Han scoffed, surprised. "Why?"

The boy didn't seem to know how to answer and just shrugged.

"Really?" Han took a step towards him and the boy shrank back but nodded, still holding the bottle out in offering. "Won't you get in trouble?"

"It's okay," was all the boy said in response to his question. "The instructions are on the tag. I... I can get more if you aren't better... after you're done."

Han took it, holding the glass bottle curiously. It was warm from where the boy had probably held it from falling out of his pocket as he chased after Han for half a block. Han looked at the instructions and back at the boy, who was watching him carefully. His eyes were dark like molten gold, skittish like a wary animal, but bright and impossibly deep. Han could tell he was thinking much more than he had said.

Suddenly, he felt a bit sorry for wanting to sling him down the stairs. Hadn't he even seen him before? Somewhere?

"Thank you," Han finally managed. "I hope he won't be angry at you for this."

The boy grimaced slightly and shrugged again, repeating, "I can get you more if you aren't better."

"I'll let you know then," Han answered awkwardly, accepting this timid boy's charity with a strange sense of guilt.

He pocketed the medicine and turned away, leaving the boy without another word. The bottle clinked lightly against the two copper coins in his pocket, and Han gripped it tight as he hopped over a large puddle in the street.

As he walked he found himself wondering about that boy. Maybe he wasn't at all like he had thought. He wasn't rich, or spoiled, or callous. Just a servant there, and one that Merik seemed to enjoy inflicting some kind of torment upon.

Curious and touched by the random act of kindness, Han resolved to find him again. After he finished the medicine he would go to the boy to get more and to learn his name.

But little did either of them know, they would never see one another like this again.

"ALRIGHT," Python crossed his arms over his chest and stared up at the mansion looming overhead. "What're we doing here."

"This is where we get the crystal," Calysto responded.

"And how do you know it's here?"

"Cause this is where I stole them." Calysto's tone was flat, intentionally void of emotion, but his whole body was tensed and stiff like a wire.

"Okay, but you said the other one was gone."

"Yes, but not yet," Calysto answered cryptically. "There's still time to take it, instead."

"Mind elaborating."

"Yes, I do," Calysto snapped, shoving his hands deep in his pockets. "Just follow my lead, and don't say anything out of turn, okay."

Python could feel the anxiety coming off him in waves. "No promises."

He followed behind as Calysto took achingly slow steps—even for him—up to the front door and knocked twice, before cramming his hand back in his pocket. Python could see Calysto's fist moving as if he were holding something, but before he could pay it any more attention, the door opened.

Greeting them was an elderly woman dressed in maid's clothing and squinting up at them from her aged position that bent her in a crooked curve towards the ground.

"Who's calling?" she asked in a warbling lilt.

"Acquaintances of the esteemed Dr. Merik," Calysto said. "I have an appointment."

Seeming convinced by the confident facade he had slipped on the moment she answered the door, she shrugged slightly and stepped to let them through. She was about to lead them up the long curving staircase, but Calysto stopped her with a gentle hand.

"No need, ma'am," he said softly. "We know the way."

"What is this place?" Python hissed once they were halfway up the stairs.

Calysto didn't answer and signaled for him to be quiet. They approached a large oak door decorated with ornate filigree and intricate carvings of swirling tree branches that left only a space in the middle where the words "*DOCTOR ADRIANI MERIK*" were pronounced in black hand-painted lettering and outlined carefully in gold trim. Calysto once again knocked twice.

"Come." A voice came through the door.

Calysto reached to open it and walked inside, leaving Python to feel more and more like an out-of-place tag-along. As soon as he entered though, he was hit with the strangest sense of nostalgia. Had he been here before? Once perhaps, in a previous life?

The smell of firewood mixed with antiseptic chemicals stung his nose and reminded him of a bad batch of blood he'd had not that long ago.

Damn, had it really only been a few weeks?

Looking at the mess they were in now, it was hard to believe that before all this his life had been so straightforward and simple. Eat, sleep, fuck, steal, repeat. Uncomplicated except for the times when he might have made an enemy here or there, biting the wrong wife or getting caught with his hand in someone's wallet. Though it wasn't hard to make enemies of the rich, all you had to do was threaten their hoard and they began to breathe fire.

Python wasn't too worried about offending the likes of them. The likes of this Dr. Merik who was staring at them both from across the room.

Python hovered and watched as Merik's eyes landed on Calysto and the man abruptly stood.

"No," he said, holding himself out over his desk, leaning on his knuckles. Python thought he quite looked like a gorilla.

"No?" Calysto asked.

"You're not welcome here," Merik was saying. "I told you to never return."

"I think you have me mistaken," Calysto answered.

Python was standing right behind him and thought he could feel Calysto trembling. His usually methodical pulse was erratic, like a rabbit about to bolt.

What is he so damned nervous about?

"Absolutely not," Merik barked. "Calysto, is it?"

Calysto inhaled sharply and Python heard his heartbeat stutter.

"I thought as much." Merik's glare was pinpointed on Calysto still, and murderously sharp. He righted himself and rounded the corner of his desk, approaching them with an authoritative gait. "Or do you not recall the last time you were here and nearly had my heart out? Accusing me of some... some cursed affliction you seem to wholeheartedly believe. Well, let me enlighten you, sir. There is no such thing as vampires, nor witches, or ghouls or anything of the like. You are delusional, and I do not treat the mentally ill. You need to leave."

Calysto didn't speak but he retreated back as if terrified and bumped straight into Python, who was standing there in a daze, absolutely at a loss as to what he'd heard.

"Cal...?"

"Let's go. I... I was wrong. We-we have to go," Calysto was

mumbling half to himself, but one of his hands had reached out clenching viciously tight into Python's coat. Python was nearly dragged behind him, as confusion rendered him temporarily limp. He let Calysto lead him all the way down the stairs and outside before the slap of cold wind hit his face and he regained his sense.

"Calysto!" He slapped the warlock's hand away. "What the fuck was that?"

Calysto didn't respond and bent over his knees, chest heaving up and down frantically while Python looked on. Down the street, a distant shout rang out, but nearby the roads were empty, the evening dinner hours leaving them unobserved.

"I take it that was not the plan." Python scowled. "And why does that guy know you? What is he talking about, vampires? You didn't know about that until you met me. Or did you not? Were you lying to me?"

Something clicked and he took a step back. "What... what he said... are you a vampire hunter?"

"No!" Calysto's head shot up. "No, Python I'm not! But..."

He tried to reach out to grab Python's arm and Python shrugged it away. He watched as Calysto let his hand drop in defeat and shook his head.

"But, since we've been here he's the second person to call me that. And to know my name. But, Python I have no idea what's going on. Nor am I a vampire hunter. I swear it."

Calysto's dark eyes pleaded up at him and for the moment Python was compelled to believe him. He certainly didn't *seem* the type, shit, he'd just slept beside the man. If he were a hunter that would've been the perfect time to strike. Yet, Calysto did nothing but try not to accidentally touch him the whole night.

"Second time? What was the first? Why didn't you fucking tell me?"

"I thought you might react like this, that's why! And cause it's not true! I thought it was a one-off, someone mistook me for someone else. But now I..."

"Twice is too much to be a coincidence."

"Yeah..." Calysto took a deep breath and slowly let it out.

"That guy really hates you, whoever he thinks you are."

"Well, the feeling's mutual," Calysto scowled. "We'll have to come back another time."

"And do what?"

Calysto massaged the bridge of his nose and pushed up his glasses. "I'll just steal the crystal again."

FOURTEEN

"I don't want to stay another day," Calysto protested as Python led them away from Merik's sprawling estate. "I want to do it now."

"Cal, you're shivering like a wet rat in a blizzard, how do you propose to pull this off?"

"I'll figure it out!" Calysto said, exasperated. His feet were chafing in Python's much too big shoes and the smells of the city were making him feel queazy. He stormed ahead of Python, not looking back. But also not sure where he was going, exactly.

"Fucking hell," Python grumbled from behind him, then his voice reached Calysto louder saying, "You're a fucking dick when you get hungry you know that?"

"Yeah well, you're a dick all the time!" Calysto shot back. "And what kind of expression is that? Wet rat in a blizzard. Did you make that up?"

"I mean," Python trotted up beside him. "I could have, or I could've heard it somewhere."

"It's stupid," Calysto answered, but he was quickly losing steam.

He didn't actually feel like being mean, and he didn't want to argue. He really wanted—

"I am kind of hungry," he admitted.

"Thought as much, Sir Candy Ass," Python smirked.

"Don't call me that," Calysto snapped, heat rising in his face. "That doesn't even mean—"

"I know what it means," Python cut him off. "I saw what you did back there."

Calysto stopped in his tracks. He spun around to face Python to find the vampire already leering down at him with that infuriating smirk.

"Did what, exactly?"

"Ran away," Python answered. "Just like you did when we got here."

"So what if I did?" Calysto grit his teeth, he was nearly at his limit with this fucking asshole. "It must be really nice for you to have buried everything and forgotten, but I haven't. I hate it here, and it's worse than my memory because it's real. And you're an idiot if you're not afraid."

"*I'm* an idiot?" Python's face fell, the amusement at Calysto's expense suddenly waning. "Well, you're a fucking coward."

"And which one's worse?" Calysto bit back. "At least a coward knows not to overstay their welcome."

"You want me to leave is that it?"

Calysto paused. A week ago he would have instantly said yes. A few days ago he would have *probably* said yes. But now? In this moment as Python danced on the frayed edges of his nerves? Yeah, he still wanted to say yes.

But overall, he didn't.

Maybe he *was* a coward and Python's presence was preferable to being alone here in this place or back in the present. Maybe he was lonely and this was better than nothing. Maybe he kept pushing Python away only to see if he'd come back. Testing him, trying him. Trying to trust him.

Calysto heaved a small breath and rubbed his nose underneath his glasses.

"No," he answered. "I don't. You're... you're right, okay? I'm..." He pinched his lips tightly together.

"What?" Python asked, still sounding impatient. Guarded.

"I'm scared," he murmured. He could barely get the words out. He turned away from Python then. "I'm scared we won't... we can't..."

"Fuck it, man," Python cut him off. "Let's just find the tavern. You're driving me nuts with your fucking attitude."

Calysto sighed.

Should've expected as much in the way of sympathy.

"Fine, sorry."

"Whatever." Python walked ahead, crossing the wide cobbled street without another word.

"Um..." Calysto wiped his mouth on a cloth napkin and took a gulp of beer, all while Python gnawed on the pickle Calysto didn't want.

"What," Python said between open-mouthed chewing.

"I ... I guess I *was* hungry."

"Yeah, no shit," Python scoffed, loudly slurping the juice from the pickle's edge. "You get really... uh, what's the word?"

"Hm?" Calysto stuffed a piece of sandwich crust into his mouth.

"You know, when people get mad 'cause they don't eat."

"... Hangry?"

"Yeah," Python bit the pickle in half. "That. That's you."

"I refuse to believe you don't get the same way," Calysto scoffed. "Don't you die without food?"

"Yeah so do humans, Cal," Python chuckled. "Or you know... you."

"Alright," Calysto sat back, relaxing into the booth they shared.

Python finished his snack while taking in their quiet late evening surroundings. The tavern had mostly cleared out of its occupants. The small two-man band had long since played their set and packed up and left. The bartender leaned tiredly on the countertop, flipping through a book with a glazed-over look on his face. He probably really wanted to go home, right about now.

A couple in the opposite corner stayed hidden in the dark from anyone but the likes of a vampire. He watched with slight amusement as the man kissed the woman's neck where he thought no one could see.

"We should go," Calysto said, interrupting his voyeuristic fun. "It'll be dawn soon."

"Ah, fine," Python reluctantly agreed, and dug out the purse he'd stolen to throw more than enough money on the table without counting it. He'd just as easily come by more the next time he needed to really eat.

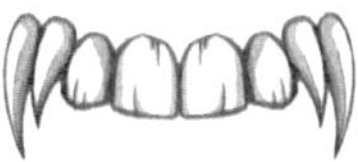

EARLY MORNING AIR sent a shiver down Calysto's spine and he pulled his coat close around him. It was beginning to reek faintly of mildew and somewhere along the way had lost the distinct perfumed air of Python's wardrobe. The smell was alright, Calysto had realized, when it wasn't freshly sprayed in overabundance into every article of clothing the vampire owned. Python said it was to 'get rid of the rotting smell' which was a little more information into Python's anatomy than Calysto had the time to think about, so he just decided to chalk it up to vanity.

"Think the innkeep's gonna kick us out?" Python stamped his feet in the mud and visibly shivered.

Why can he even get cold? Isn't he already cold?

"Huh, why?"

Python looked up at the sky and answered in a singsong voice,

"I'm sorry sirs, this is just too indecent I can't allow it! You'll have to pay for another room!"

Then he craned his neck down at Calysto and continued, "What do you think, should I eat him when we get back? Saves money."

He gnashed his teeth in a rapid series of mock bites then smiled wide, watching Calysto's face closely as he did.

Calysto didn't react.

"No, I don't think you should," Calysto finally said. "Do you just bite anyone who bothers you?"

"Eh," Python shrugged. "Not all the time."

Calysto bit his lip, considering what to say next when—

"Hey! Hey mister Calysto!"

They both jumped to attention and Calysto was met with the sight of that same woman from the night before, trotting down the alleyway after them.

"I can see you!" she called out, and ran up to them. She slowed to a stop and stood with hands on her hips.

"Hello," Calysto answered, haltingly.

"Who's this?" Python said from behind him. The sun was starting to peek through slats in the cityscape roofs and Calysto could see him squinting. He probably couldn't stand to be outside much longer, and they were still a few blocks from the inn.

"It's alright," Calysto spoke to him. "You head back, I'll be there later."

Python hesitated but barely, before shrugging. Like he was trying to play off his urgency for lack of interest. "Okay, see ya."

"What is it?" Calysto asked her once Python was gone.

"I found what you asked for!"

She closed the space between them with one step. She smelled of leather and rose. It was nice, sweet, warm.

"The vampire den," she whispered softly into his ear, breath tickling his hair.

"The what? I didn't even know they had... I didn't ask for that."

He slowly put his hands on her shoulders and pushed her away, ignoring the way her stare lingered. "What about it?"

"It's a place for, well..." She bit her lip, eyes searching his own as if trying to read something about him before sharing more. "Maybe I should just show you."

"You went into a vampire den alone?" He realized. "You shouldn't have done that."

Her small mouth fell open. "But you said if I found it, I could be your apprentice! You promised!"

"Did I?" he mumbled.

Oh, he must've been really drunk.

He must've made something up to get her off his back.

Is she lying?

Shit.

As if it weren't bad enough that he'd gotten them trapped in the worst point in the past possible, he was supposedly some infamous vampire hunter with his same name, who everyone seemed to have strong opinions about one way or the other. Case in point, the woman across from him was looking at him with a mixture of eagerness and something else... like she was one simple invitation from gladly devouring him.

"I must've forgot," he said apologetically. "You did catch me in a state the other night."

She grinned and shrugged, instantly accepting it.

"S'alright. You do want to know where it is, yeah? I'll take you. I can show you right now! I'm even ready to go!" she exclaimed and opened the inside of her long coat to flash an assortment of knives and instruments dangling from leather straps.

In the same instant, a pair of patrolling officers turned in their direction down the side street, and at the sight of her excessive array of weapons combined with two well-dressed patrol officers looking for an excuse to exercise their power, Calysto panicked and grabbed her in a hug, effectively closing her coat and smashing her against his chest. He awkwardly caressed her back and tucked his head next to hers, pretending to be the mock of a boyfriend comforting his distraught lover. As the officers made their way by he looked up, and gave them a 'what can you do' kind of shrug, and their grimaces of sympathy were all he needed to know he sold it.

Maybe he wasn't as bad at interacting with others as he thought.

At least that's what he told himself in this moment.

We know better though, don't we?

He looked back down at her and she was already gazing at him, wide grin in place. He loosened his arms, ready to release her, but she snaked her arms around him instead.

"My hero," she teased, and squeezed him tight, snuggling her head into his shoulder. Calysto turned rigid as she leapt up and kissed him on the cheek, then let him go with a small laugh.

His face was burning and he was immensely thankful she'd turned away to watch the policemen go.

"So, what do you say?" she said, twisting back to look at him. "Shall we go hunt some vampires?"

"If I say no, will you just go on your own?" he asked in defeat.

"You bet!" she laughed.

"This is a terrible idea," he insisted, one last time.

His head was beginning to pound from lack of sleep and his limbs felt heavy and awkward. Even if he were actually a vampire hunter and knew what the fuck he was doing in such a dangerous situation, he doubted this was the condition to do it in.

But she was determined, and he couldn't very well knowingly let her run straight to her probable death without trying to stop her, or at the very least drag her out of it if things got too hairy.

He looked her up and down, as the slow dawn of sunlight spread down the stone walls at their back. She was young, only twenty or so. Yet such an age at this time made one much more mature than they appeared. Her black hair was pulled back in a long braid, and she dressed in a fashion that reflected more that of a man of the era. But despite her confident and flirtatious demeanor, her face was still soft and rounded with youth. Skin slightly tanned but not worn with age or exposure, he couldn't tell where she could've come from or who she was supposed to be. Didn't she have a trade? A family? A spouse?

She was self-assured and independent, certainly not traits desirable in an obedient woman. So likely not. He felt a pang of sympathy at the sight of her eager eyes. How could he blame her for wanting to make her own way in a world that clearly didn't fit her? He just wished the way she chose wasn't so fucking dangerous.

"I don't have any of my weapons," he finally spoke, accepting that for now, it was best if he played this part. Even if just so he could tag along with her, and hopefully keep her from some horrible demise. "Got any to spare?"

She perked up, excited to be of help, and whipped open her coat again. "Take your pick!"

He gingerly selected a long knife from her coat, careful not to brush into her side as he did.

"I didn't catch your name," he said.

"I didn't tell you!" She smiled. "It's Aeris!"

MUCH TO HAN'S SURPRISE, the medicine had actually started to work. Instructions, written in a tight and precise hand, indicated the patient should take a tablespoon by mouth twice a day, once with an early meal and once before bed.

Well, Han didn't remember eating breakfast once in his entire life and he certainly didn't have any idea of what a tablespoon was, so after he'd left the boy behind and resumed his work, he'd slipped into an alleyway, shrugged, popped the cork, and took a swig straight from the bottle—and immediately almost threw it up.

It burned like coal and burst up through his sinuses with the vengeance of a hot pepper, instantly making his nose run. Down his throat it went, scalding as it landed in his empty stomach where it rebelled with a vengeance, churning violently and making his entire torso turn to flames. He blew his nose into his hand and in the same instance doubled over, gagging into the gutter.

After a few intense moments of nausea and watering eyes, it began to settle and Han wiped his palms on his pants, smearing them with snot and soot, and stood. Then, he noticed he felt oddly clear-headed and a weight in his chest had lifted.

What the hell was that stuff? Whatever it was, it certainly was attempting to do the trick.

He looked at the bottle curiously as if to find some answer within the etched facets of blue glass. There was nothing, not even on the back of the label, to explain its purpose or what was in it.

Han had a moment of doubt, that perhaps it was some kind of poison and the heat traveling down his belly was about to make him shit himself to death. But then he reconsidered. The boy had chased him down, bottle in hand. Stolen from the stores of a master who was clearly no more kind to him than Han's was to him. Brave, stupid. Oddly kind. And he was willing to do it again for him.

Han hoped that the boy knew what he was doing and wouldn't get caught. He couldn't imagine what that Merik would do if he found out his medicine was being given away for free.

In the public eye and from behind his polished mahogany desk, Merik was the picture of a professional. A gentleman. But Han had lived long enough in this world to recognize the hidden malice behind a man's eyes. The lie of an altruistic facade torn down by an absence of coin, or the simple privacy of a closed door, the lack of an eye that would judge. Not that if Merik truly did abuse that boy in front of others would anyone bat an eye nor lift a finger to help.

He deserved it—they would say.

Scum, servant, peasant, nameless boy.

He should be grateful to even be in the house of such a man. What a good man, taking him in like that. Just disciplining the wild out of him. He has to learn somehow. Not a bright boy, one who can only learn with the rod and the punishment befitting his simple-minded mistakes. 'My mother spanked my bum once with her palm and I turned out fine.' He got what was coming to him. Ungrateful he is, to be such a disobedient student. A student, even!

What luck he has been given, to study under a doctor of all people. Would if I could give him punishment of my own, to remind him of how much worse it could be.

Gutter waste, refuse in fancy shoes, it's a wonder Dr. Merik puts up with him at all. The charity of that doctor is honorable, don't you think? I could never do such a thing. Letting a dirty little rat like him sleep under my roof. Much less teaching him my trade. Wouldn't you be afraid he'd steal you blind in your sleep? Is it not the nature of such trash to leave their masters lying in a pool of their own blood? Only to be found days later by a concerned housemaid, or a friend and colleague come calling, traumatizing their poor sensibilities for life.

Oh yes, I asked him once what he was doing with such a child. Of course, as to be expected his answer went much over my head, but I do know he thinks the boy is special. In what way, well that's unclear. Perhaps he just needs a tool at hand, one with its own hands to assist him in his inventions and work. If the boy doesn't drop everything he holds, what an idiot! Look at him! Not a thought behind those empty eyes. Unnerving isn't it?

Oh no, he's all anger and spite that little one, best the good doctor beat that demonic streak from him before it festers and works its way in. Who knows what such a thing would be like, should it be allowed to grow? Goodness, where he gets off acting in such a manner is beyond me.

Han's imagination got carried away and he only snapped too as he accidentally bit down on his tongue in anger. He swore under his breath. He knew he was right about them. He'd heard it enough to feel their hypocrisy in his bones. Their gossip dug into his mind, eating at his confidence and fueling his anger.

What if they're right? What if we are trash? What if I will never be more than what I am? What if I'm doomed to this life? Oh fuck, I'm doomed, I'm doomed. Aren't I? This is it for me. This is all it'll ever be. I'm going to die here, like this. As this. My one life wasted inside the walls of an ungrateful aristocrat's house. I'm never getting out, oh fuck oh—

A sharp edge of the bottle in his pocket nicked his hand and he gasped, putting the small cut to his lips. The medicine. He wasn't doomed. He wasn't going to die. He could be cured, by the mercy of a young boy who cared not for the coffers of his cruel master. He could live. Soon, his cough would be gone, ridding his body of the toxins that threatened to strangle him from within.

He could take his money—he had saved enough, hadn't he? He'd take his money, his ragged coat, and his hopes and dreams. He'd find Gabriel in that cellar that had become a second home and place of reprieve, and he'd get them out of here. They could run away, somewhere nicer, warmer, kinder. A place where they could be themselves, and live together, open, free, happy. Yes, that was his plan.

Han considered downing more of the medicine to speed up the process but ultimately decided against it. It was okay, he could wait another week, or two. It would give him time to squirrel away a bit more, here and there.

Besides, his stomach was still churning.

PYTHON COLLAPSED HARD on the bed, sprawling out to his heart's content now that Calysto wasn't there. It bothered him that he couldn't have stayed and he tried to play it off, but part of him really didn't like getting separated from Calysto in this place.

That nagging was becoming much more insistent these days—filling him with rather irritating thoughts, such as, wondering what that anxious little warlock was doing.

Is he okay? Who was that girl?

Anxious. Yeah, Python had noticed *that,* too. Since when did he give a shit? He'd spent the last centuries not caring who or what he ran into, as long as he got his way.

Well, okay, to be fair, he cared *a little*.

Python never stole from anyone who appeared less fortunate than the richest in the room. From those, he took everything his hateful claws could get away with. Blood, money, clothes, food, shelter, time, sex, even love. Well, he'd let them believe it was love. He took a certain kind of pleasure from stringing along some spoiled brat until they finally fell. Then, he'd disappear off into the night with credit card numbers written on the same hand that had held theirs just a day before.

His conscience was lighter than the stolen shirt on his back, and he couldn't give less of a fuck about the misfortunes of the wealthy. He had hoped if he could leave any kind of legacy in this endless life of his, it would be a trail of broken trust fund babies' hearts.

But Calysto was different—he wasn't rich or stuck up. He didn't act spoiled or entitled. Granted, he was rude as hell and could be a right ass. But Python was beginning to be able to see past this hard exterior of his traveling companion, a little bit more with each passing day. Calysto tended to shy from Python's eyes and shuffle around with an avoidance he could easily mark as nervousness once he got enough outside of himself to notice. Calysto answered him in short, clipped responses that held an edge he didn't seem to mean. As if he wasn't used to being talked to, and expected even less for the listener to care. Did Python? Care?

He wasn't sure yet.

Calysto had lived alone in that house for all this time after all, but Python hadn't thought about why. Not until now, not until lying here unable to help with whatever shit the warlock was about to get himself into. Not until he realized he might miss the fucking guy.

Why was he alone? Python rolled over on the bed, tucking a pillow under his head, and stared up at the dust-covered canvas canopy. What had he done to run off anyone he could have had in his life?

Then Python remembered the execution and Calysto's strange

almost numbed reaction. He said he knew them. He also had said once that all of his people were dead.

Python sat up.

And what had he said back?

Good.

Good. I'm glad you're miserable and alone, scared, and poor.

Python cursed between his teeth.

Fuck. That was stupid.

Calysto clammed up at the smallest hint of rejection. At any breath of being an annoyance he would make himself scarce whether he would actually leave the room or not. His cold shoulder might as well have been a defensive mile-thick block of ice with the way he shut down, becoming entirely unlike the few hints of who he *really* was that Python had gotten a glimpse of.

Shit.

He *did* like the guy. At least enough to think this much about how he must feel. *That* was a first for Python in a very, very long time. Something inside him had hardened over the years, crystalized into a stone where his heart had once been. Whatever once could have resembled it.

What had it been? What had done it?

Python sometimes had a hard time piecing it together now. The memories were so faded and jumbled, he couldn't tell if they were all from the same time, or place, or people. He got glimpses—like those moments he saw that vampire hunter woman's face, sneering at him with a hate so ripe it could only have been caused by a personal wrong. But he didn't know what it was. She had been chasing him for such a long time, their little game of cat and mouse twisting and turning them through the years. One gaining the upper hand, then losing it. One chasing, one running. It didn't matter who was who, they were at each other's throats and Python had no idea why. He knew her name though.

She had almost caught him once, that long cedar stake pressing into the sensitive dead skin of his chest.

"Aeris," she had hissed. "Remember me?"

He didn't. He didn't. It would be better if he did. He fought her out of self-defense, but damn if it wouldn't be nice to know the reason. All these years and she hadn't given up and he didn't even know how long it had been.

Other images came from the depths of his memory. A man in white, the taste of something sticky and warm, the heat of a kiss. Lips on a face he couldn't place. Why couldn't he remember?

Why can't I remember?

"Aeris, you shouldn't do this," Calysto insisted once more, following behind her and bowing slightly against the bitter morning autumn wind. She slowed to walk beside him, coat buttoned around her and head held high. Her feigned confidence was clearly an act for his sake or rather, to try and impress him. It didn't fool him though—as someone who spent most of his time nervous and uncomfortable in the presence of others, it was easy for him to sense the same waves of anxiety coming from another.

"You don't need to prove anything to me," he spoke again when she didn't answer, but the corners of her mouth twitched as if she were considering it. "Really, if this is what you wish to do with your life, I will... I won't try to convince you otherwise but, know it's incredibly dangerous."

"I know that!" She snapped suddenly and halted. Mud splashed out in front of her boots. Calysto stopped too and raised his brows in surprise. She hadn't talked to him in such a manner before, and he wasn't exactly sure which part of what he said garnered such a reaction. He waited.

She deflated slightly as if realizing he wasn't going to retaliate towards her outburst.

"I just... I can do it," she said. "I can prove it."

"Why the need?" he asked, softening his voice. "This isn't about me, is it."

"No..." She looked out across the sprawling expanse of buildings down the muddy street. He could tell her thoughts were far away from here. "But, I need your help to do it, don't I."

"To prove something to yourself, you need another's help?" Calysto asked. He wasn't trying to be rude, he was just having a hard time following. But it quickly became apparent that this was the wrong thing to say as her attention snapped back to him, re-alight with indignation.

She might not be someone to fuck with if she got the chance to get good at this.

"It's not like I've killed a vampire before," she bit the words out as if it pained her to admit. "Just show me the ropes, and then I'll do it myself."

"I haven't either," he said softly. Maybe now was the time to get her to listen. "Aeris, I'm not who you think I am."

"Look, I know you weren't a part of the raid in Purvel," she huffed impatiently. "That was all just slander to get you on the vamp shit list. I know that."

Oh god, she's still not listening.

"Won't this be a perfect way to prove you've still got what it takes? That you're not prey, you're predator!" she continued, getting more excited the more she talked. "Take down a den while they still think you're towns away from here! They'll never suspect you would be so bold with such a reputation and bounty on your head!"

"Bounty?" he asked, heart suddenly in his throat. "What bounty?"

"You haven't heard?" She sounded as surprised as he. "There's a huge price on your head. Those vamps are certainly mad about you."

"And... and you're taking me straight in there, Aeris?" He was about one more sentence of bad news from teetering on the edge of a panic attack.

Where is Python? Damnit. Why did I think of that?

That asshole hadn't done shit to make him feel better, ever, at all.

No, that wasn't true. Despite his terribly crass exterior, and the way he simply said shit without thinking about who would hear it, Python had a heart in him. Calysto could tell. As much as he resisted even paying attention to such a thing.

But, Python had tried to reason with him when he was freaking out and thinking all of this wasn't real. Okay, maybe he still thought that a little bit, but not so much anymore. He accepted that what he was seeing for the time being—whatever this was, whatever was happening—was much more real than any dream. Too strong and prolonged to be an illusion, and a shared one at that.

Shared with a vampire with a tongue like a whip and a stare so hypnotizing that when Calysto looked too long it dug away at the edges of his carefully built defenses. Walls that had thus far held up quite fine with the wear of time and trial alike. Ever just so slightly Python might have gotten through. A realization that both terrified and soothed Calysto in equally unquantifiable measures. He resisted the urge to bolt, to clam up inside his shell or sling a biting remark where he knew it would hurt.

Why do I know what hurts him?

Though in those rare moments—when neither one had said something to put off or offend the other, when the suspicions faded and for a moment whatever collective issues they had fell away, and they were just themselves—it seemed like they could be something. Something like friends, maybe.

It was frankly a bit painful to watch. Centuries-old creatures of myth with a myriad of mysterious powers between them, bumbling over the most simple of human interactions and slamming straight into each other's every insecurity along the way.

They were learning though, weren't they?

"Hey!" Aeris' sharp voice broke through the tangent of thoughts he hadn't realized he'd gone on. That was another thing good to be said about Python—he did seem to be able to help him focus, stay on task, stop zoning out into some other reality, or imagining something much more interesting than the present moment.

Living alone will do that. As the surroundings settled in, became mundane, repetitive, empty and cold, they held him in by their four walls and the fear in his heart. The only way to escape without going out, was going in. In and in and in, until every memory, every experience, cruel and kind, was played to warping like a worn-out tape. Turned this way and that, seen from all angles and felt from the same, over and over again. With no absolution, no answers, no closure. Only the remnants of pain that became duller over time, cooling from their once heated state into a solid diamond crust, impenetrable to feeling by even the thought of them.

But here and now, cracks had begun to appear. At first, only a hairline fracture across the surface, as quiet and invisible as he himself tried to be. Under the strain of constant companionship, they had started to spread, inching their way out like splinters of fragile ice under a brazen foot. Working their way down through the solid layer of his self-imposed reticence and into the tender place underneath, where a damaged organ of flesh and blood lie. Where it was meant to be protected, guarded, safe. Now, it was left vulnerable to the elements—the turn of his endless time on earth, the chafing winds of life ever-changing, the fire of another's words, the raw ache of exposure.

Not the influence of a loud-mouthed vagabond could entirely have this effect on him though, for without the reality of where he was now would Calysto really see the entirety of it. Of what he'd become.

He had ceased to feel not out of apathy or distance or time, but because he simply couldn't stand to do it. The deep and soul-wrenching pain of a world so terribly wrong he ran from it, hid from it, the moment he found his glimmer of a chance. The injustice he'd faced came back to him again tenfold with his older eyes.

When he was young it was hurt, it was shame, it was cold. It was suffering of a different kind. The sort that doesn't bite with the knowledge that life could be anything else. A child's hurt, a formative pain, a molding of bones on opposite limbs, a malformation for life before one can know what to consider normal, to accept as acceptable. A mind put in backwards and a heart upside down, given to expect the cruelest of intentions from those who should care most.

Though he wasn't that child anymore, the remnants of it lived in each of his careful and cautious actions. He was nearing centuries old and what had he learned?

Placed here, trapped here, within the confines of a world he so desperately tried to quell the ache of, he realized he hadn't learned a goddamn thing. If there was anything to be gleaned it was that the world never truly changed, it only shifted shape. But that didn't mean there wasn't good, there wasn't something, or someone, worth finding joy and solace in.

Solace?

His mind had wandered back to Python. The first vampire he'd ever met and consequently, the one who opened to his mind to so much more than the existence of other mythical creatures.

Python was the epitome of what one would think a scoundrel, a menace to society, a freak with a mean streak. But, to Calysto he slowly—ever so slowly—was becoming more.

There Calysto stood, on the precipice of what would be his second encounter with Python's kind, and he was preparing to kill them. Or at least let this woman do the killing.

No, it wasn't right. The status, the state, the manner of one's birth —or re-birth—did not automatically determine that they should die. It didn't mean they offered no value, had no merit, and couldn't be better to him than anyone else he'd ever met.

Well, not *everyone* he'd ever met.

He looked up to meet the eyes of this eager young woman, a mere fledgling in his aged eyes, and stroked the small deer statue clenched tight in his fingers concealed deep within Python's coat pocket.

"What's that?" she asked, tipping her chin in the direction of his pocket.

"Nothing," he answered. "Just a good luck charm."

"Oh? I didn't really take you for the type." Her brows raised in surprise.

"And what," Calysto pinched his lips in a complicated mix of annoyance and worry. "Did you take me for?"

"Not sentimental, that's for certain."

Then you don't know me at all.

Calysto thought it, but he didn't say it. For once he held his spiteful tongue, choosing not to spread the pain that had been done unto him. He shrugged and tried to right his thoughts back on the topic at hand.

"Are we close?" He motioned to the neighborhood behind her, and she turned to follow his hand.

"Just about." She grinned then. "Don't worry Master Vampire Hunter, I'll take good care of you."

Calysto prepared his sleep-deprived brain for action in the likely case he'd have to shut this girl up and haul her out of there. He could sense from a mile away that this was a terrible idea. But just how terrible it would be, well certainly he could have no clue of what was really coming. He sighed and reluctantly continued to follow her lead.

Gabriel sat with his full weight on Han's lap, legs slung over to one side, chin resting on the crown of Han's head. A tipsy haze had settled over them both as they enjoyed their second drink of the night and found a cozy corner couch to cuddle on. Gabriel had been humming softly along to whatever song was being scratched out from an old music box, and occasionally pausing to kiss Han's hair. Their gentle state was comfortable and soft, just between the two of them.

Even in this place always bustling with life and laughter, shouts and singing, kissing and sometimes not-so-discrete lovemaking, they squirreled away a corner of their own. A small sanctuary against the world and anyone who wasn't them. Han felt safe here. Cared for. Loved in a way he'd never felt before. It was new, it was terrifying, but most of all it was everything he'd never allowed himself to want.

That was, except for one missing thing. The way they were here, together, true and authentic, they could be no where else. Their lives were a carefully built lie. A public facade of two friendly acquaintances. But acquaintances didn't drag one another fervently into the dark of an alleyway to kiss, just once, just one passionate kiss, before a long days work. They didn't intertwine their fingers together, so different yet so much the same, behind the old water tower on the outskirts of the landfills that surrounded their town. Their town. But it wasn't, was it. It was simply a place, a place they lived and worked and breathed. But it wasn't theirs. It would never be. Not until they could be like this. Anywhere.

"I've been thinking," Han said, running his hand up under the back of Gabriel's soft cotton shirt. "What if we got out of here?"

"What do you mean?" Gabriel asked, his thin lips pursed in a slight alcohol-induced frown of confusion.

"I mean, let's leave this town. Me and you," Han repeated, leaning up to speak into the curved shell of his ear. "I hear there's other places... that'll be... be okay with us."

"Leave?"

"Yeah listen." Han pulled him close, relishing in the comfort between them and the warmth of Gabriel's body on his. He wanted this always, in any way he could have it. If that only meant here, then so be it. But he couldn't help but grasp for more, always more, something better. Images of them like this—but surrounded by others and the open sky—filled his mind. Gabriel's lips, free for the taking, wherever he pleased, with no one to spare a second glance. Expressing his love and desire anywhere it suited him, and to simply hold his hand.

He couldn't help but want it. Maybe he was selfish for it, greedy.

Maybe he should take what he could get. But the unfairness of their lives here continued to eat away at him until the obsessive dreams of a better one dug in like a parasite in his brain, feasting itself on his desires and growing stronger with the manifestation of each new one. There was nothing he could do but ask. To see if Gabriel wanted those things for them, too.

"Listen," he said again after taking a drink from his glass to clear the sudden dryness of his throat. "I've been saving up, here and there. If I'm right, I have enough to get us a carriage over the mountain, and enough for a place in a town near the coast. It wouldn't be anything really nice, not until I could find steady work again. But I'm sure there's something I could do, I hear there's plenty of opportunity for us—"

As he spoke, he watched as Gabriel's face twisted from one of surprise, to skepticism, to a frown.

"What?" Han asked softly. "What's wrong?"

"So you want to run away?" Gabriel asked, sitting up and breaking the comfortable place where their chests had touched.

"I want to live in a place where we can be together, really together. Don't you want that?"

"And what will you really find but more of the same?"

"Gabe... what do you mean?" The scratch in Han's throat had come back, and he resisted the urge to cough against it.

"So, you saved up for now. To get there, you'd be broke once again. And who's going to hire you?" Gabriel was speaking faster now, his gaze intense and burning into Han's desperate eyes. "You said it yourself you don't have an education. Hell, I barely do. We'll never be more than what we already are, Han. That's the way of the world."

"What?" Han tried to pull Gabriel back to him, but Gabriel resisted, placing a firm hand on his chest.

"You and I both know we can never be. Not really. We'll both marry some nice girl who we can stand enough not to be completely miserable, have a couple of ill-produced children, and hope to spread our meager wages even thinner to feed them more than a scrap of bread for each meal. That's what our lives are—are destined to be, Han. Besides, you like girls, too. It won't be hard for you."

"It doesn't have to be!" Han leaned forward, pleading now. "If we get away! I don't care if I have to do the same damn thing forever, not anymore! Not if I can be with you. Not if I can *really* be with you. That's what will be different. It doesn't have to be like what you say, it doesn't!"

"It does, Han," Gabriel scooted off of his lap to plop down heavily beside him on the couch. In a breath, the distance between them grew, the physicality only a symptom of it.

"No, it doesn't!" Han argued, scooting himself up against the sink of the cushions. "And I don't want a girl, you know that, I want you!"

"Yeah, but you'd be okay with it if I were one, wouldn't you."

Han swallowed hard. Gabriel wasn't wrong exactly, but to hear it said like that, he didn't know what to say in return. What could he say to someone who didn't understand and didn't want to? Someone who wished Han were more like him? He suddenly wondered if he'd ever find his place. Here underground, or there, up above.

"That's not the point!" He leaned towards the man who had first touched his heart."Besides, wouldn't that make you want to go more?"

"It's not worth it," Gabriel sighed. "That's the difference between you and me, Han. I'm okay with this." He motioned to the room. "I don't want people to know that side of me, and this is enough."

"I don't believe you." Han's hand was sweating around the outside of his glass, half full of liquor and melted ice, long forgotten. "You don't mean that."

"I'm not like you," Gabriel emphasized with a pinch of his lips, and took a swig from his own glass. "You want the world to see you, to witness all your splendor and you want payback for what they've taken from you. I get it, I do. But, that's not me. I just want to live in peace."

"What is that peace worth?" Han said spitefully, as a wave of bitterness overtook him. "Your true self? Me? You don't want to be seen with me? You'd rather we were a secret forever? I don't want that Gabe. I want to be allowed to love you. I don't want to be afraid of it."

Gabriel stared at him long and hard with unreadable eyes. Then when he stood and spoke his words drove an ice-cold knife into Han's heart.

"Then let me relieve you of the burden of it, Han. You don't have to do anything you don't want to. Including be with me."

"What!" Han shot to his feet with his heart in his throat, grasping at Gabriel's empty hand. "You know that's not what I want!"

"Do I?" Gabriel wouldn't meet his eyes.

"I just said I want to run away with you, that's the exact opposite of this!" Han pleaded and dared to take a step closer, ducking his head to avoid the basement ceiling's tinsel decorations. "Please, Gabe, just think about it. I know you're afraid. It would be a big change, I'm not denying that! I don't want to be the world's most famous couple, I just want to kiss you under the sun. Wouldn't you like that, too?"

"...Yes..." Gabriel whispered the admission, barely loud enough to be heard over the music. "I would."

Han sighed, feeling the jittering of his nerves. "I'm not asking you to decide right away. I just want you to know what I want. And it's you, all the time."

Gabriel's hand that had been limp tightened, squeezing his back. "I'll think about it."

Instantly, Han grinned and took a swig from his watered-down drink as if in celebration.

"Don't get so excited," Gabriel grumbled, but a smile played on his lips. "I haven't said yes yet."

"Yes, but you didn't say no."

Han pulled him close again and between their kiss, they didn't notice anything else. Not the fragile nature of their truce, nor the way in which their hearts were clinging to hope while still drifting further apart, and certainly not the two people who then entered through the cellar door.

"May I emphasize once again what a bad idea this is," Calysto protested wearily.

The sun was barely dawning still but thick clouds of black and grey mixed with the low smog of the city, blocking out most of the impending morning light. He found himself wishing Python had stayed, at least the vampire could probably pick Aeris up and sling her over his shoulder with ease if things went south.

As it stood now, Calysto could *maybe* stand a chance of getting himself stabbed by pissing her off at the suggestion of leaving. Sure, lest we forget, Calysto was a warlock. He had power of his own. But no overpowered inhuman strength like Python, and certainly nothing he could really utilize without exposing himself to more danger. Especially in a vehemently close-minded town such as this one.

They were standing together in a small backyard area between the narrow-guttered alleyway of two homes. It didn't seem like there was much around at all, just a small square of mud, a few sad patches of green and yellow grass, and a half-rotted mostly collapsed fence to section it off. But Aeris had stopped here, a determined look etched on her face and hands once again on her hips.

She eyed him carefully as if trying to decide if he were serious, or nervous, or trying to talk her out of it for a reason he wasn't willing to explain. He was definitely all of those things, and his feet squelched in the mud as he shifted uncomfortably under her intense scrutiny.

Then her gaze began change, from one of analyzing to one that indicated she liked what she was seeing.

"What?" he asked, noting the shift in expression across her face.

"Oh, nothing," she said, taking a step closer and closing the distance.

Her hand grabbed his arm and she used it as leverage to pull him to her while leaning into him at the same time, slamming her lips roughly into his. It was warm, wet, forceful, and extremely awkward. His lips crushed into his teeth and he winced as his eyes instantly widened.

She had kissed him.

"What was that for?" he managed, between being tongue-tied and an aching lip.

She pursed her lips then smiled, offering no other explanation than, "You're sweet."

"... Sweet?"

Who the hell is she talking about?

Certainly not him.

"And just in case we die," she giggled. "I wanted to make sure I'd be able to do that."

He winced, not liking the sound of dying here, now, at the hands of a vampire, in the past, with her, or at all.

"Um... Okay... Can we just get this over with?"

"With pleasure," she winked and headed towards the house. She knelt down at the cellar door and knocked twice loud, twice soft, and after a short wait it opened, and they went inside.

HAN BROKE AWAY from their kiss still grinning with the feeling of Gabriel's lips on his teeth. He knew now with that single kiss, that things would be okay. They would be okay, they'd make it. All was right and there was hope, sealed with a declaration of love and desire. They would have one another, come what may.

Then he heard the shattering of glass. Not an uncommon occurrence in a cramped space filled with dance and drink and colliding bodies. But then there was another, and a shout, and finally Han tore his eyes from the soothing sight of Gabriel's face and was filled with a sudden dread.

Near the stairwell stood a woman dressed entirely in dark shades of leather, with a long black braid twisting out from beneath a tricorn hat. In one hand she held a long shotgun, in the other what looked to be a curved silver sword.

What the fuck?

Though she wasn't dressed like a patrol officer or a constable, she still looked like absolute trouble. Han instinctively moved in between her on the other side of the room, and Gabriel beside him.

"Listen up!" He heard her say. Then she cleared her throat and shouted. *"LISTEN UP!"*

Voices stopped, music ceased, and chattered died down, as those who weren't already watching this weaponized woman with wary eyes turned to take her in. Rosa, resident butch bartender, hopped down from her typical post atop the picnic table and pulled a cigar from her mouth.

"Whatcha doin' with the sword, sweetheart," she said carefully.

Her voice was low and confident and commanded a sense of comforting authority, soothing the anxious fervor the other woman's unnerving and threatening presence created in the room.

"I'm not here to hurt you," the mysterious woman replied. "That is if you aren't a vampire."

Someone barked a loud, disbelieving laugh. A few murmurs traveled throughout. Gabriel slipped his hand into Han's and held it tight. Rosa ashed her cigar on the floor then took a slow puff.

"I think ya got the wrong joint," she said slowly. "Ain't nothin like that here."

Then Han noticed someone else take a slow step down the cellar stairs. A golden haired man in a red coat emerged from behind the woman and whispered something in her ear. The woman shook her head.

"No."

The man frowned and fell silent, but kept a close eye on her regardless.

"Look," she spoke again. "All ya gotta do, is one by one, touch the blade of this here sword. If you aren't vampires, you've got nothing to worry about."

"She's out of her mind," Gabriel murmured to Han, who nodded once in agreement. "Let's get out of here."

"Okay."

Han slowly placed his glass down on the low coffee table and tugged Gabriel's hand as they snuck to the edge of the crowd and around the outer edge. They approached the exit, with Han keeping his tall frame carefully in front of Gabriel, hoping to sneak past and up the stairs. No such luck.

"Not so fast." The woman snapped to attention while whipping her sword in their direction. "Pass my test."

Gabriel emerged from behind Han's back. "Then we can leave?"

"Don't," Han whispered.

"Of course," The woman smiled, but her black eyes did not.

"Okay."

"Gabe," Han warned.

Gabriel took another step forward and placed his palm on the flat of the blade. Nothing happened, of course. But still, it was as if everyone breathed a sigh of relief.

"Alright." The woman nodded. "You can go."

Gabriel turned back and reached his hand out to Han, who instantly took it.

"No. Just you," the woman barked. "He can follow after, if he passes."

Gabriel met Han with wide eyes. "I'll wait for you, right outside."

"Okay," Han whispered, then watched as Gabriel tipped his head to acknowledge the woman's quiet companion and climbed up the stairs into the overcast morning light.

Before Han had a chance to follow, the realization that the way out of here and away from this woman was as simple as what she'd promised, created a massive push toward the front and Han was swallowed within it. He was shoved up against the cool cellar wall and couldn't wiggle through to the front. After a moment of struggling he gave up trying, deciding to worm his way around the other side.

He stumbled out from the rear of the crowd and climbed up over the back of the couch over to where Rosa now stood up on the table, trying to see over the heads of people pushing towards the stairs. One by one they exited, given leave by the woman and watched carefully by the man at her side.

Han stepped up onto the picnic table bench, which brought him above eye level with Rosa. She shot him a look.

"As if you needed to be taller."

He responded with a halfhearted smile then nodded toward the exit. "Anything like this ever happen before?"

"What, some knife-wielding lady lookin for vampires?" she guffawed. "Can't say that it has. Thems bout as likely to exist as the witches the constables burnin' in the square for having too many herbs in their kitchen."

Han nodded in agreement, and they both looked on at the slow procession of people as they made their way up the stairs and out the door. He was hoping Gabriel was still waiting for him. Often times they would spend their evenings here, accidentally staying too late into the night, and were forced to sneak back to their respective homes to begin their work days empty of sleep, but full and happy on each other. It had happened so often at this point that Gabriel had taken to bringing his white uniform, carefully stashed in a clean sack, and stuffed behind the mirror in the bathroom to keep it safe from spilled drinks and the perils of evening revelry.

Han didn't have to worry much about what he looked like, except that he wanted to look good for Gabe. All he had were his dusty chimney sweep clothes and his worn grey coat anyway.

Gabriel had never appeared to mind, wiping the dust from the creases in his skin with care and kissing the spots left cleaned. Now that Han's cough had begun to subside and the strange sores faded as well, Gabriel was happy that he was healthy and found that more attractive than the state of his clothing. So for now, it would suffice.

Though Han swore one day he'd wear what he pleased, no matter the cost, no matter the style. He wanted to be free to choose, that was all, he argued. Gabriel had laughed.

"I know you just want to wear a skirt," he'd said.

"What if I do." Han had grinned back. "They look comfortable."

"It's okay, I think you'd look nice in one."

"Really?" Han hadn't expected his unwavering acceptance.

"Of course," Gabriel had smirked and pulled Han close. "One day I'll get you all the skirts you want, Han. Plus..." He'd leaned close, eyes glimmering. "Easy access."

Han had laughed out loud and ducked down to place a kiss on Gabriel's neck, and then another, but not before leaving a few bites in their wake.

Han shook his head, bringing himself back to the present. This strange woman was keeping to her promise and one by one the room was clearing. Gabriel was right—it was best to do what she said and get out unharmed. He jumped back off the bench and weaved through tables and chairs to the bathroom to retrieve Gabriel's uniform. Plenty of new and strange faces came and went here, but certainly, there was no such thing as—

A strange hissing sound filled the air, then a scream, then more voices, more shouts. Han acted on instinct and without looking back he slipped into the bathroom and slammed the door shut. It was small, no bigger than the room needed for a hole in the floor and a wash basin on a table. He crouched on the cold ground, bracing his back against the wall and his feet against the door. Should anyone try to get in they certainly wouldn't be able to budge him. Or so he thought.

Outside he heard the scuffle of feet, shouts here and there, the breaking of glass, and the slam of the cellar door. There was still that hiss, like the leak of a water pipe. Han clutched Gabriel's clothes to his chest and his whole body stiffened as he tried to stay perfectly still.

Nearly as soon as it began, it ended, and silence fell. Han waited, counting the seconds along with the rapid beating of his heart, then slowly began to climb up from the floor. He stood, took a deep breath, and ventured back out through the door.

Sunlight from the cellar entrance streamed in vibrant golden beams, casting long shadows across the abandoned basement stone. On the stairs were large piles of what Han perceived to be the familiar sight of soot and ash. The cellar was nearly empty of people. The tipped-over picnic table was surrounded by drinks that spilled and puddled in-between broken glass strewn across the floor. Rosa was no where to be seen, in fact, there were only four figures in the room. Han, the woman with the sword that was now dripping with blood, her companion who had the woman wrapped in a hold she was struggling to release herself from, and a strangely postured man who lurked in the remaining darkness, leering over at them.

"Come here, sweetheart," The man in the corner said into the open air, and the two struggling near the staircase froze. They all turned to face Han's direction, noticing him for the first time.

"Me?" Han managed. Before he could blink the man was at his side, a vice grip of extraordinary strength digging into his shoulders.

"I could hear that sweet pulse of yours from a mile away."

His breath was ice against Han's ear but Han was already too frozen to move. "Don't worry, all your little friends escaped."

"Now pay attention," the man continued, his voice riding the edge of malice that chilled Han to his core. But he wasn't speaking to Han, his eyes were fixed on the woman instead. "You should listen to your friend there, and get out of here before things really get nasty."

"Aeris, let's go!" the man behind her pleaded. The sunlight glinted off his broken glasses and Han caught the sight of desperation in his eyes.

"Maybe..." Han nearly choked on his voice. "Ma'am, perhaps you should listen."

"Shut up!" Her retort was sharp, like the end of her dripping blade. "What are you, his lackey? His pet? One of them?"

"Not yet you're not," the man murmured so low that only Han could hear.

He didn't know what it meant, but the simple tone of the words made his stomach twist in knots.

"I'm giving you one last chance," the man spoke up. His hand dug further into Han's goose-fleshed skin, but his words were still for the woman across from them.

"Then give it your best shot!" She barked back and shook herself loose of her companion's grip, sword at the ready.

What happened next was only a blur.

Han was thrown backwards as the two opponents lunged, clashing in a whirlwind of blade and claw. She slashed toward him at the same moment his mouth opened in a yawn, stretching unnaturally wide. Han watched unable to believe his eyes as the man ducked around her in an invisible flash and leapt straight for her throat. He pinned her to the wall and blood began to pour from her neck. She let forth a weak shout and fell limp, her fight instantly dying out.

The man released her and she hit the floor with a thump. Then his attention focused on the golden-haired man who was gripping the banister, as paralyzed as Han felt. Within a blink, the ice-cold man was at his throat and threw him to the ground. Then the man wavered, his confidence shaken.

"What are you..." Han heard the strange man murmur as he wiped his lips.

The golden-haired man stumbled into the wall, holding the gaping wound in his neck. Blood dripped through his fingers at an alarming rate but his eyes were wide and bright.

Han's heart stuck in his throat and he could hardly process what he was seeing, but still he forced his feet to move across the room and over towards the woman, slumped over on the ground. More specifically her sword. He scrambled nervously to find the handle, slippery and sticky with blood and held it up in his shaking hand.

"Stop," he said, the blade trembling limp as a wet noodle at the end of his arm.

The man slowly turned around, achingly slow, and only then did Han get a good look.

His mouth was etched in a wide sickly grin, rows of teeth jutting jagged and sharp glistened crimson with viscous blood. His chin and lips were stained with it, stark against deathly pale blue skin that clung to the hollow curves of his bones.

But what struck Han the most were his eyes. They were completely black, dipped in ink and overflowing. Worst of all, where an iris should be were only glimmering rings of iridescent yellow and red, shimmering against the remaining candlelight like that of a cat, and staring Han down like his next meal.

"Stop?" the man hissed back, hideous smile growing longer.

Too long. Unnaturally so.

He approached Han one long creeping step at a time, crossing the distance between them careful as tracking prey. As he reached the sword he pinched the tip and with two fingers yanked it forward, dragging Han with it until he was inches from the man's bleeding maw.

"Are *you* going to stop me?"

His voice slithered cold and wet in Han's ear, who could do nothing but stand stock still in horror. The man clicked his tongue then pulled away, looking Han up and down.

"No, you're much too pretty to kill. Much too pretty."

A glimmer of hope loosened the vice on Han's throat and he managed to find his voice enough to ask, "... I... I can go?"

"Oh no, sweetheart." The man's grin returned, dripping with such a sinister air that it made Han's knees nearly give out from under him. "You're staying with me forever."

Han had no idea what he meant.

Only before he had a chance to ask, the man lurched forward and latched those terrifying teeth onto the delicate skin of Han's neck and bit down hard. Pain shot through him like a thousand razor blade cuts. He heard the ripping of his skin as it was torn to shreds and his own voice involuntarily cried out.

Plap plap plap.

Droplets of blood hit the concrete floor, hot and wet, and Han's head swam. He grasped weakly at the man's shirt as if it could make a difference against the incomprehensible strength he seemed to possess. He heard the man swallow loud and full, then groan against him, as if he'd tasted the most incredible morsel.

Cold seeped through the back of his shirt where long clawed fingers rested against his spine, holding him upright. Weaker and weaker he became, his futile protests slowly softening until all he could do was hold on, limp against the thing that drained his blood, his life. His life. Rapidly fading.

As darkness blurred the edges of his vision and a soft hanging lantern light swam before his clouding eyes, he realized.

I'm going to die. I'm going to die. Gabriel, oh no, Gabe I ... I...

And with those final thoughts, Han's weary eyes slid shut.

SIXTEEN

Calysto scrambled up from the ground; his head was spinning and a vicious ache throbbed through his neck. He must've passed out. Where was Aeris? What the fuck had happened?

His hand was still pressed firmly against his throat. He was surprised it hadn't fallen away when he lost consciousness. He quickly realized why, for when he went to move it his palm nearly ripped the skin with a glue made of dried blood. He winced and yanked off the small kerchief necktie Python had let him borrow and pressed it hard against the wound as it began to bleed anew.

Python.

Oh shit. What time is it?

Where was he? He looked up at the cellar door, still gaping open for anyone who passed to see the massacre inside and noticed the sun slowly fading behind low clouds.

How long had he been out?

Taking a few breaths Calysto blinked and rubbed his eyes, steadying his feet underneath him. He made his way around the sloping alcove behind the stairs and grasped onto the rail. But his foot met something soft and he halted, drawing back. In front of him on the floor was Aeris, lying face down in a pool of her own blood. His heart stopped short.

The thick, hot stench of copper entered his nose and he instantly felt ill, stomach lurching against a sickening concoction of realization and sensory overload. Calysto gripped the railing tighter with his blood-crusted hand and heaved. He hadn't more in his stomach in the past few days besides, well, mostly alcohol and a small sandwich, and it came up thick in his throat, bubbly with bile. He choked, leaking spit from his lips and weakly gasping. He squeezed his eyes shut in a juvenile attempt at erasing what he'd seen, hoping he'd open them and something else altogether would greet him.

Alas, unfortunately for Calysto, all was still the same.

Aeris was dead and she'd gotten herself recklessly killed. All because he'd failed to stop her from walking straight into a vampire's den and pulling a fucking sword out.

What was I thinking? Oh, this is a fucking mess.

He looked down at her body splayed out on the ground, her hand in a loose fist where the blade had been, and sank to his knees beside her. A soft moan carried up from his throat, an involuntary whine, and he wiped his lips with the back of his arm to muffle it.

Then the light across her body shifted, and he was brought back to the reality of where he was. This was a vampire den, fangs-out hangout, bloodsucker lunch club, whatever you wanted to call it, and the sun was about to go down. If Calysto had learned anything from the vampire with which he was most familiar, any vampire who was lucky enough to escape under the cover of early morning clouds would be back to find their vengeance. They liked that kind of thing, it seemed. Being violent, creepy, selfish, loud...

Calysto realized it was extremely likely that there were also some still down here now, sleeping and lying in wait for just enough darkness to wake and finish with him what the other one had started. The thought made his gut lurch in fear. Determined not to throw up again he gulped down the growing knot and inhaled a shuddering breath.

On quickly weakening legs he climbed to standing, but not before whispering a solemn apology to the young woman lying amidst the destruction she'd created.

Aeris, whom he'd failed to protect.

"Where the fuck have you be—" Python shouted at the opening of the door, but the sight that met him cut his words off in his throat.

Calysto's entire front was covered in blood, some dried and brown, some black-red and fresh. He had a hand clenched in a half fist on the side of his neck, holding a soiled piece of cloth against it, and his face was smeared with dirt and more streaks of blood. The neat ponytail that Python had styled for him had come loose and golden hair hung in bedraggled matted clumps. His glasses were smeared and stained, seeming only to cling to his nose by sheer willpower. He barely looked at Python as he stumbled across the room, his eyes cloudy and distant.

Python was up off of the bed in a flash and over to his side, guiding him forcefully to sit on the edge of the mattress. "What happened to you?!"

"Uh…"

"Let me see that." Python pulled his stiff hand from his throat. "Goddamned fuck Calysto, did you get *BIT*?! Did you… Shit! How the fuck did you run into another vampire of all things?"

"I uh…" He could tell that Calysto was having a hard time focusing, but the warlock nodded unsteadily. "I'm… it was a…"

"Fuck." Python pinched his lips together while tilting Calysto's neck to get a look at the wound. "Damn this is deep, did you…"

His voice faded as he took in the details of the jagged skin and torn flesh. He felt that unfamiliar feeling of concern, along with a healthy jolt of recognition mingling with muted terror.

"Cal, what did this vampire look like exactly?"

"I didn't..." Calysto slumped forward, color draining from his face, and Python swore again.

"Alright, hold on."

He scooted up next to Calysto's side and in one quick motion, tilted his head and landed a sloppy wet lick across the entirety of the wound. Then again. Calysto jumped slightly underneath his hand and likely would have protested if he hadn't been so near the edge of fainting.

It worried Python that he didn't. He didn't like this weakened version of Calysto who didn't have a little bit of his own kind of bite. The pulse beneath his tongue was slow and strong though, which served to ease his nerves. Finally, he drew back and watched closely as the skin began to stitch together. This was a handy trick for covering one's tracks, but also for occasionally saving a life. Python wasn't exactly in the habit of licking any poor injured person he came across but he wasn't about to let Calysto bleed out, or end up with another nasty scar. A scar like his own.

Assured that the bleeding had stopped, Python pulled Calysto out of his overcoat and vest. As he bent down to take off his boots, the top half of Calysto flopped back, splayed out flat on the covers and a soft moan escaped him. Python noticed a strange sensation. His lips and mouth were tingling lightly. He paid it only one single thought of attention—it was likely from the myriad of shit all over Calysto's skin.

Fucking gross.

He jerked Calysto's feet free of the blood-soaked shoes and forced himself not to jump to any wild conclusions or leap up and rattle Calysto to consciousness to get some answers. It's not like he could anyway, Calysto wouldn't be able to form a coherent thought until he got some rest and probably food.

Ah, food. Shit.

He'd have to go downstairs and ask for some. Come to think of it, it's a wonder no one saw Calysto in such a state. He added 'cover-our-tracks' to his quickly growing mental list of tasks. First, was to get Calysto coherent and talking.

"Hey," he called, leaning over Calysto's face. Calysto's unfocused eyes slowly tracked the low-hanging canopy above the bed before landing on Python's face. That slight permanent frown that he usually wore was softened at the edges. But not in a way that Python liked.

"I'm going downstairs to get you something to eat. Stay awake, okay?"

Calysto continued to stare without speaking and Python growled impatiently, giving him a gentle slap on the cheek.

"I need you to answer me, Cal."

"... Mmmuhh yeah...."

"Okay, good enough." Python sighed. "I'll hold you to it."

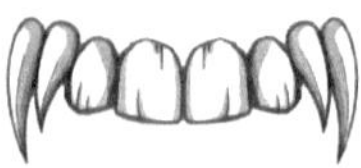

"Here, drink this."

Python tried not to watch too carefully as Calysto sipped from a cup of watery soup held in shaky hands, but he stayed prepared just in case the cup went tumbling into his lap. Calysto could take care of himself. Or could he?

Python reached over, took Calysto's glasses from his nose, used some spit and the now-soiled duvet to scrub away flecks of dried blood, and returned them to Calysto's face.

Then he leaned back and rubbed his temples. His already thin patience was quickly waning.

"Want to tell me what the hell happened?"

Calysto let the mug rest in his lap as his deep-set frown returned. Python felt some reassurance at seeing it, even if it did mean Calysto was about to be his insufferable ass of a self. But what he said next went against Python's expectations.

"I... I made a mistake," he barely spoke, staring down into the murky depths of oily broth. "Remember when Merik called me a vampire hunter?"

"... Yeah, that was like a day ago."

Calysto let out a tired breath. "Well, that lady who approached us? She was the other one, to call me that."

"Okay so?" Python sat up, trying to get a glimpse of Calysto's expression that continued to face away from him. "And?"

As if sensing it, Calysto looked up and meet his eyes. They were bloodshot and glassy but met Python with an openness he hadn't seen on the man before.

"Uh..." Calysto rubbed his face, flaking off chunks of dried blood in the process. One fell into his cup. "When we were getting drinks the first night... this woman approached me, saying I should teach her to hunt. She said I was some famous hunter. She knew my name, too. I swear I don't know what..."

"It's fine Cal, I said before that I believe you," Python held up his hand, then motioned for him to continue.

Calysto swallowed. "She wants... wanted... to be a hunter she said, and was all hell bent on proving to me she could do it. Said she found some... some den or something. I couldn't convince her not to go, and she went in there causing a huge fucking fuss. I thought she was wrong you know, that there wouldn't be any vampires, or she wouldn't actually go through with it. But she did... uh, she got some. Ultimately, the one who bit me got her too, I think. I'm not sure, it's... I woke up after..." He fell silent with a grimace.

"Cal, I need you to tell me something." Python's expression was grim as he observed his... friend. "Who bit you? What did he look like?"

"How'd you know it was a he?"

"I have hunch about something, will you humor me. Please." Python's voice took on a desperate edge and he wondered if Calysto could hear it. If he did he gave no indication, but still answered all the same.

"I didn't get a really good look honestly, it was dark but, about my height, black hair, um... thin? He had long claws, or nails, I don't know. Uh, dark green dress coat and wore lots of lace. Was real cocky, seemed stronger than the rest to be honest. I don't know how that works but... um, he was pale, not like you but more like..."

"Blue? Dead?" Python whispered.

"Yeah," Calysto nodded. "You know him?"

Python stilled on the bed, so stiff he could've been a corpse. He didn't answer for a long, tense breadth of silence.

"I did, once."

Calysto's voice softened, "Who is he?"

"Dangerous," is all Python said. All he wanted to say. No, he wanted to say more. But what was there to say? It was so much, too much, and he was suddenly consumed with the nervous itch to get the fuck out of there as soon as possible.

"Remember what we talked about before we split?" he asked, changing the subject.

"Uh-huh," Calysto sipped from his cup then made a face and set it down on the side table. "That's not good cold."

"It's not good cause you got shit from your face in it." Python sniffed.

Calysto rubbed his neck then looked down at his hand.

"You healed me? How?"

"Licked you, remember." Python shrugged.

Calysto winced slightly. "Oh... Okay. I wasn't sure what that was for."

"I don't lick for fun without consent, Cal." Python winked, but his joke felt flat with a lack of enthusiasm.

"Well..." Calysto's eyes darted from his face to his hands back to his face. "Thanks. I wasn't sure I'd make it back to be honest."

"I'm surprised you weren't killed," Python said, dropping his cheeky act. "That vampire is nothing to fuck with, trust me. We have to get out of here, Cal, tonight. I mean it."

Calysto pushed his glasses up and looked at him, expression surprisingly soft. Genuinely curious. Careful. "Did he do something to you?"

The whole moment caught Python off guard and he looked away, letting loose one nervous laugh. "Does it matter?"

Calysto reached out halfway between the distance on the bed, testing the space between them. "I've never seen you so shaken up before, Han. Not through all this, not until now."

Whatever words Calysto said went right over Python's head. All except one. He shot up as his whole body reeled and instinctively, he jerked away.

"What did you just call me?"

"Oh..." Calysto had been leaning toward him but he quickly pulled back. "What? I... I thought."

"Don't ever call me that," Python snapped.

Suddenly he felt cornered, anxious. All at once the room was too small, the space between them too strange, too familiar, too unfamiliar, too real, the walls too thin, Calysto's stare too...

Everything was too much. Much too much.

What's wrong with me? Am I panicking? I don't panic. What the fuck is...

"I have to get out of here," he managed to wheeze. The words slipped out through gritted teeth.

His chest heaved with an intense reflexive breath, it did nothing but simulate a humanity he'd lost long ago. A humanity that... that...

"Hey wait," Calysto said. His sympathetic tone might've been comforting to anyone else. But to Python, well, it just pissed him off. "I'm sorry. I didn't... I was just..."

"Calysto. Shut up," Python bit out, and Calysto stilled entirely.

He could hear Calysto's heart pounding hard, but the warlock didn't move or speak a word. He had shrank back into the pillows, making himself as small as possible.

Python's hand gripped the bed frame so tightly within his anxious fist that the wood creaked and splintered under the strain. As it broke off in his hand, he leapt to his feet and bolted from the room without another word.

Han woke to find himself lying in a pool of his own blood, so much blood in fact that his clothes were soaked through and his head felt fuzzy with faint. A near-deafening ringing in his ears was accompanied by pain that shot straight down from his temples to his jaw to his neck. His entire head was buzzing and aching like a hangover or a punch in the teeth.

His mouth was on fire and a near unbearably sharp raw nerve shot through the roots of his gums. An ache had blossomed in every tooth all at once, the kind that required a kick in the skull to knock someone out and a pair of ruthless, dirty, rusty pliers.

He slowly opened his eyes to an instant pang of regret. They were dry as bone and sensitive to even the slightest hint of light seeping in through cracks in the closed cellar door and barely flickering candles left burning on the low basement beams.

Squeezing them shut again against the continuous throb of maddening pain in his skull he rolled to his side and let out a groan. His blood-covered hands gripped the sides of his head as he tried pressing his palms into his jaw to ease it. Anything that would help. He moaned again, barely able to think past the ringing that kept swirling round and round in his head, bringing with it wave after wave of brutal burning pain.

Han curled in on himself, his whole body nearly shaking with the sheer willpower it took not to begin sobbing into the blood-soaked rug beneath him.

"It will pass." A voice crept through his semi-consciousness with a slight laugh. "Don't try to fight it."

Han couldn't even move his near lock-jawed mouth to try and respond. He resorted to tucking his knees to his chest, clenching tighter and tighter to keep himself from falling apart. Then, inside his mouth he felt a strange movement, and whatever awareness he had instantly snapped to attention. He knew what this was. Somewhat, somehow, it rang a familiar chord.

For a few months now, Han had experienced a reoccurring dream.

A pleasant dream at first.

It was a farmer's market in the crisp early morning, sunlight beamed down through thinning swathes of fog and warmed the world beneath it. Sights and smells enticed him as he made his way through the stalls, holding onto Gabriel with one hand while the other gripped tight to a breakfast pastry he was intent on devouring. Flaky crust crumbled onto Han's fingers and he kept his eyes on his feast, letting Gabriel lead them as he pleased.

People buzzed around, talking, congregating, selling, buying. Smiling. Smiling at him and at Gabriel and not paying a single mind to the connection between them. Gabriel would turn and give him a wink, and that irresistible confection became impossible to swallow.

Then in a blink, Gabriel's hand was gone. He was gone, and Han would be alone.

Alone in a crowd that darkened at the edges with a piece of food that turned to rot and swarmed with flies in his anxiously clenched fist. Suddenly, the whole place smelled of refuse, sick and damp, much too cold. Dread seeped in with the loss of light, as the once sparkling fog became a heavy blanket of choking smoke pressing down around him.

"Gabriel? Gabe?!" He would call into the frozen air. Everything was stock still and dead around him. The once delicious treat melted away between his fingers and he wiped his hands desperately on his pants. But this only proved to cover his hand in slime and soot blacker and darker than the odd sense of faint and sharp pang of panic crowding into his mind.

He would try and open his mouth again to call, but this time his voice didn't come, and his tongue felt odd against his teeth. Still, he tried again, and again. Nothing.

But as he spat, forming words on soundless lips, a tooth would come loose. Painless and sudden it plopped into the mud, sparkling like a lost pearl. His hand clamped down over his mouth and he would feel it sink in a bit too far, all his teeth tumbling onto his tongue in one smooth motion.

Teeth would rattle between the meager remainder of molars hanging by a thread. Cautiously, not daring to breathe, he would open his mouth and let the teeth fall loose and wet into his palm. Spit dripped through his fingers as he felt around carefully with his tongue. He teased at the few that still loosely wiggled in his gums.

Faced with an impossible dilemma, he would think to call out for Gabriel again, but cherishing the teeth that were left and near petrified with the shock of his mouth in his hand, he always decided against it.

Instead, he would begin to walk one foot after the other, down a street now lined with abandoned market stalls that appeared to have no end. He walked and he walked and he walked, but he never saw anyone near, as if they'd all been swallowed up, as if they'd never been there.

Alone, alone, with no one to call for and no voice to speak, Han would continue on in this dream, sparing one look behind him only to see that it mimicked the same sight in front of him.

Mocking him.

No different in any direction in its endless dismal nothing.

With nowhere left to go but forward, Han would trudge towards an impossible goal, tongue gently exploring the ragged edges of his abandoned jaw, teeth clattering in his palm like a cruel game of dice. It went on and on and on until the loneliness was deafening, until the smoke closed in around him and he could no longer even see his feet, until he began to choke and cough and choke and cough and finally wake, heaving beneath a blanket made of the same black that walled his failing lungs.

But this, now, this wasn't like that dream.

Gabriel was gone, but Han wasn't worried—Gabriel had promised to wait for him. It was something else, it was those teeth. Though still, it was different.

This was real, this was real, and this hurt.

Han could hear the grind of his teeth shifting in his mouth, felt his gums pinch and bleed as they moved on their own. That terrifyingly familiar sensation of smooth bone landing loose against his tongue made him gag and he spit them out, only to catch himself on something sharp. Razor sharp. He hissed and drew his tongue back, hand clamped against his bleeding lip.

"It will pass." That voice slithered out of the darkness again, somewhere behind him. "You will learn."

Han froze with a frigid fear that was making an unwelcome home in his bones. His hand slid from his mouth to his neck, feeling around for where he was sure he had been bit. Instead, his fingertips brushed a slightly raised scar and he traced it cautiously, unsure of how he should feel. But what was underneath this scar was even worse.

Or what wasn't.

Nothing. Absolutely nothing. No warmth of human skin, no rise and fall of breath, no pulse. No fucking pulse.

Despite the way his body screamed in protest against him, he shot upright and flipped over onto his hands and knees. Frantically he crawled his way across the dirtied, glass ridden floor, barely registering the cuts that sliced into the nigh resistant flesh of his palms. Without thinking, he head-butted the bathroom door and it swung open at high speed, slamming into the opposite wall and leaving a long crack in the stone. He paid it no mind, more intent on dragging himself up from the ground to look at himself in the tarnished mirror.

Feet unsteady underneath him, he gripped the edges of the porcelain washbasin in trembling hands, looked up, and let out a horrified scream.

There, facing him in the mirror was... no one.

Only the empty washroom at his back and the gaping black hole of the *Molly and Tom*—usually teeming with life—lying silent as the grave behind him. A soot-stained shirt was all he could see, with the outline of a body beneath it holding its ragged shape. But nothing else. No hair, no eyes, no face. He glanced down and frantically blinked. He saw his hands slippery and wet, unstable on the slick ceramic bowl. Panicked and confused he spun around, looking back and forth as if his surroundings would provide some kind of answer, as if they could.

"What's going on?" A whimper of confusion escaped his throat, hanging limp in the dead air around him. "What's happening to me?"

He hadn't really been asking. Not expecting an answer, anyway.

But then out of the shadows, one came.

"Something wonderful." That voice came slithering once again. "A gift. From me to you."

Han was looking back into the mirror and startled at the sound, no one had appeared in the room behind him. But when he turned around, a figure was there. That horrible pale blue man with the razor-sharp mouth was leering up at him. A whole head shorter, but with presence enough to suffocate the air out of every inch of the tiny shithole bathroom. Han leaned back as the man approached until he felt his head touch the silver-coated glass behind him.

"Who... who are you?" he stammered, terrified of those teeth and those bottomless, soulless eyes.

"Lord Richter, at your service." The man flashed that eerie smile and did a slight mocking bow.

Richter. Han had heard that name before but where—he couldn't place. It was familiar, but right now everything else wasn't, and something like a nobleman's name wasn't exactly top on his list of things he gave a shit about, not even on a good day.

And it was definitely not a good day.

"What did you do to me?" Han brought a hand to feel his neck again. "What... you bit me..."

"Yes," Lord Richter responded, his dead lavender lips twisting in amusement. "I bit you. But I also did so much more."

"W-what did you do..." Han asked again, slowly finding that he was afraid of the answer.

"Come now." The man clicked his tongue in what was becoming a habit of his. "What's your name?"

"H... Han."

"Han, Han..." Richter rolled the word around in his mouth like a treat, and Han cringed at the way he savored it. "Lovely. Really, it's wonderful to finally meet you."

He invaded his way into Han's personal space with a smooth twirl of his coat. Then looked up his nose at him and said, "How about we go somewhere else, where we can talk. Just us."

"I... I'm supposed to be meeting someone."

Han was violently confused, in pain, and certainly not wanting to go anywhere with this man.

He might be dressed nicely like the Lord he supposedly was, but you can put pearls on a pig as they say. His hair was long and black, wavy and curled in intricate knots and rolls on the sides of his head with a braided ponytail down his back. The stench of perfume, too much of it in fact, wafted off of him and carried a sickly-sweet odor not only of flowers and spices, but of rot.

"Who?" Richter frowned, his mock-friendly demeanor slipping away. "That little milk boy with the funny nose? The one you're always sticking your lips to in the corner over there?"

He extended a long clawed fingernail towards the salvaged couch where Han had been so happy, only a day before.

"Gabriel, and he's a milkman."

And Han loved his nose. But he didn't need to justify anything to this asshole. Then something else Richter said caught his attention.

"You've been watching me?"

Richter sniffed, crossed his arms and leaned against the grimy bathroom wall. "Well, obviously. I noticed you the first night you came in. All tall and lean and dark and rugged. I knew I had to have you. But you're always with that little... shit."

"Don't talk about him like that." Han felt heat rise in his chest. "And if you liked me so much why didn't you ever say anything to me? I've never even seen you here before."

"I knew I'd have my chance," Richter smirked. "I'm a patient man. And look, here we are. Just me and you. Together forever."

"Stop saying that. I don't know what you mean, and I'm certainly not sticking around to find out. I don't know you, and I don't want to. You.... You fucking bit me!"

Richter sighed. "This again. Yes, and you're not curious what for?"

"I'm assuming this is some kind of fucking kink of yours. Something you want me to be into?"

"On the contrary," Richter pursed his lips. "It's simply a matter of survival."

"Will you please tell me what you're on about?" Han rubbed his forehead with his bloody hand. The skin felt strange underneath his fingertips but right now, that was only another weird thing on the ever-growing list of bizarre happenings, and definitely not a contender for the top-ranking spot.

"Come with me," Richter beckoned. "And I'll tell you all you need to know."

Resigned to the fact that this slimy nobleman was determined to get his way, and nigh exploding with questions he so desperately needed answers to, Han had no choice but to reluctantly obey.

SEVENTEEN

The door slammed shut and Calysto was alone, stunned and half slumped into the pillows. Python's sudden absence left a gaping hollow in the room, a silence carved out with such sudden intensity Calysto barely had the chance to process what had happened before Python was gone.

Calysto took one look at the broken bedpost and buried his face in his hands.

What did I do wrong? What did I do?

He'd only called Python by a nickname, something that slipped out of his mouth unprompted, un-premeditated. He hadn't really even meant to say it. Besides, Python called him 'Cal' all the time, 'Han' felt like the obvious choice to the awkward task of shortening 'Python'. Han, Hon, what was the problem?

It was Calysto's small attempt at indicating familiarity between the two of them, as Python was grappling with something Calysto didn't fully understand. It seemed there was still more to it he wasn't privy to.

Python had said he didn't remember anything from his life before. Was that a lie? Or was he starting to remember? Calysto really wished he would have stayed. He was conflicted with not only being uncharacteristically concerned for the vampire, but also the horrible depths in which the rejection had sent him spiraling into.

He shouldn't have tried and he should have known he'd fuck it up somehow. The things he felt in his heart never came out of his mouth the right way round and he was certainly extremely out of practice with it. Even extending half a hand in Python's direction sent a bolt of anxiety through his chest. If it should be rejected, if it should be unwanted. Well, it was bravery enough that he offered an olive branch, or should I say, leaf, between them. But to have it scorned in such a manner, he nearly wanted to curl up and die in shame.

Not only was it a digging embarrassment that he had put himself out there on the line like that, but most of all, the sense that it wasn't good enough. He wasn't good enough, to reach through to Python in a moment of need.

Useless, inadequate. As always.

To make matters worse, Python had snapped at him in a way he hadn't heard before. It hadn't been with the general annoyance or dismissiveness that Calysto could handle from anyone and let roll off him without a single care. It had been with venom.

Python's name really did suit him, didn't it?

That biting force of his vehement hatred. Straight at Calysto and the stupid thing he'd said. And now Python was gone. Calysto thought for a moment that they had made some kind of progress between them. He almost liked having Python around now, and the vampire also hadn't been a complete ass to him either when he'd returned blood covered and bleeding.

Hadn't Python even saved his life?

And this is how Calysto would repay him.

But he'd only called him Han.

It was familiar to Python, as if he'd known what it meant. What was it? Calysto again wished desperately that Python hadn't left. But then again, he was glad he did. He wouldn't be able to bear such refusal and sit there in the midst of it, faced with his failure and the one he had failed. And it wasn't even the first time now.

The guilt was digging at him more and more with each passing hour they spent stuck in this hell hole of a town. It's not like this whole thing wasn't his fault to begin with.

And now he'd participated in a vampire hunt. Or some sad excuse for one. He might not have held that silver sword directly, but nevertheless he contributed to the slaughter of Python's kind. It was one thing for Python to not like other vampires, but it was another to kill them.

Calysto wondered how he felt about that kind of thing. He hadn't had a chance to ask.

Calysto took a deep breath from between his fingers and scrubbed his weary eyes underneath his glasses. If there was one way to make all of this right, it was to get them the fuck out of there as soon as possible.

Despite his shaken confidence, the blood-loss-induced exhaustion, and the way his stomach felt like a pit of puke and despair, Calysto forced himself up off of the bed.

He slipped his coat and boots back on and headed towards the door. He took one last look around the tiny room he and Python had shared, and for a moment, wished he'd had better memories there.

At least now, at least with him.

With a sigh and shake of his head, he closed the door and set out on his own to carry out what needed to be done.

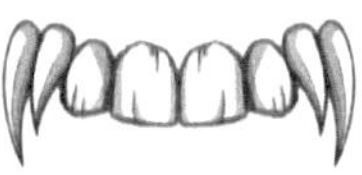

Outside, cool night air rushed through Python's hair as he ran. He ran, and ran, and ran. He ran all the way through Industry, across the long causeway to Purvel, through Purvel, and up into the woods. He didn't stop until he reached Calysto's house where it sat quiet and abandoned by them only days ago.

Days that felt as arduous as months. Months he usually spent alone, hopping from town after town and burning everything in his wake, and why? Why?

Python slowed on his approach and though he was barely winded he collapsed to his hands and knees. A scream tore from his throat, so loud it startled a nearby animal into scurrying away through the brush. He screamed again, until his dead lungs were empty and his throat was raw. He didn't even know why he was doing it, it just felt good, it felt right. It felt pent up beyond compare. As if he didn't realize he'd been holding it in for a hundred long and lonely years.

Han. Han. Calysto had called him Han. He had *been* Han, once. A long, long time ago. He was Han, he was Han now, and he'd always been. He'd forgotten, tucked all of it away beneath a barrier of hate and loneliness and time. So much time that now felt like only moments ago.

In the past when he'd fled that miserable town with vengeful blood in his teeth and ill-gotten gold in his hands, he swore to never look back, to never go back, to that wretched place and time. Yet here he was, a part of it all over again. And he had pretended he didn't feel what it meant to him; he had tried to let it lie.

But as his broken heart mended the cracks with blackened tar made of spite and rage, he buried those memories of Gabriel along with his human life and everything that came with it. All the suffering and the pain it had caused him. But also, the good—he'd forgotten the good. He'd convinced himself there was no such thing as that to remember.

But there was so much good, wasn't there?

Even if it was in secret, even if it was only in a fanciful daydream.

There was good. There was joy. There was love.

He had loved once, and as he heaved against the weight of countless memories he realized, he might again. The feelings were familiar, though the faces weren't the same. He hadn't put it together before but there it was, nagging at him from underneath the peeling corners of his hard exterior. Love. Just a little bit of it. Begging to be felt, to even be acknowledged.

But he couldn't. Not against the pride and pain in his heart. He wouldn't. Not when something so wild, so out of his control, could be his undoing.

Had been.

It didn't matter. There was nothing he could do now to stop it. Once one turns towards that realization in their heart, they will never be able to turn back. Not even if they wanted to. Even the stubborn and callous vampire Python was no different.

He had always loved *so much.* So passionately, so blindly. With such unbridled abandon. And that's exactly what had ruined him. He'd forgotten what it was like. Yet there it was, staring him down, demanding to be seen.

Finally, he couldn't help but look. He faced straight into its burning, unbearable gaze and he knew.

He was so unbelievably fucked.

Calysto.

Shit!

Python recalled the words he said before he left, and the way Calysto had immediately clammed up in resistance. Python was struck with a chilling realization. No matter how he felt now, it may be nigh impossible to reach Calysto like that again. He had held a moment of rare vulnerability between them, Calysto had *handed* him that, and he'd slammed the door shut in his face. Literally.

Python climbed up from the ground, wiping his knees of the dirt with trembling hands as his emotionally-induced claws slowly retracted. His gums ached and his head was throbbing. He hadn't eaten in over a day now and it was beginning to feel like it. The panic-induced jaunt across two cities probably didn't help matters either.

He took a long look at the cabin in front of him, where deep blue moonlight glinted off the thick uneven glass of the windows. The rest of the home was bathed in black, the rotted wooden slats were nearly entirely covered in thick layers of mold. Where Python before had found this place wanting, it now struck him as kind of charming. This house was a perfect representation of his weird warlock companion. Hidden away, doing its best to blend in and go unnoticed. Neglected, abandoned, and used to it. Persevering in spite of it.

Guilt.

That's what Python felt.

An emotion he was becoming all too familiar with recently, despite his well-fought battle to keep it at bay for longer than most others had been alive.

The intense realization washed over him as he wished he hadn't said what he did, and frankly, he had no idea what to do with such a feeling. With such a weight. The responsibility of what another felt was not a thing he was accustomed to, and had no doubt intentionally made it so.

So, what could he do?

Well, for starters he knew he needed to go back. Likely to act like nothing happened, or try to smooth things over if Calysto's defensive spikes had retracted even a little bit.

Python took one last look at the cabin, finding that he wished he could go inside, lie down, and have a snack. Maybe in the company of one very annoying, unfairly attractive, extremely irritating, but endlessly interesting, warlock.

Fucking hell.

He swore under his breath, spun on his heel, and headed back toward town.

I had to get attached, huh? I just had to.

This is a nightmare.

Calysto leaned against a dark shop window on the empty street and took a long pause to stare up at the cloudy night overhead.

Another few blocks away was the wealthier district where the manor of one Dr. Adriani Merik sprawled in all its extravagance.

Inside Calysto's pockets, his fists opened and closed; left one clenching tight around the small deer statuette and biting into his palm. The subtle pain brought him back to center, helped him ground his overwhelmed senses, and soothed the reeling of his psyche.

He had to do this, he had to make it right.

It wasn't like he was afraid.

Not afraid of getting caught, or of going back into that cursed house filled with scents and sights and memories all too familiar. No, he wasn't afraid of that. Damned if he wasn't afraid of seeing that man's face again though.

Merik, who had shaped his young and already fragile and bruised mind with a sculptors tool made of sadistic sneers and empty eyes. A face more familiar to him than that of his own mother's, whose cruelty existed in his mind only as a vague vignette of his introduction to the pain of this world. She lingered there as a reminder, no, as a first lesson, to what his life would bring. Pain, hurt, and pain again. The prologue to a textbook filled with examples to prove that anyone who existed within his limited orbit was bound to harm him eventually.

He couldn't believe he had almost let himself forget such an engrained teaching driven in to him over and over again. He had almost let his guard down. He had almost let someone in.

But yet again, his mother's words were right. The sting of her slap and the ring of her voice in his ear was stronger than the memory of her face. Useless and inadequate, pathetic, alone. She was right, and she was... blonde? No, she had dark hair. Not like him. He looked like his father, she had said. He didn't know. He had never met the man. But when she spat that fact like a curse he had sometimes wondered if that was the reason she hated him.

Was it a painful reminder of loss to look at his amber skin and golden hair? Or was it simply a matter of his magical inability? It was probably both. He had asked for neither yet was punished for it all the same.

A warlock in the image of his father. Ideas he could hear and nearly touch, but never feel.

The chilly evening breeze tickled the hairs of his neck and pulled loose strands from his ponytail. Within his hands he conjured a small, weak light, to warm them. The heat seeped into the metal deer and slowly, slowly it soothed him. Calysto prepared to stand when an ice-cold hand met his shoulder, pressing him back against the wall.

"Hey mister, you really shouldn't wander these streets alone at night." A cheeky quip slithered out of the shadows. "Don't you know there's vampires in this town?"

Calysto pinched his lips, glaring in the direction of the familiar voice. Python's glistening eyes widened a fraction and he breathed a low whistle.

"Geez, tough crowd."

"What do you want, Python."

"Just what the fuck do you think you're doing?"

Great. Exactly what he needed right now, the current embodiment of his failures tagging along to make sure he didn't fuck another thing up too bad this time.

"Let me go."

"You're not going by yourself, are you?" Python moved closer beside him and didn't remove his hand.

"Why do you care," Calysto hissed between his teeth. "You want to go home, right?"

"Yes, but..."

"Okay then," Calysto cut him off. "I'm going to get you home like I said I would."

"Calysto," Python's voice fell, and something about the tone made Calysto turn to meet his eyes. For a moment he thought he might have seen a softness there, a hesitation. But then Python spoke, shattering any illusion Calysto might've foolishly thought was true.

"I'll do it. There's no way you're getting out unheard with the way you drag your feet."

Calysto sighed. "Do you even know what you're looking for?"

Python wrinkled his nose, frowning at nothing over the top of Calysto's head.

"No," Calysto answered for him.

"Why don't you tell me then?"

"I can't. It's too specific. I need to find it myself."

"I'm not gonna let you walk in there to, I dunno, get shot or something. That Merik guy seems like he'll do it, too."

"He'll do more than that," Calysto mumbled under his breath.

This was taking too long, and Python was distracting him, again. But he had to admit the conversation had served to take his mind out of its downward spiral and soothed his nerves.

"Listen, let's... let's just both go."

"I have an idea."

Python's lips spread into that type of smile that Calysto was quickly learning meant he had something that was surely invented to torture Calysto specifically hidden up his sleeve.

"Climb on my back."

"What? I'm not doing that."

"Come on!" Python grinned even wider. "I can go fast and run quietly, you can't. Get on my back and I'll take us both. Got a better plan?"

Calysto rubbed his forehead and pushed up his glasses. "You've got to be fucking kidding me..."

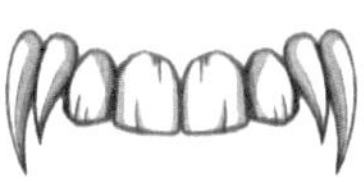

Hours, weeks, months.

Han didn't know how he'd been trapped in a limbo of moonless night and sleepless day. Locked in a room with no windows, no candles, no light. Though that didn't particularly seem to matter anymore, as now he could see perfectly fine in the dark without it. It was as if his eyes had reversed their function, for when the door to his strange prison would open, the candlelight from beyond nearly blinded him and he shrank into the now comfortable shadow.

The idea of escape had crossed his mind, but he'd barely the strength to crawl across the floor much less try to fight his way out. He didn't even know where he was.

All he knew was Richter had led him here and tossed him in.

"For your own good," he had said. "Until the early symptoms have passed."

Symptoms of what?

But he quickly found an answer, slipped down the letterbox of his sandpaper throat. Hot sweats, flashes of chills that left trails of prickling sticky sweat in their wake. Feverish fits lasted so long that the accompanied delirium was a welcome reprieve for his mind as he lay tortured by the eternal damp of this strange room.

Cold concrete walls surrounded him on all sides and the space was furnished with only a small metal framed bed. Han spent most of his time curled up on the thin mattress, clutching an army-green woolen blanket around him. He didn't let it go, even as it soaked through with what surely was more sweat than all the water his body contained.

When the door did open and someone entered, they placed a tray down and quietly left, speaking not a word to acknowledge or reassure him. He forced himself to turn and see what was brought, surprised to find it was only a cup.

Han reached toward it with a hand he had taken to not looking at too closely, as the strangeness of the glimpses of his appearance made him heave.

Skin—though usually imperceptible through layers of coal and dirt—that once was a pale amber blushing with life, now was translucent as the gauze over a windowpane, blue veins trailing through every finger making him much too aware of what lie beneath.

Nails turned black and cracked, some peeling, some bleeding, had healed with the added addition of what had become claws, thick as knife blades and tapered to a vicious point.

Han felt an awful flex under the flesh of his fingertips when they slid in and out of their own accord. He really hoped they would stop doing that, or at least that he could learn to *make* them stop.

He sat on the edge of the creaking cot, blanket tight around his shoulders, and cautiously sniffed the contents of the cup. To his surprise it smelled good. It had a strange metallic tinge that burned his nose, but in a welcome way like a bottle of spices or a strong tea. Warm to the touch it permeated through the cup into hands that now ached with a chill he couldn't shake. Finally, after thoroughly enjoying the way it felt, he took a sip. But the moment it hit his tongue, he froze.

Han was a street dweller, a boy who had viciously fought for what meager possessions he owned.

Han was an orphan raised under the tutelage of a master with an iron fist.

Han was a chimney sweep. A profession he survived much longer than most by clinging to his life with a bitter persistence.

Han was a fighter, you see—and he knew the taste of blood.

But instead of the twinge of copper on his tongue igniting fight or flight, that primal urge to swing out with his fists or cower away from one coming his way. Instead of the blood on his lips being a distinct sign of warning. Instead of it tasting of fear or malice or rage, it tasted of life. And he liked it.

Though Han had sampled his own blood from a busted lip or cracked tooth many times before, it had never been quite like this. Thick and sticky, it was unbearably salty in one moment and tooth-achingly sweet in the next. It coated his tongue like honey, viscous and hot, nourishing a primal desire that had awoken with the budding arrival of his animal teeth.

Han salivated uncontrollably, craving a sensation he'd never had but suddenly, desperately needed. He swallowed the contents of the cup and it warmed his chest twice better than the medicine Dr.

Merik's boy had stolen for him. It stung, cayenne and chili pepper, spreading through him and lighting up every nerve.

Come to think of it, that coal-coated cough was gone. No longer spitting up fluid and black earth, he breathed clearly. Well, he didn't breathe at all. But when he inhaled just out of habit, it was air and nothing else.

Han licked the edge of the mug and hissed, drawing back as he cut his tongue on those newly found fangs. They emerged as he indulged, his body turned beast with the scent of meat, of iron, of blood. He wanted it, more of it. Ravenous, he couldn't have enough of it.

He could very well have taken the time to be disgusted, somewhere in the back of his mind. But the sheer hunger that even when he was alive was stuffed down, ignored, tolerated, familiar, now reared its head and howled louder than any small protests of *this is weird, this is bad, what is happening to me?*

Bloodlust and want still overcame him, and the empty cup in his hands was slowly crushed. As soon as he noticed what he'd done he let go, peeling his fingers from the dents. A part of him felt apologetic, he didn't know whose cup this was and he had clearly ruined it. It was smashed so flat the basin was now a thin slit, rimmed in blood like a shining wound. Yet the hunger he hadn't known lived deep within him, still lay unsatiated.

Then, filled with the sudden strength to move around he decided to explore and stood on legs surprisingly steady for all their recent time passed wasting away in the hazy clutches of death on the shitty little bed.

If you could see him now, it might be a little bit funny—

He was wearing the clothes from the night before, when he'd done his best to dress his best. One needed to look the viable part to ask one's secret love to run away with them, after all.

He had worn his black coat with all the missing buttons, frayed suspenders held up poor-fitted trousers tucked into cuffed leather boots, and his old shirt was now stained at the neck with blood and at the hems with dirt. His long black hair fell into his face where it slipped from the ribbon that held it, and he shrouded himself in the blanket like a cape.

He made the picture-perfect stereotype of a vampire, if a low-budget and sweaty one. Not to mention the fact that he was skulking around the edges of the room in the dark.

Han walked from corner to corner, slouching beneath the low height of the ceiling. He realized it must be a basement. Pipes ran overhead and it had the same slightly musty smell of the *Molly and Tom*, though the permeating mold wasn't being covered up by various perfumes and crowds of folk. It was only him in there, alone in the frozen damp.

He saved the most interesting stop for last in this dismal little cell and finally approached the door. He had to hunch further to peer through the few barred slats near the top, but there wasn't much to see there either. Just a corridor and an old wooden staircase that led to the landing outside. On a small table near the door was a candle and when Han glanced to look at it, the warm gentle glow nearly knocked him off his feet. It was shockingly bright and he hissed, flinching back and squeezing his eyes shut as sparks flew behind the lids.

What the fuck.

This wasn't just some long-term hangover or feverish illness that he had yet to shake. This was something else. He realized it now, slowly putting pieces together of the series of strange events.

Richter, it was Richter. He said he'd given him a gift, but what was it? Why was he being kept here? Where the hell was that guy, anyway? Han hadn't seen the man once this whole time.

Maybe Han had come down with some kind of strange disease and was being quarantined from others. Richter was a lord after all, he probably had more access to knowledge on the goings-on in the town than people of Han's status did.

Right as he thought of this, he heard footsteps above, much louder than what one would normally hear with regular ears. They traveled over his head, then got louder and closer as they descended the stairs.

Han quickly scrambled back onto the bed. A movement that he completed in a split second without so much as thinking. His mind raced as he waited. The steps reached the landing. The sound of a lock clicked, and the door creaked open.

Blinded again by the slight candlelight seeping in through the door Han pulled the blanket close around his head, hunching down and shrinking back.

"Oh, let me get that for you," came a voice. Then, there was a small puff of air, and the light bleeding through Han's burning eyelids went out.

"Better, yes? I forget how sensitive one is at the start of such things."

A weight sunk down next to him on the mattress and Han peeked over to be met with the face of Lord Richter, as clear as day in the dark.

"What things?" Han managed to ask. "Where have you been? What's going on?"

"Those are all heavily loaded questions, my boy."

Richter grinned at him, and Han nearly gagged on the nauseating scent of rotten meat that came from his mouth. He smelled strongly of old blood and dead skin and was much too close for comfort.

"But now that the worst has passed, why don't we get you out of here? Come join me upstairs."

Only then did Han realize Richter had left the door open, exposing a perfectly good route to escape. He cast one glance at the man beside him and decided he'd much rather make a run for it than spend any more time in this cage or hear any more fucked up semblances of answers come from the guy's putrid mouth. He jumped to his feet and without another word, bolted toward the exit.

He made it in half a second flat but was instantly stopped by an iron grip on his forearm, and Richter's voice creeping right up behind him, cold like a blizzard's howl in his ear.

"I thought you might try something like that," he hissed slowly, sounding only half-amused. "But trust me, should you run out now, all you'll meet is a painful death. That's no threat, but a simple promise from the sunlight. But even if it weren't, I would catch you all the same."

Han didn't answer but relaxed to show he wouldn't fight. He had always been strong, but Richter was stronger, and those teeth of his had left their mark not only forever on Han's skin but on his mind. He was terrified. And now more than ever, he was alone. No one was coming to help him. No one even knew where he was if they wanted to try.

No, whatever happened next was completely up to Han to handle all on his own. Through the force of the claws on his arm and the way Richter spoke, Han could sense the danger he was in. And so once again, he reluctantly complied.

"Good." Richter chuckled, slightly loosening his hold. Though his nails stayed firmly etched into Han's skin, and he didn't let go. "You'd do best to listen to me where such matters are concerned."

CHAPTER

EIGHTEEN

Richter's palm sent chills down Han's back as he let himself be led up the stairs into a darkened dining area. The only window in the room was blocked with a thick curtain, leaving no indication to Han that it was daylight aside from the fact that Richter had told him so. Richter guided him to a decorative wooden chair at the side of a long dining table, then seated himself at the head.

Han stayed quiet but watched Richter with careful eyes as he settled down and crossed his legs, leaning back in his chair like a king on his throne. Han decided he really didn't like this man. Though for now he had no choice but to comply. A fact that already ate at him more and more with each passing moment. Taking orders from noblemen was not his way and a task he always carried out with a begrudgingly bitter heart. Dependence on this man wouldn't change that—but only serve to make it worse.

"Ah," Richter sighed, breaking through his thoughts. "This is better, don't you think?"

"Sure," Han finally spoke. "But why keep me in a fucking cell to begin with?"

Richter leaned his forehead on lazy fingertips, and the lace from his cuff fell open to reveal a slender wrist. Han still couldn't understand how he was so powerful when he resembled a withered corpse in nearly every way.

"It's safer for everyone that way. When one goes through the changes."

"What changes?" Han snapped, the confusion and itching hunger eating away at his patience. "Will you just tell me what the fuck is going on?"

He realized with the rising of his anger his gums began to ache, and his tongue licked against budding fangs. His lips curled back and a soft growl rose in his throat. He didn't even mean to do it. It was as if his body had taken over an instinctual edge of its own, and Han was simply being led behind it.

He was met with another mocking laugh before Richter turned a sharp glare on him.

"Oh, so you really haven't figured it out at all? My god Han, use your head, will you?" As he spoke that fake grin disappeared and his voice dipped low, dripping with a sudden malice.

"But here's something you can learn right now," he said.

He uncrossed his legs and leaned forward, eyes sparkling in the dim candlelight with a deadly emptiness. The haunting sheen of a cat in the night sent shivers down Han's spine.

"Don't you ever bare your fangs at me again, boy. Do you understand? You are fresh, so I will forgive it this once. But you'd do best to keep your disrespect in check around your maker."

He finished with a sneer, then sat back into the velvet curve of his chair, relaxing again as if nothing had happened. That amused smile returned to distort his pale lips.

"Now, what else do you want to know?"

Han leveled him with a look of his own. He wasn't going to let this asshole intimidate him. Still, he tried to calm himself, and as he did, he found those new teeth of his retracted. So they responded to his emotions too, then.

Weird.

"What are you?"

"What do you think?"

Han swallowed hard. What he thought he knew was simply impossible, and he wasn't ready to say it.

"I... don't know."

"Come on now," Richter huffed, scratching a clawed nail on his cheek. "I think you do."

"Yes but, that's not real."

"Real?" Richter barked a laugh. "You'd do well to forget about what you think is real, Han. When you let that little notion go, a whole world awaits."

"So..." Han's hands gripped the wooden arms of his chair and it creaked beneath them. "I... died?"

"Yes."

"And I came back to life?"

"Indeed."

"What was in that cup?"

"What do you think was in that cup?"

"... Blood?"

"Ahhh, he's catching on!" Richter waved his hand lazily through the air and let it land with a thump. He was quickly losing interest and Han wasn't sure what he'd do when he did. "Just say the word, won't you?"

"What..."

"Oh, stop playing dumb!" Richter snapped. He slammed his palm down and sent a long crack through the length of the table between them.

Han jumped at the sound and cursed himself for doing so.

"Spit it out, boy!"

"Vampire?" Han's voice was meek, barely above a whisper. He hated himself for his fear.

"There! There, he finally said it!" Richter laughed aloud, his mouth wide open and long fangs on full display. He snapped it shut with a click and leaned across the tabletop, pursing his lips in a cruel twist. "Now, you can accept it."

Han stared. He couldn't think of anything to say since the room had suddenly started spinning. As the breath that lay dormant and unneeded in his lungs caught and tangled his dead throat. The heart he now knew he didn't have anymore could have leapt through his chest if only it still beat.

Everything smelled of blood, of death and decay, of rotten wine and molded food. The air was full of it. Every sensation of touch and every scent, every sight and sound, became all too much, much too much. He clenched the arms of the chair tighter in his aching fists and they all but disintegrated with the force. Splinters broke off into his hands and dead flesh instantly rejected it, spitting rotten black blood and healing the wounds.

He stank of it—the odor of death. He knew that now. He had thought, maybe, perhaps, it was just the fever. The passing ache of that sickly sweet sticky salt-sweat of sickness. It seeped into his clothes, pooling cold in yellowed armpits and a bloodied collar, creasing his pants into crisp lines that cracked when he sat as if they were starched in a way he could never afford.

It clung to his hair, knotted in strings tied to that feverish memory, a strange transformation that he'd imagined was all a dream. A bizarre fantasy he'd had while spinning out sick and half-drunk on the cold basement floor of the one place he'd ever felt at home. For why else? Why else would this be happening?

There was no such thing as monsters, demons, vampires, witches. It was all a horrible game. To find someone to blame, someone to place one's hatred upon.

They didn't *actually* have magical powers.

Magic was a myth, like the promise of a better life he had so carefully held in his pockets and placed coin after coin into that small hidden pouch behind the walls of a place that slowly killed him. It was all a fairy tale, whimsical nonsense told to children to make them dream, to give them a sense of wonder, to drive them on when everything else told them this world wasn't worth the fight.

Imagination though, she was real, and what a powerful lover she was. More than once she had coaxed him into her bed when the thought of anything tangible was much too hard to bear. She opened her arms and embraced him when all else was falling down. He could escape into her soft and welcoming bosom and breathe in the scent of possibility and hope, and lie there for a while, feeling it, listening to her promises. And believing them.

Just for a moment, she could make his dreams real.

Just for a moment, everything else could fall away.

But now she had abandoned him, her comfort turned hard as stone, offering him no reprieve. She had lied and told him there was a place of safety in the realm of the impossible.

The line between fantasy and reality blurred before his eyes as he stared down at once-tanned hands turned much too pale. Bruised and shriveled veins tracked the undersides of the skin, like cracks beneath thick layers of ice. His body as lifeless as a frozen lake in winter. His tendons bulged with the force of his grip on the chair, jutting out in a skeletal stark-white reminder. This one simple fact visible on protruding joints and fingernails gone decrepit blue—he had died, but he had also lived.

No, he was dead, and he was nothing more than that. Richter had killed him and cursed him to be a living corpse of some perverted design.

Han heard himself gulping for air that made no difference to calm him, as it would have if he still had working lungs to breathe it in. He wanted to scream but it trickled out as a wheeze, whimpering through lips that tasted as rotten as his tongue. Flat and dry he licked them, pinching them between his teeth in hopes of stimulating some return of feeling. It didn't ease the tingling. The numb. The cold.

Han released the chair and in one panicked motion flung it behind him and sprang to his feet. He spun frantically around looking across the room.

Quiet dying embers smoldered in the large arched fireplace and even that was still too bright. He looked away and chose not to think of what a place like that meant to him. Irritated that after it all, even in the midst of this, his thoughts went straight to the mechanisms of his trade.

Smother the embers, sweep out the ash, collect it in a sack, climb the chimney, back against one wall, feet on the other, broom in hand, face covered with a meager cloth. Shimmy, shimmy, careful not to bend too far or go too fast, don't let your knees get ahead of your neck. If you get stuck you won't ever get out. You'll suffocate, you'll die, and your remains will be yanked free with a shovel and poker and hook and you'll be replaced by another who will soon meet a similar end. If you want to live you'll remember these words. Go faster, go higher, hurry it up boy, there are more houses to do, don't want to keep the nobles waiting.

Nobles.

Nobles who feigned delicate coughs behind perfumed handkerchiefs at even the sight of him. As if somehow, their wealth afforded them a more sensitive form of humanity, a worthiness to be coddled and cared for, an innate need for all these luxuries they built around them on the backs of people who, with the right amount of coin, they'd consider to be just like them.

Han didn't want to think of that now, but it came all the same. Lord Richter, *Lord*.

He had taken everything from him, and not only in life.

He had taken his chance at a merciful death, an end that one in his position would eventually find. He had snatched away the one thing that Han fought so hard to control.

That space between life and death.

He had fought so hard to live, he had fought so hard to not give in and become another boy who choked to death on the opulence of the rich. And he would have done it, too. He was so close. To getting away, to being free, to choosing the life he wanted to live.

And Richter was the one to tear it out of reach. Not even giving Han the courtesy of a true and final death.

Han ran from the table and towards a far wall where he glimpsed a glimmer of silver sheen hung near a bookshelf laden with dust. There in front of the mirror he looked again, and again he saw nothing. The room behind him was empty as if not a single living soul was present. The place where Richter sat was void, but his mocking laughter carried over all the same, the only thing to confirm he was really there.

Any hope Han had left that perhaps he would wake up and find himself in that previous life—the one he'd hated and taken for granted, the one he'd tried so hard to escape—was finally crushed.

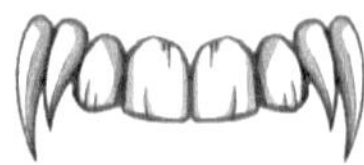

"Hang on tight," Python called quietly to Calysto.

He was clinging to Python's back like a monkey, trying to muster the remaining scraps of his dignity through the furiously pinched expression etched on his face.

"I hate this," Calysto answered. "Just for the record."

"You don't gotta tell me that," Python chuckled, and hiked Calysto up to get a better grip.

"Hey!"

"Would you rather I drop you in the street?"

Calysto's blunt nails dug into his shoulders. "You could pick me up with one finger, couldn't you? So, doubt you would."

"Got me there," Python snickered again. "You are gonna have to hang on with your legs though, I gotta use my hands."

Calysto reluctantly complied, crossing his ankles over Python's waist.

"Stop enjoying this," Calysto protested, wiggling himself as much as he could into a more comfortable position.

"Cal, you look like a half-drowned cat with that miserable frown, I can't help it."

"Can we just go!"

"Alright, alright." Python took a bit of mercy on him. "But listen, once I get going don't let go Cal, I'm serious. If you fall with how fast I'm going, you'll smash your skull open."

Calysto swallowed and jerked a nod, his hands coming up to wrap around Python's neck.

"Alright."

Python took off at a speed that came with an almost natural ease, but the buildings on either side of them turned into a smeared blur of black and brown. Calysto wasn't sure if Python could make out any details, but he must be able to since he was navigating with some semblance of knowing where he was going. The ride on his back was surprisingly smooth, not like a typical piggyback that was a silly and slightly humiliating attempt to cling on to someone about to topple over.

Instead, Python was solid and sure beneath him, and while he ran it was at such an even pace that Calysto wouldn't have felt it except for the wind tearing through his hair and stinging his eyes.

Even though Python had told him to fold his legs around him, Python's hands were still holding him above his knees. Firm and sure, but not gripping too tight in that way he did with most things—as if he didn't know his own strength. Calysto's kitchen table was evidence of what Python's claws could easily do when he wasn't thinking.

But he held onto Calysto with what must have been an intentionally human-strength-level grasp. His large palms nearly wrapped around Calysto's legs and the chill from his body seeped through Calysto's pants and caused him to shiver. He huddled closer to Python without thinking, only to find that the rest of him was just as lifeless.

He wondered if Python felt it, or if he felt anything at all. Did Python's hands feel as cold to him as they were to Calysto?

Calysto hated being cold, especially in his fingers. He wondered if Python did, too. It always caused Calysto to be clumsy and make stupid mistakes in the middle of tinkering with something important. And there were few things, other than most people and an unnamed vampire, that annoyed him more.

He unfurled his grip from around Python's neck and placed a hand over one of Python's on his thigh, covering it at much as he could. Though the moment he did, Python stopped running and they came to halt. Calysto realized what he had been doing and jerked back, letting his arm dangle in midair.

Without a word, Python released Calysto's legs and knelt. Calysto took the hint and hopped to the ground. He found his legs were wobbly and reached out to grab Python's coat. But instead, Python took his hand gently, holding him steady.

"I got you," he said quietly, his strange cat eyes glimmering fiercely in the dark. "How was that?"

Calysto was momentarily stunned, focused on where their hands were folded together. It took him a second to realize Python had spoken, as he was noticing that indeed, the heat from his own skin was seeping into Python's deadened limbs.

"Uh…" His lips felt numb. From the wind, no doubt. "Fine, fine. Uh, not what I expected."

"What did you expect?" Python was still looking closely at him.

"I don't know."

Calysto's thoughts were mostly consumed with not moving his fingers a single centimeter nor flexing one bit of muscle underneath Python's large hand.

"What, was it fun?" Python tried to tease, but to Calysto it sounded a little strained.

"I…" Calysto pushed his glasses up with his free hand and met Python with the slightest, almost imperceptible half-smile. "Yes, I guess it kind of was."

Python might've twitched and he quickly looked away. "Okay."

"Not going to make fun of me?" Calysto eyed him skeptically through the low fog hanging in the air.

Python just shrugged.

He was acting strangely out of character. He almost seemed nervous. Distant. Too serious. He would, that is, if Calysto didn't know him any better.

What's wrong with him?

Calysto didn't know how to ask. So instead, he said something else.

"Give me your other hand."

"What?"

"Just give it," Calysto beckoned until Python slowly lifted it and placed it limply in Calysto's control. Calysto took both of Python's palms, faced them together, then sandwiched them between his own. There was no one around so Calysto let a tiny spark of that magically warm red light bloom between them. Python's skin glowed all the way through and Calysto quietly marveled at the way he could see the tiny veins and long, spindly bones, the sinew of lean muscle and knobs of gnarled knuckle all lit from within.

"They're really cold," he said in some half-hearted attempt at explanation. "Don't they feel cold?"

"I uh, don't really notice anymore." Python stood very still, not meeting his eyes.

"Does this help?"

"Mhmm." Python nodded once, quickly. "It feels... nice."

"Are you okay?" Calysto blurted then, without really meaning to ask. *Damn it.*

"What?" Python's gaze flickered to his face, and then away just as quick. "Yeah, sure."

"You're acting strange," Calysto continued. *Ah, shut up! Stop asking!* But he couldn't help it. "Are you tired? Do you need to eat?"

"I'm fine, Cal," Python answered, still barely moving. "We should get going, yeah?"

"Yeah, okay," Calysto agreed.

Only then did he look up and realize where they were.

In the street outside of Merik's estate.

The house was dark, windows covered with no semblance of lamplight or movement. It was the perfect time to strike.

"Now what?" Python pulled his hands back, crossing them over his chest.

Calysto was reminded of what had happened between them earlier and had to make effort to speak around the sudden lump in his throat.

He's acting weird because of that, and he doesn't want to talk to me. Obviously.

"Uh, well," Calysto started. "It's likely in his office."

"Where we went the other day?"

"Yeah."

"Okay so..."

"It's that room," Calysto pointed and Python's eyes followed his finger to where he indicated. Near the roof on the top floor, a large arched window loomed. It was nearly fifty feet off of the ground.

"Think you can get up there?" Calysto asked hesitantly and was immediately met with Python's scoff.

"I would rather end my immortal life than spider-crawl up into that asshole's window, Cal. What the fuck do I look like?"

"Like someone who can scale walls and therefore bypass the front fucking door?"

Calysto was followed by a string of curses directed specifically at him and this whole place and Merik and the world at large, as he made his way across the street and led them up to the house.

"What would you even do without me," Python spat as he looked up at the window high above their heads. "Did you even have a different plan?"

Calysto frowned and decided not to answer. "So, can you do it or not?"

"Yeah," Python growled. "Yeah, I can fucking do it, Cal."

"Good, then we shouldn't waste any more time."

NINETEEN

Young Calysto heard the sound of Merik's voice demanding his presence from down the hallway. Like his mother's call of 'boy' this was the same, and as close as it ever got to his actual name. So much so, it would leave Calysto wondering sometimes if he'd ever had a name at all.

Calysto felt like a title he had given himself, a figment of his imagination, an alter ego that he kept close and that no one cared to see or know was there.

Not much different than his outward self then, yeah?

Sometimes he would imagine that Calysto was another person entirely. Well not entirely. Only a better version of himself. He imagined Calysto was a grown man, tall, strong, capable, and unafraid. Calysto was the master of his own world, with the glorious power of magic at his fingertips to call upon at any time.

Young Calysto would lie in his rickety bed—tucked between rows of maids aprons and cleaning implements in the storage closet near the kitchens—and stare at the cobweb-covered ceiling, imagining what he would be, could be, and wanted to be. Not small and afraid, not seething with a buried anger that caused him to act out and talk back, that caused him, in consequence, to get put back into that small and afraid place.

He wouldn't be like that he had decided, not when he was older. He would be everything he wanted to be and more. He would be something he'd never been given, except by one boy many years ago. He would be kind; he would be good. He would help those in need no matter the cost. In fact, there would be no cost. The magic he kept inside him would not be a source of fear for others, and there would be no *need* to fear him because he would help. And if he did enough, if he was good enough, if he tried hard enough, maybe, maybe they could like him. Love him, even.

Maybe, he could have that thing that he saw so many others have.

The way the maids clucked about in the kitchens, mouths full of gossip, stolen treats, and affectionate kisses. The way the hands of one of Merik's patients intertwined with another's when they received news, good or bad. The way people's eyes lingered on the ones they cared for, the silent unspoken comfort of shoulders touching and palms brushing. A gentle press on a lower back, a whole universe communicated in a glance with a complexity that not even those who spoke their own specific language could entirely grasp. Calysto saw it, and he wanted it.

But, would he ever believe he could have it? No, not without earning it, first.

For Calysto was only a boy, made to believe he was even less than that. He was nothing to anyone but a tool. Though even people have their favorite tools, the ones they pick up time and time again. The ones they choose first, the ones they feel a fleeting sadness to lose. And if he could be that, at least. A favorite, for a short time. Worthy, for a little while.

Maybe he could have a taste of it, as much as he was allowed, anyway.

Yet how does one go about earning such a thing? Through service —silent and reticent. Through a diminishing of the soul, the self. Through becoming an empty shell that lives only for others. That fickle, undependable thing—approval, acceptance. Crawling beneath the feet of others to get it, all the while refusing to truly let it in.

His walls were built high with age and time, now stronger with the passing of the decades spent alone, unwanted, unbothered. And as far as our present Calysto was concerned no one even knew he existed.

In his tucked away cabin, far from the reaches of a society of any kind, he lived. Quietly speaking to no one but himself in the hollows of that run-down shack. Long had the time passed when he ever hoped for any kind of response.

Nothing was disturbed or changed if not by his doing. Spiders that dwelled in the high corners of the walls were the only ones to hear his thoughts, should he bother anymore to say them out loud. No one wanted to hear, no one wanted to know. All his effort had amounted to naught, and here he remained, untouched and alone.

Quietly he whiled away the years, one by one, until they blended together in an indecipherable haze of day and night, sun and no sun, sleep and no sleep. From one project to the next, he moved in a daze. Not thinking of anything else, or not trying to, other than what was in front of his hands. What he could make, what he could fix, what he could give.

That tiny sense of purpose, the obsessive focus that came with solving a problem, is what got him through. For nothing else around him could bring any kind of satisfaction or joy. There was no one there to share in his accomplishments, so even he stopped focusing on such a thing. It was almost as if the closer he got to completing a task, the closer the looming dread and yawning emptiness of his vacant life came.

He began to make lists. What to do next, what needed to be done, what thing he could shift his focus to as soon as he completed something else. No time for rest, no space for outside thoughts, no room for the room to feel too empty.

But before this century of solitude, Calysto was under the care and tutelage of Dr. Adriani Merik. Or that's what it was supposed to be. If anything, he was a glorified errand boy, maid, and verbal punching bag for the man.

While Merik may have only ever struck him a few times in what he would later call 'a moment of weakness' while straightening the cuffs of his sleeves and pulling down his waistcoat, he certainly still found many ways to humiliate the boy instead. For the wounds of words strike as deep as a blade on a young, undeserving heart.

Though Calysto received no real education from the doctor, and followed in his shadow doing his best to keep his head down and his presence unacknowledged, he was still a curious boy. And a bright one at that.

With dark solemn eyes, he watched. With sharp ears and an even sharper mind, he listened, and on his own, he learned. About the medicines Merik made, about who was prescribed what and why, and even about simple things like what notes to make when things went wrong, and what chemicals should never be mixed under any circumstances.

Calysto taught himself to read from the handwritten labels and the scribbling of notes scattered across the doctor's desk that he was tasked with cleaning, organizing, and straightening. He had known the basics before, through peeking in spell books and watching over his sister's shoulder as she received an education he wasn't afforded. But in the company and servitude of Merik, the knowledge surrounding him and passing through his fingertips with his daily chores began to catch his attention.

He watched as people were turned away—out of lack of money, mostly. But also, sometimes, because Merik claimed there was nothing he could do for them. If there was anything like a respect for the man that Calysto might've had, it was worn away with every instance like this.

Therefore, Calysto became determined.

He would be the one to fix them—he would be the one to find the answers that supposedly were just 'too much trouble to bother with' for 'people who would die soon anyway'.

Then one evening when he was still a young boy, not yet grown into his hand-me-down breeches, he stole his first book.

It wasn't a good one. Well, it wasn't one he could understand. He had been dusting Merik's long bookshelves for the hundredth time and there it was, tucked near the bottom.

The faded soft leather cover peeled at the edges and withered old pages crinkled with the brittle sound of age. Embossed letters nearly wiped clean with time appeared under his fingers as he smeared the dust away, creating a powdery streak on the surface.

HOMEOPATHY is all it said. He had no idea what it meant.

With a quick look over his shoulder around the empty study, he took a peek inside. Contained within the crisp yellow-brown pages were illustrations of plants, roots, leaves, and fungus. All labeled meticulously in a clean but age-bled typeface. Most of the words made no sense, speaking of remedies and concoctions, poultices, and salves. It didn't matter though. Between the drawings, the potential for knowledge, the musty smell of parchment rife with age, and the history of many hands before him, Calysto was captivated.

So much so, that he almost didn't notice when the doctor entered a moment later. In a flash Calysto slammed the book shut, and still crouched near the floor facing away from the door, he tucked it into the front of his pants.

Later that night in his storage closet bedroom, illuminated by the nub of a candle he'd swiped from the kitchen trash bin, he poured over the letters he didn't understand. Running his cracked work-worn fingertips over the surface of the pictures, flipping back and forth between pages to memorize their differences.

The next day he stole a clean piece of parchment and the next a discarded quill. He stuffed blocks of charcoal from the fireplace into his pockets, hurrying in any free moment to stash them deep beneath the shelves behind his cot, in a place they would be hidden but also wouldn't be crushed. Too many times the burnt wood had turned to dust in his pants before he had the chance to take it out, marring his hands with blackened powder and his mood with sour thoughts.

His fingers became increasingly sticky as the days wore on and soon he had an only-slightly-cracked vial, a small wooden holder, a cork, a handful of charcoal, and a pocket full of gummy sap.

Young Calysto's first experiment—the beginning of countless thousands that would define his life for ages to come—was the attempt to make ink.

And he failed. Over and over.

Water with charcoal was too thin, grainy, and all the soot would settle at the bottom of the vial. Charcoal mixed with resin gum was better, but too thick and sticky, coagulating into a wad that stained everything it touched, and nearly adhering itself permanently to the in-between spaces of his fingers.

Since he still had no way yet to write down his findings, his thoughts, and his ideas for a different approach, he kept the notes tucked inside his head as he tried again and again.

And again.

This particular night though, it was different. He had swiped a mortar and pestle from the kitchens, intent on sneaking back late in the early morning to return it before anyone noticed it was missing. Crossed-legged on the cold stone floor, knobby growing knees pressed up against shelves of flour and corn, a broom and a mop, he placed his implements in front of him.

Mortar and pestle, a lump of charcoal, the last remnants of the stolen resin gum, a small tin cup of water, a capful of alcohol, the vial, and to the side a quill and parchment riddled with evidence of his past attempts.

Carefully, one by one, he added the ingredients into the mortar, measurements made with a watchful eye that was aware of where he'd gone wrong before. The pestle crushed the hardened gum into a fine dust and the charcoal soon followed. Then carefully, drop by drop, he added the water, then the alcohol in smaller measure. Slowly, slowly. He never took his eyes off of the swirling black paste that began to form, as the soft grate of the pestle filled the small space with its quiet stone song. Then seeming satisfied, or perhaps now a bit impatient, he grasped the quill and dipped it in.

His breath came in slow even strides as he tried to keep himself calm but could barely anticipate seeing the results. The quill laden with his experiment ran down across the paper in one straight line. And there it lay, a clean trail of smooth solid black.

He had done it. He had made ink.

Calysto nearly broke the quill with his sudden burst of adrenaline and a good few seconds were spent in celebration, as he wiggled excitedly and muffled a small yell behind his hands.

This was it. A rare moment of joy he had created all for himself. By himself.

It was the most exhilarating and satisfying thing he'd ever done. He took a few deep breaths to calm himself before carefully pouring the ink into the vial and the vial into the holder. He rushed to the kitchen on quiet bare feet, washed the mortar and pestle in the dish bucket, dumped the blackened water outside of the kitchen door, returned the tools to their rightful place, then made his way back into his room.

Finally, finally, with all of his worries cared for and his tracks covered, he sat down again on the floor. This time with the quill, steady in his hand.

Calysto.

Calysto is what he wrote. The first word created with the fruit of his labor and the careful deductions of his mind. The name he was never called, that often felt like a figment of his imagination and just a silent wish for something to be acknowledged by. It was real, right there in front of him. His name.

He wrote it again. He looked down as the ink slowly sank in and spread into the pulpy fibers of the paper, drying with each small breath from his mouth as he leaned closer to inspect it.

Calysto.

It was real.

He was real, he existed, and here was the proof. No longer an accessory in another's life, a servant without a name that ever passed the lips of anyone he knew. The moment he wrote it down he could feel it. He was more than that which they saw him as. He was this. He could be. He would be.

Calysto's inquisitiveness had always gotten the better of him— asking things when he shouldn't, peering into boxes and books and jars that were not his own, eavesdropping through doors on conversations of Merik's and the maids that were personal and professional alike. Just to see, just to know, just to hear, just to be included.

But with these tools of his making at his fingertips he wouldn't have to store all those mysterious misunderstood words in his mind, where he turned them around and around searching for meaning. He could write them down—if he could figure out how to spell them. He could remember, he could decipher, he could learn.

There wasn't anything that would stop him now. Not Merik's berating words that rang so much like his mother's with the familiar weight of his inadequacies. Not the limits of his own ability to read.

He had observed Merik deep in thought, drawing from the pages of a book lined with terms and what he called 'definitions' long enough to know how to find the meanings for those lost words, and where to store them.

He was supposed to be Merik's apprentice, but ultimately was his uneducated lackey and receptacle for any outlet of frustration. Whether for something as petty as the result of a missed payment, failed experiment, misplaced item, or the scissors and the spectacles switched places on the exam tray. Instead, in his own time Calysto would become that apprentice, yet in this secret and obsessively observant way.

He learned through the pages of stolen texts and overheard ramblings that Merik would mumble until they began to make sense. Calysto would sift through Merik's notes as he organized the doctor's desk at the end of each day, taking what knowledge he could, absorbing anything as quickly as his eyes could read, and feigning the busyness of his hands.

Merik still treated him the same, barely sparing him a glance or a moment of humanity or time. But as Calysto grew he moved past the need for these things from such a man. All he wanted was his mind and keeping himself as small as possible and out of the way had proven the best way to access it.

The doctor was none the wiser, carrying on with his carefully structured routine in his neatly pressed shirts and waistcoats embroidered in the finest golden silk thread, eating his meals made of meats and vegetables that most could never afford, making his notes on precious parchment only to wad it up and throw it in the trash. Yes, Merik carried on as normal, not knowing or caring that his little apprentice who grew taller and lankier and longer than his clothes more and more every day, had also outgrown his childish mind, and had become as inquisitive and knowledgeable almost as himself.

That is, until the day that Calysto made a mistake.

Merik was seeing a patient—a young woman in her thirties, with soft amber curls peeking out from underneath a silk bonnet. She was dressed to the nines as if coming to see the doctor were as big of an affair as a fancy dinner party in which one was trying their best to impress their guests and piss off the hired help. Still, she sat on the cold paper-covered exam table the same as all who passed through these doors, button-booted feet crossed daintily at the ankles, with velvet-gloved hands folded in her lap. Her thumbs fidgeted nervously as she watched the doctor stand from his seat and walk away behind his desk.

Her eyes caught on Calysto staring at her, silent as a ghost from his usual position in the corner. She jumped slightly and stilled her hands, then shot him a nervous-polite smile that he didn't return. He didn't see the point in smiling for no reason.

What did she hope to achieve? A feeble attempt at comfort? To soothe herself by reaching out for kindness from another? Well, kindness didn't come for free. Young Calysto had learned that much. And he didn't particularly like being used for another's anxious grasp at validation either. Plus, she was clearly wealthy. He didn't have a reason to care about her.

She could buy her reassurance somewhere else.

Calysto looked away and focused his attention on Merik instead. The doctor didn't speak as he picked up his quill and tapped the tip once on the table before writing something down in his large ledger, blowing the ink until it dried, and closing it again.

He stood, straightened his sleeves, and made his way to a large locked glass cabinet that held a various array of medicines. Treatments of all kinds lined the shelves inside small cotton pouches, wrapped in tiny waxed paper foils, filling jars and vials stopped with small corks. Merik reached inside and pulled out a pouch of powdery capsules that smelled of wet earth.

Calysto continued to watch as Merik gave the pills to the woman, with instructions on how to consume and care for them. The woman took the small satchel, tucked it neatly underneath the contents of her handbag, and made her way to the door.

All was still after she left as Calysto slowly emerged and began to change the paper on the table where it had wrinkled from the woman's bottom nervously twitching upon it. His brows were furrowing in a thoughtful frown, and he was chewing over something heavy on his mind. Finally, after he changed the paper, he took the soiled pieces over to the fireplace and threw them in. He stood there watching the waxed bits melt and the paper shrivel up and disappear.

Then, said in a tone as if he couldn't hold it in any longer, Calysto quietly spoke, "Doctor?"

"What is it," Merik barely acknowledged him.

"Considering the symptoms, wouldn't Milk of Magnesia be a better treatment for the woman? Certainly, if there is another more serious underlying cause to her discomfort, it would be best determined if first ruling out the more obvious causes such as monthly menstruation and ovulation cycles that cause varying levels of pain and abdominal upset."

As soon as he said it, Calysto knew he'd done wrong. The crackle of the fireplace was suddenly deafening in his ears as the sound of Merik's quill on the parchment scratched to a halt.

"What did you just say to me, boy?"

Calysto swallowed hard, realizing the magnitude of his mistake. But he didn't want to back down. He cleared his throat once, then turned towards the desk and spoke again.

"I just think it would be a better option than the dandelion extract you gave her."

As Calysto looked up he met Merik's eyes and saw them flash with surprise and disbelief, that, as he watched, hardened into boiling anger.

"Snooping in my cabinets when you shouldn't be then, are we?" Calysto didn't answer before Merik continued, "Or is it the libraries, the study? Don't think I haven't seen you spending more time dusting those shelves than is reasonably required."

"Why shouldn't I?" Calysto blurted, feeling emboldened. "I'm your apprentice, am I not? Or did you forget the purpose of that, too?"

He should have seen it coming, he should have watched his mouth, he shouldn't have said anything in the first place.

These are all things he told himself later when he had time to reflect and his tongue wasn't one step ahead of his rational mind.

But should've's and could've's can't change the past.

Merik's heavy leather chair hit the shelf behind it with a loud bang, and before Calysto could move more than two steps backward Merik was upon him. His back pressed against the hot stone of the fireplace and Calysto winced as Merik leaned in, looking him up and down from inches away like a vulture inspecting the carrion gripped between its talons for a nip at the juiciest bite. Calysto pressed his lips together tight against the pain and refused to show the discomfort across his face. Still, his heart was thundering beneath his thin cotton shirt as he waited there, resigning himself to his fate.

"Apprentice, hmm? Is that what you think you are, boy?" Merik pulled away, meeting Calysto's watery yet defiant glare. "Who told you that?"

"You did," Calysto bit back.

"Oh? When? When that crone you called a mother sold you to me for less than the price of the clothes on your back? Is that what you thought? That I'd teach you something?" Merik jostled Calysto in his hand. "Clearly, you haven't learned much, then."

"Then what am I," Calysto scowled. "To you."

Merik sucked in a quick breath then let it out with a mocking bark.

"You must be joking. Your mother claimed you had magic and yet you have never shown it. Not once in all these years have you given me an ounce of what I've asked for. A simple task for someone as supposedly powerful as you, wouldn't you think? So do you think you're anything to me, boy?"

Despite it all, it still stung a little bit for Calysto to hear and he stammered, "N-no."

"Good. Don't get any other ideas."

Merik backed off, and the pressure released from Calysto's chest. But before he could right himself the doctor turned to him again.

"And don't you correct me again, do you understand? Snoop all you'd like, but don't you dare presume to know more than me."

Calysto could let go of the fact that Merik thought nothing of him. He had always known that anyway. He could accept that he was useless, that he'd in part created his own suffering by refusing to perform parlor tricks of magic on metal to help the greedy old codger get his gold.

But this, this he couldn't accept.

"Why not? You didn't say I was wrong."

The tension between them grew palpable as Merik pinched his lips tight before forcing a halting response.

"You want to learn something, boy? Well, listen to this then. Wealth is not made off of charity, nor is it made from healing the sick.

Naturally, that woman would benefit from Magnesia, which she will receive once she returns next to week to complain of the dandelion not working and that the pain remains. She will begin to worry more, fretting over the persistence of her condition, afraid of the possibility of it being an incurable ailment. She will pay more for whatever I suggest, should it truly be the cure or not. Medicine is a business, not an altruistic pursuit."

Calysto listened, hands pressed behind him on the rough brick of the fireplace, not taking his eyes off of a loose thread dangling from Merik's waistcoat.

"So..." he began after Merik was silent. "You will cure her only after you've robbed her blind?"

Merik turned again to face him, this time with a sneer etched on his moustache-covered lips.

"And who's to say she can be cured? It's nothing but a game of dependency, boy. Magnesia will make her feel better for a time, but soon it will cease. By this time, we will have built a rapport and she will put her trust in me. The medicine that gave her some relief came from my hands, after all. But her symptoms are clear, and she will be dead within the year. She has no use for the wealth she possesses."

Merik's words sank in with a sickening dread, as Calysto began to understand just what he was saying. He thought of the woman with her pale face drawn tight, and the way she looked to him for reassurance. He heard what kind of pain she was in and offered her no relief. Despite his resentment of her status, he began to feel a bit guilty that he had been so callous. Granted, he hadn't known her case was so severe, perhaps he would have been nicer, then.

She had come here with the hopes of trustworthy treatment from the city's most respected doctor and yet was met with a con man, a dishonest thief who would swindle her out of every penny, all the way to the sheets of her death bed.

Calysto resented Merik for a lot of things—and rightfully so, as we have witnessed—but Calysto had also never loved himself. He had never seen the worth that he held, simply by the fact that he existed. That need to earn it was buried deep within him, and the cruelty he experienced at the hands of others he always had thought, at least a little bit, that he'd deserved it.

Even if indignant and stubborn, even if outwardly a bit rebellious towards the authority imposed upon him, it was near impossible for him to survive such a place, such a situation, such abuse, and escape completely unharmed—completely secure in himself and his choices. And young Calysto, with no one to tell him otherwise, took all the blame onto himself.

No one had ever shown him he deserved any more than that.

So in spite of this bitterness towards his master, he still didn't often feel the urge to stand up for himself.

It's hard to say what was different this time from all the other days that Merik had turned a poor patient away, or diagnosed someone incorrectly, or simply spoken in a manner that talked down to those in need, those in pain. But suddenly faced again with Merck's cruelty—and not only towards him—Calysto was angry.

Near the fireplace still warming the backs of his legs and crackling against long shadows on the red stone, Calysto clenched his fists. His ears began to burn hot beneath the shaggy cut of his golden ponytail.

"You're a fraud," he said softly through clenched teeth.

Dr. Merik spun around, this time with a barely controlled anger behind his sharp eyes.

"Say that again, won't you, boy."

It was a warning, one that Calysto purposefully ignored in favor of stoking the coals in his aching chest.

"You're a fraud," he said again. "You're a killer. You sell people what, false hope? For money? You greedy bast—"

This would be only the second time that Merik would hit him, but it would also be the last.

"You ungrateful shit," Merik growled over the figure of Calysto as the boy held his cheek. "Without me you'd have been bones in a manure pit years ago. I took you in…"

"Yeah," Calysto spat between the pain in his teeth. "For a price."

All at once he was being dragged by the arm, stumbling over his feet and bleary-eyed from the slap. Calysto nearly fell as Merik half-hauled him down the long redwood staircase. The vice grip on his bicep was biting sharp, digging in to leave bruises that would ache for weeks to come. Finally, as he gathered himself and recovered from the shock, he began to protest.

"Hey! Let me go… Let me go!"

Merik didn't respond. He only continued to drag the boy along by an arm thin enough to be entirely engulfed by his meaty palm. Down the winding staircase, into the foyer, tripping across the lavishly embroidered floral print rug, through the kitchens—where the maids stopped and gawked, but none dared interfere—and down the hallway to the storage closet that was Calysto's room. Merik shouldered the door open and with one strong heave, and slung Calysto's wiry frame inside.

Calysto fell against the shelves with a crash, his face nearly missed colliding with a solid canvas bag full of flour. Something rolled onto the floor and broke and between it all he heard Merik's voice behind him.

"I don't know where you get off presuming to speak to me in such a manner, boy. But you will do well to remember your place here."

Calysto breathed hard, seething anger steeling his stare as he looked up at the doctor looming in the doorway.

"I do not want to see you again until you do. You will stay here until you learn to keep your obstinate mouth shut, do you understand?"

Before Calysto could find the words to retort, Merik had slammed the closet door shut, bathing Calysto in darkness. He heard the distinct click of a lock, and with it came the cold realization of fear spiking through his chest. He scrambled towards it grasping at the handle, but it wouldn't budge.

"Hey!" he yelled, pounding his fists on the rough wooden door. "Let me out! You can't... you can't leave me in here!"

The only response he received was the sound of footsteps slowly fading away down the long empty corridor.

PART THREE
RESONANCE

TWENTY

"Alright, if I'm doing this, you're coming with me," Python grumbled.

"Naturally, I assumed you could carry us both," Calysto responded and walked behind Python, preparing himself to once again jump onto his back.

"Well, obviously I can, but do I want to? That's a different story."

"Will you stop complaining!" Calysto snapped. "We need to hurry!"

"Fine, fine," Python sighed and crouched. After Calysto leapt, Python grabbed his calves and pulled them closer. "Hang on tight, okay? If you fall from that height, you'll die."

"What, you're not gonna catch me?"

"No, bitch, I'm not gonna catch you. I'll be hanging on to the fucking wall. Want me to fall, too?"

"Okay, damn, I'm not gonna fall."

Python took a moment to gaze up at the long ascent in front of him. It was a vertical climb of gritty red brick evenly placed with thick grey mortar. A bit above eye level were decorative metal sconces of wrought iron filigree, cut into the brick in an unnecessary show of wealth and decorative extravagance. But above where one would naturally look was only solid stone blocks. One window was visible from where he stood, and another singular one even higher above that, nearing the awning of the curved shingled roof.

"Which one, again?" he asked without looking away.

"The top one."

"Of course it's the fucking top one," Python responded, before sighing and fitting his fingers against the stone. "Let's go then."

He felt Calysto's arms tighten around him as he began his ascent. It was easy enough. He had made a bigger deal out of it than it needed to be and barely exerted himself even with the tips of his fingers and toes to support them both.

Yet he went slowly, as each bit of the climb was accompanied by grout and gravel from the wall loosening and falling to the ground beneath them. If anyone walked by it would be a clear yet strange giveaway, and might cause them to look up.

"Hey Cal..." Python broke the silence with a soft whisper between them.

"Huh?" Cal's breath brushed the back of his ear.

"How do you know this guy? Like, present you, I mean."

"Uh..."

He heard Cal swallow before he answered.

"I knew him as a kid," Calysto said, with a tightness in his voice that made it clear it was much more than whatever he was willing to give away.

"Oh." Python got the hint for once and didn't pry.

"He's a fucking asshole," Cal continued. "I don't know if you've noticed."

"Ha, I definitely did." Python grinned even though Calysto couldn't see it. "Even if he thought you were someone else."

"I told you I don't know what that's about."

"Yeah, yeah I know." Python stopped to rest his feet for a moment on the first windowsill. "Just... what is he, your dad or something?"

"... No," Calysto said slowly. "He um, bought me."

"Bought?"

"Mm."

"Oh, um, sorry."

"It's fine now."

"Is it, though?"

Calysto didn't answer right away. The fingers clasped under Python's chin fidgeted with the hem of his collar.

"Not really."

"Thus the sneaking?" Python asked.

"Thus the sneaking," Calysto agreed.

"Okay, well we're almost there."

"Good."

CALYSTO WONDERED if Python could feel the pounding of his heart beneath his shirt, and the nervous sweat that was accumulating in his palms and pooling in his pits. One brief encounter with Merik was e-fucking-nough thank you, and now they were about to break into his house via vampire-facilitated wall-climbing tactics. If they were caught... well, Calysto didn't want to think about it.

Sure, they could easily escape, but what about the confrontation that came beforehand? Even the simple idea of it made him want to curl up in a ball and roll away into the nearest gutter. He glanced down far below him and decided that a quick plummet to the ground would be preferable.

"Hey," Python hissed back at him. "Calm down, it's gonna be fine."

Shit.

"Y-yeah. Sure. I know."

"Yeah, okay," Python scoffed. "You straight up sound like an entire snack right now, so sorry if I doubt that a little bit."

"Didn't you just eat yesterday?"

"That's why I said snack."

Calysto could feel Python's cheeky grin beaming at him even in the dark. His cheeks suddenly felt wind chafed hot against the cool of the night and he frowned, squashing his lips together as he did. Even still, despite how Python teased, he didn't feel afraid that Python would actually eat him, somehow he even doubted it. So why then, was he getting so flustered?

He readjusted his grip around Python's neck and decided not to think about it. He buried his face into the bone of Python's shoulder, waiting for it to be over.

"Alright, um," Python spoke up after another quiet moment of climbing. "Looks like no one's inside."

Calysto popped his head up and realized Python was standing with feet straddling the high windowsill, his arms outstretched and bracing himself at the top. Then, he realized something else.

"I don't know how to get down," he admitted.

"What? Oh, shit," Python half-laughed. "I didn't think about that. Um... here. I'll climb to the side and you just step off into the edge."

As he spoke, he moved to cling to the wall outside of the sill.

"Okay, go."

Calysto suddenly gripped tighter around him. "I'm... I can't. I'm gonna fall."

"You won't fall," Python said.

"Python, I can't." Calysto tried to keep his tone steady but inside he was sure he was near to shaking apart.

"I won't let you fall, okay?"

"I thought you didn't care," Calysto bit out through gritted teeth.

"Yeah well, I lied!" Python snapped. "Just fucking trust me. Get on the fucking sill, Cal."

"Fucking hell."

Calysto tried to force his fingers to unfurl from Python's coat and release his legs which were beginning to ache from the effort of being clenched around him in a vice grip.

"Go slow, I've got this," Python murmured. "Don't look down."

"Saying not to look down makes me immediately want to look down, thanks."

"Sorry."

Calysto didn't respond and concentrated on shimmying a foot out onto the windowsill.

"Fuck me," he whispered with a shaky breath.

Python might've snorted behind him but he was much too focused on slowly extracting himself off the vampire's back and onto the balancing beam fifty feet above a rock-hard gravel street below.

Oh, okay. Nope. Not thinking about that right now.

Finally, he scrambled all the way over and gripped the edges of the window frame with shaking hands. Python immediately joined him, slipping a protective arm around his waist.

"S-sorry." Calysto stammered. "Uh, if I was squeezing you too tight."

Python chuckled in his ear. "Don't worry about it. So, what're we doing? Breaking the window?"

"That seems way too loud of an approach, but..." Calysto leaned forward towards the frame. "Will you... keep holding onto me, please."

"I got you." Python flexed his hand on Calysto's hip as a reminder.

"Okay, um, if I remember correctly there's a..." Calysto reached into the pocket of his coat and produced the squished pack of cigarettes.

"Oh, that's where those went," Python remarked. "Remind me that I want to smoke the whole pack when this is over."

Calysto opened them up, ripped off the paper lid, and reached over to tuck the box into Python's front coat pocket.

"There," he said quietly.

He took the square piece of cardboard and flattened it out with more stable hands. Python's gentle grip on his waist was admittedly a reassuring presence and allowed him to focus on what was right in front of him and not the... *Nope.*

Right in front of him, only.

From his other pocket, he pulled out the small light wand he carried with him, and murmured softly at it and it began to glow.

"Woah..." Python's iridescent eyes widened in the warm subtle light as he watched.

Calysto crouched slightly towards the windowsill edge and using the light to guide him, slipped the paper between the frames. He shimmied it slightly up and down, quietly working but hyper-aware of Python watching his every move. Then, there was a muffled click and the window popped open slightly by an inch.

"There," Calysto whispered.

"How did you... Never mind, tell me later," Python whispered back. "You go first."

"So chivalrous, thank you," Calysto deadpanned.

Truly he was grateful, as he realized he would absolutely rather jump into this room and be the one to scope it out first, rather than tumble backward the moment Python released him.

With one last deep breath, he pushed the window open all the way and slipped into Merik's office.

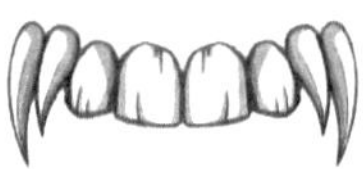

THE SUBTLE ORANGE-YELLOW glow from Calysto's magical flashlight-wand-stick-thing created a warm bleed onto the floor around them, dimly lighting the surfaces of the room. Python was completely out of his element, having no idea what they were really doing here, or what they were looking for. Calysto had said a crystal, but that could be anything. There were a lot of types of crystals in the world.

So, as he slowly followed Calysto around the study on quiet feet, he took in the surroundings, looking for anything that might resemble such an object.

On one side of the room was a patient exam table covered in

brown leather, worn to bleaching and riddled with cracks. To its side were tables neatly clothed in waxed paper and exam instruments arranged in a meticulous manner atop them.

The walls on all sides were lined with shelves. Some were closed and locked, with glass cabinetry doors sealing various arrays of jars, vials, and beakers away. Python caught the sight of a gelatinous mass floating around in of them and wrinkled his nose. Other shelves were riddled with books, all as neatly arranged as the instruments on the table. But what Python noticed the most was the pungent odor of chemical cleaners and preservatives wiped over the scent of blood.

"Cal!" he hissed. "Just what is this place?"

Calysto didn't answer so Python turned to find him. He was crouched in the corner near the floor, holding the light out over a pocket-sized brown leather book.

He was very, very still.

"Cal?" Python approached in a flash and crouched near his side. "What is it?"

"Oh," Calysto frowned, seeming to break out of a subtle trance. "Something I thought I'd lost," he said cryptically while tucking the little book into his pocket.

"Sorry, let's go. It's not here. We have to go downstairs."

"What?" Python hissed. "Downstairs like, in this house? What the fuck did I climb the wall for?"

"I said sorry."

Python shot a look at him and stood. "Alright, whatever we need to do to get back I'm doing it, so lead the way, doctor."

"Don't call me that." Calysto abruptly walked away towards the door. "I'm nothing like him."

"Okay, touchy."

"Be quiet!" Calysto hissed. "Keep an eye out, will you?"

"Have been, will do." Python waved his hand around the room. "Vampire sense, remember."

"Oh…" Calysto cleared his throat. "Right. Okay, follow me."

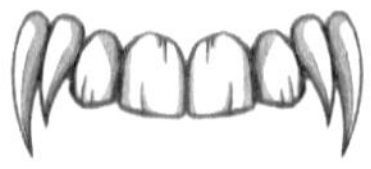

CALYSTO STUCK to the edge of the long winding wooden staircase, with one hand carefully skimming the railing of the banister. Python tracked silently behind him, and Calysto wondered if he hadn't been intentionally stepping in places he knew the stairs wouldn't squeak, if Python would still be as quiet. It was as if his feet never touched the ground, or something about being a vampire made him extra sneaky and weightless, floating right above the surface of where normal people influenced by gravity couldn't touch.

At first, he'd found it a bit creepy, that Python's mouth was the loudest thing on him and the rest lingered around like a ghost, dead and haunting. But now in a strange sense, it was comforting. He liked the feeling of turning around and finding someone there, even when he didn't expect them to be. Like Python always had his back, just like he did on the windowsill.

It was a bit odd. To find himself thinking this way about it, when Python didn't seem to give much of a fuck about anyone.

It was artificial and he knew it.

Python kept coming back to him because they were in a strange place, in a fucked up situation, in their own goddamned past, and not only was it Calysto's fault to begin with, he was also Python's only hope of getting back.

Still, he had to admit that even if it was a farce, the feeling of companionship—albeit a headache-inducingly antagonistic one— regardless of being unfamiliar to him and mostly bothersome and completely disruptive to his creative process and generally loud and annoying and pushy and irritating... was kind of nice.

He wasn't alone anymore. Someone actually answered him when he spoke aloud, even if it was mostly with a condescending and unhelpfully sarcastic remark. Python wasn't all bad though, and his constant presence became a reassurance that Calysto was starting to expect.

This was extremely dangerous territory of course, for Calysto knew the moment Python left—which he certainly would once they got back—that his comfortable cocoon of solitude and silence would suddenly fail to feel right. Like that one time he'd accidentally tossed his favorite sweater in the laundromat dryer and had to suffer through nearly a week straight of wearing it when it was too tight until it fit again. Yeah, kind of like that.

"Hey," Calysto whispered.

"What?"

"What'll you do?" Calysto didn't want to ask, but he also needed to know. "You know, when we get back?"

Python didn't answer right away, and Calysto had a spark of doubt that maybe he'd spoken too quietly. But then he heard the vampire's response.

"Oh... I don't know," he said slowly. "Get out of your hair, I guess."

"Oh..."

"Why?"

"Never mind." Calysto waved his hand as they reached the bottom of the steps. "It's this way."

"Are you sure this time?" Python's ice-cold breath tickled across his neck.

"Yeah."

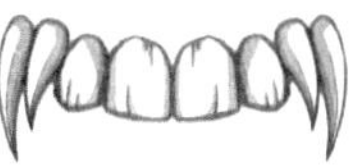

Calysto was about to step off of the staircase when Python grabbed his arm, pulling his ear towards him.

"Wait!" he hissed. "I smell smoke."

Calysto instantly froze, bicep tensing beneath Python's hand. "Smoke?"

"Yeah, um... someone could be awake," Python sniffed again as the scent grew stronger. "That's definitely a fire of some kind."

Calysto stiffened even further. "I... Uh, it's probably just a fireplace, right?"

"Probably, Cal. But that means someone's awake, doesn't it?"

"There's seven fireplaces in here, not to mention the kitchen hearth, they could be anywhere."

"Okay, just think it's best if we be careful."

"Yeah, yeah," Calysto swallowed hard.

Python went to release him, expecting Calysto to jerk or step away and was surprised to find he didn't. Calysto stayed very close, chest brushing his arm. He hesitated at the mouth of the living area and was tense to the point of nearly shaking. Calysto hadn't seemed calm before, but it was quickly escalating.

"Cal!" He shook the little warlock slightly. "Keep it together."

Calysto bit his lip and scowled.

"Look, I know this is fucked up," Python continued. "I don't know exactly what you're worried about, but I'm not gonna let anything happen to you, alright?"

That caught his attention, and he met Python's eyes.

"You won't?"

The warm orange glow from his wand illuminated the planes of his sharply featured face and his eyes were as just as molten. Python studied him back, and for a quiet moment they both seemed to forget about much else besides trying to read into one another's eyes. To find the truth of how the other felt beyond all the attitude and the spite and the lies.

"No," Python finally answered. "I won't. But the longer we stand here the more likely we are to get caught, right?"

"Oh." Calysto nodded. "You're right. Let's go."

Before they had a chance to move any further Python pulled Calysto closer again and hissed, "Wait."

"Mm?"

His whisper came out more insistent, and urgent, "I was wrong. That's not a fireplace... it's ..."

"It's... what?"

"That's a fucking fire alright."

He stepped around Calysto, placing his body in front of the warlock on the steps and sniffing the air like a cat.

"Like a house fire, I'm sure of it. Tastes like chemicals."

Calysto didn't answer.

"I'm going to check it out."

"No!" Calysto blurted, a little too loud. "Don't."

"What? Why not?" Python spun around and took a long look at him.

His amber eyes were glassy and shifting nervously, and the expression creeping across his face was closely resembling a muted terror.

Python could smell it—that sour stench of adrenaline sweat—oozing from his pores, building with every breath, seeping a spreading poison through his veins with each panicked flutter of his rapidly beating heart. The man standing before him, usually a bit neurotic and clearly full of his own particular quirks and peculiarities, was not ever this nervous. Even when they actually traveled back in time into their own goddamned past, he hadn't acted like this. It didn't make sense, exactly. Sure, Python had freaked out then in his own way too, though thankfully his dead heart didn't give him away. But this, this was different. Calysto looked on the verge of some type of collapse, gripping the banister with white knuckles as if it was the only thing to keep him upright.

"Cal!" Python shook him to attention. "What is it?"

"I can't..." Calysto ground out between clenched teeth. "I can't do this, I'm sorry, I can't I..."

Python looked at him and back over towards the far hallway, where the smell of smoke was beginning to grow, wafting over to where even Calysto's normal nose could detect it.

"What do you mean you can't?" he snapped impatiently. "Someone is definitely going to notice this soon, we gotta get your shit and go!"

"No!" Cal shook Python's hand loose. "I w-won't... I won't..."

"Fuck Cal! I'll fucking do it. Tell me what to get!"

"I... Uh..."

"Calysto!" Python barked his full name. It caught Calysto's attention, and their eyes met. "Focus!"

Calysto rubbed his temples with the hand that he wasn't using as a lifeline to keep himself standing. "Uh, yes. Um, purple... Um, large purple crystal. Do you... Do you remember the one in my house?"

"Yeah, yeah, I remember."

"There's two, in that room um... somewhere, I know there's a um... just grab one." He motioned with his head down the back hallway that Python could see was slowly filling with smoke.

"Okay, okay fuck it. I'll find it." Python took a step down and paused. "Wait for me outside."

"Yeah uh... yeah, okay..." Calysto swayed a bit before slowly jerking his head in a semblance of a nod.

As soon as he saw Calysto stumble in the direction of the front door, Python flashed across the front living area and down the hall. The door to the room in question was spewing smoke from underneath the gap near the floor, and Python could feel the heat permeating through the wood. With no time to waste, he kicked the door in and at the same time heard a scream. It came from inside.

Shit! Someone's in here!

As the door swung open smoke billowed out into Python's face. He winced against it but it didn't bother him like it might have once have when he was alive. Even then, he was so used to it by the time he died that smoke was as much a part of him as it was second nature to breathe it in. He waved his hand to clear his sight and stepped into the midst of it.

The flames were blinding, already climbing the walls and nearly covering the floor, red and orange creating their own harrowing glow and lighting the otherwise dark room.

Glass was scattered on the floor and wooden shelves fell to the ground, sending more jars and vials crashing down. It looked to be a lab, or storage room of some kind, full to the brim on all sides with shelving and cases, long rows of supplies and vats, barrels and jars. All of it quickly being consumed by the flames. The sound was deafening to his sensitive ears, and Python tried to focus, looking around at the items that remained in the firelight.

Everything's already fucking destroyed!

Python wasn't immune to fire, but he was more resistant than most. So he took his steps in a hurried but cautious manner, smoke blinding him at every turn. The room wasn't that big, it shouldn't be that hard to find the stones if they were even still in there. He wasn't sure what to do if they weren't.

Then he heard it again. Not a full-bodied scream like before, but a small one, one that was choking on smoke, near a whimper. Someone was definitely in here.

"Hey!" Python called out over the growing roar and sound of crackling wood. "Where are you?"

"Help...!" a small voice replied. It came from a far back corner. "Please!"

Another whimper reached his ears, and with the crystal forgotten Python dashed over in the direction of the voice.

He reached out through the smoke. "Grab my hand!"

A small trembling hand reached back and held his fingers. It was a boy. Python reached out and scooped him up while shouting, "Hold on, I'll get you out of here!"

The boy came easily into his arms and gripped his shirt tight. Python heard soft whimpers against his shoulder as he frantically searched for a way out.

"Back door," the boy in his arms choked out. "There's a back door!"

"Got it!"

Python gripped the boy tight and ran toward the far end of the room. Sure enough, he found a wooden door now licked clean to collapsing with flames. He kicked it, and a burst of fresh air hit his face. In a flash, he bolted outside and down the street, far from the house which was quickly being consumed outside the confines of the room.

He slowed to a stop as he reached a small alleyway. The boy hadn't made a sound the entire time, only clinging tightly to Python with one hand and the other wrapped tightly around his middle.

"Alright." Python went to set him down. "You're safe now. Are you hurt?"

The boy released him and immediately clenched both hands around his stomach, hiding something. Python's eyes were still stinging from the smoke and he rubbed them before taking a good look at the boy. He looked to be about sixteen, but extraordinarily thin, long and lanky like he hadn't fully grown into his proportions just yet. His eyes were streaming with silent tears, and staring up at Python in a mixture of fear and perhaps disbelief.

He was badly burnt and the cotton shirt he was wearing stuck to large wet blistering welts across his torso, and the side of his face was bleeding in rivers down his neck. But the boy didn't even seem to notice. He just kept watching Python carefully, squinting in silence.

Something about it felt familiar, *but what?*

"Shit, you're really hurt, we need to get you to a hospital," Python breathed, concern lacing his tone.

The boy shook his head, wrapping his arms further around himself, coughing a few times and sniffling thickly.

"Don't worry," Python said carefully. "I'm not gonna hurt you, I just want to help."

The boy still didn't answer.

"Uh... okay..." Python was beginning to feel a bit awkward. Helpless. "What's that you've got there?"

The boy's eyes widened and he shook his head, curling his knees into his oozing chest.

"Look, I'm not... it's okay, alright? I was... I was looking for something in that room, and maybe you can tell me where to find it? It's like a purple crystal or stone or something... I'm not really sure. It's for a friend, it's... it's important."

Then the boy paused. He trembled with every movement as he slowly opened his arms and revealed what he guarded against him. Wrapped in a canvas cloth were two dark lavender crystals, both similar in size.

"Oh, shit..." Python breathed. "Why do you have those?"

"Why do you need one?" The boy finally spoke, his throat husky and raw.

"Uh... my um, my friend and I need to get back home. He said he needs one of those to do it, that's all." Python shrugged. "I really don't know how it works, kid."

"You... you saved me," the boy said then, sounding surprised.

Python wasn't certain, but it might've been a question.

"Well, sure," Python answered. "What, you think I'd let you die in there?"

"... I dunno..." The boy looked down and shivered, pinching his lips and closing his eyes.

"Hey, kid, seriously, we should get you to a doctor, okay? What about Merik, won't he help?"

"No!" Even through his pain, the boy was suddenly alert. "No, no don't... don't take me back!"

"Shit, alright, I won't then..." Python raised his hands in defense. "But you've been badly burnt kid, let me take you somewhere to get help."

"I can fix it," is all he said in response.

"What? How?"

"I just can!"

"Alright, alright," Python sighed. "I can't leave you here, though."

"Yes, you can." The boy squinted up at him, then he seemed to be thinking hard and frowned slightly. "My name's not... not kid."

"Oh?" Python quirked a small smile. "What is it then?"

The boy was silent again, staring at him and breathing slow, raspy breaths, as if gauging whether or not he should answer. He was in shock, and seemed to be trying to make out Python's face in the dark through bleary eyes. His spidery fingers fiddled with the facets of the crystals in his lap.

He grabbed one and held it out to Python.

"Here... for... for helping me," he said softly, not meeting his eyes.

Python took it carefully. "Thanks, kid."

"My name's Calysto."

Despite its importance and the precious nature of its limited existence, Python nearly dropped the crystal in the street.

TWENTY-ONE

Calysto bolted out of Merik's front door and didn't look back. He didn't know if Python was fireproof but he sure as hell wasn't, and he wasn't about to get anywhere near exactly what he knew was about to happen. Why did it have to happen like this? What kind of god awful cosmic timing was he cursed with? Stuck in a situation built specifically for him to be the butt of some cruel and elaborate joke.

Not only did they fucking travel back in time and come back to his past, but it had to be this specific time, this specific thing. He didn't *know* this was the exact time they'd come back to, but it was just his fucking luck, wasn't it?

Calysto ran all the way down the street, not stopping until he was completely out of breath. His vision was swimming as his glasses slipped down the sweat on his nose and his eyes filled with terrified tears.

He pushed up his glasses and ran his hand down his face, trying to calm his frantic panting. His fingers slid over the smooth-skinned scar on his cheek that trailed beneath his clothes and all across his chest. He had healed it on his own, with the knowledge he'd gleaned from his time living with Merik, but he couldn't exactly remember how. Or where he'd been. It'd been so long now the whole memory was wrapped in a flaming blur.

He panted hard, leaning back against the cool stone of a building behind him, and let his head fall back as he stared up at the sky. It was a night like this, wasn't it? He remembered something like this. The cool breeze against his burning skin. It had stung when it touched the raw flesh and blisters leaking plasma into his shirt. Brushing against the stinging nerves, it ignited the burn all over again with each gust. He had looked up to the sky like he did now, and watched the clouds pass over the waning crescent moon through vision blurred by smoke and tears and the loss of his glasses. He had swallowed the pain, barely crying out, not asking for help, finding his own way.

He recalled setting the fire, that much was clear. He had grabbed the crystals from the shelf, wrapping them and keeping them close in one hand while holding up a lit candlestick in the other. He had almost turned to leave, sulking to his room with his stolen treasures when he stood in the doorway and glanced back. Out in the hall, he heard a small noise like the sound of footsteps and he retreated into the storage room, closing the door. In his haste to go undiscovered, he bumped into the rickety work table behind him. A small wooden container filled with corked vials wobbled, teetering on the edge of falling, as Calysto attempted to right himself.

But as his hand met the tabletop the candle, poorly fitted into the candlestick, toppled out of his hand, rolling away after it softly thunked onto the table. The next seconds played out in slow motion like they had every time Calysto recalled it for decades to come.

He was never sure why he remembered this part in such intricate detail, as if the most horrifying moment of his short life was the thing that was doomed to be imprinted in his mind forever, haunting him, ready to jump to the forefront at the slightest provocation.

The candle fell, its sticky body soft from the heat and dented slightly on the side, and left a piece of hardened wax on the wooden tabletop. He turned then to try and catch it only to spin too far, bumping his elbow on the corner and toppling the array of vials spilling green and blue viscous liquids into thick puddles of goo that oozed onto the table, reflecting orange fractals of the still-lit candle that rolled right into it. The table went up in flames.

At first, Calysto backed away, intent on running straight out of the door. But the fire had already begun to spread, creeping out and pouring over, crawling down the table legs and falling in flaming wet globules onto the floor.

A bit splashed onto his bare foot and he yelped, frantically trying to shake it out, but it wouldn't extinguish. To his left the wall began to catch as flames licked up the shelves braced against the wall. Calysto retreated until his back met the door and with eyes locked on the quickly growing blaze he felt with his hand for the knob.

But then something exploded and glass met skin and he lost his bearings as he flinched, covering his face with his arms. He stumbled away, looking for cover with anything he could find as smoke began to fill the space and blind his already blurring eyes.

Calysto's breath was coming in desperate pants as he tried to maintain some sense of orientation and calm, tried to keep his wits about him. But as he flailed towards the back door the tattered sleeve of his worn cotton sleep shirt snagged on a nail and the flames devoured the chance at a dry and fleshy meal.

All sense of rationale lost, Calysto screamed. Fire ate its way across his shirt and torso, lapping up the oils of his skin and the crisp fibers of the shirt. His consciousness teetered on faint as the fire dug into his flesh, climbing up his right arm and across the sensitive skin of his chest.

A sharp smell met his nose, rich and crisp, hot and hearty, as the scent of warm roasted meat filled the air. Later when Calysto would look back, recalling this memory that kept him up at night, he would realize that there had been no feast, no meal. There was only him. As he was burnt alive in his own skin.

As quick thinking as he usually was, he didn't have a sense of that now, and as white-hot panic consumed his senses along with the growing pain he screamed again, falling to the floor. He collapsed, landing against the sharp crystals still in his hands. He crawled across the wooden floorboards, eyes wide, gasping loud and dragging his raw and bleeding skin across the splintering wooden ground.

His decisions were erratic. He had no sense of what he was trying to accomplish, but if in this moment his instincts took over then they knew what to do. His wild flailing was only a weakening attempt to escape but it began to smother the fire underneath him. He rolled away into the corner and hit the far wall with a hard thud.

His nerves likely had died now, or perhaps he was in so much pain and charged with instinct that for the time being, he ceased to feel it. Young Calysto lie there on his back, half curled in the corner of the laboratory, half burnt and half alive. As he breathed in large gulps of smoke that smothered his lungs, he was sure this was how he was going to die.

Then, a hand he would dream of. A hand he would never cease to remember in the reaches of his memory as clear as his recollection of the rest. Someone had saved him, but he couldn't see who. His glasses had fallen, broken, somewhere on the floor, demolished along with everything else. He hadn't tried to rescue them, more worried about saving himself and clinging to those precious crystals. Yet he always remembered that hand.

He couldn't ever see a face, even as he recalled the unbearable sting of cool midnight air chafing his raw skin. Even as the man had spoken to him with some kind of curiosity and awe. Even as the man saved him.

Him.

Calysto, the little worthless boy who no one cared if he lived or died.

He had never seen him. Flashes of white, silver, red, pale, pale skin. His savior as much a mystery to him as the purpose of his life.

He remembered everything else, each little detail like he was watching a movie play out over and over and over. But try as he might, he couldn't remember what happened afterward. He couldn't see that face. He couldn't hear that voice. He couldn't remember if he'd ever heard a name.

It didn't matter, he had been saved nonetheless and by a stranger, no doubt, someone who didn't know him, who shouldn't care for him at all.

He hadn't died.

As he lay there watching the ceiling blur and fill with flames, young Calysto had accepted his fate. He had wanted it, the release from it all, the end to the suffering that consumed his life from the start to this untimely and fittingly painful end. He had nearly wanted to die, to give up here and see what lay beyond. It felt right, to follow his mother and his sister in such a way, just the same way they had gone. He would die how he lived: unloved and alone.

That is, that is until...

"CAL!"

Python's voice met his ear, and he jolted up from his place on the wall.

"Fuck!" Calysto gasped between his already stuttering breath.

He had still been leaning back staring up at the sky, trying to calm himself from the precipice of a certain type of panic he hadn't felt in more decades than he cared to count. Python appeared quick and quiet and out of fucking nowhere and was staring at him with some strange intensity.

"What?" Calysto asked, becoming quickly irritated at a scrutiny he didn't understand.

He didn't want Python to see him like this, and certainly would have cleaned himself up beforehand if he had a chance to know the vampire was coming.

Python was intrusive that way—just butting in into everything.

Into his life, his house, his fucking bathroom when he was trying to *shit in peace, Python!* And now he couldn't even escape to have this anxiety-induced moment of I'm-a-huge-fucking-coward alone without those red cat eyes watching his every panicked-hiccupping move.

"Will you stop fucking staring!" Calysto choked out. "Don't you have other shit to do?"

Python didn't answer, but instead he reached out a hand at a snail's pace as if approaching Calysto in slow motion, and placed it on his shoulder. His glassy marble gaze was watching him much too carefully. It made Calysto feel squirmy and overly-seen. Still, he found he regretted snapping and was too tired to keep his irritation up.

"What's going on?" he finally asked, when Python still didn't respond. "Did you get it?"

"Cal... I..."

Python's attitude was totally off.

Calysto knew him enough by now to tell and it unnerved him. Python had struck him as someone near unshakable. Sure he was impatient and reckless, but whatever trouble those traits got him into he shrugged off with a carelessness that surely came with being an incredibly powerful and immortal creature. He wore his confidence like a second skin, fitting him as neatly as the skinny jeans he was so keen on wearing as snugly as possible.

Maybe Calysto didn't know him though, and had only seen the aspects of him he chose to show. A concept that he was ashamed to realize he'd only now thought of.

Python might be a drifter, a vagabond, and a self-proclaimed scoundrel. But he was also as old as Calysto was, and one doesn't live that long without seeing much, much more than they would ever say aloud. There had to be more to him than his cocky persona, his teasing way of brushing off any topic that threatened to get too deep, and his unquenchable restlessness that seemed to stem from a need to never sit too still for too long lest something, anything, god knows what, caught up with him.

Python was running, and running, and running. From the last town he'd ravaged, from the lover's bed he'd killed them in, from the memories of his past, from the threat of feeling anything, from the possibility of thinking too long about anyone else, and especially from himself.

He was running from himself.

Whatever the fuck gave Calysto such insight into him in this moment completely distracted him from his fire-induced panic. That, combined with the dead chill that Python's hand was seeping into his shoulder.

Calysto cleared his throat and pushed up his glasses before speaking softly. He tried for something compassionate, understanding, even just calm. He wasn't sure if he succeeded.

"What happened?"

Python shook his head and out of the dark he produced his other hand. In it was a lavender multi-faceted crystal wrapped in charred canvas cloth.

"I got it."

"Oh!" Calysto pushed himself up off of the wall. "Great, let's go then."

"Alright, Cal." Python nodded, dropping the crystal into Calysto's hands.

Calysto looked down at it and for a moment he thought about saying something, asking something, reaching out. But he didn't know where to even start.

How are you? What'd you do? Why are you being weird? What's wrong with you?

He winced slightly at the idea. For a second longer, he overthought the whole thing with a few more possibilities before ultimately coming up blank. He was never too good at comforting others, and all of those options sounded slightly insulting.

So, as he wrapped the crystal back up in the cloth and shoved it in his coat pocket, all that came out of his mouth was, "Why are you fucking wrong?"

"What?"

Calysto froze, only then realizing what he'd said, and decided he'd very much like to die instantly, on the spot, *right now. Thanks.*

"Nothing," he mumbled, his ears burning hot. "Let's go."

Oh, fuck me. Goddamnit.

Calysto didn't look back or try to talk again, the whole way across town.

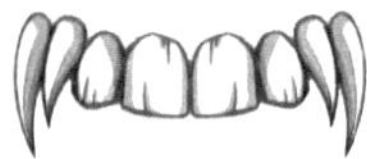

PYTHON'S THOUGHTS WERE RACING. He looked at Calysto beside him in the dim crescent moonlight and saw the glimmer of smooth skin on his cheek. It was certainly the same Calysto. It had to be. How many Calysto's could there be in the world? And in the same town, at the same time? With the same bronze skin and curly golden hair. Same eyes and squinty little irritated stare when caught without his glasses. A habit he realized that Calysto had carried over since he was young.

Fuck, that *was* him back there.

He had just broken into the house that Calysto grew up in with Calysto, Calysto had left, then he had what, saved Calysto's life in the past? Did that mean this had always happened like this? Without him, Calysto would have died in that fire, wouldn't he? That made no fucking sense. Or, it made perfect sense, but it was simply too much to take in.

He couldn't take his eyes off that scar, that evidence, that perfect proof that this was all tied together somehow.

"Cal?"

"Mm."

"Where'd you get that scar?"

"Why." Calysto sounded hesitant.

"It was a fire, wasn't it?" Python felt that asking so directly wasn't going to get him anywhere, but shit, he had to try. Calysto came to a halt beside him, not looking up from the ground.

"Why?" he nearly whispered.

"I uh..." Python licked his lips and pushed back his hair before continuing. "Look something... something happened."

"What?" Calysto turned to him then, and Python saw in him a glimpse of genuine concern. Calysto's hand that was shoved deep in his pocket was suddenly reaching out, closing the space between them. It caught him off guard and suddenly he felt overly observed, strangely seen. Cared for. By Cal?

Calysto didn't care for anyone it seemed, and certainly not him. Calysto liked being alone and Python was an annoying distraction that he was hoping would go away soon. It's probably why Calysto was so insistent on finding this crystal and bringing him back, so Python could finally leave him be. Yet Python couldn't deny that the emotion he saw in Calysto's eyes now, was one he hadn't seen from anyone else, in an immeasurably long amount of time.

He swallowed hard and opened his mouth to respond when a bell rang out, cutting sharp through the quiet night. Calysto flinched, quickly drawing back.

Fire! Fire!

Suddenly the street was lit up with the sound of shouts and a large carriage led by two glistening horses came clambering down the cobblestone street ringing an alarm. Python instantly grabbed Calysto by the coat collar and dragged him out of the street, off to the side and into the dark.

"That shit really went up, huh?" Python said over the sudden commotion. "Let's get the fuck outta here, yeah?"

He felt Calysto nod near his shoulder. "Yeah, yeah."

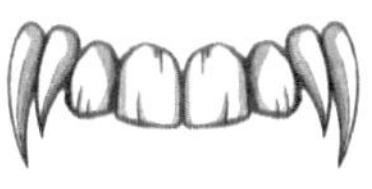

Calysto's house still sat quietly in wait, tucked away beyond the reaches of the outer city. As if from its own awareness of needing to hide, the house had begun to grow vines across the old wooden-slatted walls, and it appeared from their perspective as they approached, the small shrubs and trees around it had leaned in, shrouding the house further from sight.

It was silent here. Only the soft rustle of cool evening breeze through the treetops and their footsteps on frosted grass could be heard. Much more peaceful than the innards of a bustling industrial city that barely ever slept.

The fire that started in Merik's estate would soon grow out of control, consuming the home and everyone in it. It spread from Merik's house and on through the garden, reaching other homes in a mere matter of minutes until the whole district of mansions had gone up in flames. The great fire that burned for three days spread nearly all across the city of Industry. By the hands of a young boy who was only looking for an escape.

When the fires were finally put out and rubble was riffled through it had become evident that only a few maids managed to escape with their lives. The doctor and his young apprentice were lost. The manor had fallen and along with it the city of Industry would follow swiftly behind.

Now, it was quiet between them as well. Interrupted here and there by Calysto's footsteps and occasional sniffle or heavy breath as they trekked. Python was as silent as he ever was when he was keeping his mouth shut. And it was one of those rare times. As he walked and thought, he realized he didn't know how to bring up the fact that he had most definitely just met Calysto's younger self.

He wondered if Calysto remembered him. It didn't exactly seem likely, as the warlock showed no recognition when they met. And besides, it'd been over a hundred years. Still, Python wanted to ask.

Despite the fact that they didn't talk the entire time back, he couldn't find the right moment. At first, he felt it'd seem too eager and if he blurted it out and Calysto didn't answer, then it'd be fucking awkward the whole rest of the way.

Then as they kept going, it felt weird to break the silence that had accumulated into something that might be considered comfortable.

When he saw the cabin in the distance Python started to feel rushed, like there wasn't enough time to say everything — if the conversation *did* start — before they'd get interrupted.

So, Python opted to say nothing, leaving those mysteries for another time, another day when he could figure out exactly what to say. He told himself it wasn't a good time yet.

An easy excuse.

To be fair, Calysto was a right prickly one to approach, I'll give him that.

Calysto increased his stride as the house came into view, and Python watched as he approached a vine-coated wall and gave it a targeted thwack with the side of his palm. The house quietly shuddered and a door that wasn't there a moment before materialized and slipped slightly open. Calysto didn't speak a word and quickly went inside.

"Cal!" Python called as he shut the door and followed the lanky little warlock up the stairs. "What're you doing?"

"Taking us back," he said over the sound of his borrowed boots scuffling on the floor.

"Yeah, I know but, wait!" Python grabbed Calysto by the coat sleeve. "Why are you rushing?"

"Don't you want to go back?"

"Well, yeah. But..." Python trailed off.

What exactly was he trying to ask? He couldn't place it. The desire that drove him to act was too foreign, leaving him clueless in the face of it.

When they went back to the present, he'd leave like Calysto wanted. Back to his life of running and being on the road. Back to freedom and detachment and doing whatever the fuck he pleased.

All of this time travel magic house grumpy warlock weird shit would be over. It would all be over. That's what he wanted, right?

Calysto was still staring, halted mid-stride by Python's hold on his coat.

"But what?" Calysto asked, his voice hushed.

He seemed to want to say something else but stopped, biting his lip and squinting at Python in the dark.

"... Nothing. Nothing, you're right." Python let him go. "Let's get the fuck outta here."

Calysto gazed at him a half-breath longer before nodding once and continuing down the hall.

Fuck. Fuck!

Calysto paused in front of the boiler room and took a deep breath. Python clearly wanted to leave, and he was always going to anyway. Calysto knew this and had anticipated it since the day that irritating vampire burst through his front door. He looked forward to it. So now, that the time drew near, why the fuck was it bothering him so much? He scoffed quietly at those nagging thoughts. It wasn't bothering him. It fucking wasn't.

At least he would try to keep telling himself that.

He shouldered open the door and a cloud of dusty soot puffed out. He waved it away with his hand, and holding the crystal carefully tucked against his chest, he reached into his other pocket for the light. He spoke to it softly and it dispersed, lighting up the lanterns around the small, charred room. Behind him, Python whistled softly under his breath. The vampire had run into the kitchen for something then charged up the stairs behind Calysto in a flash, and was now barging his way in behind him.

"Your magic is real fuckin' cool, Cal."

Calysto shrugged it off.

A little part of him was still glad to hear it, though. Maybe his magic *was* impressive, but to him it was lackluster and pathetic. At least Python seemed to like it. That did feel kind of good. Then, he had an idea.

"Want to hold it?" he said, turning towards Python and waggling the wand in his direction.

Python's mouth fell open slightly. "What, really?"

"Sure," Calysto shrugged. "It won't hurt you, nor can you hurt anything with it. It's just light."

"Oh..."

Python reached out carefully, a bit awkwardly, tangling their fingers in a mess as he tried to grab it at the exact place where Calysto was gripping it. His skin was so cold, still. Again. Something about that bothered the warlock in a way he couldn't name.

"Here, wait," Calysto pulled back. "Just hold out your hand."

Python stilled and did as he asked. Calysto passed the wand over, handle first, and placed it into Python's palm. Then, he closed Python's fingers around it and held them there.

"There," he said, hoping to warm Python's skin a bit at the contact. "Hold it like that, like a flashlight."

"I've never used a flashlight," Python responded.

He wasn't even looking at the wand, but at the place where their hands met. Calysto almost moved away but Python hadn't yet so... so maybe it was okay? Python's skin was warming beneath his touch, and he liked the feeling of being able to do that for him. Calysto didn't want to let him go.

"Oh..." Calysto finally answered. "I forgot you don't need one."

"No, but..." Python's low voice was quiet between them in the dim glow. "I'll hold it for you, y'know... if you need."

"Yeah, okay thanks. Just... all you have to do is aim it."

"Okay."

He could let go now, he should let go now. Python was a grown-ass man who didn't need help holding a stick upright. Still, he didn't want to.

The stillness between them was turning palpable, so Calysto cleared his throat and slowly slid his hand out of their grasp, turning towards the charred table in the corner.

"Over here."

Calysto carefully placed the crystal down on the table then paused to take off his glasses.

"Uh." He fiddled with them for long enough to sound nervous when he finally spoke. "Will you hold these too, real quick?"

"Sure." Python took them.

Calysto stripped off Python's coat and vest, revealing a worn-thin black t-shirt full of moth holes underneath. He had brought it along this whole time and changed into it once the itchiness of a ruffly shirt collar got to be too much for him. No one could tell beneath the other clothes anyway.

A rip at the right shoulder left the sleeve barely hanging on from the armpit, and the neckline was nonexistent, dangling open near to the middle of his chest. He could feel Python staring but chose to ignore it. Instead, he threw the coat on the floor, tucked the vest under his arm, and reached out feeling for Python's hand to grab his glasses back.

"Damn, Cal," Python huffed. "If I didn't know you any better I'd say this shirt was a stylistic choice, and I'd say it looks kinda cool."

"It's not."

"Yeah, I'm aware."

Calysto scowled slightly and put his glasses on. Then, he waded up the vest and used it to wipe the broken table clean, swiping away bits of debris and the layer of soot from the surface.

"That's what you needed to take that off for?" Python scoffed.

"It's fabric," Calysto said back. "It's multi-purpose."

"I guess," Python half-laughed. "You're a weird one, Cal."

"So I've heard," he mumbled, unsure of how exactly he should take that. It didn't seem to be as much of an intended insult as some of the other things Python had said before. "So are you."

Python really laughed then, causing the light in his hand to bounce all over the room. "I guess we… haha… I guess we do make quite a strange pair…"

Calysto shot a look at him, and something about the genuine smile on Python's face made his own lips quirk up as well. Reluctantly, he felt like it was actually a bit funny.

"I suppose so," he agreed. "A vampire and a warlock in a time-traveling house, who would believe it?"

Python laughed again. "It does sound made up, right? That's hilarious."

"It is…" Calysto smiled. "Isn't it."

Python paused and looked at him, glassy teeth and glistening eyes shining in the dim light. "Hey, you're smiling!"

Calysto instantly felt his ears turn hot and he rubbed his face as if to wipe it away. "Yeah, yeah… Stop distracting me."

"Sorry."

Python's grin didn't falter and he didn't seem sorry in the slightest.

Calysto peered up at him for a moment longer before turning back to the table. Suddenly, instead of feeling amused, he was irritated and confused. Embarrassed, even. He couldn't remember the last time he'd laughed and at first it had felt good, maybe better than he'd felt in a long time. Someone else had made him laugh.

The reality of how long it'd been set in, and the pang of guilt at feeling any semblance of joy and the shame of exposing his true feelings, burned on his face.

It was fucking humiliating. And as much as that in itself bothered him, it also nagged at him that he didn't know why this was. Why couldn't he just feel, be, happy? Without some instant twisted regret digging into his heart? Didn't he deserve happiness, too?

He hadn't ever really thought about it.

Happiness was ten hundred steps away from anything he'd ever considered for himself. The desire for acceptance was one thing—at least he felt that might bring him some peace.

But to be happy? Content? To feel loved and liked in the presence of others? That wasn't even a possibility in his mind. It was something he'd given up on barely wanting a long time ago anyway. He didn't even think of it now, and the reminder of the ability to laugh was also a reminder of these things he'd forgotten he'd wanted once. He thought he'd gotten rid of the idea that happiness was attainable for him.

Why did it still hurt?

It didn't matter now. Not like he could have it here. This was a temporary, fleeting moment, in the midst of an endlessly empty and lonely life that would soon go back to the way it'd always been.

He stood and shuffled off to his workshop with a mumbled 'stay here' before returning with an armful of tools and his tablet which miraculously had a little bit of battery left. The blue light screen cast his face in an eerie glow as he set it down. He knelt down near the table, took the crystal in hand and flipped it over.

"What're you doing?" Python watched quietly, crouching down beside him and holding the light over his work area.

Calysto mumbled some kind of unintelligible response and kept about his work. It would take three times as long to explain as it would to just do it and get it over with. He could feel the frigid cold coming off of Python's skin even through the few inches of space between them and it made him shiver. If Python noticed he didn't comment, and stayed very still watching his every move with those iridescent eyes.

"Oh hey, is this yours?" Python reached around him and snatched up Calysto's tablet.

"Whose else would it be?" Calysto said back, barely paying attention.

Python turned the screen on and laughed. "Is this a picture of your house?"

Calysto glanced up. "Yeah."

He heard Python chuckle under his breath before speaking again. "What's your passcode?"

"Why?"

"C'mon, I'm bored, just tell me," Python whined.

"1796."

Silence. Then. "Ah, no service."

"We're currently still in the eighteen fucking hundreds if you didn't happen to notice," Calysto said from around a screwdriver dangling between his lips.

"Oh yeah." Python shut it off and set it down on the table, then started digging around in his pocket. "Care if I smoke?"

"Nu-uh." Calysto heard the sound of a lighter before he even finished answering. He huffed and shook his head, not able to help his amusement. "Let me have it."

"Huh?" Python puffed, and the smell of tobacco stung Calysto's nose. "The cig?"

"Yeah." Calysto took the tool out of his mouth and turned to Python, plucking the cigarette from his fingers.

"Didn't know you smoked," Python said with a half-smile and eyebrow raised.

"We're about to try to move this house back to the future," Calysto reasoned, sitting back to lean against the wall. "I have no idea if it's going to work, or how to make it work since I didn't mean to the first time and if I can't get us back... I'm... I think I can... I can smoke a little bit."

"Okay yeah, shit. Go ahead," Python agreed quietly. "Look... Cal..."

Calysto heard the hesitation in Python's voice and took a long drag while he waited for whatever the vampire was about to say next.

"If... If you can't, you know. Get us back uh..."

"I will," Calysto cut him off. "I'll make it work, okay?"

"But I mean, if you can't... it's... it's okay. It's my fault we're here anyway."

Calysto exhaled and released a small cough. "No, it's not."

"I mean... it kinda is..." Python sighed, taking the cigarette back. "That hunter? She's been after me for... shit, forever I guess. I really didn't think she'd track me down all the way to your house, but... I mean I should've known."

Calysto's interest was piqued. "Is that why you're always on the run, then?"

Python shot him a look of half annoyed, half surprised he'd asked. "Uh, yeah, pretty much. I mean, yeah."

"Why? I mean, what'd you do to her?"

"I don't know."

Calysto scoffed and raised a brow. "So, you're not going to tell me?"

"No, Cal, I really don't know." Python shrugged, handing the cig over. Calysto took it, inhaling again and enjoying the way it made his head feel slightly fuzzy. "She's almost caught me a few times here and there, over the years. But damn if she won't tell me what she wants. She just hates me. I dunno. Maybe I did something I don't remember."

"Like what?"

"Hard to say," Python laughed sourly, sending smoke billowing from his teeth with the exhale. "I've stolen a lot of people's shit but I couldn't tell you who, and never enough to warrant this kind of vendetta. I don't think?"

"Have you tried asking her?" Calysto was curious in spite of himself.

He gave Python his smoke back and returned to his work, scooting around to lean under the tabletop while he listened.

"Yeah, once or twice. She's usually way too mad to listen though, and it's a bit hard to have a conversation when I'm trying to avoid getting staked."

"Oh..." Calysto frowned. He was focusing on securing the crystal through the hole in the table and was entirely underneath it. "Is that how you die? A stake?"

"Why?" Python's voice muffled slightly through the wood, but Calysto could still hear his thinly veiled nervous chuckle. "Want to kill me?"

"No!" Calysto bit back forcefully, then picked his head up from under the table to make his intentions clear. "I'm just asking, Python."

Python shot him a halfhearted smile and took a drag the volume of which would obliterate any normal man's lungs.

Calysto sighed, pushed his glasses up, and asked, "Do you really think I'd want to kill you?" He wrinkled his nose and continued before Python could answer. "Look, Python. I don't hate you, alright? You're annoying as shit and you eat all my fucking chips and crashed in my house but, I don't want you dead. I don't wish anyone dead."

"I do, sometimes." Python shrugged. "Wish people dead, that is."

"And what happens?"

"Well, mostly I kill them," Python grinned.

"Be serious," Calysto sighed.

"I am."

"Oh." Calysto set down the tool in his hand and started sliding them one by one into a little leather organizer belt. "Well, okay. Well... I'm not gonna kill you."

"I'm not gonna kill you either."

"Yeah?"

Calysto was only slightly shocked to hear it. As much as he had become used to the vampire's company and the fact that he *was* a vampire, he still couldn't shake the thought that Python might up and eat him at some random time of his choosing. Maybe. It was hard to tell where Python's head was at a lot of the time.

"Yeah, weirdo," Python huffed. "Besides, who else is gonna get us back?"

"Oh..." *I should've figured.* "Yeah, well... it should be good to go now, I think. I mean, it's not gonna get any better."

"Oh shit, already?" Python jumped to his feet. "Okay, what do I gotta do?"

"Get out."

"Oh..."

"I dunno," Calysto shrugged. "Just go sit downstairs or something."

"Is it gonna be like last time?" Python waved the wand around while he spoke, sending light glinting off of Calysto's glasses.

"It's likely," Calysto stood as well, snatching the wand back and putting it out. "So, hang on."

"Alright, here, well... eat these real quick." Python paused, ashing the cigarette against the doorframe and letting the butt fall to the floor. From his pocket he pulled a packet of cookies and tossed them in Calysto's direction. "Yell if you need anything. Or if the house is gonna explode."

"You'll be the first to know," Calysto mumbled, and shut the door.

TWENTY-TWO

Python paused outside of the door weighing if he should say something else. Then before he got too lost in thought, he remembered the last time the house traveled through time and he ran downstairs in a flash. He jumped on the couch and pulled a blanket over his head, lying in wait for the inevitable earthquake that was about to come.

Then it came.

Whatever Calysto was trying was certainly doing something. The walls began to rattle like the first time, and he heard the sound of trash and bottles and cans sliding to the floor from the kitchen table. The lanterns mounted into the hallway corridor—that Calysto had kept lit since Python arrived—all went out, bathing the entire front room in darkness.

Python peeked out to see the eerie fluorescent glow from the kitchen overhead light right as the refrigerator door swung open and slung its contents all over the foyer with a chorus of carbonated hisses.

Cal will probably be pissed about that.

A door upstairs that was left half-open slammed over and over against the wall, creating an anxiety-inducing shotgun shell of a bang in rhythm with the frantic vibrations. Python pulled the blanket back over his head and found himself wondering if Calysto was okay.

What if he does that glowing thing with his hands again? Will it wear him out like last time?

When Calysto first moved the house back to this timeline he had looked near to fainting, his scrawny body collapsing against the copper boiler and his golden-brown face had paled beyond what Python had assumed possible for his complexion. His hands had glowed—one of the only times Python had seen to any extent what his magic could do—something Calysto clearly didn't want him to witness, evident by his ridiculous denial of it even happening and the way he had, just now, kicked him out to do it alone in peace. As if his magical ability was something shameful and not the most magnificent thing Python had ever seen.

He thought about telling Calysto that. He had told him it was cool, but that's not the same as real praise.

Maybe he should. Maybe it would make him feel good to hear it? He wasn't sure.

Because on the one hand, most normal people would like to be complimented on their abilities. Shit, that was damned near the most surefire way Python had wormed his way into anyone's house or wallet or pants in the past. But Calysto wasn't exactly a normal person, and he certainly wasn't an easy one to figure out. In all the places where Python would typically know exactly how to act or to get someone to behave how he wanted them to, it was as if Calysto was entirely immune.

Either it was through his stubborn exterior or callous nature, or maybe he was still completely oblivious to all of Python's attempts since he clearly didn't know how to socialize to save his fucking life. Python laughed quietly at the thoughts that also served to distract him from the house threatening to fall down around him. Though as he pondered it further he sobered.

He realized now why Calysto had freaked out in Merik's house.

After little Calysto handed him that crystal and told him his name, he had understood. Python had dragged Calysto back through probably what amounted to the most traumatic moments of his life, all for what? All so Python could run away again?

So what if Aeris wanted to kill him? Didn't he deserve it a little bit? Didn't he want it, a little bit? And besides, Calysto had a perfectly peaceful if albeit boring life, before Python came along. And Python had clambered in and fucked it up, hadn't he?

Shit.

Python wasn't big on debts and certainly not on paying them, but he suddenly felt that if they made it back in one piece, he would owe Calysto a hell of a lot.

The house began to still, and as Python's thoughts continued to race the room around him fell into silence. He sat up, removing the blanket from his head and shaking off a cloud of dust. At least nothing huge or dangerous had fallen onto him.

Slowly he stood and looked at the mess. Surrounding the old couch were all his clothes, likely strewn about even before the house shook itself into the future. His collection of cosmetics and care items had rolled off the rickety coffee table and a tube of lipstick had popped open collecting dirt and dust, rendering it useless. Python felt a little pang of regret at the sight, it was a pretty nice color and he had no idea where he'd gotten it from.

He stepped over the mess, once again observing the ways in which he'd completely trashed Calysto's life, and headed to the stairs. He halted halfway up and waited, listening for the sound of Calysto in the distance.

"Cal?" he called. "You alright?"

A shuffle, the sound of something falling and a grumble gave him all the response he needed but then he also heard. "Yeah."

Python hazarded to climb the rest of the stairs, rounding the corner to the hallway when he heard the boiler room door open. Calysto emerged, first in total darkness, then illuminated by the warm magical lamplight through his little wand. Python really wanted to know how that thing worked.

But at the sight of Calysto's face all that creeping, annoying guilt came back.

Calysto looked tired, more so than usual. Bits of soot were smeared in finger lengths across his neck, and the black t-shirt hung off of him like a shroud and exposed his long golden arms speckled with charcoal dust. His hands were still softly glowing, as they had before, with that gentle orange hue. He didn't seem like he was going to fall over this time.

"Feeling okay?" Python asked as he approached.

"Uh, yeah." Calysto nodded while rubbing his palms together, making the light disappear from view. "Thanks."

"For?"

Calysto looked down and Python could see his cheeks turn a dusty shade of pink. "I think it works better when I've uh, eaten something."

"Oh, hah, most things do." Python grinned, but then it faltered. "Hey listen... um... wait it worked right?"

"Yeah, I think so," Calysto answered slowly and lifted the edge of his shirt to wipe his face, giving Python a clear view of not only his entire scar but the body that lay beneath it. Python bit his lip, not realizing he was staring until Calysto let his shirt fall back into place.

"Uh, yeah well..." Python righted himself. "I should probably get out of your hair then, yeah?"

He saw Calysto's throat rise up and down as he swallowed, watching him carefully before he answered with a sharp, "Okay."

"Okay." Python wasn't sure what he'd hoped for. But he probably shouldn't have expected much more. "Well, uh, yeah I'll get my shit then."

"Fine, Python."

He felt Calysto's hollow eyes follow him all the way back down the stairs.

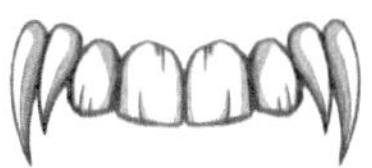

He was leaving. Python was really going to leave, just like that. The realization that the time had come sent Calysto's anxiety spiking. He used a hand to hold himself up against the wall as a subtle bout of dizziness overcame him. That was probably from the whole moving the house back to the present thing.

Python's near-silent footsteps retreated back downstairs and Calysto was at a complete loss for what to do. He took a few deep breaths and decided he should at least follow him down, and say goodbye, right? That's what people did in these kinds of situations, didn't they? See each other off?

"Python?" he called quietly, unable to make himself speak up any louder for fear of sounding desperate.

"Yeah!"

"Oh." Calysto reached the bottom step to the sight of Python shoving clothes haphazardly into a bag. "You're still here."

"Don't worry, I'll be outta here soon," Python mumbled.

"No... I didn't mean..." Calysto frowned.

He had no idea what to say. What should he say? Shit. With every passing second Python was getting closer to leaving and he just stood there like a silent idiot, watching him.

"Python."

"Huh?" Python turned.

"Do you um... have somewhere to go?" Calysto grimaced as he said it. *What am I fucking saying?*

"Nah, Cal, that's not really my style."

"What, you just, figure it out as you go?" Calysto asked. "Isn't that dangerous?"

"It's what I've always done." Python shrugged, stuffed a shirt into his bag then paused, craning his neck to face Calysto. "Why?"

"Uh..." Calysto wanted to say it, he *really* wanted to say it. He also didn't want to seem pathetic, even though he certainly felt it. "I just mean. If you wanted to... stay. For longer. You could... do that."

He winced and closed his eyes, certain that Python would laugh at him. When he didn't hear anything, he hazarded a peek, and what met him was Python's face stuck in a quiet o.

"What?" Calysto asked cautiously.

"You really want me to?"

"I didn't say want!" Calysto immediately covered. "I just said you could!"

Python broke out into a grin and his bag hit the floor as he blitzed right up to Calysto's chest. "You want me to stay. Don't you."

Calysto grimaced but didn't back away, choosing to stare straight at Python's neck rather than meet his eyes. "I'm just saying if you... if... can... can you back off?"

Python snickered and took half a step back.

"I'm just saying if you needed, a place, still. You can... stay."

"I thought you'd never ask." Python's lips curled even further, then as Calysto met his eyes the vampire's smile suddenly vanished. "Are you sure though?"

Calysto paused. Was he sure?

"... No, not really," he finally answered. "But you don't just have to rush off."

Python bit his lip, looking uncertain. "Listen Cal, I'm... shit, I'm not trying to be a bother anymore, you don't have to..."

"It's not a bother, alright?" Calysto blurted before he could over-think it and take it back. He rubbed his neck, smearing more soot across his skin. "... Look, don't worry about it. Just... do you want to, um... get something to eat or ... I'm, I'm still hungry I guess."

Python hesitated, but ultimately he smiled that familiar Python smile and leaned back. It sent a bolt of relief through Calysto, knowing he'd bought himself a little more time.

"Yeah, I could eat."

"Cool."

"Shit's all over the kitchen floor, though." Python waved over Calysto's shoulder.

Calysto followed his gesture and saw the energy drink and soda cans scattered and leaking onto the pock-marked concrete. He sighed and rubbed his brow.

"Oh... do you... want to go get... more?"

"Tell you what, Cal," Python moved in closer, and Calysto felt the cool air he brought with him. "How about since you're so kind as to let me stay, I take you out for a real meal. My treat."

"You don't have any money." Calysto rolled his eyes.

"So? I'm the fastest dine and dasher the world has ever seen," Python winked. "And I've got experience in carrying you with me."

Calysto huffed, slightly amused in spite of himself. "Alright, fine. Lead the way."

"You have *got* to change first," Python answered, heading back to the couch and dumping out his bag. "Here, you can borrow something of mine."

"Your shit is too bi—"

A loud crash hit the living room wall and they both jumped. Calysto froze to the spot and Python ducked behind the couch.

"What the fuck is that!" Python hissed.

Another bang louder this time, another, faster, traveling across the walls.

"Oh shit..." Calysto took a step back. "Oh no, no..."

"Cal!" Python called. "What's going on?"

"Python I..." Calysto's heart was suddenly in his throat and he could hardly speak as he realized what had happened. What he had done.

"We came back but... Oh shit, I'm sor... it's the exact same time we left."

PYTHON BARELY HAD time to register what Calysto said, and no time at all to comprehend what he meant, before that poor rickety wooden door that had barely clung to life by its rusted hinges for a hundred years burst open, splintering with projectiles that flew across the room. One clipped Python's cheek and he hissed, ducking further down. Why the fuck vampires weren't invulnerable to pieces of wood of all things was not only an entire mystery but an extremely annoying and inconvenient fact. Black blood began to ooze down his face, but he was too distracted to notice it because a figure was behind the demolished door.

Aeris.

Like emerging from a dream, her tall hunter's frame appeared, creating an odd silhouette in the backlit moonlight of the doorway. Her long coat fanned out at her calves, and stood proud and pointed at her strong shoulders. Long boots added inches to her height and folded near the knees, and on her head she wore a hood held in place by a tricorn hat. In her hand, outlined in a soft silvery light from the night outside, was a double-barreled shotgun.

"There you are," she growled, her dark gaze landed on Python who, realizing the ridiculously humiliating position he was in, slowly stood and brushed himself off. He cleared his throat and tried to smile.

"Hey."

"Fuck you," came her retort and she lifted her shotgun, holding it straight out in one hand. "Are you finally ready to die?"

"Uh, excuse me."

Calysto's voice made them both jump. In his panic Python had completely forgotten he was there. Aeris turned as well and what came out of her mouth was nothing he could've expected.

"You, too!" She turned the barrel of the gun at him and Calysto took a quick step back.

"Do I know you?" Calysto asked, his eyes wide behind his dust-smudged glasses.

Python watched as Aeris crossed the space between the doorway and stairwell in two quick strides and pressed the shotgun to Calysto's chest, pushing him into the wall. Calysto winced but didn't try to fight her, simply standing with his hands raised.

"Oh, don't tell me you've forgotten me, too?" she snarled. "So you're just as fucking hopeless then, aren't you?"

"Hey!" Python called. "Leave him alone, Aeris! This is between us."

"Aeris?" Calysto breathed.

"Yeah, Calysto honey," she spat. Her free hand reached up to remove her hat and push back her hood. Black curls tumbled loose and Python saw Calysto's eyes widen. "Who else."

"I thought..." Calysto spoke in halting sentences as if he couldn't believe what he was seeing. "I thought you... you died."

"Cal!" Python took a few steps toward them, as close as he'd dare get to Aeris with a shotgun and the assortment of knives he knew she carried. "You know her?"

Calysto's eyes shot over to him then back to her then back to him again. Python could hear that tell-tale flutter of his heart in his throat. He was some combination of confused and afraid, and Python really didn't like the sight of the gun on his chest.

"She uh..." Calysto shifted his back. Aeris poked the barrel in further and he winced.

"Tell him, Calysto," she snarled. "Tell him about how you left me to die."

"You *were* dead!" he said. "Aeris, you were dead! I... I checked!"

"*Not* dead, asshole! Un-dead!" she raised her voice. "Of which you're going to cure me!"

"W-what?" Calysto stammered.

"I know you have it! I've read all the papers, all your research, I know you figured it out!"

"I..." Calysto's glasses were sliding down his nose as a thin sheen of sweat ran down his forehead. "Aeris I really don't know what you mean."

"Oh... Motherfuck—"

Python should have seen it coming. At this point, he should've seen *her* coming but well, Python doesn't get any points in this story for being perceptive. Not until he's actively hit over the head with what he should already well be aware of. Even years of being chased by Aeris didn't give him any better idea of what she could do, or would do, to get what she wanted.

In a flash she reared back and whipped Calysto right across the temple, knocking him out cold. Then she turned to Python and pulled something out of her coat.

"A flashlight?" Python laughed, but there was still a twinge of nerves and he glanced at Calysto, listening to make sure he was breathing. "Really?"

"Not just any flashlight, a modern vampire hunters dream." Aeris grinned right back and he heard the flick of the switch.

A searing hot pain tore across his skin and before he had a chance to react, his mind went blank as his vision turned white.

TWENTY-THREE

Han righted his ruffled collar and smoothed down his vest. He was getting used to this, in a way, being Richter's little side-piece trophy boy. Richter had a lot of them that wandered here and there, in and out of his extravagant mansion at all manner of hours of the night. But Han was his newest, his prettiest, his favorite, he liked to say. Being used to it didn't mean he liked it, though.

If anything, he tolerated it.

To his left was a wardrobe, specifically outfitted and tailored to him in Richter's style of how he wanted to see Han dressed. There were shoes of satin with golden buckles, crushed blue velvet and lined with tight laces, stockings and garters, clothes of complete impracticality that couldn't withstand even the slightest provocation. Things that Han would have never dreamed of wearing even if he could've afforded them. No wonder nobles never stepped foot out of their extravagantly built manors, when that foot would instantly become soiled by refuse and mud, destroying not only the handiwork of some exquisite and underappreciated craftsman but sullying the entirety of a chimney sweeps life wages in a single step. Not that the nobles cared about such things.

His long hair was smoothed back, combed with sweet almond oils and rose water to shine and accentuate the natural waves. No longer did it hang clumped in strings of dirt and soot, blackened from the buildup of tar and coal dust. It didn't itch anymore either, and neither did his skin. He was bathed and clean, skin smooth and clear. Though his complexion was paler than before without blood running through his veins or the sun to warm him through.

His cough was also gone, along with those weeping sores that had begun to plague his body. Merik's apprentice had essentially saved his life with the medicine before Richter did the most, by taking it. But either way, he would have survived, thanks to the boy.

Though he couldn't see his face through the polished shine of a silver-coated surface, he could look down at his arms, his chest, his legs. He could run his hands down his face and feel the tinted fleshy pink color of rouge on his lips that surely turned him into a gross and blushing pantomime of his once-alive self.

His feet were clumsily stuffed into shoes that supposedly fit better than anything he'd ever owned, but felt cramped and stupid, crushing his toes and his ability to run. Though he had already learned his lesson in defying Richter, or trying to run away at all, he resented it all the same. He was dressed up like a little doll, perfectly packaged to Richter's liking from head to toe, the pinnacle of noble desirability and attraction. And he hated it.

He stood in front of his wardrobe and observed the blues and purples, crimsons and whites, lace frills and satin fronts, and smeared that humiliating shade of waxy pink on his fingers between angry palms. Just as he'd expected, the door behind him opened, and none other than the esteemed Lord Richter crept his way inside.

"There you are," he crooned in a sing-song tone. "Looking smart as always."

Han didn't answer but his spine stiffened at Richter's arrival. He slowly turned, anxious and tense. As Richter approached it only served to worsen, as those creepy always-slightly-too-watery eyes slithered over his skin in such a way that Han felt it might as well have been Richter's tongue.

Then Richter looked at his face and frowned.

"You've smeared your makeup, idiot."

The small gust of wind from Richter's swift approach made Han involuntarily shiver. Richter pulled a kerchief out of his breast pocket and gripped Han's chin tight, roughly wiping away the smeared lipstick from around his mouth.

"Really, I thought you'd have the hang of this by now." Richter *tsk*ed while finishing his work and tucking the cloth away.

He held the vice on Han's chin a bit longer before releasing him. Then he petted Han's cheek with the back of his hand, looking up at him and licking his thin wormy lips with a sickly predatory smile. Han hated that look.

It was nearly as bad to be in Richter's favor as it was to not be. Han had seen and felt the effects of both by now, and he still couldn't decide which was worse. At least a pissed-off Richter didn't breathe that putrid rotten breath so close to his face through a weaselly leering smile that spoke only of conquest and lust.

Richter's sharp fingernail tracked his jaw, scraping softly against the smooth skin that no longer grew hair, tracing down to his neck. Han stayed stock-still, letting it happen with the knowledge of what would happen if he didn't.

"As pretty as a picture," Richter purred. "All dressed and fed and well-kept, aren't you?"

Han nodded once, intently staring out and studying the carved wooden decorative notions on the wall behind Richter's head.

"Aren't you?" Richter's purr pitched to a warning growl, and Han realized he failed to answer.

"Yes," he managed.

Beneath his lips his gums tingled with agitation as they usually did when Richter was around, leering at him and touching him. But he wouldn't dare show them to Richter again. Not if he didn't want to get his fledgling ass slung around the room like a rag doll, like the last and final time he did.

Han was a vision of obedience, though he couldn't entirely hide his flinches and the occasional grimace. For brewing beneath his buttoned-up breast was a resentment and anger so well fed, a fire of bitterness stoked near to roaring flames so hot, he feared it would bleed through onto his face.

He pretended the best he could—to play along. To be the little pet that Richter wanted, no, forced, him to be. He stood like a gilded statue at Richter's side through evenings of parties and early morning indulgent feasts. Feeding on what he was given, feeling out of the corner of his eye the ways in which Richter garnered sick pleasure at watching him eat from the throat of someone quickly dying. Like a man who perceived himself a god. As if he had, in every way that mattered, molded Han to be everything that he was now.

His creator, his maker, his master.

Sometimes Han would imagine those delicate human veins beneath his aching teeth were Richter's flesh instead and bite down too hard, ravenously ripping at the skin and killing the unfortunate nameless victim who had fallen into their trap. Around others Richter would laugh—a young little vampire Han was, reckless and careless, like a newborn child unaware of the blessings of strength he now possessed. Laughing off his mistakes with a wave of his spidery fingers. Excusing him. Having mercy on him.

But in private, Richter was ruthless.

Like now.

"How could you embarrass me like that?" he growled. His tone quickly turned dangerous and his rage took a candlestick across the room with it. "Some fucking refinement you have!"

Han retreated to sit on the edge of the bed, out of the way of Richter's pacing tirade, and to settle himself in for an outburst which, with Richter, usually proved to be for the long haul.

"I should have known!" he spat, his grey tongue working behind his fangs, likely tasting a variety of insults and selecting just the right one to add to the words he would throw Han's way. "To adopt a gutter rat into the fold! Even your blood tasted of swill when I turned you!"

"And you would know what swill tastes of?" Han hissed back and instantly cursed his tongue. Fuck.

In a flash Richter's nails were digging dangerously into Han's exposed neck. Richter had jumped on top of him, stranding his waist and pushing Han down into the soft down feather bed that threatened to swallow him up on all sides from the pressure.

Their gazes met, with Han struggling to keep his from seeming wide with a terror that threatened to climb to the surface, and Richter's boring into him as if he were trying to make him break. Then Richter grinned and Han's heart sank.

"I only need to taste you again to remember," he hissed and dove down, pressing a crushing, biting, kiss to Han's lips.

His stomach churned, instantly rising up in his throat at the taste of his own veins bursting into his mouth against his hidden fangs and Richter's rotten teeth. Richter's scent was overwhelming like old perfumed skin, embalmed and decayed, soaked in oils, and stretched beyond recognition to simulate some semblance of life still remaining. But Richter wasn't alive, he was as dead as Han, but more so he was void of the thing that made any of them remotely human anymore. A heart.

Han's might not still beat in his chest, lying as empty as he had begun to feel, but it was still there, guiding him, nagging him, getting him in trouble. Trouble like this. Trouble like not keeping his mouth shut, like trying to keep his dignity intact, like still being driven by the desire to live his own life. Outside of this decorative box that Richter kept him in.

He couldn't stand it.

He lie there, enduring the way that Richter kissed him, reciprocating him only by existing. With fists clenched at his sides, his body was a plank of coffin wood—stiff and carved into a prison to house the dead. Dead dreams, dead loves, dead life.

He watched the bed canopy carefully as if it too would bite, as Richter's claws dug into his flesh, teeth moving to his neck. He barely felt it. Instead preoccupied with counting threads and following that paisley pattern up above with his eyes, around and around and around. The blood on his lips dripped slowly across his cheek, leaving sticky trails to dry on his face, to pool in his ear, to clump in his hair. He wouldn't wipe it off until much later. He was more used to being dirty after all. Better an outward stain than the one that Richter left crawling across the insides of his mind. Tainting him, making him afraid, making him hate.

He wasn't sure how long it'd been now as time stretched on in a seemingly infinite loop of sleeping and eating and parties and boredom. The city had burned around them and yet they'd stayed, carrying on under the cover of darkness as if nothing had changed. It felt to Han like nothing ever changed now. His life was eternal yet he lingered here, stuck, imprisoned with less possibility for escape than the options his limited mortal life had presented him.

He stared at the walls, memorizing them in all their intricately ornate extravagance. The way the ceilings climbed higher than any mortal man could reach, decorated up to the curved corners and trimmed down the sides.

Once he had scaled them like a chimney, peering around at the floor below from his strange upside-down perch, staying perfectly silent as a maid came and went, never noticing him hanging there. He marveled a bit at the way he never got tired of doing this; like his limbs were made of steel. He'd find himself peering at the upside-down flames of the fireplace, and thinking about the ways in which sweeping would be so much easier now. He'd almost wanted to try it, if only to see.

Part of him was also glad he had left all that behind. There were no vampire chimney sweeps, not as far as he knew, anyway. His mortal life had already felt endless and stagnant, stuck in the class of his birth, his occupation, his fucking city.

But it wasn't his city and they didn't want him here, yet he was trapped in a different way all the same.

No, he didn't suppose any self-respecting vampire would want to spend another eternity within the bowels of a fireplace, just because they could.

He stared at the bookshelf, tracking the shapes and colors and heights of the books, the widths and the lengths, the textures of the covers. Sometimes, he would pick one up, flip through a few pages, and even try to read one a little bit. But Han was near illiterate—for what use did a chimney sweep have for words? And even if he could read well, he wouldn't like what they said.

The books were about a range of subjects. Though mostly about commerce and nightlife. Long whining treatises on the ways in which the poor were a detriment to society and should be punished for their lack of fortitude—their lack of wealth—books from other parts of the world in various languages speaking of the latest fashions and trends, what one must have to be considered a true up-to-date socialite.

So yes, perhaps it was better he couldn't read, for it would do nothing but fuel the frustration and unrest building within him.

He stared at the mirror, as it showed him everything but himself, watching the clothes rise and fall with movements he knew he made, but couldn't see. The mirror in a way, was a perfect reflection of him now—nothing, no one. He didn't exist. Not to the sun or the day, not to the people who once saw him, spoke to him, loved him. He didn't belong in their world anymore, and he didn't even know if maybe, indeed they did think he was dead.

Did anyone even notice he was gone? Had he really existed then, either?

He had to know—did Gabriel forget him?

Did he look for him?

With that thought he shot upright, catching Richter by surprise and slinging him off of him onto the bed. Blood ran onto his clothes, blood he had only recently drank that now coursed through him simulating a fragile facade of life.

"I need to go out," Han gasped, breathing heavily from racing thoughts. "Right now."

Richter had already leapt up and collected himself, glaring at Han with something wicked prepared to say on his lips. But it didn't seem that he was expecting Han to say this.

"You're not going anywhere," he snarled, wiping his mouth.

Han got to his feet. He was taller than Richter, and for once he used it to his advantage. He leaned over into Richter's smelly fucking face and sneered right back, "Yes, I am."

Richter wasn't intimidated in the slightest, and as Han turned to leave he grabbed his arm, hard. Hard enough to break the skin. But Han was good at ignoring the ways in which Richter hurt him. For now.

"No, you're not!"

"Yes, Richter, I am," Han snapped. "Don't worry, I'll come back and still be your little pet once I'm done."

Richter was momentarily shocked, but then his lips twisted into a smile and he placed his hands on his hips, looking Han up and down.

"Well, well, someone's bucking up, aren't they? Growing some hefty little vampire balls, are we?" His laugh was a mocking bark. "Alright, pup. But if I don't see your skinny ass here by sun-up I'll find you, and kill you myself."

Han stared at him long and hard, trying to watch his tongue, then finally nodded. "I'll be back."

As he left he heard. "If you fuck anyone else, I'll kill you for that, too."

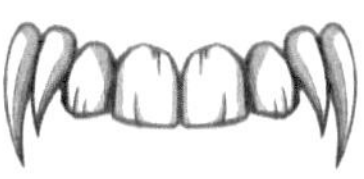

THE NIGHT WAS hot and sticky midsummer warm as Han paced the streets of the inner city, looking for... looking for what? Gabriel's milk route was long over, and he certainly wouldn't be traipsing around in the middle of the night in his little white uniform.

Han went to the only place else he could think to find him. The *Molly and Tom.*

He stood outside of the cellar door for a long while, listening to the muffled sounds of revelry and feeling the resonance of the last time he'd been there. The memory of what had happened. Of how much had changed. Without even really thinking he bent down, knocked, and was let inside.

Later he would realize that it shouldn't have surprised him, but still it hurt to see Gabriel with another man. He paused on the staircase, unseen by most in the darkness of the guardrail and dimmed mood lighting. The music was humming as it always was, rattling the beer bottles and shot glasses on Rosa's picnic table bar, where she still sat straddling the bench with a cigar between her lips.

Han made his way through the crowd, sticking to the shadows and weaving his way over to her. Her face dropped in surprise as she spotted him and he slipped up on the bench next to her as she said, "Well where in the name of all that's unholy have you been?"

Han shrugged, grimacing before answering, "It's a long story."

She observed him with dark eyes through a billow of smoke hissing out of her lips. "You alright?"

"I dunno, Rosa." Han leaned his elbow on the tabletop, rubbing his forehead then motioning through the crowd in the general direction of where he had seen Gabriel. "Do I look okay?"

Her lips pinched in thought before she responded.

"You been gone awhile you know that? I know that shit hurts, but you can't have just expected him to wait around."

"How long has it been?"

"What, you mean you don't know?" She took another drag, chasing it with a shot of something from the bar.

"No, I..." Han hesitated.

There was no way he could tell her, or anyone, what had actually happened to him. But he also hadn't taken the time to come up with any kind of viable excuse. He didn't even know what to excuse himself for. Had it been a week? A month? He was so confused, trapped in that timeless prison under Richter's forceful thumb.

"I'm... I just..."

Rosa's lips turned down even more.

"Where you been?" she asked again. She placed a hand on his arm and jerked back. "Fucking hell, Han! You're as cold as ice! You been living on the street or what?"

"I just need to talk to him," is all he could manage to say.

He moved to stand and she followed his movements with her eyes, peering up at him through pinched brows.

"Don't go getting in more trouble," she warned, but she sounded more concerned than anything.

Han sighed, staring out at the small crowd, then bent over and kissed her cheek.

"It's nice to see you, Rosa," he said softly, struggling to keep the melancholy out of his voice as he thought of the way in which he'd probably never see this place again. "I hope you find you a pretty lady who loves you."

She laughed and smacked his ear. It didn't hurt.

"Shut your mouth. I got more game than anyone in this whole joint combined."

"I know." Han smiled sadly as he straightened out. "Take care of yourself."

She watched him, gaze careful and searching. "You too."

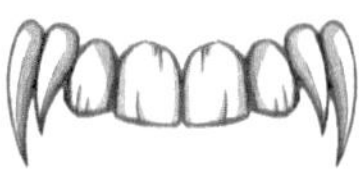

"GABE!" Han called, pushing his way through the small sea of bodies and over to the familiar face.

"Han?"

Han could see Gabriel's expression fall in surprise and the man he had been dancing with looked up as well.

"What is it?" Han heard the man ask.

"It's my... it's my old beau," Gabriel stammered, his expression one of muted shock.

"Old, huh?" Han asked. He stuffed down a well of insult that overtook him at the idea and raised his voice over the music. "Is that what I am? I want to talk to you!"

Gabriel glanced between him and the man at his side and seemed conflicted. He turned to the man and said, "This'll only take a minute."

He ignored the way Han scowled at him when he did.

"A minute, huh?" Han said once they were outdoors in the warm night air. "Moved on already?"

"Han," Gabriel shoved his hands deep in his coat pockets, not meeting Han's eyes. "You've been gone for months. I thought you were dead, killed by that rabid lady with the sword."

Han stared. Hearing what Gabriel was saying and not entirely taking it in.

Months. Dead. Killed.

He found his voice beneath the flurry of emotion and managed to speak.

"You thought I died, so you... what, mourned my memory with a new squeeze?"

"Where have you been, Han?" Gabriel ignored him. "Why don't you tell me that? Why didn't you come find me like you said you would? I was worried fucking sick. I came back and everyone was gone and there was just... there was..." Gabe took a deep breath and dug into the depths of his coat. "There was blood everywhere, and... and I found this so I thought..."

In his palm he held a tiny emerald green droplet earring on a long silver chain, once a signature accessory of Han's. He'd picked it up from a gutter ages ago and never thought to try to sell it. One could easily get themselves thrown into jail for owning something they obviously couldn't afford that they 'must've stolen'. So, he'd taken to wearing it under the cover of night in the safety of the club. Now, he didn't even realize he'd lost it.

"I thought you were gone." Gabriel sounded truly solemn.

"Well, I'm not," Han's retort reeked of bitterness, and he bit his lip. "You could have waited a little longer."

"I waited for a month Han!" Gabriel's voice rose. "A month! I heard nothing from you at all! What was I supposed to think? And now... now you just show up here with no explanation as to where you've been?"

"I..." Han deflated. Gabriel had every right to be upset, to try to move on, to be angry with him. "It's hard to explain, Gabe. You wouldn't believe me."

"Why don't you try telling me." Gabriel frowned and handed over the earring. "Here, you should have this."

Han grabbed it without thinking and instantly let out a small shout, dropping it into the grass. He looked down at his hand where the seared imprint of the earring lay like a fresh brand in the middle of his palm. Silver.

"What's wrong with you?" Gabriel let out an exasperated sigh, crouching down to pick it up. He stood and went to give it back.

"N-no," Han didn't take it. "You keep it."

"I don't want it," Gabriel said, still holding it out to him.

"Well, I don't either!" Han snapped.

It's not like he could actually explain the truth of his actions.

"Well, I don't want *this*," Gabriel said, softer now, as his arm fell to his side. "Han. I was never going to run away with you, okay? I was already thinking of ending things before you disappeared."

"What?!" Han took a small step forward. This was news to him. "Why?"

"You know why, Han." Gabriel pleaded. "This isn't right for me, it's not going to work. We're too different. It was fun but, it's not what I want."

"What so... me dying was an easy out, is that it?"

"No! Wh—" Gabriel scowled. "I mourned you, you ass."

"But you never really loved me, is that it?"

Gabriel pinched his lips before looking down at the dirt and giving a noncommittal half-shrug.

"Wow." Han scoffed. "Well, fuck me."

"I'm sorry Han, I really am. You're a great guy I ju—"

"Oh, don't give me that bullshit!" Han snapped. "You might not have given a shit to tell me the truth before now Gabe, but I *do* love you. I came here to see you because... because I thought... I needed to know... but you moved on. You forgot me."

"I'm sorry," Gabriel said again. "I don't know what to say."

"I think you've said enough," Han deflated. He'd gotten his answer. "You've said enough Gabe."

"So..." Gabe said after a moment of awkward silence. "What now?"

Han looked at him, then down at his palm slowly healing over from the silver burn. This place wasn't for him anymore. This wasn't his life, and he wasn't wanted. He was forgotten, and the world he knew had moved on without him.

"Nothing," Han said quietly, still looking at his hand. He swallowed hard against a sudden tightness threatening to take hold. "I hope you find what you're looking for."

He spun around, leaving the yard and the remnants of his old life behind, without another word.

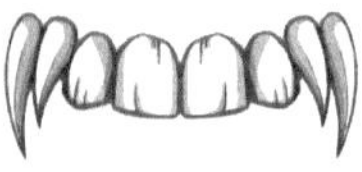

HAN RETURNED TO RICHTER, head hanging low. He should have fucking known, he should have seen it coming, he should have expected it. But what could he do? Even if Gabriel *had* loved him, even if Gabriel had waited for him, Han couldn't be part of his life. Not anymore.

He wasn't sure what anyone would do if they discovered what he was now. He still couldn't even bear to say it aloud, the reality of it only truly settling in during moments like this. When he would realize just how different he was, how impossible it was to go back. He had to find a new way forward, and apparently, that way was with Richter and his posse of stuck-up assholes that he hated.

He opened the large front door as the sun was beginning to rise, nearly missing the precious window of time before he was no longer safe outdoors. As he made his way to his room, his feet dragged across the luscious carpets, weighed down with bone-deep exhaustion and a broken heart. He was ready to collapse on his bed for as long as he could.

But he would have no such luck or sense of peace this morning. For on his bed, waiting for him with a borderline venomous scowl was Richter.

"Where the fuck have you been?" he instantly demanded.

"You said before sunrise." Han rubbed his temples. This was not the time for this. He was completely over Richter's shit—even on a good day. "It's before sunrise, isn't it?"

"Don't get smart with me." Richter jumped to his feet, meeting Han near the door with a snarl twisting his already repulsive features.

"I'm only saying what you said," Han sighed, and tried to move around him to get to the bed. "I'm really tired, Richter."

"As am I," Richter shot back. "Tired of your shit."

"*My* shit?"

Han quickly swallowed the rest of the words about to escape as he caught the look in Richter's eyes. He wasn't trying to get into some long-winded argument right now, or another fight of a more physical nature. But Richter was pushing it and Han was getting weary of not pushing back.

"That's it," Richter snapped. "That's the last time you go out alone. Where were you, huh? You smell like cigars."

"You know where I was," Han answered, and watched as Richter's scowl showed fangs.

"You piece of shit," Richter growled. "Him?"

"Yeah well, it's over now. So, don't worry."

"It should have been over the moment I turned you." Richter grabbed him, nails digging into his forearm.

"It was! It is!"

"It is what!" Richter gripped him harder.

"What?"

"It is... what."

"Over!"

"You forget your fucking place." Richter spun around, taking Han with him and causing him to trip over the carpet, stumbling to keep up in his stupid too-tight shoes.

"You don't own me!"

Han tried to pull back, but those nails dug deep into his skin nearly ripping through like knives.

"Oh?!" Richter whipped around to face him, jostling Han as if to shake him to his senses. "Don't I?! Who's the one who made you? Who's the one who took you out of the streets, out of your scummy life, and gave you all this?! Was it you?! No! You would be dead without me!"

"I wish you would have left me then!" Han yelled back, yanking his arm from Richter's claws and leaving flesh under his fingernails as he did. Blood dripped down into Han's palm and poured from his fingertips, quickly soiling the rug beneath their feet. "I would have rather died than be stuck here with you for an eternity!"

"Is that so?" Richter leered. "What do you know of eternity, boy?"

"Don't call me that," Han snapped.

"Boy?" Richter took a step towards him. "That's what you are, isn't it? Do you know how old I am? I could be your great-grandfather, your great-*great*-grandfather. I could have fucked your grandmother and made your mother and fucked her and made you, too!"

"Shut up." Han backed away, his patience quickly reaching its limit. "Just shut up!"

"WHO ARE YOU TO TELL ME TO SHUT UP?"

Richter's voice bellowed off those stupid fucking decorated walls.

He rushed at Han, hauling him by the front of his shirt and slamming him into the bookshelf. A misplaced tome tumbled to the floor brushing Han's shoulder just as Richter's leering voice hissed in his ear.

"I *MADE* you. You're *mine*. You can't escape me. You might as well accept it now, before the *real* eternity sets in."

Han's head was ringing. The night had already been bad, and now it was growing steadily worse. Anxiety pounded behind his temples blinding him with a slow-boiling rage. Gabriel hadn't missed him, hadn't loved him, had moved on without him. It hadn't even been that long.

Gabriel had abandoned him. He was trapped here, stuck with this. Stuck with *him*. Forever? Cornered, captured, and alone.

Forever.

No. No, he couldn't stand it, he couldn't take it.

He wouldn't.

No more thoughts came to him then, only the long-stifled desire to fight back.

Han whipped out his bleeding arm, slinging blood into Richter's eyes. Richter yelped and stumbled backward, trinkets and papers and ink were destroyed as he fell against a desk set in the middle of the floor. Before he could right himself Han was upon him, biting and clawing at any exposed skin. He didn't think. He became. As animalistic and primal as he felt, is how he acted.

He tore and bit and screamed while doing it, swatting away Richter's attempts to stop him with barely any effort. He was stronger now and fueled by adrenaline and rage and anguish and heartache.

Richter resisted, but he barely stood a chance as he was consumed by a monster of his own making. His claws no longer hurt the man they touched, for Han was much too far gone to feel it. Han was no longer that man.

Tendons came loose from flesh, stringy and pliant, and Han relished the taste on his tongue, the chewy texture in his teeth. Blood poured down his face, spewing from his ravenous mouth, soaking his extravagant clothes. Claws dug in deep, ripping and shredding and breaking, using the harvested bones as makeshift tools.

He was consumed by it—the blind rage that fueled him. That exhilarating sensation of freedom found past the tipping point of having had enough. There's no other way to describe what he felt besides that of pure, unadulterated, euphoria. It was a massacre. But it was beautiful. It was justice.

As Richter's body came apart beneath his hands, as his insides were clawed to ribbons and stew, as he drank up the flesh between his aching, burning, growling teeth, he went completely mad. A feral growl rose from within him as he relished in his glory.

He was finally free.

Eventually, he slowed, he blinked, and remembered where he was. What he had done. He came back to himself. Though nothing like remorse set in. Only calm realization as he looked down at the body beneath him, torn to bits by his angry claws. A strange wheezing sound was coming from the thing that was Richter and Han realized the vampire had begun to laugh.

"What's so funny," Han demanded, his body still crouched over Richter on the desk. Black blood was hot on his face, dripping from his mouth with the seething of his saliva.

"...What's... so funny?" Richter's words bubbled up through mouthfuls of spittle and bile, gurgling between the rasping of breath. "Han... you've finally... grown up. You've been waiting for this... haven't you?"

Han looked down at him, this remnant of his torment, and he felt no regret. A little bit of pity, maybe. But mostly nothing.

He witnessed what he had done and it simply spoke of a peculiar type of peace.

Han's lip twisted in a wry, humorless smile, and he repeated the words Richter had spoken to him that fateful day he took Han's life.

"I knew I'd have my chance. I'm a patient man. And look, here we are. Just me and you. Together forever."

His hands were soaking onto the polished wooden desk as he

stayed there quiet and observant watching as Richter writhed beneath him. Then, almost thoughtfully, he slowly reached a hand into the cavern he'd dug into Richter's chest. His fist squeezed around a heart that no longer remembered how to beat, how to feel.

He glanced up, meeting Richter's bloodshot eyes.

"Tell me this," Han said softly. His tone was only slightly curious, inquisitive. Detached. "Despite everything, Richter. Did you ever love me?"

Richter hiccupped, coughed, then out came another laugh.

"Of course not, boy."

When Han ate the heart he tore from Richter's chest, he relished the taste.

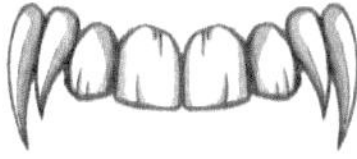

It was all a blur after that.

He remembered climbing down off of the desk on trembling legs, but what he did after it was hard to piece together. He thought he changed his clothes, but maybe he didn't. Maybe he stood still on the desktop, looking down at Richter's finally-actually-dead corpse with glazed-over eyes for long enough for the sun to go back around and sink down again. No one came to look for him, no one came to look for Richter either. The time passed in inches, stretching into miles, creeping out across his mind to freeze this moment solid. Stopping it all right in its tracks.

Maybe he was sticky with it, fingers melded together with a slurry of offal and bile, velvet shoes peeling from wood and fiber carpet and clinging to the floors. Maybe he stumbled, body alive and awake in a way, a way it had never, ever been. Not even when he had needed breath.

Maybe he felt sick with it, a little queasy, a little overly full. He had gorged himself and had to focus entirely on not puking on the rug, red and black and bone. In and out in and out, simulated breaths, artificially cultivated calm. Until he was.

Calm. Nothing, empty, mostly fine, simply stoic.

Maybe he was heartbroken, betrayed, and alone. Though if he were, he wouldn't have admitted it. Not to himself and certainly not to anyone else. To those who do not care. To us. Those who watch with the callous interest of a voyeur, the morbid curiosity of a passerby waiting to see what happens next. Peering at his torment through a screen, on a page, without lending a shoulder, offering a hand, opening a heart. More intent on knowing than seeing. More intent on seeing than feeling.

He wouldn't show himself to anyone like that. Not any longer.

At some point he wiped his hands, he burned his clothes, he stared lifelessly at the remnants of Richter go up the chimney in a sticky smoke he was sure would be hard to clean. Cleaned by someone like him, what he once was. What was he now?

He wiped his face, he combed his hair, he watched as clumps came loose that had slowly turned silver with the loss of his life, knotted with dried bits of Richter's flesh.

He found new clothes, something simple.

Something that made sense. Something comfortable, practical.

He'd always thought Richter's taste something ridiculous, something obnoxiously ornate.

He might've even eventually blocked out the memory of it, that pompous palace of indulgence and pride.

He took what he could, jewels, clothes, money, coins. Anything he could find and shove into the embroidered satchel he'd snatched, where it had been haphazardly tossed into a closet full of more luxury than he would ever see again. In this age, anyway.

Then he ran.

Through the hallway, past the den, past the living room and dining room, past the foyer and the lounge, past the fireplaces lining every accursed corner of this decorative cage. He reached the front door and didn't stop, slinging it open and not bothering to close it behind him.

Down the street, stumbling on cobblestones and sidestepping holes, more focused on keeping his head down and the sick churning copper slobbering sludge of Richter from escaping his throat.

Past townhouses, large stone and mason mansions with roofs higher than the low-hanging clouds of smog choking anyone too poor to rise above them. Past the iron fences meant to keep people like him, people who were him, from placing their unworthy feet on artificially designated hallowed ground.

Down alleyways that became more familiar to him—crisscrossing lines which never intersected with fancier roads that people here were meant to clean and never enjoy. Past smaller houses, ramshackle cabins, lean-tos and huts, quiet in this early morning night as a few hours of rest settled on the backs of those who needed much, much more.

Finally, he broke free, no more homes or horses or slums or alleys, just open field and the long empty road that led away from the failing metropolis of Industry and into rolling forest hills.

A road he once hoped to travel with Gabriel in hand, running and running. But not running away. Running towards. Something new, something better.

Han stumbled on the edge of the pockmarked cart wheel tracks, completely alone, following them as a means of escape.

He panted as he slowed—human habits, human traits. A mirage of his former self.

The sound of a carriage caught his attention, and he looked back. The dark silhouette of Industry cut the rising dawn sky into unnaturally jagged shapes, and for a moment he was frozen as he took it in. He raised his hand, hailing the carriage without even really looking. He had money now; he could buy a ride.

Everything came so easily to those who already had enough.

Hopping aboard as the sun began to rise, he shut the door, and without another backward glance, left it all behind.

For a hundred years, he would run, from himself, from that place, from memory and attachment, from love and home, from care and anyone who could offer it. The thousands of miles he crossed would soon blend into this continuous pantomime of life. Living to survive, not living to love, to be seen, to be known. His heart hardened solid as stone, and no one could touch it. Touch *him*. Know him. Vindictive and spiteful he became, hateful and empty, stealing and using, taking what he could and leaving nothing behind but a trial of emptiness and hurt as hollow as he felt.

Han wouldn't slow down, not until he found that his fleeing footsteps had led him into the ramshackle home of a crotchety warlock.

Then, now, perhaps, he was ready.

Maybe slowing down didn't seem like such a bad idea after all.

TWENTY-FOUR

Python groaned, coming to consciousness to the sensation of burning tightly wrapped around his wrists. He wriggled and realized they were tied and whatever was holding him was lined in silver. The blistering effect sizzled on the surface of his skin. He hissed softly through his teeth, attempting to adjust them to escape the sting that was quickly becoming more painful.

He was in some kind of shack, or barn, or abandoned house. Empty except for old furniture covered in cloth and layers of dust that sparkled off the slow movement of stagnant air. For a moment Python wondered if he were still at Calysto's, and maybe he'd been asleep for a really long time. Time enough for everything to look even more condemned than it already was.

It was daylight outside, and thin muslin curtains made a poor attempt at keeping the sun at bay. Small slivers of deadly light sliced in ribbons across the darkness inside. He saw a beam threatening to creep across to where his leg lay outstretched and he quickly pulled himself in, hunching his long legs up into a ball as best he could.

He was secured to one of the home's center support beams and couldn't move his upper body, except his neck to look around. The silver chains dug into his upper arms where they restrained him. He could feel their bite through his thin shirt and shuffled in an attempt to make it more comfortable somehow, to no avail.

"Cal?" he asked softly. Hopefully.

It was ridiculous to think the warlock could've done this to him. Or was it? His easily reactive heart instantly assumed he'd been betrayed. When he called out it was quiet, simply from the hesitance in which he wanted to accept that he would hear a response from the man. If it was Calysto, if he'd done this, Python couldn't even begin to imagine what he'd do. He couldn't handle it. Not again, not another friend, not his first friend in a hundred years. If he couldn't trust Calysto now, after it all, then, then—

"Don't even think about trying to escape." A voice came from behind him.

Her.

Accompanying the words were her footsteps across the floor emphasized louder by thick-heeled boots.

Aeris.

He'd completely forgotten about Aeris, again. The events before she'd blasted him with a deadly form of flashlight all came rushing back and he began to feel a gnawing sense of panic.

She walked around to face him, dragging an old wooden chair across the floor in one hand and holding her shotgun in the other.

"Where's Cal?" he asked, surprising himself with the question. "What did you do?"

"Oh, what." She plopped down, straddling the back of the chair and leveling him with a look. "You expect me to believe you give a shit about him or something? Please."

Python swallowed and leaned his head back onto the pillar. "Is he dead?"

Aeris shrugged, waving her shotgun in a lazy circle. "Not till I get what I want."

"Did you have to use so many chains?" he groaned softly. "It really hurts."

"I'm not about to let you get away, not again," she snapped in response, then flashed him a humorless smile. "This is the end of the road for you."

Python wiggled in his restraints again before responding, and tried to maintain some humor in his voice. "Are you really gonna kill me, Aeris? Really? What'll occupy all your time when I'm gone?"

"Peace and fucking quiet, that's what," she answered, leveling him with another one of her looks. He knew by now that it meant trouble, it meant he shouldn't keep running his mouth, but then he remembered what Calysto had asked him and he needed to know.

"Hey, how come you've been chasing me this whole time, anyway? You never give me a straight answer, and seeing as I'm about to go to my eternal slumber you could at least do me that favor."

Aeris scowled, her expression turning even more sour.

"You really don't know?"

Python shook his head. "Swear."

She mulled something over before slowly saying, "I thought you were just messing with me this whole time."

"Aeris, babe, I've been alive way too long to keep track of everyone I've done wrong."

She wrinkled her nose, took off her hat, and threw it at his head. It smacked him in the forehead before falling into his lap. It smelled strongly of leather and old blood.

"Python, *sweetie*," her retort came out snide and dry. "I'm not your babe. Nor am I your friend."

"Awww." He feigned disappointment. It was a ruse to hide the growing fear he was actively forcing himself to ignore. "But honey, don't you remember our little rendezvous in the old Pike hotel? You surely liked me then, if I recall correctly. I liked you, too."

"That was simply a way to try and kill you, that didn't work out as planned," she said quickly, pinching her lips.

"What kind of genius master plan to kill me involves fucking, then cuddling while watching shit TV, then drinking, then fucking again?"

"The kind where you let your guard down," she snapped.

"Ohhhh," he mused. "That's why you tried to stake me in the middle of... Oh, I thought that was just some attempt at arousing me."

"What kind of..." She raised an eyebrow. "And you just went with it?"

"Well, sure babe," he smirked. "It did the trick. Sharpened my own stake, if you know what I mean."

"I hate you," she bit back, completely unamused by his antics.

"You didn't enjoy it then, did you? You're gonna say it was really all an act?"

She studied him quietly then sighed before answering, "Since you're gonna die, I'll indulge you. On two accounts. One, yeah I enjoyed it, you're cute, a fun lay, and I was lonely. Two, you're the last one, Python. The last fucker from that god-forsaken shithole city who's responsible for all this. You're a weasel and a scoundrel and a liar, and if it wasn't you who turned me it was one of the ones with you. You're all responsible for this in my book. I swore to kill every last one of you, and I have. All except you."

Python couldn't help the grin that crept across his face. "You think I'm cute?"

"Is that all you heard of that? I hate you!"

"You said that already," he sobered. "I don't get it. I've... I've never turned anyone. Never."

"I don't believe you."

"I swear! Why would I? I... I didn't ask for this any more than you did!" Python struggled to sit up more against the wooden stake. His skin was aching to the point of creeping in and irritating his every action. His emotions, too. "I've never turned anyone, not even then... I... I didn't even stay there long enough for that." He bit his lip, as this conversation forced him to revisit fragments of memories he'd much rather forget. "Aeris, I... did you know me back then? I don't remember you at all."

She glared at him, dark curls falling around her face to frame her hollowed cheeks. "I don't believe you, Python. I know you're just trying to talk your way out of your ultimate demise, but it won't work. Not this time, *honey*." She spat that last word with a mocking smile.

"What are you going to do?" he asked, cautiously.

"Sit tight and see," she answered. She swung her leg up and around and started to walk away, dragging the chair with her. "If our little hunter friend doesn't get here by tomorrow, you'll know."

"Who?" Python squirmed, trying to turn and keep an eye on her.

"Don't play dumb!" she retorted, slinging the chair against the wall in anger, where it easily shattered into splinters.

"Really, I don't know who you mean."

"Don't tell me you just crashed in some guy's house without knowing who he is?"

"What, do you mean Calysto?" A laugh escaped before he could stop it. "He's not a hunter. He can barely keep his fucking glasses on and remember to eat like, even once a day."

"That's where you're wrong, baby." She laughed in return and she left him in the slowly brightening room, alone with his thoughts.

Python groaned as the silver continued taking a toll on his remaining energy. He really needed a drink, and soon. If he didn't get blood he'd begin to deteriorate, a decaying process that was already quickened by the strain of the painful chains. He thought about mentioning it and almost opened his mouth to call out to Aeris, certain she could hear him from wherever she went. But he doubted he'd find any sympathy from her.

Instead, he let his head fall back and closed his eyes. A mistake, really. For all it did was make him focus harder on his growing hunger, and the strange comments Aeris made about Calysto. Was Cal really a vampire hunter? He was so... reclusive... and small. He didn't even like to go outside or talk to anyone. Calysto had also, even, kind of, asked him to stay. Not to mention if Cal had wanted to kill him, he'd already had more than enough opportunities.

It made no sense.

Yet the seed of doubt was planted, and without the ability to ask or threaten the warlock into telling him the truth, Python's imagination could do nothing but spin out of control.

CALYSTO WOKE to the taste of blood in his mouth and a sharp ringing in his head that fluctuated with the pounding against his skull.

What the fuck just happened.

"Py... Python?" he called out. "Python? Aeris?"

No answer. The house was silent. Too silent. He pushed up his glasses with a weakened hand and only then did he notice something on the floor next to him. It was a note.

The crumpled napkin swayed in a blurry haze as he tried to read the words through watering eyes.

BRING me the cure to the address by Friday sunup or your little vampire fuck buddy dies.

KISSES, A.

CALYSTO PEERED close at the address: 180 6B Industry Rd.

SHIT.

It became instantly clear to Calysto that whatever this was about was obviously personal. But why him and why Python and why her and what for?

Calysto crawled up from his living room floor, his head and bottom lip crusted with blood. The sun had risen outside and shined in through the front door that still swung open, wafting in billows of cool air. He stumbled over Python's clothes in the hallway and attempted to right himself as he made his way to the door, slamming it shut. It was clear from the mess and the sunlit entryway that Python and Aeris were both gone.

Calysto was still dressed in the manner Python had outfitted him, and in a quiet display of frustration, he shucked off the thick woolen peacoat throwing it on the floor with the rest of the scattered clothing. He lit the living room lanterns with a quick wave of his hand and picked up the note Aeris had left for him.

Sunrise on Friday? He didn't even know what day it was now and never typically did. It didn't matter what day of the week it was when time was one big, continuous, endless blur. He scrambled upstairs to find his tablet. Even if he didn't have service, it was still connected to the time and date via satellite, something he had a particular passing fascination with once.

He grabbed it from under the crystal table, the case still opened and exactly where he would have expected Python to leave it—on the floor. Picking it up, he brushed off the dust and wiped his hand onto his pants before entering the passcode:

1796

The year of his birth. Or what he'd once surmised it was from a general guess.

Oh, so it was Thursday, 6:34 am.

That pretty much gave him exactly one day to figure out what to do.

He definitely considered it for a moment: the possibility that he could do nothing.

Really, what did Python's business have to do with him? Aeris was a vampire hunter and Python had clearly had it coming, Calysto had just gotten caught in the middle of whatever chaos Python had drummed up for himself. There was no real obligation to help.

Aeris had mistaken him for someone else in the past, and she had done so again now. He deduced she must be some kind of supernatural being like them as well, for her to be here and then. But still, even if she had seen him then, and remembered him now, it didn't explain what the cure was. He had worked on countless cures in his lifetime, but he had a feeling she didn't mean any of the conventional ones. Besides, how would she even know? He'd never released formulas or patents under his own name.

Bring me the cure to the address by Friday sunup, or your little vampire fuck buddy dies.

Calysto scoffed a bit at the idea. Python certainly wasn't a *fuck* buddy, he was barely even a buddy to begin with. Though Calysto had to admit the strange understanding that had bloomed between them was something he was beginning to like. Become accustomed to, even. He had even asked the vampire to stay. Kind of. But Python had agreed. And for a moment, he'd even felt a bit excited at the idea, happy even.

Shit.

He was really about to go put his ass on the line to rescue Python from whatever torturous death he so clearly deserved and had brought right down upon himself, wasn't he?

Yeah. Yeah, he was.

Calysto sighed and closed his tablet case. He decided to put on some normal—as close to modern—clothes as he could find, and while he changed, figure out what possible cure Aeris could want. Really, he needed to figure out where to start to even determine that.

But before he could begin, he heard a knock come from downstairs. It sounded like the front door. For a split second, he was frozen like a jackrabbit on a backroad in the middle of the night, not expecting for their reality to be so drastically shifted by the appearance of a two-eyed glowing speed monster.

Splat. Dead and gone before the chance to process what had happened could set it, and he could flee from the danger.

Calysto shook his head, he wasn't a rabbit, and he wasn't afraid.

There had been so much action and events around his house lately, and after decades of relative silence with the only sound made being those of his own doing, he wasn't used to all the commotion. Now both Aeris and Python were gone.

Therefore this sound and interruption brought a new thought— *Who the fuck is it?*

Calysto pushed up his glasses, tucked a stray curl of golden hair behind his ear and his tablet underneath his arm, and slowly made his way down to investigate.

The knock came again, but he didn't hurry, didn't call out to respond.

Finally, he opened the door a small crack, squinting against the still-beaming morning sunlight that glinted off of his glasses and blinded him, backlighting the silhouette that stood outside on the grass.

"Can I help you?" Calysto asked.

The person didn't answer at first and only stared as if observing Calysto as hard as he was trying to see them back.

"Oh..." the person said, seeming to find their voice. "No, I'm here to help you."

"What?" Calysto opened the door a bit more, trying to get a better look.

The person was a man of similar height, though Calysto was taller than him where he stood on the doorstep. He shifted slightly, blocking the sun with the back of his head, and Calysto could finally see him.

He was smiling, patiently waiting and in good humor. His face was narrow with a pronounced jaw, framed by long ringlet blonde hair streaked with white.

He wore a long open black sweater over a relaxed-neck t-shirt in a fashion Calysto had never seen, and well-fitted jeans. On his shoulder was a leather satchel, and the slender hand that held it wore two golden rings. But Calysto's eye caught on something else—the rippled scar on the man's cheek, that looked just like his own.

"Who are you?" Calysto asked cautiously.

"Hello Calysto," the man answered, his smile stretching wide. "I'm you."

"WHAT DO you mean you're me?" Calysto frowned. "You look nothing like me."

"Not now, I don't," this supposed-Calysto answered. "I'm not from this time."

Calysto sighed. "Don't tell me there's *more* time traveling."

"Afraid so." Supposed-Calysto shrugged good-naturedly. "We get the hang of it though."

Calysto gave the guy another good once-over before asking, "If you're really me, tell me something only we'd know."

"Thought you might ask that," Supposed-Calysto smiled. "Let's see. In this time, we really like those cherry-flavored 'Fast-N-Ener-giZd' energy drinks. They stop making them in another ten years though, sorry to say. I found a pretty good replacement, but it's not the same. Um, we first wrote our name with ink we made ourselves, at Merik's. Storage closet. We both like Python more than we let on. At least you do."

Calysto frowned slightly. "He's alright, I guess."

"You know it's more than that."

Calysto pinched his lips together. "Where are your glasses?"

"Oh, yeah we get that taken care of," Supposed-Calysto grinned again. "No more glasses needed."

"How?"

"I forgot we don't get out much yet," Supposed-Calysto said, half muttered to himself.

Calysto still wasn't totally convinced, but honestly, what could it hurt to go along with it? He'd been through stranger things in the last week, meeting his future self didn't even strike him as that weird of a possibility right now.

"Do you want to come in?"

He stepped aside, and Supposed-Calysto nodded in thanks and slipped past. Only then did Calysto notice that he was wearing... boots?

"These are pretty comfortable, actually." S.C. said, acknowledging where he was looking.

"Oh... uh, alright." Calysto shuffled away, still wearing the too-big pair that Python had given him, and led them to the kitchen. "Have a seat, if you want."

S.C. obliged, still smiling in that fondly-familiar way, and set his bag down on the table between all the trash.

Calysto paid him no mind and instead put his tablet on the counter and opened the fridge, staring inside. He picked up two of the fallen-over energy drinks that survived the recent move and palmed one in either hand, thinking hard for a long quiet moment. Then he turned and gave one to S.C. who accepted it gratefully, snapping open the lid and taking a greedy gulp while closing his eyes.

Calysto looked on, feeling a mix of curiosity and detachment, like a man witnessing events he couldn't believe and was expecting to wake up from. Or to be told it was all a big joke. Or maybe he did believe it, but it was—well, it was fucking ridiculous.

He was waiting for it to set in. For that shoe to drop and send him spiraling.

This might as well happen.

"They really stopped making these?" Calysto finally spoke, after watching S.C.'s throat bob up and down. One gulp, two gulps, three.

"Yeah!" S.C. exclaimed, setting the can down. "It's a shame really. I missed them. Thanks."

Calysto tipped his drink slightly in S.C.'s direction, acknowledging the thanks, and took his own long sip, letting his eyes graze the ceiling. He stared long and hard into the fluorescence until his eyes began to burn and a large stained spot wavered in front of his sight.

This might as well happen.

"Hey..." S.C. began.

"You said you were here to help me," Calysto cut him off. "With what?"

"Oh, with Python," S.C. said matter-of-factly. "What day is it?"

"Thursday," Calysto answered. "Why?"

"Is he gone already?"

"... Yes."

"Aeris, right?"

Calysto took another long sip, choosing to stall for time with his answer. Choosing to give himself more time to process.

"Yes," he said softly.

"I assume you've already decided to save him, yeah?"

Calysto shrugged. "Well, yeah. He might be... you know..." He shot S.C. a look. "Well, I don't know what you know, but, I just don't think he should die."

"I don't either," Supposed-Calysto smiled to himself.

"Why do you care?"

S.C. gulped from the tall can and sighed in pleasure. "You should really stock up on these."

"Noted," Calysto said, enjoying his own drink. "So um... do you have something to tell or what?"

"Oh yeah!" S.C. perked up but had enough of Calysto in him to look embarrassed at the slight display. "Why don't you grab that fold-out chair from behind the stairs, you're probably gonna want to sit down."

Calysto stared at him, contemplating the strangeness of it all, then went and obliged his instructions. Sure enough, tucked behind the staircase was a shitty metal high-school-trailer-classroom type chair, nearly rusted shut with age, and the thin, essentially-useless foam cover was chewed through with small rat-shaped teeth marks and riddled with mold. Calysto wrinkled his nose as he pulled it out, wrestling with it slightly. It popped open with a loud creak and a small puff of dust. He shuffled back into the kitchen and placed it down across the table from S.C.

Littered on the table was a pile of Calysto's accumulated trash but now combined, mixed within it, and scattered on the floor, were more of Python's things. Gummy worms he'd wanted to try, a bag of chips Calysto had reluctantly shared that Python ended up gobbling down the most of, gum wrappers, drink cartons and bottles, empty cigarette boxes and countless butts, the filters of which all held the distinct dent of Python's left fang, a pint of ice cream neither of them liked and didn't finish—melted sticky and solid to the trash beneath it —a crumpled-up T-shirt used as a makeshift rag, and those deep claw marks now forever marring the surface.

Calysto took it all in, finding the ways in which he associated this place not only with himself anymore but with the presence of another.

"Yeah, me too," S.C. spoke up, breaking Calysto out of his thoughts by speaking them aloud. "Never really thought I'd like him, either."

"I don't—" Calysto stopped mid-sentence.

It didn't feel right to say he didn't like Python. But it also didn't feel right to say he *did*. He didn't know.

This shit was confusing.

But S.C. gave him another one of those pitying half-smiles laced in a complicated air of nostalgia, so he didn't attempt to answer.

"So," Calysto cleared his throat. "Can you finally tell me why you're here?"

S.C.'s golden-eyed gaze lingered on him a moment longer before he seemed to wander back to the present and he lit up.

"Ah! Yes. Saving Python." S.C. nodded. "So, I take it by now you've gathered that Aeris is a vampire."

"Figured as much, yeah."

"Well, she's had it out for him, for like a hundred years."

"He told me that."

"Oh yes," S.C. answered, a bit wistfully. "It's hard to recall just exactly how things happened back then. Now."

"Shall I catch you up?"

"No, no, let's not waste time." S.C. waved his hand. "Just stop me if I repeat myself. Or... we... do..." He trailed off and shot Calysto a sheepish glance. "I didn't expect this to be so strange, to be honest."

"I didn't expect it at all," Calysto shrugged. "But here we are I guess. So if you already know what to do why can't you just do it yourself?"

"Well, I could, but then we would never be me, would we?"

"I... guess?" Calysto wasn't stupid, and he knew if that man was him then he wasn't either. But he was now experiencing the second time travel timeline version of himself in what, two days? So, you'll forgive him if he was having a little bit of a hard time keeping up.

"Do you have your tablet?"

"Yes... why." Calysto pinched his lips.

"And we're in the same place where Aeris found us to begin with, right?"

"... Fairly certain."

"Alright then." S.C. stood, slinging on his bag and carrying his drink loosely in hand. "Let's go."

"Where?"

"Coffee shop," S.C. said. "Bout a mile west."

"Why?"

Calysto's pulse quickened at the thought of being so conveniently located near a town. He had really landed this house in the worst possible spot to get him into the maximum amount of trouble.

"Don't overthink it," S.C. said, sounding slightly amused. "It's not as bad as you think, but we need some damned Wi-Fi, and if I recall you haven't got a hotspot just yet."

"A what?"

"Oh, you'll figure it out."

"I need to uh... I need to get my... shoes..."

"You're wearing shoes," S.C. laughed softly, forgivingly. "Come on, it'll be fine."

Calysto grabbed the blood-red peacoat that—though he didn't want to admit it—had become a bit of a comfort to him in the passing days, shoved the napkin note from Aeris in the pocket, and followed his future self out the door.

CHAPTER

TWENTY-FIVE

The coffee shop was quaint, sparsely populated, and smelled deliciously of cinnamon buns and fresh brew. Glass doors opened up into a rustic seating area fit with metal chairs that could make your ass uncomfortable simply by looking at them and were clearly chosen more for a throwback vibe than any consideration of butt-cheek longevity.

The wooden walls were decorated with coffee-flavored decor, old burlap sacks with designs and dates printed on them to mimic ages past, but likely hiding the manufactured date of two years ago on their insides, inkjet printed on a pretty tag. A rusted scythe—as if people still used, or even ever used, a scythe to cut down a damned coffee plant—hung diagonally across a long wall, framed by a gallery of local art made of recycled car parts and watered down overly-saturated acrylic paint selling at prices nearly identical to that of the menu's version of hype over quality.

S.C. took the lead as they entered, bringing them both up the counter and catching the hawk-eyed attention of two baristas lingering behind the bar.

Both were uniformed in faded leather aprons, artificially wear-worn to masquerade like they served in an elite guild of craftsmen hammering swords or making tools, rather than shelling out stomach-acid flavored liquid diarrhea under the guise of an artisan label. It didn't take a genius or a microgram scale to make a decent fucking cup of coffee, but here it did, and if you didn't like it, well, you just didn't get it.

Calysto stayed behind, not particularly interested in even perusing a list of coffee drinks that were all essentially the same, over-priced, and tasted like shit. Besides, with a low-end price point of six dollars, even the cheapest thing in here was six dollars more than he had.

S.C. ordered, rattling off a mouthful of words that had no real-life applicable meaning and only served to make this place think higher of itself, then turned to Calysto.

"Hey," he said. "Get whatever you want."

"No, I'm good," Calysto mumbled in response, not really wanting to attract the judgmental stare of the beard-oiled barista impatiently tapping his fingers on the tablet POS system in a caffeine-induced frenzy. Humans were so sensitive to the stuff, he wondered how they managed to consume so much of it.

S.C. leaned towards him. "I'm buying."

"You have money? How?" Calysto asked, eyeing him suspiciously.

"Order first, then I'll tell you."

Calysto reluctantly shuffled up to the counter and stared long and hard at the plastic-coated list of bullshit he didn't care to understand.

"Can I just have a coffee?" he asked.

The barista sniffed as if he'd heard this question a thousand times before and still hadn't lost his disdain for it. When he finally answered, his tone dripped more condescension than Calysto thought was possible to get away with under the guise of customer service.

"Coffee comes in light roast, single-origin, medium, dark roast, nitro cold brew, cold brew, iced medium roast, and locally sourced."

"The fuck is a nitro cold brew?" Calysto murmured. "Nitrogen? Nitro-glycerin? Nitric acid? Are you trying to kill people?"

"Medium roast, iced, with cream and extra hazelnut syrup," S.C. spoke up, apparently taking pity, or mercy, on him.

"What did you get me?" Calysto asked suspiciously.

"Same thing I got me." S.C. smiled. "You'll like it."

"If you say so."

They made their way to a table, as tucked away from the few others whose numbed asses and lukewarm half-finished cups of bile hadn't made them give up their work for the comfort of their own homes quite yet. Calysto slid in, immediately mourning his legs still filled with a semblance of life, and flipped open his tablet, typing in the 'for paying customer's only' password into the BREWHAUS_Guest Wi-Fi.

"Okay, now what," he said quietly.

Though it was sparsely populated, he kept his voice to a low whisper. Not only was he a private man and not accustomed to being observed or overheard, be he also didn't trust a place built off the backs of a poor community turned bougie gentrified strip mall with no remorse. He wondered how S.C. could be okay with it.

"I hate this fucking place, for the record," S.C. whispered back. Oh, so there was his answer. Maybe they were the same person, after all. "But it's the closest thing."

"Please tell me you don't still live around here," Calysto spoke under his breath.

"Fuck no," S.C. replied, turning to dig something out of his bag. "Besides if I were, you would've landed the house right on my house. Our house."

"Oh, that does make sense."

Calysto fiddled with a peeling piece of faux leather on his tablet case, waiting for S.C. to set up his own and produce a huge stack of papers along with it.

"What is all this?"

S.C. shot him a patient look that told him to 'wait just a second' as the barista came around teetering both of their coffees in thick faceted glasses clearly meant for some type of equally shitty IPA rather than caffeine. It was the other employee, the one who had looked more like she just needed the job and simply played the part of an espresso enthusiast, rather than being one of the pillars of fraudulent counter-culture that held this place up with its trust fund money.

Calysto glanced over and caught her eye. She gave him a polite smile and set their glasses down. She turned to leave, then hesitated for a moment before looking back and leaning over towards them.

"Sorry about him," she said in a hushed tone. "He just... really likes coffee. If you don't like it, I'll get you a refund no problem."

Calysto nodded and murmured a small, "Thanks."

She went to walk away but Calysto spoke up again, "Ah, sorry. Could we get um, cinnamon buns? Two?"

He gave a glance at S.C. who nodded in enthusiastic agreement.

"Sure thing," she agreed and left them be.

"Good idea," S.C. said. "Might cut the bitterness of this shit."

"I thought you liked it?"

"Well, I think I will," S.C. shrugged. "Sounded like the most normal thing in here."

"Doesn't mean it won't— "

"—taste like shit, I know."

Calysto quirked a small smile in spite of himself.

It was kind of nice to talk to someone who got him.

Oh yeah, he was talking to himself. But who better to get him, than anyone else?

He stared at the dust glimmering in air-current swirls through sunbeams near the front window and his mind drifted to a certain silver-haired absence at his side, before he shook his head, cleared his throat, and turned his attention back to the task at hand.

He reached into his coat pocket and produced the crumpled-up napkin note and smoothed it out onto the table, careful not to get the cold condensation that dripped from his glass on the edges of the paper.

The scribbled handwriting and what could be a dried dot of blood on the edge reminded him of where he was and what was at stake.

"Do you know what this cure is that she's talking about?" Calysto asked.

"Vampirism," S.C. explained, reaching for his drink and taking a sip. He grimaced slightly and set it back down. "Oh, that's vile... Aeris is looking for a cure for vampirism, that our father was supposedly working on."

"Our father?"

"Oh... yes," S.C.'s brow furrowed. "Shit, I really should've thought of a better way to explain this. But essentially, yes. Do you remember when you went into the past with Python, and you were mistaken for someone else who looked like you, sounded like you, had your same name?"

"That was my father?" Calysto mimicked S.C.'s expression.

"Yes, it's... well, here."

S.C. began separating the large stack of papers from his bag into smaller piles, and presented Calysto with an array of handwritten notes, long manuscripts worn and yellowed, indented with the impact of typeface from a typewriter, old computer print-outs with ink—never meant to be permanent or archived—slowly bleeding together and muddling the words, scraps of receipts and corners of parking tickets scribbled with words and phrases, cardboard thermal coffee sleeves, something that looked like it was once a wrapper to a candy bar the company of which had long since gone under. Articles from newspapers as far back as Calysto had been alive, an old leather bound journal, and stacks and stacks of information that all were clearly written and collected and contrived from the mind of someone possessed.

"He *was possessed* with this... need to find a cure," S.C.

explained. "For vampirism. From what I've gathered, especially from this journal here..." He tapped the leather bound book softly. "He was turned and... well... maybe you should read it for yourself."

"Was? How do you know all this? Is he dead?"

"Well, as far as I know, he's probably still alive, though having searched for a couple decades now I haven't been able to find him. Whatever research he did, and whatever obsession drove him, it died out, or he died, or he went into hiding. I can't say for sure, to be honest."

"He's... alive?" Calysto grabbed for his glass if only to have something to hold onto.

"If you haven't gathered yet..."

"He's a vampire, too?" Calysto finished his sentence with a half-statement half-disbelieving question.

"Yeah. You're gonna want to read this," S.C. pushed the journal towards him. "Well, we don't really have that kind of time but... here..." He flipped through to a page marked with a crumpled neon sticky note and handed it to Calysto who, after wiping his coffee-cup-damp hand on his pants, took it into his lap. "Just go to the pink tabs, for now."

The barista came by with their cinnamon rolls, waving her hand and saying they were on the house when S.C. tried to pay.

S.C. immediately dug into his treat, picking off bites from the outer edge and working his way inward, licking his fingers of the frosting and scrolling on his phone with the other clean hand. He looked up occasionally as if studying Calysto's face as he read, or to see what part he was on, then sat back and continued staring at his phone, typing and smiling slightly to himself.

Calysto didn't notice any of it because the moment his eyes locked with the words on the page, everything else fell away. The coffee in his hand served only as a grounding presence into the present, as he chewed methodically on the end of the plastic straw, gnawing it into unusable oblivion. There was nothing on his mind besides absorbing the information.

Calysto had always been a sponge, soaking up anything and everything he could get his hands on. History, news, science, medicine, literature, bookbinding was especially fascinating to him though he never got around to trying it just yet, infectious disease, current events, TV shows, biographies, documentaries. Anything that could teach him about the world or about others, he devoured with a fervor untainted or tamed by the long lonely decades alone. But, something that could teach him about himself? Well, he'd simply never come across it.

There wasn't any literature that wasn't some false amalgamation of randomly made-up ideas about what a warlock was. It was all simply fiction, those places in which he saw what he was, what he was supposed to be. An old man, complete with the floor-length robe and a comical hat and equally ridiculous beard and wild eyes, showering magic from his hands with no consequence, no struggle, and usually on a quest for domination or power.

It was funny in a way, the stereotypes that he'd seen.

Or maybe they weren't stereotypes, maybe that really was what a warlock was supposed to be?

He couldn't say. He was the only one he'd ever met. But still, it seemed unlikely. He didn't possess any power even close to something like that. He'd never seen anything about vampires either and certainly had always thought those were a myth.

He'd always liked the idea of them though and fancied himself a bit of a vampire having lived so long in relative hiding. He didn't really eat, didn't really sleep, and lived a lonely solitary existence. For as far as he knew he was immortal, or something of the sort, and rarely ever saw the light of day.

Now, he was facing more sunlight than he had in decades, and all because of an *actual* vampire. Kind of funny, that. And currently, that actual vampire was in deathly trouble and needed his help, apparently. He was the only one who could help, even. The only one who knew how. Or, was going to know how, somehow, from this book in his lap.

With the journal in hand, he was suddenly presented with more true knowledge on both subjects than he ever could imagine. His father, a vampire? Him, a warlock? How did these two even overlap? How did Supposed-Calysto know and he didn't? He tried to clear his racing thoughts and focus on the pages in front of him.

ENTRY 173:

NOTHING TO REPORT TODAY.

Experiments with human genome unsuccessful still, hard to find test subjects or willing participants in this endeavor. Only able to go out at night, only able to lurk in the shadows, I am a back alley death dealer rather than a researcher, a man desperate for a cure. Will I ever find it?

CALYSTO FLIPPED THE PAGE.

ENTRY 189:

MERIK IS OF NO HELP, *the old bastard.*

I am nearly convinced he is one himself, the way he hoards up in that castle. The knowledge at his fingertips could help more people than he knows. Including me, the ones like me.

ENTRY 190:

I WONDER SOMETIMES *if she misses me.*

Or, missed. I read about it in the papers what became her demise and I feel sorry. Sorry that I didn't say goodbye, sorry that I ran away, sorry that I couldn't even tell her. But, it was for the best, wasn't it? I hope she felt it, the fact that I loved her, that one last time.

This life isn't for me and certainly not for anyone else. I had no choice. I had no choice.

CALYSTO FUMBLED for the next tab.

ENTRY 245:

THE LONELINESS IS NEARLY UNBEARABLE.

I distract myself with the work, the research, the fight. The blood of the others like me stains my hands, I have decided I can do no more of it. I can only try to find a way to let us die, let us rest, let us be human again. I cannot kill myself, and therefore, who am I to kill those who are exactly as I am?

ENTRY 386:

A CURE IS IMPOSSIBLE.

Now, for what must be the thousandth time, I find myself defeated. Sitting at my desk in this darkness, peering at the window which could be my undoing, and considering pulling the curtain back. It would be so simple, and it is the only way in which I can take my life into my own hands. All choice was taken from me. That night feels so long ago it is all but a dream. The last dream I'd ever had.

I am nothing but a husk, a shell of a former self that existed for less time than this creature I now am. I have nothing, no legacy, no friends, no love, no life. Only this pursuit, for which there is truly no answer. A fruitless journey. One that I cannot turn from, for there is nothing to turn to, there is nothing else.

ENTRY 426:

*W*HOEVER TURNED *me must still be alive.*

Who turned them? And them before them? Is this ancient blood curse a lineage passed down like a virus from age to age, from the beginning of the history of humans on earth? Further? Though, one cannot exist without the other, can it? I feed on the life of those with so little life to give, to sustain this enteral sprawl. What is my life worth, in comparison? Who am I to deem myself worthy of their essence, to prolong my own?

I am weak without it, I am unstoppable within it, but it does nothing to enhance my mind or my knowledge, only this body which forever hangs on the brink of decay. It helps me not in finding a way out, for myself and for the others so unfortunately forced into this half-life of misery. If only this eternity didn't move so slow. If only I could find the key.

ENTRY 427:

*T*HE ONLY WAY OUT *is death.*

The key is the sunlight and the release from this immortal toil. I no longer hold out hope for anything else, but for the day in which I am brave enough to let it warm my face.

ENTRY 503:

· · ·

*U*NSURE OF WHAT *year it is, anymore.*

I have lost track, and no longer wish to try to do so.

ENTRY 507-508:

*I*T IS TODAY, *I think, that I will part with life.*

This bittersweet fruit plucked while ripe, and turned to rot and mold and left to linger past its prime. I can no longer hold out for hope, for companionship, for a sense of normalcy or pantomime of life. I don't wish to continue on like this. So alone.

I haven't spoken to another, or even seen another's face, in a countless span of days and nights. I haven't fed in what must be a week. I cannot stand to hear their cries, the sound of their heart as it quickens and slows, the taste of their coppery offering on my tongue. I long for the taste of bread, of a meal not made of another but only by another's hands. I have been this creature longer than I was a man, and no longer do I wish to be either. This is no life, not without all the things that make it so.

For who do I turn to but myself, in times of need? Who will listen to me, hear my voice and prove that I exist? It cannot be me, for I am myself, and this thing that is myself is empty and hollow and void. Unchanging through the ages, stuck in stagnation, with no one but the walls and this worn-out paper to hear me.

I have come to the conclusion that there is no other way out.

There is no end in sight, so for that I say, I must make one.

The sun is rising, and I can see its deadly glow creep from beneath the front door.

I think I am brave enough now, to let it in.

· · ·

CALYSTO FLIPPED to the next page to find it blank, and the next, and all the way to the end.

He looked up to S.C. with questioning eyes, who was watching him carefully in return.

"That's why I said I don't know," S.C. said softly. "He may very well be dead."

"It's a suicide note if I've ever read one," Calysto answered, equally as solemn. "He was so lonely... and he never found a cure."

"No, he didn't," SC agreed. "Whatever cure Aeris thought... thinks... he had, he never found. He tried, that's for certain. This here is only a portion of the research and information I was able to find of his, collected over time. There is no cure for vampirism, as there is no 'cure' for life as much as death. It simply is, and must be as it is."

"That's one way to look at it," Calysto nodded. "But what about ones like him? Who hate it? Who want a way out?"

"Don't we all hate it sometimes?" S.C. shrugged. "Being alive, that is. Is it any less cruel to live as a human being, feeding off of the earth and each other..." He cast a glance around the cafe as if it proved his point. "Than it is to drink their blood? Life is meaningless without purpose, without direction, without a reason to go on. We all must find it somehow."

Calysto pushed up his glasses slowly. "Yes, but... they didn't choose that life."

"Neither did we." S.C. smiled slightly, without humor. "No one alive chose to be, did they? But they make the best of it. Whether that be by stepping on their fellow man to give themselves a sense of superiority and soothe that terrified little ego that doesn't want to be reminded that they are going to die just like everyone else, or they find something better. Something more meaningful, more real, and more human than anything else."

"What's that?"

"I think you know," S.C. smiled again, genuinely this time. "It's what our father lacked, and what drove him to his despair. Not the vampirism, not the drive for a cure or the inability to find one."

"Someone to talk to," Calysto said, quietly. "Someone who cared, someone who he could care about in return."

"Purpose," S.C. agreed. "Passion. Love."

"I wish he could have found it," Calysto murmured, then after a moment's hesitation added. "It's terrible to be alone."

SC nodded. "It is. But we don't have to be him. Through no fault of his own, he couldn't find that way out, but we can."

"How?" Calysto started gnawing on the straw again.

"Take this journal to Aeris, show her the truth, and save our little vampire friend from certain death."

"What is this," Calysto grumbled. "A fucking quest?"

"In a sense, yes," S.C. chuckled. "Think of it as a quest for what we've always wanted."

"What happened to your hair? Do... do I really age?" Calysto asked suddenly.

S.C.'s eyes widened before he focused on the greyish-white ringlet in front of his eyes and his face turned a soft crimson.

"No, we don't age," S.C. tucked the curl behind his ear. "It's ah... It's a bit embarrassing."

"Isn't everything?" Calysto grimaced slightly but tried to make it sound encouraging.

S.C. laughed softly. "You certainly are me."

"So...?" Calysto waved a hand at the hair.

"Oh, yeah," S.C. quirked a smile. "Python bleached it years ago... said it would look cool. I like it so, he just keeps doing it."

"Python dyes our hair?"

"Bleach, but, yeah," Calysto answered. "He's not so bad, you'll see."

"... I think I already have," Calysto murmured, suddenly desperate to change the subject again. "So, how do I even find them?"

"I made you a map," S.C. sat forward, leaning across the small cafe table. "Oh, and while you were reading I set this up for you."

S.C. handed him the phone he had been playing with. "Here, it's got some minutes and some data. Should last a little while."

"You're not coming?"

"Oh no." S.C. waved his hand. "I have to go back, people are expecting me."

"Can't you just travel back to the exact time you left?"

"Huh," S.C. bit his lip. "I suppose so. But either way, I think this is something you should do alone."

"But... Wait, I have one more question."

"Hmm?"

"How did you find all this stuff? About our father?"

"You showed me. Well, I did. Like this."

"But then, who showed you... me?"

S.C. gave a wrinkled wry smile that bordered on a grimace. "You know. Maybe I haven't got this *whole* time travel thing figured out just yet."

Calysto stared, overwhelmed with the information and finding himself at a loss for what to say. S.C. began combing all the papers back together and shoving them into his satchel.

"I should get going, and so should you," he was saying. "It'll be Friday morning by the time you get there at this rate."

"Wait..." Calysto stopped, swallowing back what he wanted to say.

"What?" S.C. looked up.

"Why..." Calysto frowned, picking at the edge of his coat sleeve. "How... how are you me? Are you really me? You're so..."

"What, happy?" S.C. offered.

"... Yeah."

Their eyes locked, dark and solemn, staring into one another's. There was a long, long pause and neither moved, simply taking the other in. Calysto stared and only saw himself, mirrored in a way he never had dared to imagine.

Was it possible? To be what he'd sometimes hoped, that desire he'd long since buried? S.C. blinked, finally, breaking the strange energy between them and when he spoke, he once again, smiled.

"You'll find out."

CALYSTO STOOD on the side of the road, waiting for the car he'd ordered through some app that S.C. had downloaded. The autumn sun beat down relentlessly against the blacktop, the season not yet cooled enough to cut through the parching afternoon heat. Baking heat turned the blacktop into a steaming haze and chased all those around going to and from, into the safety and shelter of any air-conditioned relief in the white suburbanite strip mall behind him.

He found himself wishing he'd prepared for this and not worn a fucking coat.

Then again, he hadn't prepared for any of this at all. If he would've known he was leaving he would've packed... something. He would have at least warded his door. But it was no use now, and there was no time to do anything but move forward and find Python before it was too late.

He stared down at his hands in silent contemplation as if they could provide more answers on top of what he'd already learned.

S.C. was long gone, packing his iced coffee into a plastic to-go cup all while quietly laughing. Saying something about how Python would love to get a taste. Apparently, they liked to shit on shitty things together, or something of the sort.

Calysto scuffed his boot against the rough grain of the sidewalk, looking down the road for any sign of the car. He was growing antsy, impatient, nervous. Just because the Calysto of the future had an alive and well Python at his side, did not mean that him, the Calysto of right now, couldn't fuck it up for everyone involved, past, present, and future alike.

A huge weight pressed upon him as if the happiness of all his selves hung in the balance.

Was Python really the thing that had created this for him?

Calysto stood on the precipice of the curb and on the edge of finding out, determined like never before to be able to do so. If he had a chance at doing something that mattered, then he always tried to take it. And if this were the answer, if this were the key, then he'd chase it until it bore fruit, rotten or otherwise.

In the distance, a car approached, glistening with the falling early evening sunlight off of a shiny black hood. Calysto waved a hand and as it slowed, rolling to a stop as the window lowered with a quiet hum.

"Cal-ees-toe?" the driver shouted, spelling out the word with the pace of someone unsure of any unconventional name in their mouth.

He really didn't need to yell, the car was quiet as was the road around them.

"Yes," Calysto answered simply, and slipped into the back.

As it drove away he settled down into the cushioned bucket seats and leaned his head on the tinted glass window. The stark change in temperature at first made him shiver, as sweaty clothes began to cool like wet plaster on his skin. But the cold air was soon soothing, blowing softly onto his face and lulling his worries away. Or, he got too tired to even think of them anymore as the rumble of the blacktop hummed him to sleep.

Entry 386
Now, for what must be the thousandth
time, I find myself defeated. Sitting at
my desk in this darkness,
window which could be my undoing
pulling the curtain back.

TWENTY-SIX

His skin was falling off his body, slipping down and melting away like a flesh-colored candle. It was drying up, sticking to his bones, clinging to them with muscle and flesh dehydrated. Cracks were slowly forming, first at the sensitive bits, the junctions of his fingers, the corners of his lips, the raw areas where silver touched skin. Then they spread, fissures tracking out in painful lightning strikes brittle to the touch. It peeled away as if he were an orange left half-skinned on the countertop. A vineyard of grapes in the sun.

His cheeks were sunken, and his eyelids felt stretched to breaking with every blink. A few fingernails lie on the floor beneath rotting hands turned wrinkly blue. He couldn't feel his legs, his arms, but his body was on a slow burning simmering heat. He felt turned round and round on a spit over the open fire of decay that came swift with starvation.

Aeris approached, unchaining him without a word and forcing him to his feet. He was too weak to resist and let himself be hauled toward the door.

"... Aeris," he managed through lips that could barely move. He groaned in a manner more akin to a zombie, words slurring on dry tongue. "Aeris, I'm... I'm really dying."

"I know, honey," she said, her voice clipped. "This'll make sure of it."

She yanked open the front door, and cool early pre-dawn air hit his face causing the raw skin to burn.

"Come on," she said.

He stumbled beside her in the death grip she held on his arms.

They walked, dragged, shuffled, in silence all the way across the field outside of the house, down through a ditch, splashing mud on them both as she ruthlessly tugged him along. They were essentially in the middle of nowhere. Python wasn't even sure how they'd arrived there, or where they were. Certainly, no where anyone else could easily find.

Finally, another clearing appeared. Soft dewy grass was long and unkept and wildflowers sprouted up within it. In the middle of it was a tall wooden stake, rooted to the ground as if it were a striped tree trunk left to grow away from its companions. Aeris kicked Python's legs out from under him and he fell straight onto the ground, knocking the back of his head against the pole. She began to chain him again and he tried between bouts of empty-stomached nausea and bleary-eyed delirium to speak.

"Don't need to tie me up... I don't think..." he murmured.

"Not taking any chances with you," she answered, tightening the silver against his skin. He barely registered the burn of it anymore. Soon the burn of the sun would take its place, anyway.

"Aeris, I'm... I'm sor—"

"Don't try n sweet talk your way out of this, babe," she said. "Only way you're gettin' out is if that old vampire hunter himself shows up with what I asked for. And I'd say by the looks of the dawn, that ain't looking good for you is it?"

"He... he's not a..."

"Maybe you shouldn't make an enemy of everyone you ever

meet," she said as she stood. "Otherwise, you might've stood a chance."

He didn't answer, trying to focus on staying conscious.

She sighed and seemed to hesitate a moment before she spoke, "I'm sorry, Python. I really am. After all this time, it feels a bit of a shame. But this'll finish it for us both, I promise."

He listened as her footsteps faded away and left him there to face the sunrise, alone.

He hadn't expected Calysto to come for him, not really. What more did that weird little warlock owe him anyway?

Nothing, not even to begin with.

But maybe he had hoped, deep down, that Calysto might care about him back. He had already gone through his own reluctant acceptance of the way he felt... fond... of the man, still, he'd resigned himself to leaving Calysto alone forever if that's what he'd wanted.

Though to his surprise, Calysto *hadn't* wanted that. He'd even done something as unexpected as to *sort of* ask Python to stay. That didn't mean that Calysto would go as far as to save his life, though. Or even go out of his way to try.

Python didn't exactly know what Aeris wanted from the warlock, or who she thought he was, but he was fairly certain Calysto didn't have it.

He thought back on how confused Calysto had been when Merik had called him a vampire hunter, and how insistent he was that he wasn't one. It didn't make any sense.

Whatever Aeris wanted from him, she wouldn't get. And even if by some altruistic miracle Calysto showed up to save him, he would fail to appease her and so, Python was going to die.

He'd heard it was quick—to die by the sun. As soon as its face hits a vampire's skin, it was near-instantaneous. Only a slight ache like a hand on a hot coal, then nothing.

He could do that. He'd felt the heat of flames enough in his life to not entirely fear it.

It didn't sound so bad, he thought.

Not compared to this wasted eternal life. It wasn't even like he had anything to lose. Nothing to leave behind. There wasn't much to remember to begin with.

What could he do about it now?

Everything he'd done in his life, all the running and stealing and fucking and fucking up, had all led him right here, to this inevitable moment before the dawn.

This was his legacy—wasted potential. Forgettable, forgotten.

And he had no one to blame but himself, in the end.

The regret could consume him if he let it, and what else did he have to do now but feel everything he'd wished he'd ever done?

As the soft chirp of birds waking from their slumber whistled from between the far-off trees, Python leaned his head back and closed his eyes.

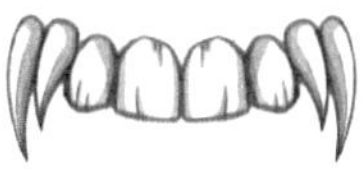

CALYSTO WOKE with a jolt as the car hit a pothole and quietly cursed as he roused himself. How could he have fallen asleep? With everything on his mind, he would have usually never been able to sleep.

Rather if he were at home, he would spend this time anxiously pacing around, up and down the stairs, back and forth between the windows, mumbling to himself all the while. Looking into the fridge for the hundredth time as if it would produce different results, and slamming it in frustration, personally offended that it hadn't magically conjured something for him to nervously gnaw on.

But here, in the back of someone else's car he had managed to be lulled into the kind of half-slumber that left him slipping in and out of dreams, riding the verge of wakefulness and sleep before his head hung too far forward or his skull bounced off the window, jerking him back into semi-consciousness only to be dragged back down again. Creating a vicious cycle that served to be more exhausting than the effort it would take to force himself to stay awake.

To be fair, Calysto hadn't slept since... since... shit, he couldn't even remember. And his habit of head-desking as soon as he couldn't keep his eyes open surely didn't come in handy for this Python-esque on-the-road lifestyle he had acquired over the last few weeks. Even before he had moved the whole fucking house into the past, Python had kept him distracted and occupied outside of his regular routine more often than not.

Python definitely wasn't used to slowing down, and had a hard time finding anything to do around Calysto's house that wasn't 1) pester him 2) make a mess 3) eat 4) sleep, or 5) dress up in various outfits and, you guessed it, pester Calysto.

Which one looks best? Does this go together? Why am I asking you, you dress like a raccoon who wandered into the middle of some clothes in the trashcan. But really, Cal, look I'm sorry, hey, come on, is the red or the white one better?

Calysto shook his head and smirked slightly in spite of himself. But as his smile slipped down so did his mood. It was very possible, that right here and now, was his last chance to prove his worth. Ever. To prove he cared about something, and that what he wanted was worth fighting for. Worth saving someone else from dying for.

What if he couldn't find Python in time?

What if he couldn't do it?

What if Aeris didn't listen, didn't take his word for it and threw the book back in his face? He could have forged it after all. She would probably think that, in her desperate search for a cure for her unfortunate life. Calysto wasn't entirely sure if he should feel guilty about that. He had tried to stop her, more than once, from getting involved in this. Then again, she had thought he was someone else, probably trying to test her resolve or throw her off the path. Still, she had been turned and he hadn't.

As his thoughts began to race, Calysto's leg bounced up and down with increasing rapidity and the sleeve of Python's woolen coat unraveled with the worrying of his fingertips, riding up over his wrist, fraying and spreading bits of fluff onto the backseat. He realized it, felt a bit worried that he was being inconsiderate somehow, gathered up all the fluff, and began pulling that apart in his hands instead.

"Uh..." he cleared his throat. "Sir? Are we almost there?"

"Ten minutes," the driver called back.

Ten minutes. Ten. He could do that. He grabbed his tablet, stuffed it into his satchel—gifted to him by himself—and righted the strap over his chest. He wadded up the tortured remnants of his sleeve into a ball and squished it down, shoving it into his sweatpants pocket. Then in both of his hands, he held the book and couldn't stop himself from fiddling with the edges of the cover, rubbing the textured tan leather between his fingers and tying and untying the cord that held it all in place.

The pink sticky notes were dirty at the edges, bent at all angles, and curled in on themselves. Likely from where S.C. had studied and marked it and carried it around for ages. Well, however many ages had passed between now and whenever he was from. So much had happened that he'd forgotten to ask from how far in the future S.C. had come.

That was another thing that was worrying along the sensitive edge of Calysto's nerves. Supposed-Calysto had teleported. Not in his house, but simply by himself, of his own will. And not by accident either. He had traveled on his own, to a specific time and place of his choosing. And he'd gotten it right.

This really was him from the future?

This man who appeared not only competent, and dare he guess, confident. But also happy and oddly fulfilled. At peace. It really didn't seem likely. Calysto was content being miserable and had been for so long, he couldn't imagine being any other way.

Though he wasn't content was he? He had confided in a moment of rare vulnerable honesty to S.C. that being alone was horrible. He hated it. No, he had never been happy with it. Why else do you think he watched so much TV? It wasn't only to keep up with the times—like the excuse he'd made up to Python—but because any bit of personal interaction made him feel like he could know what it was like. To make him feel like someone else was there.

How many pirated versions of the same off-shoot of some shitty reality show had he left on in the background? They may be vapid, empty versions of people who're barely able to activate a quarter of their brain capacity, and he may spend his entire time listening to it arguing back at their stupid decisions or staring in disbelief at the absurd extent of drama that could arise over a can of soda. Nevertheless, it didn't feel like nothing.

He had always craved it, really. That sense of belonging, of knowing what and where he should be. Knowing he had a place in the lives of others, and that they wanted him there in theirs. He'd never had it and so he had forgotten the want, buried the need, and carried on. As lonesome and solitary as ever.

Maybe now he really had a chance at something. Something that could change that, and it all depended on two things. The leather-bound journal in his hands and—

"Here ya are!" the driver called out, jerking the car to a stop and Calysto back to the present moment with it.

He peered out of the window at the near dawning sky casting subtle beams of coming light over a deep silhouette of tall evergreens still quietly sleeping. In front of him, a long backroad led into the forest, disappearing into the darkness beyond.

"This is it?" Calysto asked. "I don't see a house."

"Just down that road, half a mile," the driver said back, in a stern manner that communicated he wasn't about to be persuaded to drive the rest of the way.

Calysto took the hint and a deep breath as he opened the door and stepped out, boots scuffing sharply on the gravel road. He waited another long moment until the car had rolled away and out of sight, then started to walk.

All was silent, except the sound of his lonely steps as he picked up his pace and fished in his pocket for his light. When he produced it and murmured the words that brought it to life, it glowed brighter than it ever had before. Soft orange light traveled down the handle, seeping into his hand. Or, from it?

Calysto nearly dropped it in surprise, but regained his bearings and gripped it tight. This was normal—this was supposed to happen. This was a better time than any to practice what he had learned. What S.C. had shown him.

He walked faster, squinting through smudges on his glasses and looking for anything, a house, a car, a driveway, a mailbox. Any signal he was getting close.

Thick cool fog dampened his clothes and began to bead with the effort of his steps in droplets on his forehead. Curls of hair slipped loose from the ribbon at the base of his neck, obscuring his view and sticking to his lips. Irritated, he pushed it back, tangling the mess further and catching his frazzled coat sleeve on the sharp rim of his glasses. They fell off, slung away and clattering across the ground.

"No! Shit!" he yelped, frantically holding up the light and crouching down, feeling out blindly with his free hand. "Fuck! Fuck, come on!"

Between the blurry outlines of gravel and weeds he saw a small glint and scrambled over, nearly throwing himself across the sharp pebbles in his frenzy to retrieve them. They were bent at the nose, the thin age-old metal nearly snapped in half by the force of the throw. What once was a small crack at the tip of the left lens was now a twisted fissure from top to bottom, spidering out like a lightning bolt and rendering the whole thing near useless. Calysto groaned, cursing loudly where no one could hear, and carefully tried to clean them on the offending peacoat. He shoved them back on his face and climbed up from the ground, and in his hurry stumbled forward half crouched as he frantically forced himself on to continue on.

Birds were beginning to sing, slowly waking to the rapidly growing sunlight that reached out over the horizon of trees, casting pink and orange beams of deadly vampire-eliminating light. It cut the fog to shreds that quickly dissipated with the coming heat.

He was beginning to sweat beneath his clothes again and his

mouth was sticky. He realized for once that he might be dehydrated, and two large caffeinated beverages for what constituted yesterday's lunch and dinner weren't exactly what one should consume to go on a lifesaving hike through the forest.

His heart was near palpitating, and he felt jittery and sick, like his empty stomach had given up hope of ever being full and was about to expel itself to go in search of its own sustenance. Calysto couldn't find himself to blame it, if it did. He had never been exactly too kind to it.

He tried to shove the feeling down, anyway. Now was not the time to throw up or get winded by a bout of vertigo-inducing nausea. So, he swallowed hard against the cotton in his mouth and continued on, searching the edges of the road for any sign that he might be getting close.

Was it simply anxiety? A case of exhaustion and low blood-sugar-frazzled nerves? Or was it the fact that he was deeply afraid that Python would die before he had a chance to speak to him one more time? To see him, one more time. To be kind to him, for once.

He could be kind. He wanted to be kind.

The little light in his hand glowed while he walked and burned brighter the more he thought about the vampire.

"Oh, what," Calysto said towards it. "You like him, too?"

It glowed a bit more. Calysto scoffed and shook his head.

"Well now, I guess we've *got* to find him then, hm?"

Finally, in the distance, he saw it. What amounted to be a single-story version of his own cabin, complete with mold and fungi growing on the outside walls and vines crawling up around the windows, and a singular door. Calysto nearly tripped as he picked up his pace on wobbling knees and ran to the entrance. He didn't stop himself in time, and the momentum carried him straight into the solid wood. Apparently, it wasn't locked or even closed that tight, because instead of slamming his face directly into the door and likely breaking his glasses for good, it swung open and he tumbled inside, limbs flailing.

"Oh, you actually came," Aeris' voice slipped out of the darkness. "Python must have a friend after all."

Calysto found himself peering around in a night blacker than the one quickly transforming outside.

"I did," Calysto said, holding up his light. "Where are you?"

A few heavy footsteps fell and he saw her silhouette appear. "Why use the light?" she asked, sharp gaze sparkling within the hazy glow.

"It's dark in here," Calysto answered. "In case you didn't notice."

"No, it's not..." she approached, studying him a bit too close for his comfort. It was the first time he was able to see her in detail in the present. Her eyes were just like Python's. Slit like a cat and shiny like an oil spill. "It shouldn't be for you anyway."

"Well, it is," he snapped as the anxiety built in his chest. "There's not a lot of time, Aeris."

"Do you have what I asked for?"

"There's no such thing," he answered, quiet.

She hissed and her curious stare turned cold. "I should have fucking known."

"It's not what you think. Neither am I." Calysto fished the book from his satchel and handed it to her. "This will tell you everything you need to know."

She took it, suspicion written all over the sharp features of her face. "What is it?"

"It's my father's journal..." Calysto cleared his throat. "Apparently, he looked just like me. Minus the..."

"Looked?"

"Just read it will you," Calysto waved his hand. "I'm telling the truth."

She palmed it, looking at the outside thoughtfully and flipping it back and forth. "You came all this way to give me a book?"

"No," Calysto shook his head. "I came all this way to stop you from killing Python over something that doesn't exist, Aeris. There is no cure, whatever you're looking for, my father never found it, and I have nothing to do with it."

Aeris was silent and turned away, walking again into the ink-black darkness of the room. He heard the sound of a chair scrape on the floor and a thump as she sat down heavily atop it.

"So?" he asked. He was trying to keep his patience but was also becoming increasingly aware of the way the light under the door crept forward inch by inch the longer they talked. "Aeris, please. Read the journal. Just... just, I don't know what you and Python have between you but..."

"No!" Her voice carried out from the shadows. She was angry that much was evident, but her voice trembled on the verge of tears. She cleared her throat loudly and said again, "No, Calysto. You don't, do you? You don't know shit about me. You left me in that basement and I was turned and my whole life was stolen! Ruined! And I won't... Python, he... I..."

Calysto swallowed hard.

"I'm... I'm so sorry," he began. "I didn't lie when I said I thought you were dead. I checked. I guess I just didn't think that..."

"You didn't think about shit!" she snapped, but he heard her sniffle quietly behind it. "No one thinks about me! What about what I want? I don't want this! But I'll be damned if any of those fuckers who did it will outlive me!"

Oh.

"Did... Aeris?" Calysto took a few hesitant steps forward into the dark, and his little light fluctuated rapidly as if trying to get his attention. "I know!" he hissed at it quietly.

"Did Python do this to you?" He tried again.

She didn't answer.

"Aeris, please," Calysto bit his lip against the words he was about to say. "Please, tell me where he is."

"Oh, so you two really are in cahoots, aren't you?" she answered bitterly.

"No..." Calysto was starting to feel desperate. He briefly considered begging. Then he *really* considered it. "... Please, I don't want... I don't want him to die. Please, Aeris. I swear to you, I'm not lying. Just... if you want to kill him still, I'll bring him right here and you can stake him yourself. Isn't that... wouldn't that be more satisfying? Or something? Look, how about... his life in exchange for the truth, okay? Please Aeris, please don't kill him. Not yet."

Not till I get to tell him—

All was silent, as his pleading words hung in the air between them. For a moment he wasn't even sure if she were still there. Had she gotten up and walked away? Was she just outside the scope of his light and about to pounce on him and rip his throat out?

"Where is he, Aeris," Calysto said, softly, coaxing.

She was still silent, and Calysto wasn't sure if she was going to answer. He steeled himself to ask again. Then she spoke.

"You're lucky you're cute," she said, but he didn't stop holding his breath. "The clearing two miles west of here, follow the road, go across the ditch, and you'll find him. But you might be too late."

Her voice was solemn and quiet, and he felt another pang of sympathy for her. But, that would have to wait.

"I'll be back," he answered.

It was all he could think to say before he turned and bolted out of the door.

TWENTY-SEVEN

The past.

Aeris awoke to a burst of nigh unbearable pain in her head, and a burning in her neck. Her limbs lie crumpled beneath her. The cold basement floor of the *Molly and Tom* was sticky under her palms as she pushed herself to sit, fighting against the near-swoon of wooziness that made her feel sick. On the floor where she'd lain, there was a scattering of teeth smeared about with thick clots of bloody synovia and bile. Her coat and vest were covered with it, and strands from her long black braid stuck to her neck in clumping clots that tugged roughly at the skin. But she barely noticed it, for the pain of her waking was all-consuming.

She looked around for Calysto, expecting to see him in a similar state, but found no one at all. The basement club was dark—she could tell that much from the way the lanterns and candles were unlit—but somehow she was still able to see clearly. More so than she had been when she'd entered here a night before. All the way to the back and all the usually darkened corners of the club were as clear as day to her, but a strange oily ring surrounded every object as if they gave off their own auras or were gently vibrating in the air.

Aeris blinked and rubbed her eyes. They ached to the touch.

Her sight remained the same, shimmering at the edges. She looked up at the open cellar door at a cloudy night sky and touched her hand to her neck, then her mouth, then her face. A slowly building dread seeped into her every pore as the realization overtook her.

No, no no no nononnoonono.

Her panic rushed from her head calcifying into a single pinpoint in her chest and she shot to her feet, swaying violently before catching herself on the handrail.

FUCK. I can't have been turned, I can't!

How had she managed to let that happen? Well, she hadn't managed at all, in fact, it was the opposite of that. She had run into this overeager and unafraid. Too bold for her own good, she'd ignored Calysto's warning in an effort to prove herself, her worth.

She'd been too hot-headed, too stubborn, reckless.

Though in this moment, she didn't take the time to acknowledge such a thing as her terror turned to indignation in the face of the empty room.

Calysto had left her. He'd *left* her. *Alone.* Some fucking hunter; some fucking companion and protector. And now she was a vampire, too?

This didn't play out at all like she'd imagined, and her delusions of grandeur and perceived status or fame were wiped away in this bitterly painful instance.

She leaned against the guardrail as frustration and anger boiled over, becoming too much to bear. And so she was incapable of taking the blame onto herself. Or even, more mercifully so, onto the unfortunate circumstances of her life that had brought her to take such actions in this direction. Onto the way in which life simply becomes what one cannot expect nor desire or dream to anticipate. For was it truly her fault that she was born into a world that valued her only for the manner in which she could be subservient and bow to others? Was it her fault that she would never be given reprieve from it until she was forced to find her own way, alone, without guidance? Was it her fault she, with such limited support, had become obstinate in the face of what she was told she couldn't do?

Perhaps. In a sense. Though one cannot be blamed for the ways in which they fill the holes that a lack of love leaves.

They can instead, be blamed for the result of their coping. The ways in which their subsequent actions affect others, the way in which responsibility is shirked for a sense of self-righteousness. A refusal to acknowledge harm created to smother the hurt that attitude was born to protect.

Aeris found herself there, now. At the crux of a crossroads between grief turned to anguish or grief turned to anger. And Aeris had always been a bit hotheaded, hadn't she?

A YOUNG MAN with silvery-greying hair walked down the long staircase that led into a courtyard in front of Allistar Manor. His face was pinched in a semblance of disgust and frustration as another man clung to his arm and spoke loudly of something hard to understand as his voice reverberated into distortion off of the long walkway of stone.

Aeris watched as they walked past her, neither of them noticing her hiding place in the shrubs. Her hand itched around the handle of her silver sword—she had been careful to wrap the hilt to protect herself from touching it—at the thought of taking them both down, right here, right now. Though she didn't recognize the younger of the two, she knew the older. Richter. The one who had turned her.

Not only was he a powerful older vampire, he was nearly untouchable surrounded by his posse of servants and admirers. Not to mention the others he'd turned and familiars wishing for such a gift one day in return for their undying loyalty and servitude.

Therefore, Aeris' vendetta did not involve him—not yet, that is. She had grown in the past few months. Her time in the shadows, hiding out in hotels and basements and boxes and inns had given her plenty of time to think and seethe and scheme. She may have been turned into this monstrosity, taken from the waking world without a choice, but what was in her power was to prevent it from happening to anyone else. And to take down all those responsible for what happened to her that fateful night.

She waited, until Richter and his current pet had passed by, then ran up the long staircase in a blink. The moon was high in the evening sky behind her, casting the long black shadow of her coat in a rippling silhouette.

A bringer of final death, she ran silently throughout the house.

In a perhaps ironic twist of fate, she was faster now, more powerful in her strength and stamina and speed, resistant to injury, and quicker to strike. Becoming a vampire herself had made her an extremely efficient hunter, even better than her rare human counterparts, and perhaps the only creature truly capable of taking on a vampire with any hope of success.

She made her way through the foyer with no trouble. A human familiar lingered half-drunk with blood loss on a chaise lounge upholstered in rust-orange velvet cushions and fell instantly to sleep under the influence of Aeris' hypnotic stare. The high ceilings were illuminated with hundreds of candles painstakingly lit and hoisted atop extravagant chandeliers, lighting her path up the stairs and on to the upper bedrooms.

Not yet did she dare again to burst into a room full of vampires unprepared. And even though she was much more well-equipped now, the memory of her turning forced to her to rethink her approach over all. Now she lurked, striking with precision and decision, one at a time. If this particular nest of vampires was on to her yet, she didn't know. Nor did she particularly care.

Whether they lie down in front of her to accept their death or fled from her sword for decades to come, it wouldn't matter either way. She would follow them to the ends of the earth. No longer did she find it interesting or exciting or any of the barely thought-out reasons she'd given to Calysto. She didn't concern herself with anything but the most personal of reasons: a vendetta. Justice. A life for a life. They had taken her by force, without choice, and she would have her revenge for it.

Every one of the vampire scum who lived as part of this little coven of Richter's making would die by her hand. She swore it.

That night was like many others in her brief past as a hunter and ended in a similar way—black blood dripping thick and cold from her sword. It made no difference if she left a trail of it behind her.

She slipped out of the house as unnoticed as she'd entered. The only ones to witness her appearance lay comatose on the couch or dead mid-copulation and confection in the rooms upstairs.

Should anyone try to track her down they would meet a similar fate. A few escaped her here and there, but they would always meet their eventual determined end. She would be ready for them—she always was.

ADMITTEDLY, Aeris was deeply disappointed to discover that Richter had been killed before she could get to him. Really though, what could a monster such as him expect? As much as she wanted to be the one to do it, she couldn't be too surprised it'd happened. It was a passing fancy to find out who had done it, but one that quickly faded when she remembered the last time she'd teamed up with a hunter.

She did, however, have the chance to witness the aftermath.

She approached the now-abandoned manor house—it seemed to have expressly cleared itself out with the absence and demise of its maker—and could smell the rotting stench of decaying flesh from underneath the bolted front double doors long before she reached them. The bolt wasn't meant to keep anyone like the likes of her out, and she easily shouldered it open to the sound of the metal lock snapping in two.

It was dark and deathly cold. Where before it had maintained some semblance of life, it was now frozen in place, a mausoleum as unaging at those who'd inhabited it. Stuck stock still and strangely silent, her footsteps that could go unheard felt loud even in their weightlessness. Her sword rested comfortably in her hand, and she explored with a caution now unnecessary but engrained from months of being near constantly at the ready.

There was no movement anywhere that she could hear. No voices or human breathing, no sounds of the drinking of blood or the restlessness of a vampire oversleeping. No shoe falls or rustling of fabric, not even the crackle of a lit fireplace or the gentle creasing of the pages of a book, slowly turned.

Everyone had gone.

That is, everyone except for Richter.

Aeris turned the corner near a long winding staircase but instead of ascending it, she continued across the polished wooden floors reflecting cool blue fractals of moonlight from the open front door. Her aim was the study, which was a sprawling library used mostly for a show of wealth than the value of knowledge or education, and the source of the foul and growing odor. As she'd suspected—it too was abandoned.

More striking than the emptiness of it was the state it had been left in. Books were ripped up and strewn across the plush embroidered rug now stained black with long-dried puddles of blood. Candle sconces were torn from stone and scattered about with chintz fabrics from ruined tables and trinkets from fallen shelves. Claw marks marred the surfaces and a long tapestry rustled in tatters against the far corner wall.

The chairs were all overturned, one broken against a wall and near smashed to splinters, others ripped apart in pieces strewn, thrown so hard they stuck out like makeshift arrows from the solid brick walls. A large mahogany desk was placed in the center of the blood-soaked rug, and from across the room Aeris saw a mangled form.

She wasn't able to make sense of what she was seeing until she approached, where it quickly became clear.

It was Richter. Or, at least what was left of him.

His face was still intact—recognizable even in this state. Yet finally an unmoving corpse. Fangs on full display against shriveled gums and dehydrated lips, his death mask twisted in a sickly smile. Smug and satisfied somehow even until the end. His body was splayed out across the desktop, arms and legs dangling off of the sides. His chest was a hollow cavern and his ribs lie open like the covers of an encyclopedia of intestinal diagrams. Blood pooled beneath his torso and head, and his wide eyes stared up, blank and cloudy towards the ceiling.

Aeris came closer, inspecting the handiwork of someone deranged, and saw that Richter's hand was locked tight around a wooden chair leg as if he had almost dominated his attacker, but was either too weak or too slow to stop them.

A stake, ready to kill.

Another vampire, then.

She ignored Richter's creepy visage and investigated further, now more curious about who had killed him than the fact that he had died. She looked around the desk for any sign that the attacker may have left behind. There wasn't much to be seen between shreds of skin and clothes and blood splattered across the desk. Then she saw Richter's other hand.

At first, it'd looked like a fist—the involuntarily stiffening of a body decomposing. Yet something shiny caught her eye. Hair. Silver and white, glimmering against the dim moonlight creeping through a slit in the taffeta. Most of it was sticky and brown, soaked through with long-dried entrails. But the parts that were clean were unmistakable. This was the same hair of Richter's most recent pet.

Aeris held the strands in her hand and scoffed.

What a way for this to end for him, at the hands of his own

creation. For a brief moment she felt a slight sense of kindred with the silver-haired vampire who'd clearly had enough and enacted his revenge against their maker.

Ultimately though, she came to her senses.

Who was he but another one? And who's to say he didn't do it to take Richter's place? He would go on to make more of them, that much was certain. For as much as a human's drive to procreate is written in biological instinct, so is the vampire's same need. He could not be allowed to live any more than the rest of them that had come to die by her sword or stake or knife.

At times she would almost feel sorry, but never enough to let it linger. Whatever higher calling she assigned to her purpose, it still boiled down to the same thing. Retribution.

Imagine Aeris' surprise when tracking Python that she'd come across the name of one who hunted not only their kind but a cure to the deathly affliction altogether. This same hunter she'd once known —that very same Calysto.

Centuries later and still alive, he must also be the same as she. Wasn't he?

She figured he must've been turned that same night. Perhaps that was why he'd left her.

In the end it didn't matter to her why, he had still done it. It didn't matter if his continued existence offered the potential of rekindling, of companionship, of someone familiar. She was well past the point of needing any of that, and deeply rooted in her solitary state. Her reaction to all things that hurt her was visceral and violent, nor would she lie down and accept surrender in the form of compromise or reconciliation.

Nor would she do so for a very, very long time.

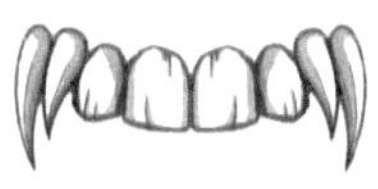

A blister on Calysto's heel popped, oozing sticky and hot down the back of his foot and the chafe of too-big-leather-boot on puss-raw skin began to burn as he ran. He repeated Aeris' directions over and over in his head, turning them into a mantra that morphed into a hum, a buzz, a smooth solid cadence that ceased to lose all meaning outside of a simple desire.

The directions led to Python, to Python, to Python. He wanted to find him and so he let his will carry him. He wasn't even sure this would work—this strange thing that S.C. had shown him. But he carried the knowledge he'd gained and trusted that it would work. It had to work.

He wouldn't have lied to himself, would he?

Focus, if you know where you're going all you have to do is focus and you'll get there.

Calysto held the directions in his mind, and with as much concentration and energy as he could muster, he willed himself in the direction of the rapidly arriving sunrise.

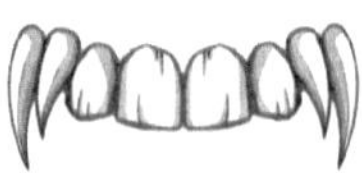

"It's really rather simple," S.C. had explained before they'd parted outside the coffee shop. But what S.C. then told him wasn't 'rather simple', it was actually really important, and if Calysto hadn't been talking to himself—and knew he downplayed everything he said and was forgetful to boot—he wouldn't have been so forgiving of the huge oversight.

"Our mother was a witch, but our father was a vampire," S.C. continued. "I don't think he meant to make us, he just got turned and he was afraid and he knew he had to leave. But he also didn't know how to say goodbye to her. He didn't know how to express it so he just... left. But not before sleeping with..."

"So that's how I was made," Calysto interrupted.

"Yeah," S.C. nodded. "An accidental farewell gift of sorts."

"I don't get it," Calysto had said, trying to piece together the threads that were slowly unravelling to reveal the truth of his life. "Why have I never felt... vampiric, then? I'm, I mean we, are pretty normal, right?"

S.C. sat forward and lowered his voice. "Have you ever noticed how, when you focus really hard you can make things happen? Almost like you don't remember doing it? Or how time passes, in the blink of an eye. Or hell, how you made the house move all this time, without ever really trying?"

"I guess, yeah."

"It's some kind of..." S.C. pinched his lips. "Warlock-vampire crossover abilities, I don't know. Not exactly a huge field of study."

"Like Python's ability to run fast," Calysto answered, working it out for himself. "And the way he supposedly can will people to obey him. But—"

"Amplified, yes," S.C. nodded eagerly. "Enhanced by the other part of us. Made more powerful with the two combined."

"Is that how you got here, then?" Calysto asked. "Willpower?"

"Basically. I thought of where I wanted to go, and I went," S.C. answered. "Just like we did before when we moved the house to a general feeling of 'where ever'. And just like how when Python asked us to move the house, we were so caught up in the panic our mind defaulted to the place we knew the most."

"It was like a psychic map or instructions," Calysto finished. "That took us there."

"Yep." S.C. sat back and reached a hand towards Calysto's abandoned cinnamon bun. "Can I?"

"Yeah, whatever." Calysto was barely paying attention to anything that wasn't the complex puzzle slowly solving in front of him. "So, are you saying I have abilities I don't know about?"

S.C. perked up even more, chewing rapidly through the huge bite he'd just taken. He held up his finger, urgently swallowing and bobbing his head.

"Yeah! Yes! Exactly!" He finally answered. "It's... it's everything the coven predicted, way back when. Only, they had no idea how it would manifest. Or that it existed this way!"

"What do you mean?" Calysto was on the edge of his proverbial seat, though not nearly as expressive about his enthusiasm as his future self seemed to be.

Odd, that.

"I mean, they were right," S.C. continued, between the smacking sound of licking his fingers. "We are the most powerful warlock their coven has ever seen, just no one knew it. Not even us. It's a different way of activating the abilities."

"How," Calysto's voice slipped out in a nervous whisper. Suddenly, he was too afraid this was a dream. A lie. A trick.

"You know how you speak to that wand with words? And how the coven used spells and incantations?"

"Yes."

"Well, it's not like that at all for us, not really," S.C. took another large bite of his pastry and spoke around a cheek full. "Obviously it kind of works, right? But, it's not all of it."

"So, it's... what? It really is just willpower?"

"Yeah, seems so," S.C. agreed. "Our magic is tied to the place where vampirism and being a warlock meet. It's entirely a mystery, really. But that's why, more often than not, we do shit without meaning to. We didn't even know we were using magic."

"That's..." Calysto's throat caught, and he reached for his coffee, taking a large gulp and wincing. "Oof, oh that *is* bad... um, that's..."

"A lot to take in, I know. But it makes perfect sense, doesn't it?"

S.C. had smiled at him, and despite it all, Calysto found himself smiling back.

TWENTY-EIGHT

Python's sharp hearing, dulled a bit by the lack of sustenance, picked up on something in the distance. Despite his carefully cultivated calm and his supposed readiness to go into the light, he cracked an eye open to look around.

Then he heard it again. Fast, messy footsteps, followed by a strange crackle, a fizzle and pop, some mumbled cursing, then more running.

Then.

"Python? *PYTHON!? FUCK!*"

It was Calysto. *It was Calysto.* Python's shock mingled with profound relief as he heard it again.

"Python!"

Calysto was shouting through the woods, stumbling and making bizarre sounds that Python didn't understand. He tried to open his mouth to answer and his throat was dry as sand. His fissured lips cracked deeper, oozing black sludge down his chin. Calysto wasn't going to hear him, and as the morning dawn warmed the tips of his boots he realized, Calysto wasn't going to find him. Not in time.

"PYTHON!" Calysto was still yelling, getting closer now. *"FUCKING ANSWER ME! SHIT!"*

There was a yelp, a splash, and more cursing and muttering before he heard Calysto take off running again.

"I'm here," he tried to call. It slithered out like a whisper. But he said it all the same. "Calysto, I'm here."

He was too late, too fucking late. Python cursed himself, feeling the way his legs began to softly burn. Calysto wasn't going to reach him until he was a husk, withered and gone. And likely pretty gross looking. Python grimaced at that. Not exactly the way he ever wanted to go. Not how he wanted Calysto to find him, or to ever see him. At least he wouldn't be here to witness the reaction on Calysto's pretty, pretty, face at the sight.

He smiled slightly and resigned himself to fading away to the sound of the messy flailing of a man he wished he'd had a chance to love.

Suddenly, the rising sun was blotted out and darkness enveloped him as a heavy cloth landed over his face.

"Oh fuck... oh... fuck..." Calysto's breath wheezed in desperate heaves. "Python? Hey..." A few more breaths. "Hey, are you... Hey, answer me."

How did he get here so fucking fast?

Python bobbed his head.

"Shit okay, hold... hold on." .

He heard the frantic beat of the warlock's pulse pumping with adrenaline and fear and the way Calysto tried to muffle how hard he was actually panting. The sweaty heat of Calysto's skin brushed close to his as Calysto fumbled with the chains around his arms. The silver fell away and a welcome relief followed it. He hadn't even realized how much it still hurt.

"... Cal..." he croaked.

"Don't talk," Calysto snapped instantly, cutting him off. "Just, shut up, okay?"

Python couldn't help but crack a quivering smile. Even when

Calysto was trying to be nice, he was still kind of mean. The awkward way in which he navigated anything besides being a complete jerk-off was endearing and almost funny if he'd had the energy to laugh.

"Can you walk?"

Python shook his head, rustling against the fabric on his face. He blinked his dry eyes and a dark red hue filled the sunlit shadow covering him. This was his coat. But it smelled like Calysto now.

"Okay... that's, that's fine," Calysto seemed to be mulling something over. "Alright, grab onto me. Hurry up."

Python willed his arms to move and dragged them around to reach toward Calysto's voice. To his surprise Calysto pulled him close, crushing his head against the warlock's chest.

"Hang on," Calysto said cryptically. "I've only done this like, three times. On the way here."

Then from underneath Calysto's musty coat—for it was definitely his now, and one that Python didn't want back—Python felt a strong electric buzz pour from Calysto's hands and into his back. A bolt of terror jerked him to attention as the thought that Calysto was here to kill him himself crossed the vampire's mind.

Before he could try to react, he was swept away.

In one instant he was sitting there in the open field, sunlit and exposed, ready to face his death. The next, they were deep beneath a canopy of thick shaded trees. The treetops overhead blocked out all of the coming dawn and they were tucked within the undergrowth for good measure.

Python felt cool damp air brush his skin and sighed, leaning his head into Calysto's shoulder.

"Here..." Calysto finally spoke and pulled the coat from Python's head. "It's safe here, right? Shade is okay?"

"... Yeah," Python could barely lift his head to nod and settled instead for lolling it onto Calysto's chest. "Good enough."

"Hey..." Calysto's arm was still wrapped around his shoulders, holding him upright. "You look like shit."

"... Thanks, darling," Python croaked a dry laugh. "Nice to see you, too."

"You really can't walk?" Calysto's voice was soft, gentle in a way Python hadn't exactly heard before.

"Not..." Python swallowed, trying to return some semblance of moisture to his mouth. "Not like this."

Calysto was silent for a moment then he shuffled to his knees, and Python whined a little in protest at being jolted around.

"Hold on," Calysto murmured.

Python felt himself be lifted up by the armpits and roughly dragged up to lean against a thick trunk of a tree. He quivered with a queasiness that taunted his half-consciousness.

How did we get here? What is going on?

"Okay...uh...how do we do this," Calysto interrupted his thoughts.

Python blinked through blurry eyes, trying to get a look at Calysto through his muddled gaze.

"Do what?" he managed.

"Uh..." Calysto rubbed his neck. "Bite me?"

"What?" Python scoffed halfheartedly.

"Well, I'm not dragging you all the way out of here." Calysto shrugged.

"You actually," Python cleared his throat. "Want me to bite you?"

Calysto grimaced, reluctance written all over his face. "Not exactly, no. But... aren't you going to... dry up without it?"

Python then noticed the warlock's glasses were more cracked than the last time he'd seen the man.

Where has he been?

"Likely," Python croaked, saving that conversation for later. "Never tried it before... not eating."

"Oh." Calysto shuffled awkwardly, his knees digging into the soft damp shadows of earth and nettles. "Okay, so..."

"Come here," Python tried to lift his hand, beckoning him. Calysto scooted over and stopped short in front of Python's outstretched legs. "You have to get... close to me," Python wheezed. "I won't bi—"

To his surprise, his little slip-up made Calysto smile, a small one, but a real one nonetheless, and he slowly relaxed. He moved in and sat down at Python's side.

"This okay?" he asked quietly. He was attempting to act like he wasn't nervous, that much was clear.

Python tried to turn and face him but his body wouldn't obey.

"Uh... Cal..."

"Huh?"

"You're gonna have to, uh..." Python didn't want to say it. He knew how well it would go over—about as well as a hot air balloon full of holes. Calysto would think he was teasing, adopt that *I've-had-it-with-your-shit* expression, and get up and leave him here to rot as soon as he suggested it. But he didn't really have any other choice. "Sit on my lap..."

Dead silence.

Python winced. "Sorry, I... I can't..."

"No, it's fine."

Calysto jolted into action and thrust himself up, landing hard on Python's legs as if he just forced himself with one impulsive action to obey.

Oh.

He was warm, really warm. Python could feel Calysto's pulse through the fabric of his jeans, and hot near his face as he leaned in. Calysto reached up, moving his hair out of the way of his neck, then continued to fiddle with a curly strand all while intentionally avoiding Python's wandering eyes.

"Now what?"

"Can you... come closer..."

If Python had the wherewithal to be a little bit embarrassed, he was. He couldn't even move his own head and was basically asking his meal—who he also had some unfortunate feelings for—to feed himself to him.

Calysto swallowed, and Python followed the movement, caught somewhere between the allure of his throat and the sight of his skin. But the pulsing vein winding beneath the golden-brown beauty was a bit more pressing.

"When I got bit back in... you know. Is it different? Does this hurt?" Calysto asked as he leaned in.

"...Yeah," Python said softly, it wheezed out like a rasp. "I'll try to be... quick."

"Okay." Calysto took a breath and braced himself against Python's shoulders. "Go... Go ahead..."

Python reached a trembling hand slowly upward and pulled Calysto down by the nape of his neck. The smell of his skin was two parts sweat, one part something Python had started to recognize as magic, and a hundred parts the sweet aroma of blood.

His starving fangs emerged of their own accord, faced with the promise of a life-giving meal.

He bit down.

As his teeth sank in, breaking through Calysto's flesh and into his veins, he felt an instant jolt of life returning. All hesitance disappeared, slipping away and quickly replaced with instinctual drive. And for a moment, hunger overtook him. Any rational thought vanished as primal thirst became a compulsion.

His whole body thrummed and something akin to endorphins sent him near tipping over the edge into oblivious euphoria. Calysto was different than anything he'd ever tasted, and it tingled his lips with bitter spices before traveling hot and pungent down his throat. It made him dizzy and he pressed in. A gazelle in the jaws of a leopard, his tracking claws scraped along the warlock's back, holding him captive.

Everything stilled as Python fed. Temporarily frozen in time, they sat locked together in a bizarre symbiotic dance. Python felt himself rejuvenate, blood rushing through his shriveled organs, restoring his hair, his skin, his strength. He was alive again, he wasn't going to die. Not by the face of the sun or the hands of this generous, beautiful, and quite delicious warlock in his arms.

Calysto had reacted as most people did when Python decided to use them for food. He displayed all the usual signs as he gasped and tensed, fingernails digging into Python's muscle. He shook slightly as a small pained whine escaped his lips. His pulse slowed and his head fell forward—only held in place by Python's palm on his neck—and his breath quickened, coming in small hiccups that bordered on panic. Calysto responded like hundreds of thousands before him. Except this time, Python found that he cared.

As soon as he returned to himself enough to realize what he was doing, he pulled away with a soft wet smack. Calysto moaned and his head flopped forward.

Then Python swallowed and tongued against the skin and the smell... that smell. It brought him back to the present.

"Shit," Python inhaled hard, licking his lips. "Hey... Hey, Cal..."

Python felt significantly better and even the small bit of blood he'd taken from Calysto had nearly completely revived him. Calysto didn't answer except to moan again, his whole body weight falling against Python on the forest floor. Okay, maybe it wasn't actually a *small* bit of blood.

As Python realized this he stiffened and grabbed Calysto, pulling him up. His face was much too pale for his typical golden skin and his eyes were half-lidded, not focusing on anything in front of him.

"Shit!" Python's throat tightened and suddenly the taste of Cal's blood was horrifying, repulsive, disgusting.

Did I kill him?

"Cal! Cal, hey, hey, hey..."

He straightened up and easily slid Calysto off of his lap to lay him on the muggy ground. Calysto didn't move, he was barely breathing, and his pulse was quiet. Much too quiet. Python wiped his mouth and cursed, leaning over into Calysto's face. He didn't know shit about fixing humans. Were warlocks different somehow? Even still, if they were, he didn't know shit about that either. He'd never really practiced restraint. Moderation and Python couldn't be more opposite.

This would have been a good time to keep that idea in mind for once, Python.

He cursed again.

If he'd killed Calysto after he'd offered up his own blood to revive him—

Python had no idea what to do. If he had a heart it was firmly lodged in his bowels and his asshole had taken up residence in his throat. Then he did the only thing he could think of.

"*CALYSTO, GET UP!*" he shouted while giving the limp little warlock a shake. A nearby bird startled at the sound and flew off into the morning air. "*GET THE FUCK UP!*"

Python stared down at Calysto's unresponsive face and had a horrible idea. What if he turned him? Really quick? Before he died, Python could make him a vampire. Calysto was already basically immortal, right? So he couldn't be mad about that part of it, anyway. Would it even work? Python had told Aeris the truth—he hadn't ever intentionally turned anyone. He much preferred to keep his personal hell his own, thanks. Though, it wasn't like it could be that hard.

He could also let Calysto die.

If he knew anything about the guy at this point, it was that he could be pretty sure that Calysto wanted that. Or at least didn't want his life.

He could just let Calysto die.

But he didn't *want* Calysto to die. He wanted him to wake up and fix him with that annoyed glare that more often than not had turned to begrudging amusement, at least in the last few days before they'd come back. He wanted to talk to him, this weird old man who lived in a cabin all alone. He wanted to know him. It was strange to realize, and even stranger to admit. But he couldn't sit here and watch Calysto fade away.

Maybe Calysto would be mad at him. He could handle that. What he couldn't handle was being alone. Not again.

So, Python took a deep breath and brought his wrist close to his lips, his long double-fangs extending to share whatever magic had brought him back to life, once upon a distant time.

Then he stopped, hovering above his wrist and realized. No. This wasn't his choice to make. His own life had been stolen against his will, suspended in an eternal limbo, all previously laid plans and loves swept away in a blink. With a bite.

He couldn't do that to another. He just couldn't. No matter his desire for Calysto to live, he knew the horror of not having been given the option. If this is how Calysto would die, Python would rather live with the shame and sorrow and guilt of that, than whatever hateful gaze Calysto would see him with for what he'd done.

Python slowly closed his mouth, resigning himself to grief at the result of his own selfish actions when Calysto let out a quiet groan. It was faint, but then he did again, stronger this time. Python watched as he lifted a hand to his eyes, spidery fingers rubbing behind his glasses.

"Mmm... Ohhuhh..." Calysto blinked a few times, and let his arm fall back down into the sharp pine nettles covering the forest floor. "The... the fuck was that?"

"Oh shit," Python scrambled closer and leaned over Calysto's face, smoothing back the hair from his forehead, feeling his skin for warmth. It seemed to be returning. "Cal? Hey, are you..."

Calysto's eyes fluttered open, and their amber sheen had never struck Python in such a way before. Glassy and bloodshot but deep as night, they looked at him with a tired confusion.

"It's okay," Python found himself babbling. "Shit, I didn't mean to take so much, I thought you were gonna die, it's okay now though, yeah? Right? Are you feeling okay?"

"Py... thon..." Calysto slurred his words, but his gaze was clearing. "I'm okay. I'm not human, remember?"

Python smiled and huffed nervously, suddenly realizing how close he was to Calysto's face. Their chests were nearly touching where he was much too far into Calysto's personal bubble. "Oh, yeah, I wasn't sure if that mattered, to be honest."

"Me neither." Calysto grinned, too—a sloppy lop-sided smile.

Then to Python's surprise Calysto started to laugh. It was quiet and shy and shook them both with small tremors. For a split second Python was stunned, watching the way Calysto's face had changed and hearing the soft whisper of his laugh. But then he felt it himself, bubbling up from his chest, and he joined in, laughing carefully between the two of them. He leaned forward, resting his forehead on Calysto's chest and the laughter slowly faded.

Calysto sighed, heaving Python up and down, before Python looked up. Once again finding himself very close to Calysto's face.

"Hey," Python said softly, as if not wanting to be overheard even in this empty place. "Are you okay? Really?"

Calysto wrinkled his nose. "Yeah. That did hurt though."

"I told you it did," Python pinched his lips. "Sorry about that anyway."

"What were you doing?" Calysto asked, bringing a hand up to rest on Python's shoulder, fiddling idly with the thin fabric of his blouse. "When I woke up."

"Oh..." Python suddenly felt sheepish. Calysto had a way of doing that to him like no one else. "I thought you were going to die so..."

"You were going to turn me?" Calysto asked. Python read his expression as he spoke, but Calysto indicated no anger. Only an amused type of curiosity. "I don't think that would work."

"Yeah...Uh, Cal, I..." Python swallowed and met his eyes.

All in an instant Python's mind raced through a hundred options of what he could do right now. A hundred outcomes of what he might *choose* to do. He could make a joke, he could brush the whole thing off. He could thank Calysto profusely and he nearly ached with the desire to embrace the man in gratitude. He could move away, clean himself up, and act like none of this even happened. Like none of it mattered to him, like he could turn away and carry on and leave this all behind like he'd normally do.

But, unfortunately for him, he couldn't fool himself with such ideas any longer.

He didn't want to leave, he didn't want to lie, and he didn't want to deny himself.

Not of this. Not this time.

Amidst all his thinking and silent indecision something like instinct won over. Or his desire finally spoke louder than his hesitation, his feelings overriding his last remaining bit of sense.

His thumb came up to brush Calysto's chin. Their gazes stayed locked. Calysto didn't look away nor did he move.

"Yeah?" Calysto breathed out the word as if winded.

"I, um..." Python looked down at his hand resting on Calysto's cheek, at the face beneath it, stubbled golden hair on golden skin. The lips slightly parted and pale blushing brown even in the dark overhang of shaded trees. The tongue that flickered in and out, nervously licking then falling still, leaving a slight glistening sheen in its wake.

This was the man who had saved him. He'd come for him, he'd traveled through time with him, given his blood for him, nearly died for him. This was the man before him, one who likely wouldn't admit to caring for him, not without a fight, but who clearly cared nonetheless. And Python liked it, wanted it, craved it. He wanted *more* of it. He wanted to show Calysto he cared in return, that he could be as good as Calysto wanted him to be.

He could do it, he wanted to do it. He could try again.

He was ready.

Python hesitated for one final breath then, with more courage than he'd ever had to muster in his endless life for any fleeting fancy or hook-up or false love, he leaned down and kissed him.

He was warm. He was *so* warm.

Calysto, as cold and icy as he tried to seem, tasted like the memory of sunlight on his lips. Soothing him, making him feel alive.

Golden, golden light. Golden boy. Calysto.

Python felt Calysto shift beneath him, responding to him, and a thirst—longer untapped than any other kind—rushed forth, and Python kissed him harder. Calysto's blood was still in his mouth and mingled between them, but neither of them noticed.

Suddenly Calysto pulled away, inhaling hard like a gasp and his head thunked onto the ground. Python froze, afraid he'd gone too far, terrified he'd made a mistake. He opened his eyes to check, fully expecting Calysto to be angry or... something.

Instead, Calysto's eyes were closed, his lips were open and panting and his brows were knitted tightly together. Python had no idea what it meant.

"Cal?" He cautiously stroked Calysto's chin. "What's..."

"...I, uh..." Calysto's words melted together. "I'm kind of... lightheaded."

"Oh." Python started to move away but Calysto's hand gripped his shirt. Not tight, but noticeable enough that Python stilled.

"I haven't... really... eaten... anything," Calysto mumbled. "Tired."

"Oh! Oh, shit... of course, you haven't... and I just..." Python barked a laugh. "Shit, I just drained all your fucking blood, too. Here, here sit up."

"I think I'm gonna... hurl..."

"I got you. Here, come on." Python lifted him up by his shoulders.

"You... do you have any... real food?" Calysto asked weakly.

Python leaned the warlock against the tree beside them and frantically pat down all of his clothes. Outer jacket, inner jacket, vest, front shirt pocket, pants.

Nothing.

Wait.

"Uh... I have... this." Python dug into his jeans and produced a half-crumbled cookie from a shallow pocket.

Calysto looked over and immediately frowned. "Was that... in your pants?"

"Yeah?"

"With no wrapper?"

"I was in a hurry!" Python scoffed. "Like you care, I saw you eat cheese puffs off the floor."

"... They were there for like... a second..." Calysto protested. "Whatever, just give it."

Python wiped the cookie on his leg trying to remove a bit of the lint, but it was a mostly-melted chocolate chip from a week ago and the dirt was relentlessly stuck.

"Ah fuck it, here."

Calysto took it and Python noted the tremors in his fingers as he brought it weakly to his mouth. It was so stale it instantly fell apart, crumbling all over his chin, worn t-shirt, and lap. Python reached over, picking up the pieces and handing them back to him. Then, he hesitated.

"...What?" Calysto was squinting at him, chewing slowly.

"You've got some..." Python motioned, then thumbed the edge of Calysto's lip wiping away the crumbs. "There."

Calysto's eyes widened a fraction and he looked away, continuing to quietly eat. They sat in semi-awkward silence, the destruction of an extraordinarily hard cookie being the only sound between them.

"I'm..." Calysto cleared his throat after what looked to be a painfully dry swallow. "I'm glad you didn't die."

Python glanced up from where he was braiding some pine needles together and realized Calysto was staring at him, hard.

"Likewise," he said slowly. "Sorry again, about that."

Calysto shrugged. "I offered."

"Yeah, you did." Python nodded. "Why?"

"You think I'd come all this way to let you die in the shade?"

Python huffed a laugh. "Okay, fair. But you didn't have to come for me at all."

"I guess." Calysto frowned, biting his lip. Python waited to see if he would continue. "But I... Well, I... I have a lot to tell you."

"You saved me cause you want to talk?"

"Something like that." Calysto was avoiding looking at him directly now. "Ugh, I don't feel good."

"Maybe you should lie down again."

"Yeah..." Calysto pushed his hair back, blinking blearily. "Yeah, just for a second."

As he leaned to the side, sliding down the tree trunk to the ground, Python saw him fish in his pocket for something, clenching his fist around it.

"What's that?"

"Huh?"

"You hold onto something in your pocket like, all the time, I've noticed."

"Oh..." Calysto pulled his hand out and gave it to Python in a closed fist. "Just this."

Python opened his hand and froze. He squeezed his eyes shut then blinked them rapidly a few times, before making sure what he thought he saw was what he actually, truly, was seeing.

"Doesn't seem to work, but, it..."

"It's for good luck," Python finished, his voice barely a whisper.

Calysto didn't answer right away, and when he did his voice was equally as hushed. "How'd you know that?"

Python stared down at the little pewter deer. It was worn and the details had faded, it was nearly smooth and one of the antlers was broken. But out of all the things he'd forgotten over the years, he'd never forgotten this.

"Where did you get this, Cal."

"Someone gave it to me... a long time ago."

"A... chimney sweep, perhaps?" Python clenched his fist around the deer until the leg dug a hollow into his skin. "At the... at..."

"How did *you* know *that*." Calysto's eyes widened and he leaned up on his elbow. "Python, what's..."

"Cal." Python could barely believe what he was about to say, and the words fell out of his mouth before he had a chance to decide if it made any fucking sense. "Cal, I gave this to you. That was me. I was... I... you were... you were that kid?... I..."

Calysto sat up fully, bringing them close back together. Python could hear his soft heartbeat and feel the heat of his skin. Again. But it was much more distracting this time. Calysto. How long had he known him? Forever? This whole time?

"In..." Calysto began, but his voice faded away again.

"Whatever you're gonna say, just say it." Python squeezed out as he gripped the statuette tight. "Say it, Cal."

"I remembered... you..." Calysto said softly. "When you came to Merik's years later. You had... you had a cough? He, he wouldn't give you the medicine..."

"That was you?!" Python's mouth fell slightly open. "That *was* you wasn't it? You were older... I didn't, I didn't even make the connection."

"How is it..." Calysto scooted across the pine needles with a small shuffle, no doubt smearing the ass of his pants with mud. He reached a hand out covering the statue, his molten skin seeping warmth into Python's frigid palm. "This is real... isn't it?"

"I think so, yeah," Python said in a hushed murmur, curling his fingers around Calysto's hand. "I think so."

"How is that even possible?" Calysto murmured. "That you... you just happened upon me like that... it *was* on accident, right?"

"Yes!" Python blurted quickly. "I swear I had no idea but I... well, listen when I..."

"What?"

"You know when we got the crystal. Uh. You were there weren't you? That's how you got this." Python motioned to Calysto's cheek. "Right?"

Calysto's eyes darted up to look at him, then away just as quick. "Yes."

"You gave someone one of those crystals, too. Didn't you?"

"I don't know."

"Cal..." Python's head was reeling and he fell back onto the soft earth from his prolonged squat. He still held tight to Calysto's hand. "You asked what happened back there. That's what happened. You gave it to me."

"W...what?" Calysto's eyes were glassy and he jolted in their grip as if he wanted to pull away. "What? No... that's... how do you know that for sure?"

"I've only met one Calysto in my whole life," Python said gently, even as his mind was racing he'd had a bit of time to realize this part of things. It was only Calysto who was hearing it all for the first time. "I put it together, I guess."

"Wait, so..." Calysto adjusted his glasses and ran his hand through his hair and down his scar-ridden cheek. When his voice emerged, it trembled. "You-you you're the one who saved me?"

"I guess so, yeah."

"I..." Calysto took a large, shaky breath in. "I always wondered who'd..."

Calysto looked up and Python saw his eyes were brimming with tears.

"Cal..." Before he could finish his sentence, Calysto had leapt up, slinging his arms around the vampire's neck.

"It was you," Calysto whispered, pulling him close. Python snaked his hands around Calysto's waist, returning the embrace. "It was you, Han. That's... that's really your name isn't it?"

Python tucked his head into Calysto's shoulder and nodded, he couldn't trust his voice to speak as he held them both there. What were the odds? How could it be that they had always been the thing the other had needed, their whole lives?

Intersecting through small acts of kindness, illuminated moments of light that inspired them to go on, brief sparks of hope in a bleak existence that proved the world could be good.

They had found those things in each other, over and over again.

Without knowing the other was the same, time and time again.

"I'm sorry, Han," Calysto said quietly, soft breath tickling Python's neck. "I'm sorry, I didn't... I was so mean."

"Me too," Python huffed. "I'm not a good person, Cal."

Calysto pulled back, meeting his eyes. His golden skin was dusted softly pink, and his eyes were a ruddy red. "That's not true."

"You don't know me," Python disagreed. "Not really. I really haven't been good. I know it. I'm not... I'm not the person you want to remember as your savior."

"But..." Calysto frowned. "You saved me just last week. The current you, saved the me of the past. That's not bad, there's... there's nothing... I... Han you, you saved me, don't you get it? You saved my life. No one has ever... ever cared, I..."

Python felt a pang in his chest at the realization. Calysto had looked up to that mysterious figure who lifted him from the fire as a symbol of hope for his whole life.

On one hand, Python was angry because through what Calysto said, he'd implied that no one else had ever been kind to him. On the other, he was ashamed. Ashamed that *he* was who Calysto's hero turned out to be, this vagabond, this asshole of a vampire who embodied the term in every sense of the word.

He wasn't really anything worth the admiration.

"Cal..." Python shook his head. "I'm not that great."

Calysto twitched as if hesitating, then, pulled Python closer and let his weight fall back, yanking them both onto the ground.

"Hey!"

"How about this..." Calysto said into his ear. "You saved me, I saved you. Now we're even, so you don't even have to worry about it."

Python rolled off of Calysto and over to his side, resting his head on the forest floor.

Calysto turned to face him. They were so close their noses were nearly touching.

"Is that so?" Python murmured.

Calysto violently blushed, and his lips parted but no sound came out.

Then Python was overtaken with a sudden glee.

He'd been so alone, so hateful and closed off, so selfish and lonely for so long. But, without him knowing it, this little warlock had been in his life from the beginning, and somehow, call it fate or destiny or pure chance, they had been brought back together.

Despite his unwillingness to acknowledge it this whole time, he'd never felt so complete, so whole, so... strangely accepted, than he did with Calysto. Even if Calysto got kind of annoyed, or closed off, or irritated at him, he'd never rejected him. Never made him feel ashamed, never was intentionally mean or truly unwilling. Calysto was as alone as him, and as unused to constant company, and he simply acted like it in his own weird way.

"Do you really want me to stay?" Python asked softly.

Calysto's cheeks bloomed an even deeper shade and he nodded. "I'd... Yeah, I'd like that."

"Okay, good." Python smiled, fangs brushing his lips. "Me too. Hey, you're not gonna pass out, are you? If I kiss you again?"

Calysto blinked. "No, don't think so."

"Okay. Good."

Python closed the breath of space between them without another word.

TWENTY-NINE

The covering of trees served as a sufficient shelter for the two well through the day and on into the evening hours as the sun returned to its rest. Calysto slept on and off in fits of nauseated exhaustion, slightly soothed by the cool touch of Python's hand on his face checking to make sure he was still alright. He was frustratingly weak and hungry to the point of irritability, but he still couldn't entirely be in a bad mood. Python *had* kissed him after all.

It was near maddening, really—this visceral juxtaposition of exhaustion and elation, frustration and embarrassment, confusion and shock and disbelief and relief. The tumultuous nature of his emotions alone was enough to keep him lying still for nearly all the afternoon hours.

They talked on and off, here and there. In bursts in which he could muster the energy, and between the times that Python decided to end his sentences with another kiss instead. Calysto felt an occasional pang of guilt that he was in no state to truly reciprocate and tried to communicate some sort of enthusiasm through his gestures. He accidentally might've let slip a nearly imperceptible moan, just once, but quickly stifled it to the thoughts of smothering himself to death with a handful of cold forest dirt. Python didn't seem to mind though, instead choosing to find it encouraging and pulling Calysto closer for more.

Calysto realized at a moment in the midst of one of these kisses, that he might've gotten himself into something he was wildly, utterly, and absolutely unprepared for. It set his heart to racing and he pulled away as his blood suddenly ran cold.

"What?" Python asked, in a gentle tone so unlike him. Yet in that moment, the tenderness of it and the rapid change that was occurring between them was somehow both reassuring and terrifying to Calysto's sensitive state.

"Nothing," he answered, shaking his head. Likely getting nettle stuck throughout the curly knots. "I... it's a lot, isn't it?"

"Do you want to stop?" Python's hold on him loosened.

"No! No, I don't..." Calysto closed his eyes. "This happened so fast, that's all."

"Didn't run all the way out here and save me just to make out with me, I take it?"

Calysto smirked slightly, in spite of himself. "Wasn't exactly part of the plan."

"But..." He heard Python hesitate. "Not unwanted, right?"

Calysto frowned and reached out blindly until his hand met Python's shirt, and he pulled the vampire close to him.

"Wh—!"

"Shut up about that will you," Calysto mumbled, and let his hand fall as he was hit with another bout of exhaustion.

"Hmm," Python's voice came closer and it'd lost its nervous edge. Now, he sounded dangerously amused. "Why don't you make me?"

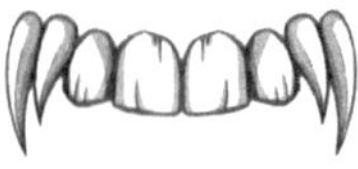

"I promised I'd bring you back to her," Calysto explained from his once again, humiliating perch as Python's backpack.

"Yeah, but you don't have to keep that promise, that's all I'm saying," Python protested, his rapid footsteps sending loose gravel flying up around them. Some flicked Calysto in the shins and he grit his teeth, trying to focus on not letting go of Python's neck.

"She won't kill you," Calysto answered, hoping that he was right. "And besides, if we run, you know it'll just piss her off, and she'll just keep coming after you. And me. I just, really think we should end this now."

"End it with me dying!"

"I won't let that happen, okay?" Calysto rested his chin on Python's shoulder. "Just let me talk to her first."

"Fine, Cal! But I'm really fucking trusting you with this, like, for real."

"I know," Calysto muttered solemnly. "I know."

Calysto instructed Python on where to go, and he quickly led them back to the ramshackle cabin tucked away off the unpaved road. He climbed down off of Python to land on shaky legs. He was pretty sure if he didn't get something to eat besides half of a stale cookie soon he was going to pass out and never wake up.

Curse Python for getting him used to eating food, now he was actually hungry more often. In a way that was hard to ignore. The liter of blood loss certainly wasn't helping, and if the tingles traveling rapidly through his limbs were any indication, he wasn't going to make it upright for much longer.

"Alright there?" Python gripped him by his bicep. "You're sounding pretty weak."

"You know..." Calysto tried to steady himself. "Even when people donate like, a tiny bit of blood, they give them more than one cookie."

Python winced. "If I woulda known I woulda planned for it."

"Have you ever?"

"What?"

"Known? Planned?"

Python had the audacity to look slightly offended and rather than the reaction being annoying, Calysto found it kind of charming.

"Sometimes!"

"Okay." Calysto's quiet laugh caught in his throat, but the ringing in his ears caused him to quickly sober and focus on the task at hand. "Okay, it's fine. I'm going to go in first, maybe... um, maybe wait out here?"

Python seemed reluctant to let go of his grip on Calysto's arm, likely worried he'd fall over without the support. And well, he almost did.

"Be careful," Python said, his lips pinching together into a thin line. "I swear Cal, if you get killed right now I'm gonna lose it. Like, I'm done."

"I won't," Calysto answered, saying it with a hint of hope that if he convinced himself of it, it would happen.

"I'm serious," Python said back, stepping in front of Calysto's path to the door. "Listen, I know we haven't known each other that long—wait, well, I guess we have. But you know what I mean."

Calysto nodded to show he was listening. He could tell that Python was trying hard to articulate something that didn't come easy to him. A feeling he understood all too well.

"But I'm not... look, I'm not..." Python growled slightly, sounding frustrated.

"What?"

"I'm not good at this, alright?" Python bit out aggressively. "But I like you, Cal. I fucking like you, and I'm... I don't *like* people, yeah? I don't. And I can't believe that I even like you, to be quite fucking honest. But I do, and damn if I'm not a little mad about it, too. Like, you could walk in there and get your dumb ass killed right now, and I would give a shit. Do you realize that? I... I would fucking give a shit!"

Python hissed and turned away, running his hands down his face. Calysto watched him, parsing out the good from the bad in the vampire's short tirade.

"So, you like me, and you care, and that's annoying?" he said slowly.

Python stilled with his claws carded halfway through his hair.

"Yeah, I guess," he finally answered.

"Oh." Calysto shrugged to himself. "Yeah, I get that."

Python shot him a look from over his shoulder. "What, really?"

"Well..." Calysto cleared his throat. "I suppose I feel the same, Python. Or... do you prefer Han?"

"Either one's fine, whatever."

"Okay, um, well..." Calysto tried to gather his original train of thought again before it slipped away into the growing fuzz surrounding his consciousness. "I like you too, I guess. Enough to... do all this anyway..."

"Yeah?" Python spun back around and approached Calysto, reaching out to grab him tightly by the shoulders. "Really?"

"Yeah." Calysto suddenly couldn't look at him directly. It was hard enough to admit to himself, or the man's back. Certainly, he wasn't strong enough to do it to his face just yet. "You're alright."

Python broke out into a wide grin. "Ha! Oh shit, that's..."

Calysto interrupted him by hiking himself up on his toes, squeezing his eyes shut, and landing a brash kiss on the vampires half-open lips. He nearly felt himself implode from the sheer audacity, but for once in the past century he let himself follow his instincts.

A want, a desire, a need.

He leaned back, suddenly afraid to open his eyes. It didn't matter if he'd already made out with the vampire a few times on the forest floor, this was a whole other thing altogether. The feelings were out in the open, somewhat. Kind of. But it was enough to add a new layer of vulnerability that had him terrified of the outcome of his actions.

"Cal," Python said quietly, sounding a bit stunned. "Look at me."

Calysto did. Through the moonlight and the ruined lenses of his glasses, the vampire's face was sliced into shining fractals, and his exhaustion-blurred vision wasn't helping matters either. Still, he looked, and he could see those dark red eyes staring down at him, searching his face, taking in the details. He was sure he appeared an entire mess, but when had he not? Yet, Python wasn't looking at him with criticism or disgust, only what seemed to be a rapidly fluctuating array of emotions.

"Just... I'll be right here, okay? If you need me, just call."

"Okay, I will." Calysto took a deep breath and backed away. He pulled his coat tight around him, and made his way up to the cabin door.

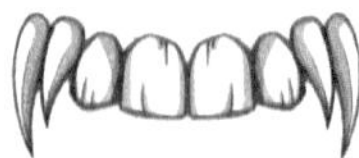

"Took you long enough," Aeris said from her corner in the dark. She hadn't moved the entire time Calysto had been gone. Or maybe she had but ended up wandering back over there to plop down, defeated. "I was wondering when you two idiots would stop crying over each other out there."

She could see Calysto clearly in the doorway, his hesitant posture and wiry frame, his baggy clothes and a coat that looked vaguely familiar to her from a long time ago. As she watched him squint around searching for the source of her voice, she realized two things. One, he most definitely couldn't see in the dark and therefore also wasn't the same Calysto she had hoped he was. He wasn't a vampire and his glasses weren't a farce. Two, he wasn't just wearing the coat she remembered, he was wearing nearly the entire ensemble. She would never forget the Calysto she met that night at the tavern, and this was most certainly the same one. But now his neck and chest were covered in blood.

"Piss him off or something?" she asked.

"Did you read it?" He asked, ignoring her question. He reached into his pocket, pulling out a thin gnarled piece of wood in the shape of a wand. The tip of it began to glow a muted orange and he held it up. She saw his eyes finally find her in the room and he slowly tracked his way across the dirty debris-ridden floor. He stopped in front of her crossed legs and equally crossed arms, and his thigh brushed her knee.

"I read it," she eventually answered, after doing her best to tamp down the emotion in her voice. "It doesn't excuse that one outside though."

"No, I suppose not," he agreed. "But you promised—"

"I didn't promise shit," she cut him off, anger suddenly rising in her chest. "You just have a hard-on for each other, you don't give a shit about me or what I want!"

"That's not true," Calysto pleaded softly. "I'm sorry, Aeris. I'm sorry I left you then. I thought you were dead, really. I didn't think I was abandoning you. Had I known you'd been turned... I would have never. I swear. It doesn't mean I didn't care."

"No..." Aeris sighed, suddenly deflating. Faced with his words that read as so sincere, her anger melted again and she felt so, so tired. "I... it's not your fault. Hell, it's been a century now? I can barely remember it all. There's... really no point to it anymore, it just is, you know? There's nothing else. Python was the last person from that night. That night that turned me. And I was chasing him for so long..."

"Now that you've got him, what do you do now." Calysto nodded.

She nodded in return and uncrossed her legs. She reached for the journal on the floor beside her and flopped it back and forth in her hand.

"I thought," she began, swallowing around an uncomfortable lump building in her throat. "I thought when I saw you two together, that I could kill two vamps with one stake, so to speak. Finish this all, and get the cure. But... but, now I just..."

Calysto was silent and she watched as he knelt down. Her knees straddled either side of his arms and despite the vulnerable position, she knew she could easily crush him with her thighs if he tried anything, so she wasn't worried. And besides, he didn't feel threatening. He never had in the brief times that they'd met, and he didn't now. If anything, it felt nice to have someone so close. She frowned at the thought.

"It's nothing like you thought it was," Calysto mused, seeming to understand the idea in his own way.

"Well, this is sweet," Python's voice cut through the moment. Aeris jerked to attention to see the other vampire leaning casually on the doorframe, observing them both.

"What the fuck do you want," she hissed, irritated at herself that she hadn't noticed him enter.

"Nothing." He shrugged. "Just want to make sure you're not gonna do anything rash, babe."

"Like what?" she snapped. "Kill your little boyfriend?"

Calysto's eyes widened but he didn't speak.

"Maybe," Python answered, and she recognized that cautious edge to his voice. Like he was deciding which mood to settle on. "Are you?"

"Aeris," Calysto interrupted, drawing her attention back to him. "You don't need to kill either of us. Or anyone, anymore. If..." he hesitated, biting the edge of his lip and resting a hand on her knee. She heard his heartbeat slow and watched him curiously. "You could come home... with me, with us. If you wanted."

"Cal!" Python sounded shocked. "The fuck?"

"If you wanted," Calysto continued, he leaned in closer to her and she didn't move. "You don't have to be alone anymore. You don't have to do this... anymore. I get it, okay? But getting rid of Python isn't going to make you happy. Or... less lonely."

His fist that held the wand still rested on her leg, and the other reached up towards her extremely carefully as if approaching a feral cat. But slowly it came to rest on her cheek, and the warmth from his hand nearly made her jolt. She remembered the one time they'd kissed—or rather the time she'd kissed him—but she'd forgotten the way it all felt. She'd been angry so long she'd forgotten that the Calysto she'd known had actually been kind to her.

That the reason he'd argued with her was to try to protect her.

He'd shut down her ideas not because he hadn't respected her choice, but because he was afraid she would die. He'd followed along behind her not to question her capabilities, but to hopefully save her from her obstinate self. She'd never been abandoned by him, only mourned. All despite the fact that he wasn't even the same Calysto she'd thought he was.

She found herself almost amused at the thought.

Calysto wasn't even a vampire hunter, then.

He must've been scared shitless.

"There really isn't a cure?"

She could barely muster up the strength to ask the question. Everything she'd meant to find was crumbling before her. There was no way out, there was no justice, there was no going back.

"No," Calysto whispered. "If that is what you really want then I'm sorry. I don't have it. And neither did my father. I can keep looking, if you wanted me to. I could. But if you decided you didn't want that anymore... well... maybe..."

"I..." She wanted to be angry, to lean back into that pain and let it take over. She thought of lashing out, rejecting him and all of what he offered. She couldn't even understand why he would offer it. She thought of killing him and Python and ending it all in one fell swoop. She thought of finding her own final sunrise. Then, she met his eyes, the color of them a glistening gold, and she couldn't locate voice.

For now, she had an option. For once she had a choice. The thing she'd always been so angry that was taken from her, he gave to her again. It all was in her hands, to live or to die. To move on, or to admit defeat. And to concede again to death just wasn't something she would do.

Besides, he was sweet, exactly as she remembered, and though their time together had been brief she'd always felt they should've had more. She was curious, damnit all, and so goddamn tired of fighting alone.

Maybe she wanted that cure, maybe she didn't. Maybe she only wanted something different.

His thumb brushed her cheek and she nodded once. It was all she could manage.

"Okay," Calysto said softly. "That's settled, then."

She felt him hesitate before he placed a soft kiss, right at the corner of her eye. She still didn't move.

"Just, no killing Python, okay?" he murmured.

Then, his hand slipped from her face and she thought he was going to move away. But instead, he slumped forward onto her shoulder, completely limp.

"Oh shit." Python ran over from across the room.

"Did he pass out?" she asked, trying to get a look at his face smashed into her coat.

"Yeah uh," Python pulled Calysto off of her. His head hung lifelessly and the little light wand rolled away across the floor. "I might've had to feed off of him."

"Oh great," she scoffed. "So you killed him, is that it?"

"No!" Python yelped defensively. "I... No, I don't think so."

"What do we do?"

She peered down at Calysto's face. His pulse was weak and his skin looked clammy. She didn't usually concern herself with after-meal after-care so this was an entirely new endeavor for her.

"I don't know," Python answered. Guess it was new for him, too. "We should probably take him home... to his house, I guess."

All in one motion he scooped Calysto into his arms and stood.

She squinted at him skeptically. "We, huh?"

"He said you could come," Python sounded reluctant, but he didn't refute what Calysto had promised. "It's his place after all."

CHAPTER

THIRTY

Python was incredibly on edge. The journey back to Calysto's house was near dead silent, and even though he and Aeris both could travel at incredible speeds it still took another hour to find the place a few hundred miles away from where they'd had been. He wondered how the fuck Calysto had found them to begin with. But finding out wasn't on the top of his list of concerns at the moment.

He shouldered open the door to the house and would almost be relieved at the familiarity of the place if it weren't for the fact that the warlock was passed out nearly dead in his arms and a vampire-vampire hunter who maybe *wasn't* going to kill him only for the time being was following right behind him.

Python lay Calysto down on the couch that had served as the vampire's bed, and subsequently on top of a lot of his scattered clothes. He pulled off the warlock's too-big boots and socks and loosened the drawstring on Calysto's pants in hopes that it would help his circulation. For once he looked at Calysto's waist and didn't think of anything untoward.

"Babe," he called behind him. "Bring me a drink or something from the fridge."

She scoffed at the pet name but didn't comment and left to find the kitchen.

"Damn, bitch, it's a mess in here!" she called out from down the hall. "You two live like this?"

"Don't rope me into it!" he called back, knowing full well he'd done his part to contribute. But to be fair, Calysto had about a hundred years or more head start. It really wasn't Python's fault for most of it.

"Hey, Cal?" He turned his attention to the unconscious form of the warlock lying much too still on the sofa. "We got you home, you can get up now."

He used the pads of his fingertips to push the hair from Calysto's face and then carefully removed his glasses.

"The fuck happened to these," he murmured, observing the new array of cracks. "What did you get into, huh?"

"Here." Aeris nudged his shoulder with the butt of a soda can.

"Fuck!" he hissed, snatching the drink. "You fuckin' startled me!"

She shrugged and sat down at the foot of the couch. She was acting much more docile than he'd ever known her to be, but he wasn't about to blindly trust it.

"Now what?"

"Hold him up." Python purposefully avoided looking at her.

He felt like if he did, he'd lose focus on the task at hand. And saving the life of the most fragile immortal being out of the three of them was definitely more pressing than possibly arguing with Aeris right now.

She grabbed the collar of Calysto's coat and hoisted him into a sitting position. His head fell back, exposing his blood-covered throat.

"Shit, babe!" Python exclaimed as he righted Calysto's head. "Be careful!"

"Be careful," she said back, her tone bitterly dry. "Says the one who ate too much off the guy he likes."

Python grit his teeth. She wasn't wrong. He decided not to answer and pat Calysto not-so-gently on the cheek.

"Cal, wake up for a sec."

He ignored the way he could feel Aeris' staring at him, and the way she gave Calysto a small shake. He was about to try again when the warlock's eyes shifted beneath the lids and he slowly blinked them halfway open.

"Hey, just drink some of this."

Python pushed the can towards him and watched nervously as Calysto tried to form a weak grip around it with his hands. He couldn't seem to lift the soda can, and Aeris freed a hand from his coat and took it from him.

"Here," she said softly, holding it up to his lips.

Python looked on silently, taken aback by her sudden tenderness. He'd rarely, if ever, seen such a side to her, and he wondered what Calysto had done to make her feel this way. It seemed the warlock had a special talent for wriggling his way into the heart of more than one cold-blooded bloodsucking motherfucker.

Calysto took a few sips and his bleary eyes shifts between the two of them.

"You're... both here," he mumbled, barely intelligible.

"Yeah." Python forced a small smile. "You offered."

Aeris snorted. "I'm not sleeping on a couch though, you better have a room for me."

Calysto nodded earnestly.

"Hey," Python protested. "I want one too, what the fuck!"

"There's..." Calysto took a shaky breath. "There's mo... more than one..."

"Python *darling,* leave him alone," Aeris chided. When he cast a glance at her she was already staring back. A smirk danced noncommittally on her lips, and her dark eyes sparkled with a hidden amusement.

"I'm gonna..." Calysto hiccuped. "I'm gonna sleep... more."

"Are you sure that's a good idea?" Python asked, but before he could get a response Calysto's head fell to his chest and he was out again. Aeris held the soda can rim between her teeth and lay the warlock back down.

Python reached out to touch Calysto's forehead. It was a little warmer than before. Reassured he slumped with his back against the front edge of the couch, and finally, he turned his attention to Aeris.

"What," she demanded, peering down at him.

"Are you really going to stay?"

"Are you?"

He shrugged. "Yeah."

"Me too, I suppose."

"You aren't going to kill me?"

Aeris sighed, leaning over Calysto's legs to rest against the back of the couch. "I thought I wanted to, for a long time," she began. "You know I got everyone in that damned nest except you."

"And Richter," he corrected.

"And Richter," she agreed. "Impressive work, that. I have to admit. I was damned surprised to see someone else had done it."

"Yeah well, I fuckin' hated him." Python let his head fall behind him. It landed on Calysto's thigh. The heat was nice and soothed the remaining edge to his nerves.

"Yeah well, I didn't know that," Aeris said, with an apologetic tone. "I thought... well, shit I guess I thought you wanted to become him, instead."

"I can't blame you for not wanting that." He rolled his head to the side to look at her. "I'd kill me too, for that."

"Well." She took a sip of soda, swishing it around in her mouth before swallowing. "You're still a right ass, babe."

"So are you," he said back, but it had no bite.

"I just wanted a choice..." she said quietly, her voice slipping far away into memory. "I never got a choice. I don't... hate this, being this. But it's not right. What we are? It was never a choice."

"It wasn't for me either," Python answered. "Do you think you would have? You know, if you had been asked. Would you have become a vampire anyway?"

"Dunno." She squeezed the can and it made a sharp metallic snap as it dented in the middle. "Doesn't matter now. I just don't want it to happen to anyone else like that."

"Me neither, hon," he murmured.

The air between them was still and peaceful, the animosity had quietly slipped away under the circumstances and left nothing but a strange sort of understanding. For a breath they simply looked into the other's eyes and shared a tired smile.

Then Python's smile slipped away and he spoke earnestly, "I don't want to fight with you, I really don't. I'm... I'm not Richter but, I could be better. I could be a lot better. I'm gonna try, I promise."

"Well, maybe I'll have to stick around and hold you to it," she said. "Figure out what I want now, too."

Python let out a pensive sigh and stared up at the dirty cobweb-coated ceiling of Calysto's little house. The place that had become some semblance of home.

He thought about the past few weeks, and what this had all become. Where it had brought him. And he found that he couldn't even look back. He couldn't *go* back. Not to that. Not to who he had been for so long. Not to his solitary, bitter, and miserable cocoon of loneliness where only the whisper of his own thoughts could hurt him.

Life would never be the same after this.

Too much had changed, too much was different. The life that was his life before felt as if he only knew of it as though waking from a dream he could barely recall. Bits and pieces of decades gone by held no meaning, simply a blur of time spent alone, alone, alone.

And now it was far more removed, belonging to a stranger he wouldn't even recognize when passing on the street.

Instead, there was this new type of nothing. This question. This hollow ache that resonated in the cavern of his chest shouting *what now, what now?*

Where do I go from here?

He knew in his heart that in this moment Aeris felt the same. Their centuries-long chase had come to an end, and all it took was a warlock and a book. It was laughably simple. It was frankly ridiculous. But it couldn't have happened any other way for this trio of lonely souls.

Python felt the shape of Calysto's leg beneath his head and listened to the soft rasp of his slow sleeping breath. He brushed his shoulder against Aeris' calf and heard her teeth scrape the aluminum edge of the soda can as she took another drink. He took a deep breath he didn't need, closed his eyes, and smiled.

Maybe he didn't need to go anywhere after all.

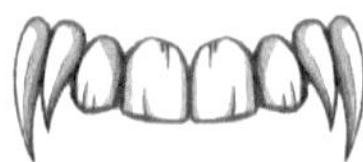

IT MIGHT'VE BEEN the middle of the night when they'd reached Calysto's house, but no matter nocturnal or not, all three of them ended up sleeping the rest of the evening away, and most of the daytime hours, too.

Calysto was the first to wake and was surprised to find both of his vampire companions passed out nearly over top of him. He reached around, feeling for his glasses on the nightstand behind him, and looked at them.

Aeris was curled up at his feet and it was the first time he'd seen her without her coat or hat or shoes. She looked peaceful and the usual sharp edges of her vicious expressions were softened in her sleep. Her long black curls fell down loose across her face and blouse and even through the cracks in his glasses he was struck with her ghostly beauty as well as an unexpected sense of relief to see her there.

Python had fallen asleep siting on the floor, with his elbows pillowed under his cheek on the couch near Calysto's waist. His mouth was open and sharp double fangs peaked out from beneath his lips. The blouse he was wearing was slightly sheer and the silver burns on his arms had all but disappeared. Calysto reached down and ran his fingers carefully through Python's snowy hair, it was soft to the touch and let off the scent of floral perfume.

"Mmm...?"

"Oh," Calysto stilled his hand. "I didn't mean to wake you."

"S'okay," Python raised his head and gave Calysto a sleepy smile. The right side of his face was tracked with upholstery lines pressed into his skin. It was a much better sight than the indents of silver chains and was even kind of endearing if Calysto could be forced to admit such a thing.

"I'm hungry," Calysto said. "You still owe me dinner, you know."

Python perked up and slapped Aeris' on the knee. "Hey, wake up, we're gonna go eat."

She instantly kicked him.

"Ow!" he yelped. "Why!"

"Be nice to me, dick!" she mumbled, rubbing her eyes.

"Oh, that's rich," Python scoffed. "You first."

"I *am* being nice," she said, as she stood and stretched. "Where are you trying to go?"

"Um," Calysto tried to sit up as his arms trembled beneath him. "There's a place close by I think, saw it... before."

Python shot him a curious look. "Before what?"

"I'll tell you later."

"Okay well, you can't go anywhere looking like that," he motioned to Calysto's clothes. Only then did Calysto realize he was absolutely covered in blood, and dirt, and probably a good sticky layer of sweat.

"Oh..." Calysto's face warmed as he realized he was surrounded by and napped upon by two very pretty vampires all while looking, and likely smelling, like a dirty napkin. "Wanna help me with that?"

Python hopped up off the floor and extended a hand to Calysto with a wide grin. "Why my dear, I thought you'd never ask."

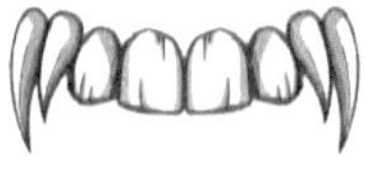

A SIGN that boasted 24/7 *BREAKFAST* hummed with the ominous buzz of a hornet's nest above Calysto's head as he waited for Python to finish his cigarette. He'd showered for the third time this month— which was likely breaking some kind of personal record— and wore a pair of black jeans he'd found under his bed, paired with a loose dark grey sweater of Python's, and some flat sneakers he'd forgotten he owned. His glasses were still cracked beyond repair, but he wore them for now and would focus on making new ones another time.

Python had swapped out his sheer top for another identical one saying something about 'if you find clothes you like, get one in each color'. Calysto had to admit he saw some logic in that and had briefly wished he had at least five of his favorite cardigan. Would save on the awkward yearly laundromat trip into whatever town was closest by.

Aeris still refused to change but opted to leave the sword and hat at home at Calysto's insistence. The sword because, well, who carries a sword to go get pancakes, and the hat because Calysto did his best to *casually* mention something about her hair being nice and so she'd left it home of her own accord. She was beside him, leaning on the large diner window covered in outdated menu items and layered scraps of sticky double-sided tape.

Python tossed his cigarette into the sewer grate and approached them, smoke billowing from his teeth like a dragon. He hopped up onto the sidewalk and reached to pull the diner door. The bell tinkled to signal their arrival, and he held it open while feigning an exaggerated bow.

"My dears," he said with a wink. "After you."

Aeris scoffed through a reluctant smile and Calysto followed after her, stopping to grab Python's sleeve and tug him behind.

A sleepy waitress guided them to their seats, but Calysto barely paid the whole event any attention. On one hand, he was fucking starving and weak at the knees, so much so the hunger had turned to a knot in his stomach and he wasn't entirely sure he'd even be able to eat now. And on the other, he was having a hard time wrapping his usually very logical and deductive brain around what the fuck was happening to him, and how things had so drastically changed.

He stumbled into the corner booth, taking the space furthest from the walkway and in between the other two, and picked up the menu without really looking at it. Python ordered them all coffee and 'also water for this one here' while motioning at Calysto.

"What do you want?" Python leaned in to look over his shoulder as if he didn't have a menu of his own.

"Dunno," Calysto answered. "Waffles or something."

Aeris hummed to herself and set the plastic sheet on the table with a clap. "Steak."

"Ew." Python looked up at her. "Diner steak is nasty."

"You're nasty," Aeris retorted.

She turned her attention to the waitress as they were interrupted by the arrival of coffee cups and bowls filled with tiny plastic containers of cream.

"How's the steak?" Aeris asked.

"Not good," the woman responded. "Especially this time of night. Honestly, it's on the menu for show."

Python stuck his tongue out at Aeris and she gave him a look that said at least a thousand insults. Calysto watched this all play out from his place in the middle, once again realizing how much trouble he was getting himself into with these two. In the same house, no less.

"Excuse me," he said quietly, breaking them up. "Can we just have a bunch of waffles and bacon? Maybe some extra syrup?"

The waitress nodded seeming relieved at the order's simplicity and left with the promise of food, eventually, sometime soon, probably.

It didn't matter how long it would take, for between the three of them they had plenty to talk about. Years of events to say and tell and hear. Things they'd never told anyone before now had the chance for an audience.

There was so much to learn about one another, but they had centuries to learn it. There was so much to do, but they had forever to do it. There was so much potential of what to be, but they had an eternity to be it.

Despite the decades of hardship and strife, despite two hundred years of fleeing and fighting and hiding away, they all had triumphed. Against all odds, all reason, and all they'd been through, they'd found a way back to one another time and time again. And while they'd passed each other by more often than not, the memories of one another had lingered all the same. But circumstance had finally smiled upon them it seemed, and time had aligned to bring about the things in which they truly wanted.

They only had but to muster the courage to reach out at accept it.

And who's to say how their lives would unfold from here—this tenuous truce, this terrifying precipice? This dive into the unknown world of companionship, and friendship and dare we hope, love?

But here and now it was just the three of them, sharing an uncomfortable booth and a meal at a shitty midnight diner. A new and tender tangle of connections that held so much prospect for a lasting harmony and hard-earned peace. A moment of respite and contentment within the present yet full to the brim with the possibilities of the future.

In the end, they were together, and they could stop running.

EPILOGUE

Some passing of time eternal later...

It was a vampire's early afternoon, and the typical waking time for one nocturnal warlock when Python stepped outside. Chilly midnight air fluttered through Python's hair from where he leaned against the porch railing, nursing a cigarette and taking in the stars.

"Love isn't real, Python. And if something like it does exist, it's conditional at best," Calysto was saying.

"Phew, who hurt you?" Python took a long drag from his cigarette, continuing to stare out over Calysto's head. He couldn't really bring himself to disagree though.

"Everyone," Calysto grumbled, snatching the cigarette from his lips and aggressively inhaling as if he could punish someone else with the ruination of his lungs. "Everyone is a massive fucking disappointment. You've been around as long as I have, don't tell me you don't know."

"Yeah, yeah," Python sighed. "Doesn't mean you can't enjoy it while it lasts, I guess."

"What's the point?" Calysto growled, smashing his teeth down on the porous cotton filter.

He was in a particularly pessimistic mood. It happened sometimes. Python was getting used to all of them taking turns at the steering wheel of cynicism and in the passenger seat of proving the other wrong.

"How can you even let yourself feel something like that if you just know you're gonna get hurt in the end?"

"I guess sometimes the hurt is worth it?" Python snatched the cig back from Calysto's lips. "It's different, too, if you... you know, want to be together. With someone."

"What do you mean?"

"Well, what about, say. You and me. We're both immortal, well, you probably are at least. It's not like, we'd lose each other in any natural way, so if we want to be together we can be, and we can promise that much. Just..." Python rubbed his temple, ash falling onto his jacket in the process. "I don't know if love is real. But I think maybe, it's just a choice. I like you Cal, and I choose to be here, I choose to be with you and around you and put up with you, because underneath it all, I like who you are. Which pretty much never fucking happens to me, by the way. And I don't see that stopping any time soon."

He glanced over and saw Calysto watching him very carefully in the dim light.

He cleared his throat and continued.

"I'm not really sure what I'm trying to say here, but... I choose you, Calysto. Just like I choose Aeris in there, who's probably getting real impatient waiting on us right about now, I should add. I choose you, and as long as I keep liking you I'll keep choosing you. And whatever of our lives happens in the meantime, I'll be here for it. I want to be here for it. I hate the idea of you doing anything alone. And I think that might be... well, I dunno. Maybe that's all love is."

"A choice," Calysto murmured softly as if thinking it over for himself.

"Yeah." Python shrugged. "What do you say?"

"... Yeah," Calysto finally answered. Python snuck another glance in his direction, and though his brow was furrowed in that thinking-way-too-hard kind of way, his golden cheeks were tinted pink. "I... yeah, I like that."

"Cool."

Python tossed the cashed cigarette out into the dark. He righted himself, pulled down his shirt, and smoothed back his hair. He tried not to overthink his actions as he took two long steps over to where Calysto was standing and watching him like a hawk.

"Wanna make out?"

Python could've sworn he *heard* the blood rush to Calysto's face, and he broke out into a grin as Calysto said, "Sure."

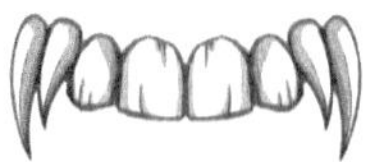

"You've got to be fucking joking!" Python exclaimed, slamming his hand onto the table as Aeris laughed.

"You're terrible at this," she teased. Her winning hand of cards laid out for all three to see.

Calysto grumbled and threw his cards down. "I'm never gonna figure this out," he said.

Aeris tsked and shook her head good-naturedly. "Maybe if either of you stopped getting distracted, you could learn something."

"Not my fault you're both pretty and the game involves getting undressed," Calysto answered.

"He's right you know!" Python chimed in. "It's extremely hard to focus with you two around."

Aeris laughed again. A real, genuine laugh. Her bare legs were crossed and draped across the corner of the table and the only clothing she had left was an open button-up top, socks, and a pair of Python's boxer briefs. Python scooted over and gnawed a playful bite onto her ankle before jumping to his feet. He wasn't exactly fully dressed either.

"I'm gonna get a snack... ah shit, hey Cal, where's my phone?" Python spun around looking for his pants in the assortment of clothes strewn across the floor.

"Workshop, I think," Calysto answered.

"Oh yeah! Be right back!"

He ran from the kitchen and bounded the stairs three at a time up to Calysto's workshop. Sure enough, right on the messy countertop was his phone, in between whatever Calysto's current investigative obsession was. Python snatched it up and was about to leave when something scraped the bare skin of his hip and caught his attention.

A large sealed white envelope stuck halfway out of a storage drawer. Python yanked the knob in irritation, preparing to stuff the envelope back in and be done with it. But when the drawer opened, he saw it was crammed full of mail. Some opened, some not, some newer, some yellowed around the edges from age. Curiosity got the better of him and he pulled out a handful, beginning to flip through them.

They were all confirmation or acceptance letters with official header logos from various medical and scientific institutes, research facilities, and production companies.

Python skimmed over the information, but they were all somewhat similar in their message.

"Thank you for your invaluable contribution to research in the field of..."

"Patent #4056 has been attributed to ANONYMOUS X in the development of..."

"The Institute for Disease Prevention extends it's gratitude for..."

. . .

"Did you find it?" Calysto's voice came from behind him and Python spun around, letters still in hand. "Oh."

"Sorry," he blurted. "I wasn't trying to snoop, one just fell out."

"It's fine." Calysto approached, taking the papers back and stuffing them into the overflowing drawer. "They're not really anything."

"Are you kidding?" Python balked. "What is all this?"

Calysto shoved the drawer shut and turned to face him. He had the gaul to look sheepish as if he were being forced to explain some horrible secret rather than the fact that he was an anonymous and prolific contributor to scientific development on a worldwide scale.

Python had now heard the long story of Supposed-Calysto, and half-vampirism—*"Wait, vampires can get people pregnant?! Ah, fuck!"*—and a teleportation trip back from a certain midnight diner had solidified the extent of Calysto's hidden abilities as well.

But he hadn't known anything about this.

"I never liked how Merik was, you know?" Calysto began, fumbling over his words. "No one should have to die cause they can't afford to live. I just... thought I could help, somehow. That's all."

Python was stunned.

"Fuck, Cal, that's like... that's like super fucking honorable."

He'd always hated the rich and their selfish blind greed, but he'd never considered there was a way to counteract it besides eating them for breakfast. Calysto had actually thought about it, and done something about it, too. He recalled the blue glass bottle of medicine Calysto once placed in his hands and nothing of the emotions he felt would find their way properly to his tongue.

He fidgeted his thumbnail on the plastic edge of his phone.

He suddenly wanted to cry. He wanted to kiss him. He wanted to hide away until did something worthy of this life he now had.

"It's whatever," Calysto shrugged. "Um, there's actually something else I wanted to talk to you about."

Calysto was looking down not meeting his eyes and scrunching his mouth in that way that said he was definitely overthinking something he wanted to say.

"What?" Python asked carefully, almost grateful for the change in subject. "Did I do something?"

"No! It's just... you..." Calysto glanced at him, then his eyes darted away. "You know I ... I love you, right."

Python laughed quickly then stopped. "Didn't you say earlier..."

"I know what I said!" Calysto snapped, his cheeks and bare chest turning a soft red.

"Okay..." Python grinned, all previous insecurity wiped away. He threw his phone back on the table and grabbed Calysto at the hip. He pulled them close then leaned over into his ear. "Well, I love you too, or whatever."

"Yeah?" Calysto's voice barely rose above a whisper as he moved imperceptibly closer.

"Yeah, dumbass." Python narrowed the space between them entirely, tucking his face into the warm skin of Calysto's neck. "Against my better judgment, I definitely do."

Calysto slipped his arms around Python's lean middle. "You're the dumbass."

"I know," Python scoffed. "I've been a dumbass for a long, long time. But I think being around you has... wisened me up a little bit."

"A little is right." Calysto smiled into Python's hair, gripping him tighter with hands dug into his hipbones. "Stick around long enough and maybe one day you'll be as smart as me."

Python snickered, then nipped at Calysto's skin. "Someone's gotta be here to keep that ego in check."

"Hey!" Aeris called from downstairs. "Stop being sappy and come here!"

"Oh," Calysto chuckled softly.

"*LOVE YOU TOO, BABE!*" Python shouted back. Then under his breath added, "Even if you do still scare the shit out of me."

"As if you don't like it," Calysto murmured, teasing him.

Aeris' laughter rang out before she answered, "*OBVIOUSLY, YOU IDIOT!*"

Calysto grabbed Python's hand and led them back to the kitchen to where the three of them spent the rest of their evening in one another's comfortable and half-or-less-dressed company. For now, their problems were easily forgotten in favor of the life they'd built together, instead.

ACKNOWLEDGMENTS

A special thank you to my editing team at Strange Suns Press and beta readers, for their thoughtful and challenging feedback that helped make this book everything it was meant to be.

To those who read and supported this book in its serialized form and who championed me in those early, rough stages. I owe you a heartfelt thanks for all the encouragement and enthusiasm that drove me to complete this work.

To my author friends, who reminded me this story is worth telling and this book is worth bringing to life. Thanks for beating back my insecurities with the logic stick.

To these characters, for pushing me to try something new, for being smartass shitheads who demanded their story be shared, for making me grow as a writer and creative, for giving me hope as I gave it to them.

Lastly, to Aeon. For all the endless encouragement, the late night rambling, and especially for gasping aloud with excitement when I said I was finally ready to write 'the vampire books'.
All my love.

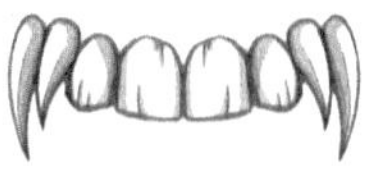

About the Author

Juniper Lake Fitzgerald is an author of Queer Dark Fantasy & Gothic tales. She is also an illustrator with a passion for bringing characters to life. Her work focuses on the raw, tragic and complex nature of being alive.

She has authored the epic dark fantasy series *The Fifth Yanai*, the gothic urban fantasy with romance *The Modern Mythos Anomaly*, and is the narrative designer of the dark fantasy video game *Shadow Rite*.

She can be found through ardentgrove.carrd.co

ALSO BY
JUNIPER LAKE FITZGERALD

The Fifth Yanai Book One: METANOIA

The Fifth Yanai Book Two: APOTHEOSIS

The Fifth Yanai Book Three: CATHARSIS

THE MODERN MYTHOS ANOMALY